Rapscallion

Rapscallion

A Regency Crime Thriller

James McGee

PEGASUS CRIME
NEW YORK LONDON

Rapscallion

Pegasus Books LLC
80 Broad Street, 5th Floor
New York, NY 10004

First Pegasus Books edition 2013

ISBN: 978-1-60598-427-8

10 9 8 7 8 6 5 4 3 2 1

Printed in the United States of America
Distributed by W. W. Norton & Company, Inc.

PROLOGUE

Sark stopped, sank to his knees and listened, but the only sounds he could hear were the pounding of his own heartbeat and the rasping wheeze at the back of his throat as he fought desperately to draw air into his burning lungs. He tried to delay his inhalations in an attempt to slow down his breathing, but the effect was marginal. Moisture from the soggy ground had begun to soak into his breeches, adding to his discomfort. He raised himself into a squat and took stock of his surroundings, eyes probing the darkness for a familiar landmark, but to his untutored eye one stretch of featureless marshland looked much like any other.

A hooting cry came from behind and he stiffened. Owls hunted across the levels at night. Sometimes you could hear the beat of their wings if you were quiet enough. Sark remained where he was, crouched low. It had probably been an owl, but there were other creatures abroad, Sark knew, and they were hunting too.

There was movement to his left, accompanied by a soft grunt. The short hairs rose across the back of Sark's neck and along his forearms. He turned slowly, not daring to exhale, and found himself under close scrutiny from a large sheep. For several seconds, man and beast regarded each other in eerie silence. The animal was not alone. Sark could make out at least a dozen more, huddled behind.

The ewe was the first to break eye contact. Backing off, it ambled away and began to herd its companions towards a clump of bushes. Sark breathed a sigh of relief.

Then he heard the distant baying and the bile rose into his mouth.

They were using dogs.

Sark glanced out of the corner of his eye and saw the sheep pause in their tracks as their ears picked up the unearthly ululation. Then, as if with one mind, the animals broke into a brisk trot. Within seconds they had vanished into the deepening gloom.

Sark turned and tried to locate the direction of the sound, but the darkness, allied to the dips and folds in the ground, made it difficult to pinpoint the exact bearing.

Ahead of him, the land had begun to rise. Sark inched forward, hoping the slope would provide the advantage of height and enable him to see further than his current position. Reaching the top of the bank, he elevated himself cautiously and stared back the way he had come. The first thing he saw was the bright flickering glow of a torch flame, then another, and another beyond that. From his vantage point he could see that the torchbearers were still some way off and that they were proceeding haphazardly. He suspected they were following the creek lines, but there was no doubt they were moving towards him, drawing inexorably closer with each passing second.

There were more lights in the far distance. They were no more than pinpricks, and stationary, and he guessed these were the masthead lanterns of ships moored in the estuary. He wondered briefly if he shouldn't have been heading towards rather than away from them, but he knew that hadn't been an option. His pursuers were sure to have cut off that line of escape.

He looked around and found he was at the edge of a dyke. The ditch stretched away from him, merging into the moonlit wetlands like a snake into the undergrowth. The smell from the bottom of the dyke was foul; a pungent, nostril-pinching mix of peat and stagnant water. There was another strong odour, too. He could see a heaped shape lying close to the water's edge; the remains of a dead sheep. Presumably the animal had placed its foot in a rabbit-hole or some similar burrow, stumbled down the bank and become stuck in the bog, unable to extricate itself.

Sark wondered how long it had taken the beast to die. He tried to ignore the mosquitoes whining about his ears, knowing even though he could not feel their bite that they had already begun to feast upon his blood.

Another drawn-out howl came looping out of the night. Sark felt the cold hand of fear clutch his heart and he cursed his inactivity. He shouldn't have remained so long in one place. He got to his feet and began to run.

He had a rough idea of where he was and the direction in which he was travelling. He had the vague notion that the King's Ferry House wasn't much more than half a mile away. If his navigation was correct and he could reach the landing and find a boat, there was a possibility that he'd be able to cross the river and hide out on the opposite shore and thus give his pursuers the slip.

Keeping low, he continued to follow the dyke's path, ignoring the stitch in his side, which was beginning to stab at him with all the tenacity of a red-hot rapier.

Another cry sounded; human this time, not more than a few hundred yards off. Sark was uncomfortably aware that the men on his trail knew the ground far better than he did. Despite the unevenness of the terrain and the latticework of waterways that crisscrossed the island, they were catching up fast.

His foot slipped and he swore as he started to slide down the side of the gulley. The desire to enter and wade through the murky water in a bid to confuse the hounds was tempting, but he knew it would hamper his progress. All they had to do was steer the dogs along each bank and they'd soon discover where he had left the stream, and they'd pick up his trail again in no time. It was best to keep moving and try to reach the ferry landing; as dry as possible, preferably. He slithered to his feet and scrambled back up the slope.

He could hear his pursuers calling to each other now, driven by the excitement of the chase. In his mind's eye he saw the hounds, eyes bright, tongues slavering, straining at their leashes as they followed his scent. Sark quickened his pace.

The dyke began to widen. Sark hoped it was a sign he was close to its joining with the main channel. Pressing down on the edges of his boot heels to give himself purchase, he pushed his weary, mud-splattered body towards what he hoped was his route to salvation.

There was a shout. Glancing over his shoulder, Sark's stomach lurched when he saw how quickly the gap had shortened. The torches were a lot closer. Beneath the fiery brands, he could make out the dark figures of men running, perhaps half a dozen in all, and the sleeker, four-legged, shapes moving swiftly across the uneven ground before them.

Another urgent cry went up and Sark knew that they had probably seen his fleeing form outlined against the sky. He ducked down, knowing it was far too late to do any good. He drew the pistol from his belt.

Then the ground gave way and he was falling.

As his feet shot from beneath him, he managed to twist his body and discovered that he had almost reached his destination. It was the edge of the river bank that had collapsed beneath his weight. He barely had time to raise the pistol above his head to avoid mud clogging the barrel, before he landed on his back in the ooze.

He struggled to his knees and pushed himself upright, and then saw the light. It was less than one hundred and fifty yards away, at the edge of the reeds. He strained his eyes. A small building began to take shape and he realized it was the ferry keeper's cottage. His gaze shifted to the landing stage jutting out into the water; in its lee, a small rowboat resting on the mud and held fast to a thin wooden post. His spirits lifted. There was still a chance he could make it.

With the mud sucking greedily at his boots, Sark struck out for the landing stage. He had gone but a few paces when the consistency of the mud changed. It was less firm now and his boots were sinking deeper with each step. It was like wading through molasses. He looked out at the river. This was one of the narrower stretches, hence the ferry crossing, but the tide was out and there was a wide expanse of foreshore separating the jetty from the water. He would have to drag the boat a good few yards before he could float it. But he could make out the horizontal black shadow that was the opposite shore and that spurred him on. He pushed himself forward.

Behind him, the noises had diminished. There were no more cries, no howling from the dogs. The night was strangely quiet, save for the squelching of Sark's laborious passage through the mud. Curious, Sark looked around and his blood froze.

They were ranged along the edge of the bank and they were watching him; a line of men, the shadows cast by the torches playing across their unsmiling faces. At their feet, secured by leashes, the hounds stood silently to heel.

The dogs were huge mastiffs, with broad heads and muscular bodies; each one the size of a small calf. As still as statues, they regarded the solitary figure below them with rapt attention. Their only movement was an occasional backward glance at the faces of the men who controlled them.

It was the moment that Sark knew he had nowhere to run.

But it didn't stop him trying.

Sark estimated he still had about fifty paces to go before he reached the boat. His legs felt as heavy as lead, while the pain behind his ribs suggested his heart was about to burst from his chest. Gamely, he tried to pick up speed but while the spirit was willing, his body was telling him it had reached the point of exhaustion.

Sark did not hear the command to release the dogs, but a sixth sense told him it had been given. He turned. A close observer might have witnessed the look of weary resignation that stole across his face.

The handlers had not followed the hounds down on to the foreshore, but were holding to firmer ground, following the line of the river bank, the flames from their torches flaring like comet trails behind them. They ran in silence.

For the second time that night, Sark dropped to his knees.

The dogs were loping rather than sprinting towards him. With their agility, and their weight distributed between four legs instead of two, making them less susceptible to sinking into the mud, it was as if they knew they had all the time in the world.

All thoughts of escape stifled, Sark gripped the pistol firmly and watched the dogs approach.

He glanced to his side. He saw that the men were now parallel to him, torches raised. They were close enough for him to make out their expressions by the light from the flames. Four of them had faces as hard as rock. The other two were grinning.

Sark's chest rose and fell. He looked back towards the dogs and raised his pistol. He aimed the barrel at the leading beast and tracked it with the gun's muzzle.

He heard one of the men on the bank curse and saw that they had all drawn weapons of their own.

Sark could hear the dogs' paws scampering across the mud. They were coming in very fast; close enough for him to see the light of anticipation in their eyes.

The lead hound was less than a dozen paces away when Sark thrust the barrel of the pistol under his own chin and pulled the trigger.

The back of Sark's head blew apart. The powder smoke barely had time to dissipate before the still kneeling body was engulfed in a frenzy of snapping jaws and thrashing limbs. As the men on the bank ran towards the mêlée, the snarling of the hounds rose into the night and carried, like the devil's chorus, down the muddy, bloodstained foreshore.

1

Outlined against the gunmetal sky, the ship's blackened hull towered above the men in the longboat like some enormous Hebridean cliff face.

The men were silent, wrapped in their thoughts and awed by the grim sight confronting them. Only occasionally was the silence broken, by the dull clink of manacles, the splash and creak of oars and the wash of the waves against the side of the boat as it was pulled through the cold grey water.

Someone was sobbing. At the sound, several men crossed themselves. Others bowed their heads and, in whispers, began to pray.

There were fifteen men in the boat, excluding the oarsmen and the two marine guards. With few exceptions their clothes were ragged, their faces pale, unshaven and etched with fear; fear caused not only by the ship's forbidding appearance, but also by the smell coming off her.

It had been with them even before they had embarked, carried across the river by the light easterly breeze. At first, the men had paid little mind, assuming the odour was rising from their own unwashed bodies, but then understanding had dawned. As the longboat had pushed away from the harbour wall they had become transfixed by the grim nature of the fate that was about to befall them. As if to emphasize their passengers' rising sense of horror, the marine guards traded knowing looks and raised their neck scarves over their lower faces.

The longboat approached the rear of the ship. High above, embedded beneath the stern windows, a nameplate that once had been embossed in gold but which was now tarnished beyond repair proclaimed the vessel to be the *Rapacious*.

Close to, the ship looked even more intimidating. The dark-hulled vessel had all the appearance of a massive smoke-stained sarcophagus rather than a former ship of the line. There was no mizzen mast and the main mast and the foremast had been cut down to a third of their original size. Only the lower yards remained. Between them, festooned from a web of washing lines running fore and aft, was an array of what, from a distance, might have been taken for signal flags but which, on closer inspection, turned out to be a selection of tattered stockings, shirts and breeches. Age, wear and constant washing had turned every visible scrap of clothing a universal shade of grey, with the majority of the garments exhibiting more holes than material.

These were not the only refurbishments that had been inflicted upon the once proud ship. Her bowsprit had been removed, and where the poop deck had been, there now stood a clinker-built, soot-engrained shack, complete with sloping roof and chimney stack, from which grey smoke was billowing. A similar construction adorned the ship's forecastle. It was obvious from her appearance that a great many years had passed since *Rapacious* last experienced the roar and thunder of battle in her search for prey. This was further confirmed by the lack of heavy ordnance; her open gun ports revealed that cannon muzzles had been replaced by immovable cast-iron grilles.

The truncation of her masts and the lack of armament

had lightened the ship's weight considerably. As a result, she was riding much higher out of the water than was normal for a vessel her size. A walkway formed from metal gratings followed the line of the orlop deck. From it a series of wooden stairs rose towards a small platform, similar to a church pulpit, affixed adjacent to the boarding gap in the ship's handrail.

Huge chains at bow and stern secured *Rapacious* to the riverbed. Beyond the ship, four more vessels in a similar state of disrepair sat moored in mid-stream, line astern and a cable's length apart, their blunted bows facing downriver.

All around, a bewildering variety of other vessels lay at anchor, from brigs to cutters and from frigates to flush-decked sloops, their yellow and black hulls gleaming, masts rising tall and straight, while pennants, not grubby pantaloons, fluttered gaily from their yardarms. They were Britain's pride and they were ready for war.

By comparison, isolated from the rest of the fleet, *Rapacious* and her four sister ships looked as if they had been discarded and left to rot; victims of a terrible and terminal disease.

Seated in the waist of the longboat, one man ignored the lamentations of his companions and gazed at the ship with what could have been interpreted as interest rather than dread. Two scars were visible on the left side of his face. The first followed the curve of his cheekbone, an inch below his left eye. The second scar, less livid, ran an inch below the first. His long hair was dark save for a few streaks of grey above the temple. His jacket and breeches were severely worn and faded, though in a better state of repair than the clothes of many of the men huddled around him, some of whom were clad in little more than rags. And while the bulk of his companions were either barefooted or else wearing poorly fitting shoes, his feet were shod in what appeared to be a pair of stout but well-scuffed military boots.

"A sou for your thoughts, my friend."

The words were spoken in French. They came from an aristocratic-looking individual dressed in a dark grey jacket and grubby white breeches, seated on the dark-haired man's right.

Matthew Hawkwood remained silent but continued staring over the water towards the black-hulled ship.

"Heard she fought at Copenhagen," the speaker continued in a quiet voice. "She was a seventy-four. They took the idea from us. Extended their seventies. They use them as standard now. Can't blame the bastards. Good sailing, strong gun-power, what is there not to like?"

The speaker, whose name was Lasseur, grinned suddenly, the expression in marked contrast to the unsmiling faces about him. The neat goatee beard he wore, when added to the grin, lent his features a raffish slant.

The grin disappeared in an instant as a series of plaintive cries sounded from beyond the longboat's prow.

Ahead, another longboat was tied up against the boarding raft in the shadow of the ship's grime-encrusted hull. A cluster of men had already disembarked. Huddled on the walkway, under the watchful eyes of armed guards, they were preparing to ascend the stairs. Several of the men had difficulty walking. Two were crawling along the grating on their hands and knees. Their progress was painfully slow. Seeing their plight, their companions lifted them to their feet and with arms about their shoulders shepherded them along.

There were still men left on the first boat. From their posture, it was clear that none of them had the strength to make the transfer on their own. Their cries of distress floated over the water. The two marine guards on the boat were looking up towards the ship's rail as if waiting for orders, breaking off to jab the barrels and butts of their muskets against the supine bodies around them.

Lasseur bared his teeth in a snarl.

His reaction was echoed by dark mutterings from the men seated about him.

"Silence there!" The order came from one of the marines, who stared at his charges accusingly and brandished his musket, bayonet affixed. "Or so help me, I'll run you through!" Adding, with ill-disguised contempt, "Frog bastards!"

A face had appeared at the ship's rail. An arm waved and an inaudible command was given. One of the marines in the boat below responded with a half-hearted salute before turning to his companion and shaking his head. At this the rowers raised their oars and they and the two guards climbed out on to the boarding raft. Turning, one of the rowers used his oar to push the boat away, while one of his fellow boatmen unfastened and began to pay out the line connecting the longboat to the ship. Caught by the current, the longboat moved slowly away from the ship's hull. When the boat was some thirty or so yards out, the line was retied, leaving the boat's pitiful passengers to drift at the mercy of the tide.

Angry shouts came from the line of men on the grating. Their protestations were met with a severe clubbing from the guards. Retreating, the quietened men began their slow and laboured ascent of the stairway.

Hawkwood watched grim-faced as the men made their way up the side of the ship. Lasseur followed his gaze and murmured softly, "We'd have been better off with the damned Spanish."

"Bastards," a voice interjected bitterly from behind them. "I've seen this before."

Hawkwood and Lasseur turned. The speaker was a thin man, with sunken cheeks and watery eyes. Grey stubble covered his jaw.

"I was in Portsmouth last winter, on the *Vengeance*. They had a delivery of prisoners transferred from Cadiz. About thirty, all told. As thin as rakes they were; ghost white, not an ounce of flesh on their bones and not so much as a set of breeches between them. Only ten of them made it on to the *Vengeance* on their own. The rest were too ill to leave the longboat. The *Vengeance*'s surgeon refused to take them. Ordered them to be delivered to the hospital ship. Only the commander of the *Pegasus* refused to have them on board, not unless they were washed first. So the *Vengeance*'s surgeon ordered them thrown into the sea to clean them and left the *Pegasus* to pick up the bodies. Most of them were dead by the time the *Pegasus*'s boat got to them." The man nodded towards the drifting longboat. "Looks to me, that's what's happening here."

"My God," Lasseur said and fell into a reflective silence as their own longboat, its way now clear, began to manoeuvre towards the ship's side.

Hawkwood regarded the manacles around his ankles. If the men on the drifting boat, who presumably had also been wearing shackles, had been thrown overboard they would have been beyond help, sinking to the bottom of the river like stones.

He took a look at his fellow passengers. No one returned his gaze. They were too preoccupied, staring up at the ship, craning their necks to take in the vast wooden rampart looming above them. The sense of unease that had enveloped the boat was palpable, as if a black storm cloud had descended. Behind their masks, even the guards looked momentarily subdued.

He could still hear weeping. It was coming from the stern. Hawkwood followed the sound. The boy couldn't have been much older than ten or eleven. Tears glistened on his cheeks. He looked up, dried his eyes with the heels of his hands and turned away, his small shoulders shaking. His clothes hung in rags about him. He'd been one of a consignment of prisoners, Hawkwood and Lasseur among them, picked up earlier that day from Maidstone Gaol. A midshipman or powder monkey, Hawkwood supposed, or whatever the French equivalent might be, and without doubt the youngest of the longboat's passengers. It seemed unlikely that the boy had been taken alone, but there didn't appear to be anyone with him, no shipmates to give him comfort. Hawkwood wondered where the boy had been captured and in what circumstances he might have been separated from the rest of his crew.

The order came to boat oars. A dozen heartbeats later, the longboat was secured to the raft and the transfer began.

The odour from the open gun ports was almost overwhelming. The river was bounded by marshland. On warm days with the wind sifting across the levels, the smell was beyond fœtid, but the malodorous stench issuing from the interior of *Rapacious* eclipsed even the smell from the shore. It was worse than a convoy of night-soil barges.

Hawkwood shouldered his knapsack. He was one of the few carrying possessions. Most had only the clothes they stood up in.

The marines set about prodding the prisoners with their musket butts. "Goddamn it, move your arses! I won't tell you again! No wonder you're losing the bleedin' war! Useless buggers!"

Legs clanking, the men started to climb from the longboat on to the raft.

"Shift yourselves!" The guards continued to use their weapons to herd the men along the walkway. Movement was difficult due to the shackles, but the guards made no allowance for the restraints. "Lively now! Christ, you buggers stink!"

The insults rained down thick and fast, and while it was doubtful many of the men shuffling along the grating could understand the harsh words, the tone of voice and the poking and prodding made it clear what was required of them.

Slowly, in single file, the men clinked their way up the ship's side.

"Keep moving, damn your eyes!"

Hawkwood stepped from the stairs on to the pulpit, Lasseur at his shoulder. A jam had formed in the enclosed space. Both men stared down into the belly of the ship. Lasseur recoiled. Then the Frenchman leaned forward so that his mouth was close to Hawkwood's ear. His face was set in a grimace.

"Welcome to Hell," he said.

2

I should have bloody known, Hawkwood thought.

Ezra Twigg's face should have given the game away. Hawkwood wondered why he hadn't picked up the signals. The little clerk's head had been cast down when Hawkwood entered the ante-room in reply to the Chief Magistrate's summons. Normally, Twigg would have looked up from his scribbling and passed some pithy comment about the marks on the floor left by Hawkwood's boot heels, but this time Twigg had barely acknowledged the Runner's arrival. All he'd done was look up quickly, murmur, "They're waiting for you," and return to his paperwork. The omens hadn't been good. Hawkwood chided himself for not being more observant. Though he had absorbed the warning that the Chief Magistrate had company.

As Hawkwood entered the office, James Read stepped away from the tall window. It was mid-morning and sunlight pierced the room. Hawkwood wondered why the Chief Magistrate, a man who made no secret of his dislike for cold weather, looked so pensive. Given his usual disconsolate manner when confronted with inclement skies, he should, by rights, have been dancing across the carpet.

The second man looked around. He was heavy-set, with short, sandy hair, a broad face and a web of red veins radiating across his cheeks. He was dressed in the uniform of a naval officer and clearly suffered from the habitual stoop, characteristic of so many seamen, which, Hawkwood had come to realize, was more a testimony to the lack of headroom in a man-of-war than any lingering defect of birth.

The officer looked Hawkwood up and down, taking in the scarred face, the unfashionably long hair tied at the nape of the neck and the dark, well-cut attire. The Chief Magistrate walked to his desk. His movements, as ever, were measured and precise. He sat down. "Officer Hawkwood, this gentleman is Captain Elias Ludd. As his uniform implies, Captain Ludd is from the Admiralty."

Hawkwood and the captain exchanged cautious nods.

"The Transport Board, to be exact," James Read said.

Hawkwood said nothing. The Transport Board had been created initially to provide ships, troops and supplies during the American War of Independence. But the wars against Bonaparte had seen the Board expand its range of activities far beyond the original borders of the Atlantic. Now, due to Britain's vast military and naval commitments, the Board was responsible for the movement of supply ships to the four corners of the globe.

"The Admiralty requires our assistance." Read nodded towards his visitor. "Captain, you have the floor."

"Thank you, sir." Ludd looked down at the carpet and then raised his head. "I've an officer who's gone missing; name of Sark. Lieutenant Andrew Sark."

There was a short silence.

Hawkwood looked towards the Chief Magistrate for guidance, then back to the officer. "And what, you want *us* to find him? Isn't that the navy's job?"

Ludd looked taken aback by Hawkwood's less than sympathetic response. James Read said, "There are other factors to consider. As you know, the Transport Board's jurisdiction extends beyond what might be viewed as its traditional bailiwick."

What the hell did that mean? Hawkwood wondered.

"The Board also administers foreign prisoners of war," James Read said. "You recall it took over the duty from the Sick and Hurt Board."

Hawkwood wondered if the Chief Magistrate was expecting a vocal acknowledgement. He decided it was probably best to remain silent. Better to keep your mouth shut and be thought an idiot than to speak and remove all doubt. He decided a noncommittal nod would probably suffice.

"My apologies, Captain," Read said. "Please continue."

Ludd cleared his throat. "Over the past several weeks, there's been a sudden increase in the number of prisoners who've escaped from detention. We sent Lieutenant Sark to investigate whether these were random events or part of some orchestrated effort."

"And he's failed to report back?" Hawkwood said.

Ludd nodded, his face solemn.

"When did you last hear from him?"

Ludd stuck out his chin. "That's just it – we haven't heard from him at all. It's been six days."

"Not long," Hawkwood said.

"In the general scheme of things, I'd not disagree with you." Ludd gnawed the inside of his lip.

"Captain?" Hawkwood prompted.

Ludd ceased chewing. "He was not the first," he said heavily.

Hawkwood sensed James Read shift in his seat. Ludd continued to look uncomfortable. "The first officer we sent, a Lieutenant Masterson, died."

"Died? How?"

"Drowned, it's presumed. His body was discovered two weeks ago on a mud bank near Fowley Island."

"Which is where?" Hawkwood asked.

"The Swale River."

"Kent."

Ludd nodded. "At the time there was nothing to indicate he'd been the victim of foul play. We mourned him, we buried him, and then Lieutenant Sark was dispatched to continue the investigation."

"But now that Sark's failed to report back, you're thinking that perhaps the drowning wasn't an accident."

"There is that possibility, yes."

"Forgive me, Captain, but I still don't see what this has to do with Bow Street," Hawkwood said. "This remains a navy matter, surely?"

Before Ludd could respond, James Read interjected: "Captain Ludd is here at the behest of Magistrate Aaron Graham. Magistrate Graham is the government inspector responsible for the administration of all prisoners of war. He reports directly to the Home Secretary. It was Home Secretary Ryder's recommendation that the Board avail itself of our services."

Hawkwood had met Home Secretary Richard Ryder and hadn't been overly impressed, but then Hawkwood had a low opinion of politicians, irrespective of rank. In short, he didn't trust them. He had found Ryder to be a supercilious man, too full of his own importance. He wondered if Ryder had been in contact with James Read directly. There was nothing in the Chief Magistrate's manner to indicate he was talking to Ludd under sufferance, but then Read was a master of the neutral expression. It didn't mean his mind wasn't whirring like clockwork underneath the impassive mask.

Read got to his feet. He walked to the fireplace and adopted his customary pose in front of the hearth. The fire was unlit, but Read stood as if warming himself. Hawkwood suspected that the magistrate assumed the stance as a means to help him think, whether a fire was blazing away or not. Oddly, it did seem to imbue an air of gravity to whatever pronouncement he came up with. Hawkwood wondered if that wasn't the magistrate's real intention.

Read pursed his lips. "It's no secret that the Board has come in for a degree of criticism over the past twelve months. It has been the subject of two Select Committees. Their findings were that the Board has not performed as efficiently as expected. Further adverse reports would be most . . . unhelpful. So far, these escapes have been kept out of the public domain. There's concern that, should word of its inability to keep captured enemy combatants in check emerge, the government's credibility could suffer a severe blow. With all due deference to Captain Ludd, while the loss of one officer sent to investigate these escapes might be construed as unfortunate, the loss of two officers could be regarded as carelessness. It is all grist to the mill, and with the nation at war any lack of confidence in the administration could have dire consequences."

Hawkwood stole a glance at the captain and felt an immediate sympathy. He knew what it was like to lose men in battle; he himself had lost more men than he cared to remember, and it was a painful burden to bear.

"What services?" Hawkwood asked.

Read frowned.

"You said the Home Secretary wants the Board to avail itself of our services. What services?"

James Read looked towards Ludd, who gave a rueful smile. "My superiors are unwilling to commit further resources to the investigation."

"By resources, you mean men," Hawkwood said.

Ludd flushed. "As Magistrate Read stated, two officers have apparently fallen prey to the investigation already. I am not anxious to dispatch a third man to investigate the death and disappearance of the first two."

Everything became clear. Hawkwood stared at James Read. "You want Bow Street to take over the investigation?"

"That is the Home Secretary's wish, yes."

"What makes him think we can succeed where the navy has failed?"

Read placed his hands behind his back. "The Home Secretary feels that, while the Admiralty is perfectly capable of assigning officers to the field, there are certain advantages in utilizing non-naval personnel, particularly in what one might consider to be investigations of a clandestine nature."

"Clandestine?"

"There are avenues open to this office that are not available to other – how shall I put it? – more conventional, less flexible departments of government. Would you not agree, Captain Ludd?"

"I'm sure you'd know more about that, sir," Ludd said tactfully.

"Indeed." The Chief Magistrate fixed Hawkwood with a speculative eye.

An itch began to develop along the back of Hawkwood's neck. It wasn't a pleasant sensation.

"I refer to the art of subterfuge, Hawkwood; the ability to blend into the background – most useful when dealing with the criminal classes, as you have so ably demonstrated on a number of occasions."

Hawkwood waited for the axe to fall.

"Captain Ludd and I have discussed the matter. Based on our discussion, I believe you're the officer best suited to the task."

"And what task would that be, sir . . . exactly?"

James Read smiled grimly. "We're sending you to the hulks."

* * *

The Chief Magistrate's expression was stern. "We've got prisoners of war spread right around the country, from Somerset to Edinburgh. Fortunately for us, the new prison in Maidstone is ideally situated for our purposes. It's been used as a holding pen for prisoners prior to their transfer to the Medway and Thames hulks. You'll begin your sentence there. From Maidstone you'll be transported to the prison ship *Rapacious*. She's lying off Sheerness. Better you arrive on the hulk within a consignment of prisoners rather than alone. There's no reason to suppose anyone will question your credentials, but it should give you an opportunity to form liaisons with some of your fellow internees before embarkation."

It was interesting, Hawkwood mused, that the Chief Magistrate had used the word *sentence* rather than assignment. Perhaps it had been a slip of the tongue. Then again, he thought, maybe not.

"Your mission is several fold," Read said. "Firstly, you are to investigate how these escapes have been achieved –"

"You mean you don't *know*?" Hawkwood cut in, staring at Ludd.

Ludd shifted uncomfortably. "We know *Rapacious* has lost four prisoners in the past six weeks. The trouble is, we don't know the exact time the losses took place. We can assume the other prisoners concealed the escapes from the ship's crew, possibly by manipulating the roll count. Without knowing the precise times of the escapes we haven't been able to pin down how they were achieved, whether it was a spur-of-the-moment thing based on a lapse in our procedures or if the escapes were planned and executed over a period of time. All we know is that *Rapacious* is missing four men. What makes it more interesting is that there have been similar losses from some of the other Medway-based ships. We're also missing a couple who broke their paroles."

"How many in total?" Hawkwood asked.

"Ten unaccounted for."

"Over how long a period?"

"Two months," Ludd said.

"As I was saying . . ." James Read spoke into the pregnant silence which followed Ludd's admission. "You are also to determine whether the escapers have received outside assistance. Captain Ludd is of the opinion that they have."

"Based on what?" Hawkwood said.

"Based on the fact that we haven't managed to track any of the buggers down," Ludd said.

"Explain."

Ludd sighed. "Escapes are nothing new. Some are spontaneous; the sudden recognition of an opportunity presenting itself: a door left unlocked, a careless guard looking the other way during a working party, that sort of thing. They generally involve a prisoner acting on his own. Nine times out of ten, he's rounded up quickly, usually because he's cold and wet and he can't find food or clothing, he's no idea where he is and he daren't ask directions because he can't speak the language. They don't last long. Many end up turning themselves in voluntarily – and not just to the military. They've even surrendered to people in the street. But when it's more than one, when two or three at a time have made a run for it, that suggests they've devised a plan, hoarded food and spare clothing, maybe bribed a guard to sell them a map so they know how far it is to the coast, and where they can steal a boat. Even so, not many make it. All it takes is one careless word; someone overhears them speaking Frog or talking English with an accent and the game's up. But these recent escapes, they've been different."

"How so?"

"As I said, we weren't able to pick up their trail."

"Which means what?"

"In my book, it means someone's definitely helping them."

"Like who?"

"That's what we sent Masterson and Sark to find out."

"What do you think?"

"My own theory? Free traders, most likely."

"Smugglers?"

"My guess is that they're passing the escapers down the line to the coast. They've got the routes all set up, they've got the men and the boats."

"That, Hawkwood, is the third part of your assignment," Read said. "If there is an organized escape route, I want it disrupted, preferably disbanded."

"It might explain why your Lieutenant Masterson was found in the Swale," Hawkwood said. "Could be he was thrown from a vessel."

"Could be," Ludd agreed. "I'd deem it a personal favour if, along the way, you could find out what happened to my men. If they were done away with, I'd prefer to be told."

"If free traders are involved, it won't be easy," Hawkwood pointed out. "They're a law unto themselves. Anyone going in and asking questions is sure to make their ears prick up. It's more than likely they'll see me coming a mile away."

Ludd and Read exchanged glances.

"Quite so," James Read said quietly. "But in this case they're going to be looking in the wrong direction."

"Hindsight's a wonderful thing," Ludd said. "Our mistake was sending Masterson *and* Sark through the front door. They were competent men, but they were naval officers first and landsmen second. In this situation they were out of their depth, no pun intended. We might just as well have dispatched a marching band to accompany them. Masterson's brief was to try and infiltrate the smuggling organizations. We thought the best way for him to do that was to have him pose as a former seaman looking for work and to make it clear he wasn't too bothered whether the work was legal or not. Trouble is, the smuggling fraternity's too closely knit. My feeling is he ended up asking the wrong people the wrong questions – and that Sark made the same mistake."

"You can take the man out of the navy but you can't take the navy out of the man," Hawkwood said.

"Something like that," Ludd agreed unhappily.

"You, on the other hand, will not be quite so obvious," James Read said. "We hope."

"You mean I'll be using the tradesman's entrance," Hawkwood said.

The corner of Read's mouth twitched. "Providing we can manufacture a suitable history for you." The Chief Magistrate paused. "My initial thought was that you should pass yourself off as a French officer, but I'm not sure that's entirely practical. While I appreciate that your knowledge of the language is considerable, could you maintain the deception for any length of time? Captain Ludd and I have discussed the matter and we believe the current crisis with the United States has provided us with the perfect solution. You will pass yourself off as an American volunteer."

"An American?"

"As you know all too well, from your recent encounter with William Lee, our American cousins are less than enamoured with us of late. Even before the recent declaration of war, a substantial number of American citizens have been drawn to Bonaparte's flag; a legacy of American and French liaison during the Revolutionary War. With that in mind, we thought you could assume the mantle of an American officer attached to one of Bonaparte's regiments who has been captured in the field. The fact that you are conversant in French gives us a distinct advantage.

"All that remains is your identity. Something credible that will pass scrutiny, preferably based on your own expertise and, ideally, involving an engagement of which you have personal knowledge. The only problem with that, however, would be the question of your whereabouts over the past three years. The most logical choice would therefore seem to be something more recent, from which all the facts have yet to be sifted. Captain Ludd and I have perused dispatches and determined that the victory at Ciudad Rodrigo will best fit the bill. Reports of the battle are still being disseminated. Are you familiar with any of the details?"

"Only from what I've read in the news sheets," Hawkwood said.

The Times had carried general reports of the battle, as had the *Chronicle* and the *Gazette*. Ciudad Rodrigo was a picturesque Spanish town overlooking the Agueda River. Only a few miles from the border, it guarded the main northern route between Spain and Portugal. Wellington had laid siege to the town at the beginning of January. The attack had been a ferocious affair. Casualties had been heavy, but Wellington had emerged victorious. Many prisoners had been taken.

Read nodded. "Very good; a volunteer captain attached to the 34th Régiment d'Infanterie Légère will be the most fitting for our purposes, I venture. The regiment was created last year, drawing men from other units, so there is every possibility they could have utilized foreign experts in the field. I'll leave you to manufacture an appropriate biography for yourself."

The Chief Magistrate reached across his desk and picked up a small canvas pouch. "These are some of the reports pertaining to the siege. Make use of them. They contain details that are not public knowledge; for obvious reasons, as you'll discover. Our own soldiers may well have emerged victorious, but they did not cover themselves in glory. Such knowledge could assist in fending off awkward questions.

Use it to your advantage if you find yourself pressed. Attack is the best form of defence. Denigrating your former comrades in arms will help deflect attention from your alias. Read the dispatches. You'll see what I mean."

Read handed over the pouch. "As an officer, you'll be permitted to carry a few personal belongings. Mr Twigg will provide you with funds. French and British currency is used on the hulks. I would urge you to be circumspect in your expenditure, however. The coffers of the Public Office are not a bottomless pit.

"The wounds you received in the Hyde case will stand you in good stead. They're recent enough to have been sustained around the supposed date of your defeat and capture. They will add to your credibility."

The scars from his encounter with the escaped Bedlamite, Titus Hyde, had healed well. But that wasn't to say he didn't sometimes wake in the small hours wondering what might have become of him had the blade of Hyde's sword been an inch longer. The razor-thin weal along the rim of his left cheek was a visible reminder that the line between life and death can be measured by the breadth of a single hair or the span of a heartbeat.

"Who else will know I'm a peace officer?"

Read hesitated before replying. "No one. Aside from myself, Captain Ludd and Mr Twigg, no one else will be privy to your true identity."

"Not the hulk's commanding officer?"

"No one," Read repeated.

"So, how do I send word if I discover something?"

"That's why you'll be listed as an officer in the ship's register. It entitles you to apply for parole. Captain Ludd recommends we make it appear as though your application is pending authorization. You will thus be required to appear before a board of assessment. Your first interview will be scheduled to take place one week after your arrival. Captain Ludd will be the officer in charge. You will provide him with details of any progress you may have made."

Hawkwood stared at the dispatch pouch and then looked up. "In that case, I hope you all remain in good health. I'd hate to find I'm stranded on the bloody ship because *you've* all been struck dead in your beds."

3

"Name?"

The question was emitted in a thin, reedy voice by a narrow-shouldered, sour-faced man seated behind a large trestle table that had been set up in the forward section of the weather-deck. The clerk did not look up but waited, lips compressed, pen poised, for Hawkwood to reply. A large ledger lay open in front of him. The seated man to his right, a supercilious-looking individual with reddish-blond hair, slim sideburns and nails bitten down to the quick, wore a lieutenant's uniform. The one standing by his left shoulder was younger, slightly built, dark haired, and dressed in a yellow canvas jacket and matching trousers. Stamped on the sleeves of the jacket and upon each trouser leg were a broad black arrow and the letters T.O., the initials of the Transport Office. His eyes roved back and forth along the line of waiting men.

Hawkwood gazed down at the clerk and said nothing. He was still feeling the chill from the dousing he had received.

The guards had removed the shackles and made all the new arrivals strip naked on deck before handing them a block of brown soap and ordering them into large water-filled barrels. The water was freezing and by the time each man had rubbed himself raw, clambered out, passed the soap on to the next man and dried himself with the rag towel, the water surface in every tub was covered by a thin oily residue.

Orange jackets, trousers and shirts had then been distributed. There seemed to be only one size, small, which left the recipients struggling woefully to fasten the jacket buttons. With most, the trousers reached only as far as mid calf. The only person to emerge from the handout with any modicum of dignity was the boy from the longboat. The jacket was too long at both hem and sleeve, but the trousers were close to being a good fit, albeit only after they had been secured around the boy's thin waist by a length of twine.

Not everyone received a uniform. A number of men, Hawkwood and Lasseur among them, were allowed to keep their own clothes, supposedly because they were officers, though Hawkwood suspected it had more to do with a scarcity of jackets and trousers rather than an acknowledgement of their rank. Certainly, it appeared that prison uniform had been passed, in the main, to those whose own apparel was beyond salvage. All soiled articles were tossed on to a growing pile on the deck. To be taken off the ship, Hawkwood assumed, and burned.

Next, canvas slippers were distributed. Neither Hawkwood nor Lasseur were deemed impoverished enough to warrant the gift of the shoes. Hawkwood noticed that both his and Lasseur's footwear were attracting surreptitious attention from some of the less fortunate prisoners and he made a silent vow not to let his boots out of his sight.

A look of irritation moved across the registration clerk's pinched face at Hawkwood's lack of response. The lieutenant maintained his impression of boredom. The clerk flicked his finger imperiously and the man standing at his shoulder in the yellow uniform repeated the question in French.

"Hooper," Hawkwood said. "Matthew."

As Hawkwood gave his name, the clerk stiffened and frowned, while next to him the lieutenant's head snapped round. His eyes darkened.

The clerk recovered his composure and turned his eyes to the grainy sheet of paper at his elbow. He ran the nib of his pen down the page and gave a small click of his tongue as he found the entry he was looking for. Hawkwood assumed it was the list of prisoners transferred from Maidstone and that the clerk was confirming his name.

The lieutenant peered over the clerk's shoulder.

The clerk sneered. "Our first American. Not so independent now, are you?" He sniggered at his own wit.

The lieutenant viewed Hawkwood with undisguised hostility as the clerk began to transfer the details into the ledger, repeating the information under his breath as he did so. "Rank: captain; date of capture: 20th January; action in which taken: Ciudad Rodrigo; date of arrival: 27th May; application for parole under consideration; physical description . . ." The clerk raised his eyes again and murmured, "Height: approximately six feet; scarring on left side of face . . . surly-looking brute. Assigned to the gun deck. Next!"

After listening silently to the description and the comment, the lieutenant favoured Hawkwood with a final grimace of distaste before he turned away.

"Damned renegade," Hawkwood heard him mutter under his breath.

The interpreter jerked his head for Hawkwood to move along. Behind him, he heard Lasseur give his name and the clerk's litany began again.

At the next table the prisoners were presented with a rolled hammock, a threadbare blanket and a thin, wool-stuffed mattress.

Hawkwood studied the armed guards ringing the deck. Their escort had been composed of marines, seconded to the shore establishment, but neither the army nor the navy liked to assign regulars to the prison ships. True fighting men were needed abroad. This lot would be members of a local militia, specially recruited, Ludd had told him. He'd seen two of the guards exchange knowing grins as they stared at the boy's milk-white buttocks during the enforced bathing. One of them had nudged the other and sniggered. "Wait till His Majesty gets a look at that!"

Hawkwood wondered what that meant.

The processing stretched over two hours. There were not that many new arrivals – three boatloads in all, perhaps forty men in total – but the ill-tempered admissions clerk seemed intent on proving how pedantic he could be. Slowly, however, the line of men began to shorten. Hawkwood was intrigued as to why they'd been herded into one half of the quarterdeck rather than escorted below. His question was answered as the last prisoner was handed his bedding.

A figure appeared at the rail of the deck above them. He was tall and raw-boned. His face was gaunt and pale. The white piping on his lapels proclaimed him to be another lieutenant, though he looked old to be holding the rank. Hands clasped behind his back, he gazed dispassionately at the crowd of men gathered beneath him. His eyes were very dark. Gradually, as the prisoners became aware that they were being observed, an uneasy silence descended upon the deck. Beneath his hat, the lieutenant's eyes moved unblinkingly over the upturned faces. The clerk and the lieutenant at the table rose to their feet.

The gaunt lieutenant remained by the rail, his body incredibly still, as he continued to stare down. Not a word was uttered. Only the sound of the gulls wheeling high above the ship broke the stillness. Then, abruptly, after what seemed like minutes but could only have been twenty or thirty seconds, the lieutenant stepped back from the rail, turned abruptly, and, still not having spoken, returned from whence he came.

"Our brave commander," Lasseur whispered. "Rumour has it he once captained a frigate, had a run-in with one of our eighties off Finisterre, and surrendered his ship. After they exchanged him, he was court-martialled." Lasseur sucked in his cheeks. "Took to drink, I'm told."

Hawkwood wondered where Lasseur had got his information. Some people had an uncanny knack of picking up all kinds of rumours. Though, in fact, Lasseur was only half right. The commander of the hulk, if that's who the lieutenant had been, was named Hellard and he had indeed been demoted from captain. But it had been Funchal not Finisterre where the lieutenant's fate had been sealed, and he had taken refuge in the bottle before the engagement, not following it. Hawkwood had been told the correct version by Ludd during his briefing; though it didn't alter the fact that Hellard had been assigned to *Rapacious* as punishment. Furthermore Ludd had told Hawkwood that Hellard's background was modest, which meant he'd been unable to call on a patron to rescue him from exile and set him back on the promotion ladder. Commanding this floating tomb was as high as Lieutenant Mortimer Hellard was ever going to get. And he knew it. It accounted for the stony countenance, Hawkwood thought. This was a man resigned to his fate, resenting it, and suffering because of it.

"Take them below, Sergeant Hook." The order came from the lieutenant with the bitten fingernails. "And do something about those. They're making the place look untidy."

The lieutenant scowled at a pair of prisoners whose legs had given way. Hawkwood assumed they were the two who had been helped up the stairs by their fellow detainees. He wondered what had become of the men who'd been left in the longboat, and whether anyone had bothered to retrieve them. No one in authority on *Rapacious* seemed interested in taking a look. It was more than likely the boat was still drifting at the end of the line.

"Aye, sir." The sergeant of the guard saluted lazily and turned to the prisoners. He nodded towards the stairway. "Right, you buggers, let's be having you. Simmons, use your bayonet! Give that one at the back there a poke. Get the bastards moving! We ain't got all bleedin' day! *Allez!*"

Lasseur caught Hawkwood's eye. The Frenchman's smile had slipped from his face. It was as if the reality of the situation had finally sunk in. Hawkwood shouldered his bedding, remembering Lasseur's earlier whispered comment. As he descended the stairs to the well deck it didn't take him long to see that Lasseur had been mistaken. Hell would have been an improvement.

Hawkwood was no stranger to deprivation. It was all around him on London's cramped and filthy streets. In the rookeries, like those of St Giles and Field Lane, poverty was a way of life. It could be seen in the way people dressed, in the looks on their faces and by the way they carried themselves. Hawkwood had also seen it in the eyes of soldiers, most notably in the aftermath of a defeat, and he was seeing the same despair and desperation now, carved into the faces of the men gathered on the deck of the prison hulk. It was the grey, lifeless expression of men who had lost all hope.

They ranged in age from calloused veterans to callow-eyed adolescents and they looked, with few exceptions Hawkwood thought, like the ranks of the walking dead. Most wore the yellow uniform, or what was left of it, for in many cases the prison garb looked to be as ragged as the clothing that had been stripped from the backs of the new arrivals. Many of the older men had the weathered look of seamen, though without the ruddy complexion. Instead, their faces were pallid, almost drained of colour.

Some prisoners huddled in small groups, others stood alone, if such a feat was possible given the number of wasted bodies that seemed to cover every available inch of space. Some of the men were stretched out on the deck, but whether they were sleeping or suffering from some malady, it was impossible to tell. The ones that remained upright gazed dully at the new arrivals being directed towards the hatch and the stairs leading into the bowels of the ship. Some of the men looked as though they hadn't eaten for days.

"My God," Lasseur gagged. "The smell."

"Wait till you get below."

The voice came from behind them. Hawkwood looked back over his shoulder and found himself eye to eye with the dark-haired interpreter from the weather-deck.

"Don't worry; in a couple of days, you won't notice. In a week, you'll start to smell the same. The name's Murat, by the way. And we call this area the Park. It's our little joke." The interpreter nodded towards the open hatch and the top of the ladder leading down. "You'd best get a move on. Squeeze through, find yourselves a space."

"Murat?" Lasseur looked intrigued. "Any relation?"

The interpreter shrugged and gave a self-deprecatory grin. "A distant cousin on my mother's side. I regret our closest association is in having once enjoyed the services of the same tailor. I –"

"How much do you want for your boots?"

Hawkwood felt a tug at his sleeve. One of the yellow-uniformed prisoners had taken hold of his arm. Hawkwood recoiled from the man's rancid odour. "They're not for sale."

There were ragged holes in the elbows of the prisoner's jacket and the knees of his trousers shone as if they had been newly waxed. His feet were stuffed into a pair of canvas slippers, though they were obviously too small for him as his heels overlapped the soles by at least an inch. Several boils had erupted across the back of his neck. His shirt collar was the colour of dried mud.

"Ten francs." The grip on Hawkwood's arm tightened.

Hawkwood looked down at the man's fingers. "Let go or you'll lose the arm."

"Twenty."

"Leave him be, Chavasse! He told you they're not for sale." Murat raised his hand. "In any case, they're worth ten times that. Go and pester someone else."

Hawkwood pulled his arm free. The prisoner backed away.

The interpreter turned to Hawkwood. "Keep hold of your belongings until you know your way around, otherwise you might not see them again. Come on, I'll show you where to go."

Murat pushed his way ahead of them and started down the almost vertical stairway. Hawkwood and Lasseur followed him. It was like descending into a poorly lit mineshaft. Three-quarters of the way down Hawkwood found he had to lean backwards to avoid cracking his skull on the overhead beam. He felt his spine groan as he did so. He heard Lasseur chuckle. The sound seemed ludicrously out of place.

"You'll get used to that, too," Murat said drily.

Hawkwood couldn't see a thing. The sudden shift from daylight to near Stygian darkness was abrupt and alarming. If Murat hadn't been wearing his yellow jacket, it would have been almost impossible to follow him in the dark. It was as if the sun had been snuffed out. Hawkwood paused and waited for his eyes to adjust.

"Keep moving!" The order came from behind.

"That way," Murat said, and pointed. "And watch your head."

The warning was unnecessary. Hawkwood's neck was already cricked. The height from the deck to the underside of the main beams couldn't have been much more than five and a half feet.

Murat said, "It's easy to tell you're a soldier not a seaman, Captain. You don't have the gait, but, like I said, you'll get used to it."

Ahead of him, Hawkwood could see vague, hump-backed shapes moving. They looked more troglodyte than human. And the smell was far worse down below; a mixture of sweat and piss. Hawkwood tried breathing through his mouth but discovered it didn't make a great deal of difference. He moved forward cautiously. Gradually, the ill-defined creatures began to take on form. He could pick out squares of light on either side, too, and recognized it as daylight filtering in through the grilles in the open ports.

"This is it," Murat said. "The gun deck."

God in heaven, Hawkwood thought.

He could tell by the grey, watery light the deck was about forty feet in width. As to the length, he could only hazard a guess, for he could barely make out the ends. Both fore and aft, they simply disappeared into the blackness. It was more like being in a cellar than a ship's hull. The area in which they were standing was too far from the grilles for the sunlight to penetrate fully but he could just see that benches ran down the middle as well as along the sides. All of them looked to be occupied. Most of the floor was taken up by bodies as well. Despite the lack of illumination, several of the men were engaged in labour. Some were knitting, others were fashioning hats out of what looked like lengths of straw. A number were carving shanks of bone into small figurines that Hawkwood guessed were probably chess pieces. He wondered how anyone could see what they were doing. The sense of claustrophobia was almost overpowering.

He saw there were lanterns strung on hooks along the bulkhead, but they were unlit.

"We try and conserve the candles," Murat explained. "Besides, they don't burn too well down here; too many bodies, not enough air."

For a moment, Hawkwood thought the interpreter was joking, but then he saw that Murat was serious.

There was just sufficient light for Hawkwood to locate the hooks and cleats in the beams from which to hang the hammocks. Many of the hooks had objects suspended from them; not hammocks but sacks, and items of clothing. They looked like huge seedpods hanging down.

Murat followed his gaze. "The long-termers get used to a particular spot. They mark their territory. You can take any hook that's free. Hammocks are slung above and below, so there'll be room for both of you. Best thing is for you to put yours up now. The rest are on the fore-deck; they're taken up there every morning and stowed. When they're brought back down you won't be able to move. You've got about six feet each. Come night time there are more than four hundred of us crammed in here. You're new so you don't get to pick. When you've been here a while you might get a permanent place by the grilles."

"How long have you been here?" Hawkwood asked.

"Two years."

"And how close are *you* to the grilles?"

Murat smiled.

"What if we want a place by the grilles *now*?" Lasseur said. His meaning was clear.

Four hundred? Hawkwood thought.

"It'll cost you," Murat said, without a pause. He read Hawkwood's mind. "Think yourself lucky. You could have been assigned the orlop. There are four hundred and fifty of them down there, and it isn't half as roomy as this."

"How much?" Lasseur asked.

"For two louis, I can get you space by the gun ports. For ten, I can get you a bunk in the commander's cabin."

"Just the gun port," Lasseur said. "Maybe I'll talk to the commander later."

Murat squinted at Hawkwood. "What about you?"

"How much in English money?"

"Cost you two pounds." The interpreter eyed them both. "Cash, not credit."

Hawkwood nodded.

"Wait here," Murat said, and he was gone.

Lasseur stared around him. "I boarded a slaver once, off Mauritius. It turned my stomach. This might be worse."

Hawkwood was quite prepared to believe him.

Lasseur was the captain of a privateer. The French had used privateers for centuries. Financed by private enterprise, they'd been one of the few ways Bonaparte had been able to counteract the restrictions placed upon him by the British blockade. But their numbers had declined considerably over the past few years due to Britain's increased dominance of the waves in the aftermath of Trafalgar.

Getting close to Lasseur had been Ludd's idea, though the initial strategy had been Hawkwood's.

"I need an edge," he'd told James Read and Ludd. "I go in there asking awkward questions from the start and I'm going to end up like your man Masterson. The way to avoid that is to hide in someone else's shadow. I need to make an alliance with a genuine prisoner, someone who'll do the running for me so that I can slip in on his coat-tails. You said you're sending me to Maidstone. Find me someone there I can use."

Ludd had met with Hawkwood the day prior to his arrival at the gaol.

"I think I have your man," Ludd told him. "Name of Lasseur. He was taken following a skirmish with a British patrol off the Cap Gris-Nez. The impudent bugger tried to jump ship twice following his capture; even had the temerity to make a dash for freedom during his transfer from Ramsgate. If anyone's going to be looking for an escape route, it'll be Lasseur; you can count on it. He's made a boast that no English prison will be able to hold him. Get close to him and my guess is you're halfway home already."

The introduction had been manufactured in the prison yard.

Lasseur had been by himself, back against the wall, enjoying the morning sun, an unlit cheroot clamped between his teeth, when the two guards made their move. The plan would never have been awarded marks for subtlety. One guard snatched the cheroot from between Lasseur's lips. When the Frenchman protested, the second guard slammed his baton into Lasseur's belly and a knee into his groin. As Lasseur dropped to the ground, covering his head, the guards waded in with their boots.

A cry of anger went up from the other prisoners, but it was Hawkwood who got there first. He pulled the first guard off Lasseur by his belt and the scruff of his neck. As his companion was hauled back, the second guard turned, baton raised, and Hawkwood slammed the heel of his boot against the guard's exposed knee. He pulled his kick at the moment of contact, but the strike was still hard enough to make the guard reel away with a howl of pain.

By this time, the first guard had recovered his balance. With a snarl, he swung his baton towards Hawkwood's head. But the guard had forgotten Lasseur. The privateer was back on his feet. As the baton looped through the air, Lasseur caught the guard's wrist, twisted the baton out of his grip, and slammed an elbow into the guard's belly.

Shouts rang out as other guards, wrongfooted by the swiftness of Hawkwood's intervention, came running. It had taken four of them to subdue Hawkwood and Lasseur and march them off into a cell.

The clang of the door and the rasp of the key turning in the lock had seemed as final as a coffin lid closing.

Lasseur's first action as soon as the door shut was to take another cheroot from his jacket, put it between his lips and ask Hawkwood if he had a means by which to light it. Hawkwood had been unable to assist. Whereupon Lasseur had shrugged philosophically, placed the cheroot back in his jacket, extended his hand and said, "Captain Paul Lasseur, at your service." Then he'd grinned and touched his ribs tentatively. "I suppose it was one way of getting a cell to ourselves."

Hawkwood hadn't thought it would be that easy.

Lasseur had managed to maintain the devil-may-care façade up to the moment he'd seen the men in the longboat being cast adrift from the hulk's side.

Around them, the other fresh arrivals assigned to the gun deck were also looking for places to bed down. The invasion of their living quarters had caused most of the established prisoners to pause in their tasks to take stock of the new blood. The mood, however, seemed strangely subdued. Hawkwood wondered if the original prisoners resented this further reduction of what was already a barely adequate living space.

Among the new batch was the boy. He was standing alone, weighed down by his hammock, mattress and blanket, utterly bewildered by the activity going on around him; though he was one of the lucky ones in as much as he did not have to amend his posture in order to move about inside the hull. He looked like a small boat tossed by waves as he was turned this way and that by the men brushing past him, mindless of his size.

The boy turned. One of the other prisoners, a slight, weak-chinned, effete-looking man with a widow's peak of thinning hair – a long-standing resident of the hulk if the decrepit state of his yellow uniform was any indication – was crouched down with his right hand on the boy's shoulder.

Hawkwood watched as a look of doubt crept over the boy's face. The boy shook his head. The man spoke again, his expression solicitous. The boy tried to squirm away from the man's touch, but the latter took hold of his jacket sleeve. The hand on the boy's shoulder slid down and began to make gentle circular movements in the small of the boy's back. The boy looked petrified. Hawkwood took a step forward.

"No," Lasseur said softly, "I'll deal with it."

Hawkwood watched as Lasseur ducked beneath the beams and the hanging sacks. He saw the privateer place his hand on the man's shoulder, lean in close and speak softly into his ear. The man said something back. Lasseur spoke again and the man's smile slipped. Then he was holding his hands up and backing away. Lasseur did not touch the boy but squatted down and spoke to him.

A voice in Hawkwood's ear said, "Right, it's all arranged; a room with a view for both of you." Murat looked around. "Where's your friend?"

"Here," Lasseur said. He was standing behind them. The boy stood at his side, clutching his bedding. "This is Lucien. Lucien, say hello to Captain Hooper and our interpreter, Lieutenant . . . my apologies, I didn't catch your given name."

"Auguste," Murat said.

"Lieutenant Auguste Murat," Lasseur finished. He fixed Murat with an uncompromising eye. "I want space for the boy as well."

Murat's eyebrows rose. He shook his head. "I regret that's not possible."

"Make it possible," Lasseur said.

"There's no room, Captain," Murat protested.

"There's always room," Lasseur said.

Murat looked momentarily taken aback by Lasseur's abrasive tone. He stared down at the boy, took in the small, pale features and then threw Lasseur a calculating look. "It could be expensive."

"You *do* surprise me," Lasseur said.

Murat's brow wrinkled, unsure how to respond to Lasseur's barb, before it occurred to him it was probably best to tell them to wait once more and that he would return.

Hawkwood and Lasseur watched him go.

"I have a son," Lasseur said. He did not elaborate but looked down. "How old are you, boy?"

The boy gripped his bedding. In a wavering voice, he said, "Ten, sir."

"Are you now? Well, stick with us and you might just make it to eleven."

Murat reappeared and, unsmiling, crooked a finger. "Come with me."

Stepping around and over bodies, heads bent, the two men and the boy followed the interpreter towards the starboard side of the deck.

"You're in luck –" Murat spoke over his shoulder "– another place has become vacant. The former owner doesn't need it any more."

"That's fortunate," Lasseur said. He caught Hawkwood's eye and winked. "And why's that?"

"He died."

Lasseur halted in his tracks.

Murat held up his hands. "Natural causes, Captain, on my mother's life."

Lasseur looked sceptical.

"From the fever. They say it's due to the air coming off

the marshes." Murat jabbed a thumb towards the open grilles. "It's the same both sides of the river. It's what most men die of, that and consumption. That's the way it happens on the hulks. You rot from the inside out."

Hawkwood noticed that the prisoners near the gun ports were making use of the light to read or write, using the bench along the side of the hull as a makeshift table. Some were conversing with their companions while they wrote. As he passed, Hawkwood realized they were conducting classes. He looked over a hunched shoulder and guessed by the illustrations and indecipherable script that the subject was probably mathematics.

"It's best to try and keep busy," Murat said, interrupting Hawkwood's observations. "You'll lose your mind, otherwise. Many men have." The lieutenant pointed. "Here you are, gentlemen. Welcome to your new home."

Compared to where they'd just come from, it was the height of luxury. Hawkwood wondered how Murat had persuaded the previous incumbents to relinquish such a valuable location. It didn't seem possible that anyone would want to do so voluntarily. Maybe they were dead, too.

They weren't, Murat assured them. "It's just that they prefer food to a view. You'd feel that way, too, if you hadn't had a square meal for a week," Murat added, pocketing his fee. "You'll learn that soon enough. If I were you, I'd guard my purse. Don't indulge in fripperies. The price you've just paid for your sleeping spot will buy three weeks' rations. Not that they give us anything worth eating, mind you. There are some who'd say death from the fever would be a merciful release. If you want to make a bit of money, by the way, you can rent out your part of the bench."

"I knew I could count on you," Lasseur said. "I had this feeling in my bones."

The interpreter permitted himself a small smile. His teeth

were surprisingly even, though in the gloom they were the colour of damp parchment. "Thank you, Captain. And might I say it's been a pleasure doing business with you."

Murat turned. "And the same goes for you, Captain Hooper. It's a pleasure to meet an American. I've long been an admirer of your country. Now, if there's anything else you require, don't hesitate to ask. You'll find I'm the man to do business with. You want to buy, come to Murat. You have something to sell, come to Murat. My terms are very favourable, as you'll see."

"You're a credit to free enterprise, Lieutenant," Lasseur said.

Murat volunteered a full-blown conspiratorial grin. "You're going to fit right in here, Captain." The interpreter gave a mock salute. "Now, if you'll excuse me, gentlemen." And with that, he turned on his heel, and walked off. To hand the money on, Hawkwood assumed, minus his commission, of course.

"I do believe we've just been robbed," Lasseur said cheerfully, and then shrugged. "But it was neatly done. I can see we're going to have to keep our eyes on Lieutenant Murat. Did you ever have any dealings with his cousin?"

Hawkwood shook his head and said wryly, "Can't say I'm likely to, either, considering I'm an American and he's the King of Naples."

"I keep forgetting: your French is very good. Murat's cousin served in Spain, though."

"I know," Hawkwood said. "And your army has been trying to clean up his damned mess ever since."

Lasseur looked taken aback by Hawkwood's rejoinder. Then he nodded in understanding. "Ah, yes, the uprising."

It had been back in '08. In response to Bonaparte's kidnapping of the Spanish royal family in an attempt to make Spain a French satellite, the Spanish had attacked the French garrison in Madrid. Retaliation, by troops under the command of the flamboyant Joachim Murat, had been swift and brutal and had led to a nationwide insurrection against the invaders, which had continued, with the assistance of the British, ever since.

Lasseur gave a sigh. "Kings and generals have much to answer for."

"Presidents and emperors, too," Hawkwood said.

Lasseur chuckled.

The boy moved to the port and stared through the grille.

Hawkwood did the same. Over the boy's shoulder he could see ships floating at anchor and beyond them the flat, featureless shoreline and, further off, some anonymous buildings with blue-grey rooftops. He heard the steady tread of boot heel on metal. He'd forgotten the walkway. It was just outside the scuttles. He waited until the guard's shadow had passed then gripped the grille and tried to shake it. There was no movement. The crossbars were two inches thick and rock solid.

"Well, I doubt we'll be able to cut our way out," Lasseur said, running an exploratory hand over the metal.

"Planning on making a run for it?" Hawkwood asked.

"Why do you think I would never ask for parole?" Lasseur said. "You wouldn't want me to break my word, would you?" The Frenchman grinned and, for a moment, there was a flash of the man who had arrived in the gaol cell at Maidstone looking for a means to light his cheroot. He regarded Hawkwood speculatively.

"I'm still considering my options," Hawkwood said.

Lasseur smiled.

The irony was that Lasseur wouldn't have been entitled to parole anyway, even if he hadn't already proved he was a potential escape risk by virtue of his earlier breaks for freedom.

There were stringent rules governing the granting of parole, which entitled an officer to live outside the prison to which he'd been assigned. It meant securing accommodation in a designated parole town, sometimes taking a room with a local family or, if possessed of sufficient funds, within a lodging house or inn. In return, the officer gave his word he would not break his curfew but would remain within the town limits and make no attempt to escape. The penalty for transgressing, if apprehended, was a swift return to a prison cell.

The rules were stricter for men like Lasseur. A privateer officer's eligibility for parole status depended upon the size of the vessel in which he'd been taken. If the ship was less than 80 tons and mounting less than fourteen carriage guns of at least four-pound calibre, he would not be accorded parole status. Lasseur's command, at 125 tons and mounted with six-pound cannon, qualified, but unfortunately for the privateer he had not been captured on his own vessel.

Lasseur's ship, *Scorpion,* was a ten-gun schooner and his eyes lit up whenever he spoke of her.

"She may not be the biggest vessel afloat, but she's as fast as the wind and her sting is deadly, and she's all mine." Lasseur had given a rueful smile. "And if I'd had her beneath my feet, we'd not be having this conversation."

Scorpion had been laid up in Dunkerque for repairs following a difference of opinion with a British fifth-rate on blockade patrol. On that occasion *Scorpion* had not been fast enough to avoid the British gun crew's aim, but with the aid of a convenient fog bank she had managed to give her pursuer the slip and make a successful run for home. While awaiting repairs, Lasseur had been talked into delivering dispatches between ports along the North French coast. His transport had been a two-masted caique or – as Lasseur had described it – a floating piece of excrement, and no match for the British sloop that had appeared out of nowhere and which, with a twelve-pounder carronade, had blown the caique's main mast and rudder into matchwood and taken her crew and temporary captain captive. Lasseur had told Hawkwood that he didn't know which would prove the most embarrassing experience, his capture or the ribbing he'd receive when he was reunited with *Scorpion*'s crew: "They will make my life intolerable."

When Hawkwood hinted that any reunion was liable to be some way off, Lasseur had fixed him with a steadfast gaze. "They know I'm a prisoner. When I escape, I will send word and they will come for me."

Recalling Lasseur's words and watching him test the strength of the bars, it was hard not to admire the man's faith, though Hawkwood still couldn't help but feel that the privateer captain was being a tad over-optimistic. He wondered whether Lasseur, confronted with the reality of his incarceration, was secretly harbouring the same thought. If he was, the man gave no sign.

Hawkwood's musings were interrupted by a sudden warning shout, followed immediately by the clatter of boots on the stairs. The prisoners seated around the gun ports scrambled to put away their paper and pens. Standing up, they moved towards the centre of the hull. Not knowing why, Hawkwood, Lasseur and the boy followed suit and watched as a dozen guards wielding lanterns and iron bars, led by a bovine corporal, thrust their way on to the deck.

4

"Here they come," a man next to Hawkwood muttered. "Sons of bitches!"

"What's happening?" Hawkwood asked.

The prisoner turned. His uniform hung off his bony frame. His hair was grey. A neat beard concealed his jaw. The state of his attire and the colour of his hair suggested he was not a young man, yet there was a brightness in his eyes that seemed out of kilter with the rest of his drawn appearance. He could have been any age from forty to seventy. He was clutching several books and sheets of paper.

"Inspection." The prisoner looked Hawkwood up and down. "Just arrived?"

Hawkwood nodded.

"Thought so. I could tell by your clothes. The name's Fouchet." The prisoner juggled with his books and held out a hand. "Sébastien Fouchet."

"Hooper," Hawkwood said. He wondered how much pressure to apply to the handshake, but then found he was surprised by the strength in the returned grip.

Fouchet nodded sagely. "Ah, yes, the American. I heard we had one on board. You speak French very well, Captain."

Jesus, Hawkwood thought. He didn't recall seeing Fouchet

in the vicinity of the weather-deck when his name had been registered. Word had got round fast.

"How often does this happen?" Hawkwood asked.

"Every day. Six o'clock in the summer, three o'clock in the winter."

The guards proceeded to spread about the deck. There was no provision made for anyone seated on the floor, nor for the items upon which they might have been working. Hawkwood watched as boot heels crunched down on to ungathered chess pieces, toys and model ships. Ignoring the protestations of those prisoners who were still trying to retrieve their belongings, the guards proceeded to tap the bulkheads and floor with the iron clubs. When they got to the gun ports they paid close attention to the grilles. The deck resounded to the sound of metal striking metal. Hawkwood wondered how much of the guards' loutish behaviour was for effect rather than a comprehensive search for damage or evidence of an escape attempt. Not that the strategy was particularly innovative. It was a tried-and-tested means of imposing authority and cowing an opponent into submission.

Satisfied no obvious breaches had been made in the hulk's defences, the guards retraced their steps. Peace returned to the gun deck and conversation resumed.

"Bastards," Fouchet swore softly. He nodded towards Lasseur and then squinted at the boy. "And who do we have here?"

Hawkwood made the introductions.

"There are other boys on board," Fouchet said. "You should meet them. We've created quite an academy for ourselves below decks. We cover a wide range of subjects. I give lessons in geography and geometry." Fouchet indicated the books he was holding. "If you'd like to attend my classes I will introduce you. It is not good for a child to while away his day in idle pursuits. Young minds should be cultivated at every opportunity. What do you say?" Fouchet gave the boy no chance to reply but continued: "Excellent, then it's agreed. Lessons will commence tomorrow morning, at nine o'clock sharp, by the third gun port on the starboard side. Adults are welcome to attend too. For them, the charge is a sou a lesson." He pointed down the hull and turned to go.

Lasseur placed a restraining hand on the teacher's arm. "Did you see what happened to the men in the boat?"

The teacher frowned. "Which boat?"

"The one before ours; the one left to drift. The men were too weak to board."

"Ah, yes." The teacher's face softened. "I hear they were taken on board the *Sussex*."

"*Sussex*?"

"The hospital ship. She's the one at the head of the line." Fouchet pointed in the direction of the bow.

Lasseur let go of the teacher's arm. "Thank you, my friend."

"My pleasure. There'll be another inspection in an hour, by the way, to count heads, so it wouldn't do to get too comfortable. I'll look out for you at supper. I can show you the ropes. In return, you can tell me the news from outside. It will help deflect our minds from the quality of the repast. What's today, Friday? That means cod. I warn you it will be inedible. Not that it makes any difference what day it is; the food's always inedible." The teacher smiled and gave a short, almost formal bow. "Gentlemen."

Hawkwood and Lasseur watched Fouchet depart. His gait was slow and awkward, and there was a pronounced stiffness in his right leg.

"Cod," Lasseur repeated miserably, closing his eyes. "Mother of Christ!"

The next contingent of guards did not use iron bars. Instead, they used muskets and fixed bayonets to corral the prisoners on to the upper deck. From there they were made to return to the lower deck and counted on their way down. The lieutenant who had overseen the registration was in charge. His name, Hawkwood discovered, was Thynne.

The count was a protracted affair. By the time it was completed to the lieutenant's satisfaction, shadows were lengthening and spreading across the deck like a black tide. In the dim light, the prisoners made their way to the forecastle to queue for their supper rations.

The food was as unappetizing as Fouchet had predicted. The prisoners were divided into messes, six prisoners to a mess. Their rations were distributed from the wooden, smoke-stained shack on the forecastle. Sentries stood guard as a representative from each mess collected bread, uncooked potatoes and fish from an orderly in the shack. The food was then taken to cauldrons to be boiled by those prisoners who'd been nominated for kitchen duty. Each mess then received its allocation. Fouchet was the representative for Hawkwood's mess.

Lasseur stared down at the contents of his mess tin. "Even Frenchmen can't make anything of this swill." He nudged a lump of potato with his wooden spoon. "I shall die of starvation."

"I doubt you'll die alone," Hawkwood said.

"It could be worse," Fouchet said morosely. "It could be a Wednesday."

"What happens on Wednesdays?" Lasseur asked, hesitantly and instantly suspicious.

"Tell him, Millet." Fouchet nudged the man seated next to him, a sad-eyed, sunken-chested seaman whose liver-spotted forearms were adorned with tattooed sea serpents.

The seaman scooped up a portion of cod and eyed the

morsel with suspicion. "We get salted herring." Millet shovelled the piece of fish into his mouth and chewed noisily. He didn't have many teeth left, Hawkwood saw. The few that remained were little more than grey stumps. Hawkwood suspected he was looking at a man suffering from advancing scurvy. Hardly surprising, given the diet the men were describing.

Lasseur regarded the man with horror.

"We usually sell them back to the contractor." The speaker was seated next to Millet at the end of the table. He was a cadaverous individual with deep-set brown eyes, a hooked nose, and a lot of pale flesh showing through the holes in his prison clothes. "He gives us two sous. The following week, he returns the herring to us so that we can sell them back to him again. Most of us use the money to buy extra rations like cheese or butter. It helps take the taste of the bread away."

Lasseur picked up a piece of dry crust. "Call this bread? This stuff would make good round shot. If we'd had this at Trafalgar, things would have been different."

"What do you think the British were using?" Fouchet said. He lifted his piece of bread and rapped it on the table top. It sounded like someone striking a block of wood with a hammer. He winked at the boy, who up to that moment had been trying, without success, to carve a potato with the edge of his spoon. "Give it here," Fouchet said, and solved the problem by mashing the offending vegetable under his own utensil. He handed the bowl back and the boy smiled nervously and resumed eating. He was the only one at the table not to have passed comment on the food.

"Do they *ever* give us meat?" Hawkwood asked.

"Every day except Wednesdays and Fridays," Millet said, with a marked lack of enthusiasm. "Don't ask what sort of meat it is, though. The contractors keep telling us it's beef, but who knows? Could be anything from pork to porcupine."

Fouchet shook his head. "It's not porcupine. Had that once; it was quite tasty."

Lasseur chuckled. "How long have you been here, my friend?"

Fouchet wrinkled his brow. "What year is it?"

Lasseur's jaw fell open.

"I'm joking," Fouchet said. He stroked his beard and added, "Three years here. Before this I was on the *Suffolk* off Portsmouth." He jabbed a finger at the tall, hook-nosed prisoner. "Charbonneau's been held the longest. How long has it been, Philippe?"

Charbonneau pursed his lips. "Seven years come September."

Seven years, Hawkwood thought. The table fell quiet as the men considered the length of Charbonneau's internment and all that it implied.

"Anyone ever get away?" Hawkwood asked nonchalantly. He exchanged a glance with Lasseur as he said it.

"Escape?" Fouchet appeared to ponder the question, as if no one had asked it before. Finally, he shrugged. "A few. Most don't get very far. They're brought back and punished."

"Punished how?" Hawkwood pressed.

"They get put in the hole," Millet said, removing a fish bone from between his teeth and flicking it over his shoulder.

Hawkwood scraped his lump of cod to the side of his mess tin. "Hole?"

"The *black* hole." Millet's tone implied that he could only have meant the one hole and Hawkwood should have known that.

Fouchet laid down his spoon. "It's a special punishment

cell; makes the gun deck look like the gardens at Versailles."

Across the table, Lasseur considered the description. He stared hard at Fouchet and said, "What about the ones who got away, how did they do it?"

Fouchet shrugged. "You'd have to find them and ask them."

"You don't know?" Lasseur said.

"Sometimes it pays not to ask too many questions."

"You've never considered it?"

The teacher shook his head. "It's a young man's game. I don't have the energy. Besides, the war won't last for ever."

"The Lord loves an optimist," Charbonneau muttered, scratching the inside of his groin energetically.

Lasseur pushed his tin to one side. "I have to ask, Sébastien: how, in the name of the blessed Virgin, did someone like *you* end up in a place like *this*?"

Fouchet smiled, almost sadly. "Ah, if you only knew how many times I've asked myself that very same question."

"You going to eat that?" Millet sniffed, indicating the remains of Lasseur's fish.

Lasseur gave him a look as if to say, *What do* you *think?* He then watched, fascinated, as the seaman reached over and, with grubby fingers, helped himself from the tin.

"I committed an indiscretion," Fouchet said. "I was a professor of mathematics at the university in Toulouse and I had a liaison with the wife of one of my colleagues. He did not take kindly to the title of cuckold and insisted on calling me out. Unfortunately for him, I proved the better shot. His friends took it rather personally. They had influence, I did not. I lost my position, along with what little that remained of my reputation. When I applied for alternative teaching posts, I found doors were shut in my face. I sought solace in the grape; a panacea not exactly conducive to the furtherance of one's career. That would have been the end of it, had it not been for a miracle."

"What happened?"

A rueful smile split Fouchet's creased face. "I was conscripted."

The grins began to circulate around the table until Millet, who started to laugh, forgot he was still trying to digest Lasseur's discarded cod. He was turning red when Charbonneau slapped a palm between his shoulder blades, bringing him back to the vertical and the rest of the table to their senses and reality.

Hawkwood guessed Fouchet's situation wasn't unique. The latter's reference to the hulk's self-founded academy and the standard of workmanship he'd observed looking over prisoners' shoulders as he'd traversed the gun deck was proof of that. It was one of the notable differences between the British and French forces. Whereas Britain swelled the ranks with volunteers – which in many cases meant felons and homeless men looking for a roof and a meal – Bonaparte's troops contained a large portion of conscripted men from all walks of life. In all likelihood, there were probably as many skilled craftsmen and teachers among the mass of prisoners on board *Rapacious* as there were in any of the small towns lining the shores of the surrounding estuary.

"I see you favour your right leg," Lasseur said. "You were wounded?"

Fouchet smiled. "Musket ball; just below my knee." He tapped the joint. "It's the devil in cold weather; doesn't work too well in the damp either."

The teacher turned to Hawkwood. "So, Captain Hooper; what's your story? How did you come to be captured?"

"There were more of them than there was of me," Hawkwood said.

Fouchet smiled. "I believe I overheard Murat say it was at Ciudad Rodrigo?"

Hawkwood nodded.

"That's a long way from home. What was an American doing there?"

The question Hawkwood had been expecting and of which he was most wary.

"Shooting British soldiers; officers mostly."

"Why?"

"Your Emperor was paying me."

Fouchet smiled. "I meant why *you*?"

"I'm a sharpshooter: First Regiment of United States Riflemen. I thought you might need my help."

"Cheeky bastard," Charbonneau said. "What makes you think France needs your help?"

Millet rolled his eyes. "Look around, idiot."

Construct a biography based on your own expertise, James Read had told him. An officer from the Regiment of Riflemen had been the obvious choice. The American equivalent of Hawkwood's former regiment, the Rifle Corps, used the same methods as its British counterpart, combining the tactics of the Light Infantry and, in the case of the Americans, native Indians, to harass and disrupt enemy movements. The first into the field and the last to leave.

"Heard that was a fearsome fight," Millet said.

Fouchet frowned. "The siege took two weeks, I think I read."

"Twelve days," Hawkwood said. "Might as well have tried to stop the tide. How do you mean, *read*?"

"It was in the newspapers. They're forbidden, but we manage to smuggle them in. Costs us a fortune. A few of us understand some English, but it's usually Murat who translates. Not that we believe *everything* that's in them, of course. You were wounded?" The teacher indicated Hawkwood's facial scars.

"One of their riflemen took a stab at me with his bayonet."

"You were lucky. You could have lost the eye."

"He was upset." Hawkwood shrugged. "We'd killed a lot of his comrades. Our cannon blew them to pieces. It didn't stop them coming at us, though."

"What happened to the rifleman?" Charbonneau asked.

"I killed him," Hawkwood said. "He died, I lived. We surrendered. The British won."

Hawkwood's manufactured account wasn't too far from truth. He'd read the dispatches. The Rifles had been in the thick of the action, providing covering fire for the Forlorn Hope, the forward troops leading the assault on the walls. The breach had been nearly a hundred feet wide, a huge target for the French gunners who'd launched a hail of grapeshot on to the attackers. It was only after the cannons had been destroyed and a French magazine had blown up that the British had managed to finally take the town. That much had been covered in the newspapers, but only the dispatches covered the aftermath, with accounts of how British soldiers, incensed by the slaughter of so many of their comrades, had gone on a drunken rampage. To prevent a massacre, officers had been forced to draw their swords on their own men. To add to his woes, Wellington had lost two of his best generals: Mackinnon of the 3rd Division and the Light Brigade's Black Bob Crauford, under whom Hawkwood had served on a number of engagements.

"Bastards," Millet muttered. "Goddamned bastards!"

The occupants of the table fell into a sombre silence.

Charbonneau broke the spell. "What about you?" he asked Lasseur.

Lasseur launched into a humorous account of his capture

and imprisonment. It wasn't long before his audience was smiling again, by which time supper was almost over. The messes began to break apart as the prisoners retrieved their hammocks from the foredeck and took them down to their allotted spaces below.

The boy had fallen asleep at the table, head across his folded arms.

"What's his story?" Fouchet asked, as Millet and Charbonneau left to reclaim their aired bedding.

Lasseur shook his head. "He hasn't said much. My guess is he got separated from the rest of his crew. So far, all he's given me is his name."

Fouchet nodded his understanding. "I suspect he'll be all right once he's with someone his own age. I'll have a word with the other boys. Perhaps he'll talk to them. In the meantime, it would be in his best interest if you kept a watch on him."

The quiet note of warning in the teacher's voice caused Lasseur to pause as he got up from the table. "That sounds ominous. Something you're not telling us?"

"The boy's young, small for his age, an innocent from what you've told me and from what I've observed. He's also far from home and therefore doubly vulnerable. It should come as no surprise to you that there are those on board who would be likely to take advantage of his situation."

Lasseur sat back down. "How likely?"

Fouchet smiled sadly. "My friend, there are over nine hundred men on this ship. More than eight hundred of them are imprisoned as much by inactivity as they are by these wooden walls. I suspect you already know the answer to your question." The teacher picked up his tin and utensils and rose stiffly from his seat.

From the look on Lasseur's face Hawkwood knew the

privateer captain was remembering his exchange with the balding man on the gun deck. Lasseur stared down at the sleeping boy. His face was as hard as stone. "I'll bear that in mind," he said.

It wasn't the first time Hawkwood had experienced the restraints of a hammock. There was a definite art to clambering into the sling, but it was a case of once mastered, never forgotten. As a soldier, he'd grown used to bivouacking in uncomfortable surroundings, be it barn, bush or battlefield. On the march, you took advantage of sleep and sustenance when and where you could, because you never knew when the opportunity would arise again. A hammock was the epitome of comfort compared to some of the places he'd had to rest his weary head.

He lay back and listened to the emanations of the four hundred souls hemmed in around him. The sounds varied widely in content and tone, from the drawn-out cries of the distressed and the wheezing of the consumptives to the groans of the dysentery sufferers and the weeping of the lonely and dispossessed. When added to the chorus of swearing, hawking, spitting, farting, coughing and general expectorations common to the male species, they formed a discordant backdrop to the physical deprivations endured by men held in mass confinement and against their will.

The human sounds began to fade as the hulk's inhabitants fell under the spell of night. In the darkness, however, the ship continued to express her own displeasure. A continuous cacophony of groans and creaks from the vessel's ancient timbers filled the inside of the hull. It was as if *Rapacious* was venting her irritation at the presence of those trapped aboard her. The pull of the tide and the sound of the wash against her sides seemed magnified a thousand-fold, as did the hypnotic slap of rope and line against her cut-down masts and yards.

Mercifully, her gun ports remained propped open, for these were the only means of ventilation. Even so, it was unbearably warm. The squeak of hammock ring against hook and cleat was a grating accompaniment to the noisy tossing and turning of the gun deck's restless residents as they sought relief from their sweltering discomfort.

Even if there had been silence within the hull, the rhythmic step of the sentries along the metal gantry outside and their monotonous half-hourly announcements that all was well was a salutary reminder that the will of every man on board, be he prisoner or guard, was no longer his own to command.

A sniffle sounded close by. It was the boy. He was lying on his back, blanket pushed down over his lower legs. His right arm rested across his face as if to ward off a blow. As Hawkwood watched, the boy turned his head, the movement revealing his right eye and lower jaw.

At that moment, a scream rose out of the darkness. It seemed to hang in the air for two or three seconds before ceasing abruptly. Hawkwood knew it had originated not on the gun deck but somewhere below, deep within the bowels of the ship. There was little or no reaction from either the sentries outside or the occupants of the surrounding hammocks, save for one: the boy. Moonlight from the open gun port highlighted a pale segment of cheek, skin tight over the bone. The boy's eye was a white orb in the darkness. He stared wildly at Hawkwood for several seconds, terror written on his face, then his throat convulsed and he turned away, pulled the blanket over himself, and the contact was lost.

The scream was not repeated. A small, rounded shadow appeared at the grille. A rat was squatting on the sill, preening. As if suddenly aware that it was being observed, it paused in its ablutions and lifted its head. Then, with a flash of pelt and a flick of tail, it was gone.

Hawkwood closed his eyes. It was interesting, he thought, that the rat, when startled, had chosen to exit the hull rather than seek sanctuary within it.

Perhaps it was another omen.

5

Hawkwood stood at the rail of the forecastle and gazed down at his new world. The view was less than impressive.

Aside from the two accommodation decks, the only other areas on the ship where prisoners were permitted to gather were the forecastle and the well deck, the space referred to euphemistically by the interpreter Murat as "the Park". Lasseur had taken it upon himself to pace out the Park's circumference. The survey did not take long. It was a little over fifty feet long by forty feet in width. It didn't need many prisoners to be taking the air to make the deck seem overcrowded. It explained why so many men chose to remain below decks. With space at a premium, they didn't have much choice.

Bulkheads at the forward and aft ends of the ship separated the prisoners' quarters from those of the ship's personnel. The militia guards occupied the bow. The hulk's commander and the rest of the crew were accommodated in the stern. At first sight, the bulkheads appeared to be made of solid iron. On closer inspection, Hawkwood discovered they were constructed from thick planking studded with thousands of large-headed nails. Loopholes had been cut into the metal-shod walls at regular intervals to allow the guards on the other side of the partition to fire into the enclosed deck in the event of misbehaviour or riot. They resembled the arrow-slitted walls of a medieval keep. With the gun deck reminiscent of a long dungeon, it wasn't hard to imagine the hulk as some kind of bleak, impregnable fortress.

At six o'clock the guards had removed the hatch covers, allowing the prisoners to carry their bedding topside to be aired. Hawkwood had welcomed the first light of dawn, still conscious of the collective reek coming off his fellow inmates. Lieutenant Murat had given his assurance that it would take only a few days to become acclimatized. As far as Hawkwood was concerned, the moment couldn't come soon enough. The gun-port location may have provided access to the elements and a sea view, but it didn't mean the smell was in any way reduced. The foul odours within the hulk had built up over so many years that they'd become engrained in the ship's structure, like a host of maggots in a rotting corpse.

Breakfast had been a mug of water and a hunk of dry bread left over from the previous evening's supper. The fist-sized block of stale dough had been made marginally more digestible when dunked into the water. It remained small consolation for what had been, despite Hawkwood's ability to negotiate the hammock, a fitful night's sleep. Though it was a soldier's lot to bed down when and wherever he could, it did not always follow that slumber came easily. The night had seemed endless. Lasseur looked equally unrested as he peered out across the choppy brown water.

Perched at the extreme north-west corner of the Isle of Sheppey, Sheerness dockyard lay across the starboard quarter; an uneven line of warehouses, barracks and workshops. Rising above these was the fortress; its squat, square outline surmounted by a grey-roofed tower. Guarding the entrance to the Medway River, the fort dominated its surroundings, a stone defender awaiting an unwise invader.

To the south, at the edge of the yard, lay Blue Town. The settlement provided accommodation for the local workforce and owed its name to the colour of the buildings, all of which had been daubed in the same shade of naval paint. Made almost entirely from wood chips left over from the dockyard work, the small houses weren't much more than crude shacks, clumped together in an untidy rat-run of narrow lanes. Even so, they were several steps up from the previous riverside accommodation. Originally, dock workers had been housed in hulks, not dissimilar to *Rapacious*, moored to break the flow of the river and reduce the loss of shingle from the foreshore. A couple of them still remained, stranded on the mud like beached whales after a storm.

Across the river, a mile away to port, the Isle of Grain was a dark green smudge in the early-morning light, while beyond the stern rail, less than two miles to the south, lay the western mouth of the Swale Channel, separating Sheppey from the mainland.

The weather had improved considerably. Despite the sunshine, however, there was a stiff breeze and it brought with it the smell of the sea and the cloying, fœtid odour of the surrounding marshes, which stretched away on both sides of the water.

A cry of warning sounded from the quarterdeck where Lieutenant Thynne was supervising the delivery of provisions from a small flotilla of bumboats drawn up alongside the hulk. Fresh water casks were being hoisted on board to replace the empty ones lifted from the hold, and one of the casks had come adrift from its sling. It was the second delivery of the day. The bread ration had arrived less than an hour before and had already been delivered to the galley.

Lasseur eyed the activity with interest. "What do you think?" he said.

Hawkwood followed his gaze to where the wayward cask was being secured. "It'd be a tight fit."

Lasseur grinned.

Hawkwood looked sceptical. "How do you know they don't check inside as soon as they get them ashore?"

"How do you know they do?"

"I would," Hawkwood said. "It'd be the first place I'd look."

"You're probably right," Lasseur murmured. "Worth considering, though." He reached into his coat, drew out a cheroot, and gazed at it wistfully.

"I'd make that last," Hawkwood said. "They tell me tobacco's hard to come by. Expensive, too."

Lasseur stuck the unlit cheroot between his lips and closed his eyes. He remained that way for several seconds, after which he placed the cheroot back in his coat and sighed. "The sooner I get off this damned ship, the better."

Latching on to Lasseur appeared to have been a sound investment. From the moment they'd been thrust into the Maidstone cell together, the privateer captain had made it clear he was looking to make his escape. Gaining the man's confidence had been the first step. James Read had been correct in his surmise that Hawkwood's background story and the scars on his face would stand him in good stead. Lasseur and the others had accepted him as one of their own. Hawkwood's task now was to find some way of exploiting that acceptance. Where Lasseur went, Hawkwood intended to follow.

Hawkwood allowed himself a smile. It was strange, he thought, given the short time he'd known him, how much he'd come to like Lasseur. It had been an unexpected turn of events, for the privateer was, after all, the enemy. But wasn't that what happened when men, irrespective of their backgrounds, were thrown together in unfamiliar surroundings? It reminded him of his early days in the Rifle Corps.

When Colonels Coote Manningham and Stewart had put forward their plan for a different type of unit, one which would fight fire with fire and carry the war to the French, the men who were to form the new corps had been drafted in from other regiments. Suddenly the past didn't matter; whether they were draftees or volunteers, was irrelevant. The men's loyalty was to the new regiment, and the glue that bound them together was their willingness to fight for their country and against the French.

On *Rapacious*, it was a similar situation. It didn't matter whether you had been a sailor or a soldier, privateer, teacher or tradesman. The important thing was that you shared a common enemy. And in the case of the men confined aboard the hulk – Hawkwood included – it was the officers and men of His Britannic Majesty's prison ship *Rapacious* who were the foe.

According to Ludd, *Rapacious* hadn't been her only name. During her years as a man-of-war, as a mark of affection her crew had bestowed a nickname upon her: *Rapscallion*, a tribute to her role in causing mischief to the French.

It was doubtful, Hawkwood reflected, looking around him, if any of the seamen who'd raised her sails, scaled her rigging and run out her guns would have recognized her now. Any beauty or sense of pride she might have possessed as a mighty ship of war was long gone. Even with the morning sun slanting across her quarterdeck, with her once graceful profile buried beneath a ramshackle collection of weather-beaten clapboard sheds, she was as ugly as a London slum.

Another cry sounded from the work party. The full water casks had all been taken aboard and the last bumboat was pulling away with its cargo of empty barrels. Several of the full casks remained on deck. The contents were needed for the day's midday soup and to replenish the drinking water tanks. The hoist was repositioned in preparation for the next round of deliveries.

Lasseur turned from the rail. "Walk with me, my friend. I'm in need of some exercise."

The number of prisoners strewn around the deck made it more of an obstacle course than a walk.

"How many soldiers are there on board, do you think?" Lasseur asked. He kept his voice low as they picked their way through the press of bodies.

"Hard to tell," Hawkwood said. "Not less than forty would be my guess." He looked aft, where two members of the militia were patrolling back and forth across the width of the raised quarterdeck, muskets slung over their shoulders. Other militia were spread evenly around the hulk, including one on the forecastle from where they had just descended. Hawkwood had counted three on the gantry and one on the boarding raft, and there was one at each companionway. He suspected several others were standing by, poised to deploy at the first sign of trouble.

The two men left the forecastle and made their way below.

"I did a count last night," Lasseur said as they descended the stairs. "Six on the grating, one manning the raft, and I could hear others on the companionways."

"You didn't waste any time," Hawkwood said.

Lasseur shrugged. "It was hot, I couldn't sleep. What else was I going to do? Besides, I've seen the way you've been looking around."

"There's the crew as well," Hawkwood said.

"I'd not forgotten. How many, would you say?"

Hawkwood shook his head. "On a ship this size? You'd know better than me. Thirty?"

Lasseur thought about it, pursed his lips. "Not so many. Twenty, maybe."

"They'll have access to arms," Hawkwood said.

Lasseur nodded. "Undoubtedly. There'll be an armoury chest: pistols and muskets; cutlasses too, probably." The privateer captain fell silent.

On the gun deck, Hawkwood was surprised by the number of pedlars foraging for business among their fellow prisoners. In their search for both buyers and sellers, they were as persistent as any he'd encountered under the arches of Covent Garden or the Haymarket. The number of men willing to trade away their belongings appeared to be substantial, though from their pitiful appearance, it wasn't hard to see why. Watching the transactions, Hawkwood didn't know which depressed him most: the fact that these men had been reduced to such penury, or the pathetically grateful expressions on their faces when a bargain was struck. Several of the prisoners who'd arrived the previous day were handing over items of clothing in exchange for coinage. They did it furtively, as if shamed by their actions. Hawkwood assumed the money would be used to purchase extra food, a commodity that had become a currency in its own right.

Lasseur read his thoughts. "I was talking with our friend Sébastien earlier. He told me that when he was at Portsmouth one of the men on the *Vengeance* set up his own restaurant and became rich selling slop by the bowl. Wherever there's a shortage of something, there's money to be made."

"Lieutenant Murat would probably agree with you," Hawkwood said.

"Ah, yes, our intrepid interpreter. Now there's a man worth cultivating."

"You trust him?"

"About as far as I can spit."

"That far?" Hawkwood said.

Lasseur laughed.

Hawkwood's attention was diverted by one of the small groups occupying sections of bench over by the starboard gun ports. It was the teacher, Fouchet, and his morning class. His pupils – half a dozen in total – were seated on the floor at his feet. The boy Lucien was with them. He looked to be the youngest. The eldest was about fourteen. Fouchet caught Hawkwood's eye and smiled a greeting. His pupils did not look up.

There were some two score boys on *Rapacious,* Fouchet had told him, ranging in age from ten to sixteen. The practice was not exceptional. Fouchet's previous ship, the *Suffolk,* had held over fifty boys, some as young as nine. Hawkwood had wondered briefly about the Transport Board's wisdom in confining children with the men. But then, the Royal Navy employed boys not much older than the ones attending Fouchet's class as midshipmen and runners for their gun crews, and so presumably saw nothing unusual in sending innocents like Lucien Ballard to face the horrors of life on board a prison hulk. Hawkwood had a vague notion that Nelson had been around the same age as Lucien when he'd gone to sea. He was reminded of some of the street children he employed as informers. Age had never been a consideration there. The only criteria he'd set during their recruitment were that they were fleet of foot, knew the streets, and kept their eyes and ears open.

"My son is twelve," Lasseur said quietly. The privateer captain was also looking towards the group by the gun port.

"Where is he?" Hawkwood asked.

Lasseur continued to watch the class. "With his grandparents in Gévezé. It's near Rennes. They have a farm."

"*Your* mother and father?"

Lasseur paused. "I'm an orphan. They're my wife's parents. She died."

Hawkwood kept silent.

"She fell from her horse. She loved to ride, especially in the early morning." The Frenchman swallowed and for a second time the mask slipped. "I've not seen my son for three months. They send me letters. They tell me he attends school and is good at his lessons and that he likes animals." A small smile flitted across the Frenchman's face. "His name is François." Lasseur turned. "You have a wife, children?"

"No," Hawkwood said.

"A woman? Someone waiting for you?"

Hawkwood thought about Maddie Teague and wondered if she'd ever viewed herself in that role; lonely and pining for her man. He didn't think so, somehow. Maddie was too independent for that. He had a sudden vision of her lying beside him, auburn hair spread across the pillow, emerald-green eyes flashing, a mischievous smile playing across her lips.

"Ah!" Lasseur smiled perceptively. "The look on your face tells me. She is beautiful?"

"Yes," Hawkwood said. "Yes, she is."

Lasseur looked suddenly serious. "Then I'd say we both have a reason to escape this place, wouldn't you?"

"As long as it's not inside a bloody water barrel."

"There'll be other ways," Lasseur said firmly. "All we have to do is find them. Fouchet said there've been a few who've done it. Maybe we should ask him *how* they did it."

"Maybe we should ask somebody who's a bit more devious," Hawkwood said.

Lasseur grinned. "You mean Lieutenant Murat?"

"The very man," Hawkwood said.

The interpreter frowned. "Forgive me, Captain Hooper, but you may recall I was there at your registration. I understood you were waiting for your parole application to be approved. Why would *you* still harbour thoughts of escape?"

"The captain's weighing his options." Lasseur kept his face straight. "No law against that, is there?"

The interpreter's brow remained furrowed. "Indeed not, but you've only been here a day."

"So?" Hawkwood said. "What the hell does that have to do with anything?"

"Perhaps you should be a little more patient."

"Patient?" Lasseur said.

"I've been patient." Hawkwood resisted the urge to wipe the condescending smile from the interpreter's face. "My patience is starting to wear thin."

"And *you've* certainly been biding your time, Lieutenant," Lasseur said icily. "How long have you been here? Two years, is it?" The privateer turned down his mouth. "Perhaps this wasn't such a good idea."

Hawkwood gazed at Murat and gave a slow shake of his head. "We thought you'd be the man to advise us. It looks as if we were wrong." He cast a glance towards Lasseur and shrugged. "Pity."

"You want to know what I think?" Lasseur murmured. "I think the lieutenant's grown a little too complacent, a little too comfortable. I'm guessing he's never even thought of making a run for it himself. He's making too good a living here." Lasseur threw the interpreter a challenging glare. "That's it, isn't it? In fact, I'd wager you're earning a damned sight more through barter and your interpreter's pay than you were as a naval officer. Got yourself a nice little business here, haven't you? You don't *want* to leave. Am I right?"

A nerve pulsed along the interpreter's cheek. "All I'm saying is that it's my understanding these things can take time – weeks, months sometimes."

"What if we don't want to wait that long?" Hawkwood said.

"We couldn't help noticing the water delivery earlier," Lasseur said. "We thought that had potential."

There was a pause. Then the interpreter gave a brief shake of his head. "You can forget the water casks. It did work, but not any more. Nowadays they're the first things they check."

"Really?" Lasseur said. He threw Hawkwood a look. "So much for that idea."

"I told you it looked too damned easy," Hawkwood said. "All right, so what about the other deliveries?"

Lasseur had played the interpreter beautifully. Like a fish caught on a hook, Murat hadn't been able to resist the tug at his vanity. Now, wanting to be considered the font of all knowledge, he shook his head. "That's been tried, too. I told you; the bastards check everything. You'll never get off that way."

Murat's gaze drifted sideways, distracted by the activity around them. The three men were seated next to one of the portside grilles. Hawkwood assumed it was where Murat slung his hammock, for the interpreter had welcomed his and Lasseur's arrival as if granting them entry into his personal fiefdom. Elsewhere, dotted about the deck, the more industrious inhabitants were engaged in a variety of pursuits. Basket makers, letter writers and knitters squatted alongside bone modellers and barbers. Some worked in silence. Others chatted to their neighbours. The scratch of nib, the snip of scissors and the scrape of blade on bone filled the lulls in conversation. Hawkwood wondered if there'd ever been a time when the hulk had fallen entirely silent. He doubted it.

"We could use the cover of night," Lasseur said. "Steal a boat."

Murat shook his head again. "They hoist the boats up alongside. They're at least ten feet above the water. One's kept afloat, but it's secured by a chain from the boarding raft and that's always under guard."

"Damn." Lasseur bit his lip.

Hawkwood addressed Murat. "How did the others get off?"

"Others?" Warily.

"There have been others, haven't there?" Lasseur pressed.

There was a noticeable hesitation. An artful look stole over the interpreter's face. "As I said, Captain, you've only been here a short time. You wouldn't expect all our little secrets to be revealed to you quite so soon."

So, you do have secrets, Hawkwood thought.

Lasseur's eyebrows rose. "Why, Lieutenant, anyone would think you didn't trust us."

The interpreter spread his hands. "For a start, there's the matter of the pot. You haven't put anything in yet."

"Pot?" Lasseur looked to Hawkwood for enlightenment. "What pot? What the devil's he talking about now?"

"Your friend Fouchet didn't tell you?" Murat said, a half smile forming on his lips.

"Tell us what?" Hawkwood sat back.

"There's a contribution taken from our food rations. It's kept back for prisoners on punishment. If anyone disobeys the rules or does damage to the hulk, they're reduced to two-thirds quota. The food we put by is used to help them out."

"Very generous," Lasseur said. "And maybe a little something's put aside for escapers as well? Is that it?"

Murat hesitated again.

"Why, Lieutenant, you sly boots!" Lasseur grinned.

The interpreter coloured.

"All right," Hawkwood said. "Let's not piss around here. What's it going to cost?"

Murat blinked. "What do you mean?"

"Don't take us for fools, Lieutenant."

"Think of your commission." Lasseur arched an eyebrow suggestively.

"And how generous we might be," Hawkwood added.

A light flickered behind the interpreter's eyes.

"Well?" Hawkwood prompted, recognizing the bright glint of greed.

Murat stared at them for a long time. Finally he sighed. "If such a thing could be arranged – and I'm not saying it could – it would not be cheap. There are expenses, you understand."

Lasseur patted the interpreter's knee. "That's my boy." The privateer turned to Hawkwood and winked. "Didn't I tell you Lieutenant Murat was the man to see?"

Murat seemed to flinch from the touch, but he recovered quickly.

Hawkwood leaned forward. "All right, how much?"

The interpreter hesitated again. Hawkwood suspected he was doing it for effect.

"Just for the sake of argument," Hawkwood said.

"For the sake of argument?"

"The three of us having a little chat, nothing more."

Murat looked around. Then, in a low voice, he said, "I'm assuming you would not be expecting passage all the way back to America?"

"You get me as far as French soil and let me worry about the rest."

Murat sat back. "Very well; four thousand francs, or two hundred English pounds, if you prefer."

Hawkwood sucked in his breath.

"Each," Murat finished.

"God's teeth!" Hawkwood sat back. "We don't want to *buy* the bloody ship. We just want to get off it. The highest offer I had for my boots was only twenty francs. We'll both be dead from old age or the flux before we'd earned enough. Are you mad?"

"The price would include all transport, accommodation *and* safe passage to France."

"For that sort of money," Hawkwood said, "I'd expect the Emperor to collect me in a golden barge and carry me up the bloody beach when we got there!"

Lasseur chuckled. Then his face grew serious.

"How the hell do you expect us to find that sort of money?" Hawkwood demanded.

The interpreter shook his head. "An agent makes contact with your families. It's they who arrange payment. Once the full fee's been paid, preparations for your departure would begin."

"How do we get off the ship?"

Murat smiled. "Come now, gentlemen; I'm sure you understand the need for discretion. The less you know at this stage, the safer it will be for all of us. I would also urge you to keep this conversation to yourselves."

"You're telling us the walls have ears?" Lasseur asked.

Murat grimaced. "It's not unknown for the British to plant spies among us, but no, sadly, there have been occasions when betrayal has come from closer to home."

Hawkwood felt his insides contract.

"Traitors?" Lasseur said.

"Not necessarily. You forget, we're not the only nationality on board these hulks. Captain Hooper is proof of that. We've got Danes, Italians, Swedes, Norwegians . . . take your pick. France has many allies. There'll be some who'd look to alleviate their misery by claiming a reward for informing on their fellow prisoners."

Hawkwood prayed that nothing was showing on his face. At least he'd discovered one thing: if there was an organized escape route, it was only available to the rich. He wondered how deep Bow Street's coffers were and what James Read's reaction would be when Ludd relayed details of the amount involved: four years' salary for a Runner.

Hawkwood felt Lasseur's hand on his arm.

He realized the privateer had misinterpreted his silence for doubt when Lasseur said, "You're wondering how you would raise the fee?"

"It's not the money," Hawkwood said, recovering. "It's making the payment."

That could prove an interesting exercise, Hawkwood thought, unless Ludd came up with a practical idea during their meeting.

Lasseur patted Hawkwood's shoulder reassuringly and, to Hawkwood's surprise, said, "No need to fret, my friend." The privateer turned to Murat. "I will cover the fee for Captain Hooper."

Murat looked momentarily nonplussed, then shrugged, almost dismissively. "Very well."

"How long will it be before we hear anything?" Lasseur asked.

"I cannot say. I'll require the name of the person you wish the agent to contact and a note to prove the agent is acting on your behalf. You'll be notified as soon as we receive word that agreement has been reached and payment made." Murat looked at them. "Are the terms acceptable?"

Lasseur and Hawkwood exchanged looks.

"For the sake of argument?" Lasseur said. "Perfectly."

"Well?" Lasseur asked. "What do you think?"

"I think Lieutenant Murat's a duplicitous bastard," Hawkwood said.

They were back on the forecastle. The stifling atmosphere below had been too much to bear. They had emerged topsides to find that the breeze, although still persistent, had dropped considerably.

"I believe we'd already established that," Lasseur said drily, and then frowned. "You're still worrying about the fee, aren't you? As I said, do not concern yourself. You can repay me when we're home."

"You hardly know me," Hawkwood said.

"That's true," Lasseur agreed. "But I'm an excellent judge of character. You'll honour the bargain. I know it." The privateer grinned disarmingly. "And if you prove me wrong, I shall cut out your heart and feed it to the pigs."

"Your wife's parents can find that amount?" Hawkwood asked. He had no idea, but he didn't think a French farmer's income was that high.

"No." Lasseur shook his head, and then said firmly, "But my men can. The name I gave to the lieutenant was one of *my* agents."

"You have agents in England?" Hawkwood said.

"But of course." Lasseur looked surprised that Hawkwood had even thought to ask. "I have a number in my employ. They keep me advised of British naval movements."

Hawkwood sensed his preoccupation with the means of payment must still have shown on his face, for Lasseur paused and then said, "What? Don't tell me you were thinking of waiting in case your parole is granted? Forgive me, but I do not see you as a man content to bide his time in an English coffee house waiting for the war to end. You said I don't know you. Well, I do know you're a soldier, and *you* know both our countries need men like us to continue the fight. That's why we're going to escape from this place. I shall return to my son and my ship. You will return to your woman and your Regiment of Riflemen, and between us we will defeat the British. You will do it for your new country and your President Madison and I will do it for my Emperor and the glory of France. One can never put a fee on patriotism, my friend, and four thousand francs is a small price to pay for victory. What say you?"

Confronted by Lasseur's earnest expression, Hawkwood forced another grin. "I say when do we leave?"

Lasseur slapped him on the back.

It had turned into a fine summer's day. The sunlight and the sharp cries from the gulls circling and diving above them, although plaintive in tone, were a welcome relief after the gloom of the gun deck. Shirts and breeches flapped from the lines strung between the yards. Faint sounds of industry carried from the dockyard: the ringing clang of a hammer, the rattle of a chain, the rasp of timber being sawn. Out on the river, a pair of frigates, sails billowing like grey clouds, raced each other towards the mouth of the estuary.

It was only when the eye returned to the deck of the hulk and on across the sterns of the other prison ships visible over her bow that the view was marred. The hulks squatted in the water as if carved from blocks of coal. Plumes of black smoke pumping from their chimney stacks spiralled into the azure sky, proving that darkness could be visited even upon the very brightest of days.

And as if to emphasize the fact, the calm was shattered by a blood-curdling howl and up on to the already crowded well deck erupted a seething tide of horror.

From his vantage point on the forecastle Hawkwood saw the throng of prisoners break apart. Sharp cries of panic rang out. He heard Lasseur draw in his breath. He wasn't sure what he was seeing at first. It was like watching beetles swarm over the carcass of a dead animal, except the creatures that were spewing out of the hatches and trampling over the Park were not beetles, they were human, and many of them were naked. Their hair was long and matted; their bodies were daubed with filth. The ones that were not naked might as well have been, for the rags they were wearing were little more than strips of tattered cloth. Some of them, Hawkwood realized, were wearing blankets, which they'd wrapped around themselves like togas. Hissing and screeching, fangs bared, they surged around the other prisoners like a marauding pack of baboons, leaping and prancing and in some cases laying about them with fists and feet. Others were beating mess tins. The noise was ferocious.

Yells of alarm echoed around the quarterdeck. As the militia gathered their startled wits and hurried to unsling their muskets, a uniformed officer materialized behind them, tall and thin. The dark, cocked hat accentuated his height. It was the commander of the hulk, Lieutenant Hellard. Flanked by the guards, the lieutenant strode quickly to the rail and stared down at the fracas below. His face contorted. Without moving, he rapped out a command. Half a dozen more guards, led by a corporal, appeared at a clattering run from the lean-to on the stern. Their fellow militia, already at the rails and secure in the knowledge that reinforcements had come to support them, drew back the hammers on their muskets. Within seconds, a battery of gun muzzles was aligned along the width of the quarterdeck.

With the ruction on the Park in full spate, the lieutenant raised his arm. The corporal barked an order and the militia took aim.

God's teeth! Hawkwood thought. *He's going to do it!*

But the lieutenant did not give the order. Instead he continued to watch the drama playing out on the deck. The militia guards' fingers played nervously with the triggers of their guns.

For two or three minutes the uproar continued. Then, suddenly, as if a signal had been given, the situation changed. The naked and toga-clad creatures began to pull back. The other prisoners started to regroup. Several, emboldened by the sight of the retreating horde, waded into their former tormentors, beating them towards the open hatchways. Some were wielding sticks. Arms rose and fell. Cries of pain and anger told where the blows landed. Driven back, the invaders were disappearing down the stairways from which they had so recently emerged, like cockroaches scuttling from the light.

Within seconds, or so it seemed, the attackers had all dispersed. Immediately, several hands were thrust aloft, palms open; a signal that the prisoners left on deck had the situation under control. The lieutenant, however, did not move, nor did he give any indication that he'd even seen the raised hands. Remaining motionless, he watched the deck. The prisoners stared back at him, chests heaving. Some were bloody and bruised. A tense silence fell over the Park. A gull shrieked high above. No one moved. It took another ten seconds before the lieutenant finally let his arm relax and stepped back. Immediately, the tension on the well deck evaporated. The militia uncocked and shouldered their muskets. The reinforcements turned about. The deck guards resumed their posts. The atmosphere on the well deck settled back into its habitual torpor. The hurt prisoners retired to lick their wounds.

Hawkwood discovered he was holding his breath. He let it out slowly.

"What happened there?" Lasseur breathed. "Who in God's name were they?"

"Romans," a voice said behind them. "Bastards!"

Hawkwood and Lasseur turned. It was Charbonneau.

"Romans?" Hawkwood said, thinking he must have misheard.

"Scum," Charbonneau said, his eyes blazing. "They live on the orlop. We don't see them very often. They prefer the dark. Some of them have been here longer than I have. We call them Romans from the way they wear their blankets, like togas. They have other names, but they're still animals. They used to be held in prisons ashore. Got sent to the hulks as punishment, I was told. Now it's the rest of us who're suffering – twice over."

"Some of them were naked!" Lasseur said, unnecessarily.

Charbonneau nodded. "They're the lowest of the lot. They'll be the ones who've gambled all their belongings away. It's how they exist. They have a mania for it. Cards and dice dominate their lives. Most start with money. When that's gone, they wager their clothes and their bedding, even their rations. Sometimes they starve themselves, hoarding their rations to sell them off and then start over again. When they run out of belongings or food they steal from others or roam the decks looking for peelings or fish heads. Even the rats aren't safe. Now and again they send out raiding parties, like the one you just saw."

"*Rafalés,*" Hawkwood murmured.

"Some call them that," Charbonneau said, eyes narrowing. "You've heard of them?"

Hawkwood nodded.

"Why don't the guards punish them?" Lasseur asked.

Charbonneau gave a dry laugh. "How? Look around. You think this place isn't punishment enough? In any case, the commander's hands are tied. They can't be flogged. No prisoner can. Direct physical punishment's forbidden, unless a British soldier or crew member is harmed."

"So he wouldn't have given the order to fire?" Lasseur said.

"Not unless there'd been a full-scale riot which threatened the safety of his men. As far as our commander's concerned, any disagreement between prisoners is dealt with by prisoners' tribunal." Charbonneau sniffed dismissively. "What goes on below deck stays below deck. It's got so that the guards hardly ever enter the orlop now. They leave them to get on with it. The rest of us don't go down there either. It's not safe. You saw what they were like."

Hawkwood remembered the scream he'd heard on his first night and the lack of reaction it had provoked. He looked across the Park towards the quarterdeck and watched as the hulk's commander removed his hat, turned his face to the sun and closed his eyes. The lieutenant stood still, letting the warmth soak into his skin. His hair was dark and streaked with grey.

After what must have been half a minute at least, the lieutenant opened his eyes and dropped his chin. Running a hand through his hair, he placed the hat back on his head and turned to go. Abruptly, he paused, as if aware that his unguarded moment had been observed. He looked over his shoulder. Hawkwood made no attempt to glance away as the lieutenant's brooding eyes roved slowly along the line of prisoners. As Hellard's gaze passed over his own, it seemed for a second as though the hulk commander's attention lingered, but then, as the lieutenant's stare moved on, the moment was gone. Hawkwood decided it had been his imagination, which was probably just as well. Clad in civilian clothes rather than the ubiquitous yellow jacket and trousers, Hawkwood knew he'd risked drawing attention to himself by making eye contact with the lieutenant. It had been an unwise move.

"Unless I'm mistaken," Lasseur commented softly as the lieutenant made his way from the deck, "there's a man who spends a lot of time in his own company."

The world began to revolve once more. Charbonneau drifted away. Beneath Hawkwood's and Lasseur's vantage point, a fencing class was being conducted. In the absence of edged weapons, the students were reduced to wielding the thin sticks that had been used to quell the recent invasion – still a risky venture given the confines of the classroom – and the Park echoed to the click-clack of wooden foils.

"Can't say I care much for their instructor," Lasseur said dismissively, looking down at the scene. "The man's style is abominable. Do you fence?"

"When the mood takes me," Hawkwood said.

Lasseur grunted at the noncommittal answer and then said, "A splendid exercise; the pursuit of gentlemen. Perhaps we should give lessons, too? Earn ourselves some extra rations."

The dry tone in the privateer's voice hinted that Lasseur was being sarcastic, so Hawkwood didn't bother to reply. He looked out across the water. Lasseur did the same. The two frigates were nearing the mouth of the river. Close hauled, yards braced, their nearness to one another suggested a friendly rivalry between the crews, with each ship determined to steal the wind from her opponent, knowing the loser would be left floundering, sheets and sails flapping, her embarrassment plain for all to see.

From Lasseur's distant gaze and by the way his hands were holding on to the rail, knuckles white, Hawkwood sensed the Frenchman was thinking about his own ship. Hawkwood tried to imagine what might be going through the privateer's mind, but suspected the task was beyond him. His world was so far removed from Lasseur's that any attempt to decipher the faraway look was probably futile.

While there were inherent dangers attached to both their professions, it was there the similarity ended. Hawkwood's world was one of ill-lit streets, thieves' kitchens, flash houses, fences, rogues and rookeries. Lasseur's, in total contrast, was the open deck of a sailing ship, running before the wind. It seemed to Hawkwood that, whereas his world was an enclosed one, almost as dark and degrading as the hulk's gun deck, Lasseur's was one of freedom, of the open main and endless skies. For Lasseur, being cooped up on the prison ship would be like a bird whose wings had been clipped. Small wonder his desire to escape was so strong.

"How long *will* it take, do you think?" Lasseur asked. He did not look around but continued to follow the frigates' progress towards the open water.

"Murat?"

Lasseur nodded.

"He has the advantage," Hawkwood said. "He'll probably be content to keep us waiting, even if it's just to teach us who's pulling the strings. It could be a while."

Lasseur turned. There was a bleak look in his eyes. "Any longer in this place and I swear I'll go mad."

"One day at a time," Hawkwood said. "That's how we have to look at it. I hate to admit it, but the bastard was right about one thing."

"What's that?"

"We should be patient."

Lasseur grimaced. "Not one of my better virtues."

"Mine neither," Hawkwood admitted, "except, we don't have a choice. Right now, I don't think there's much else we can do."

Lasseur nodded wearily. "You're right, of course. It does not mean I have to like it, though, does it?"

Hawkwood didn't answer. In his mind's eye he saw again the mob of prisoners rising out of the hatches and the mayhem they had created. Lasseur had referred to the hulk as a version of Hell. From what Hawkwood had witnessed so far, the privateer's description had been horribly accurate. In his time as a Runner, Hawkwood had visited a good number of London's gaols: Newgate, Bridewell, and the Fleet among them. They were, without exception, terrible places.

But this black, heartless hulk was something different. There was true horror at work here, Hawkwood sensed. He wasn't sure what form it took or if he would be confronted by it, but he knew instinctively that it would be like nothing he'd encountered before.

6

The interpreter had been wrong about the smell. After four days, Hawkwood still hadn't grown used to it. Grim smells were nothing new, living in London had seen to that, but in the enclosed world of the gun deck, four hundred bodies generated their own particular odour and, despite the open ports and hatches, the warm weather meant there was no way of drawing cooler and fresher air into the ship. The sea breezes afforded no respite. They brought only the damp, faecal aroma of the marshes, which hung across the polluted river like a moisture-laden blanket.

That said, Hawkwood decided Murat might have got it wrong when he'd nominated fever and consumption as the most prominent causes of death aboard the ship. From what Hawkwood had seen, it was more than likely one of the main culprits was unremitting boredom.

While a proportion of the hulk's inmates did engage in productive pursuits such as arts and crafts, giving or receiving lessons, or setting themselves up as shoemakers or tradesmen in tobacco or other goods, it seemed to Hawkwood that they were in the minority. A vast number of the ship's population opted to pass their days in idleness. Even on the gun deck, men gambled. It wasn't difficult to recognize the ones who'd fallen under the spell. The quiet desperation in their eyes as they laid down their cards or took their time lifting the cup from the little cubes of bone, knowing their inevitable descent to the deck below had already begun, was evidence enough. Others engaged in more dubious dealings: the manipulation of weaker inmates through theft, intimidation and sexual gratification, followed by threats of reprisal if their authority was questioned. Some sought sanctuary by curling up and sleeping wherever there was room – and there wasn't much room. The remainder seemed content merely to wait and to die.

In an attempt to evade the stink, Hawkwood kept to the forecastle as much as possible, sometimes with Lasseur for company. To avoid remaining sedentary, he'd lent his labour to the hulk's work parties. This had drawn comment from some of his fellow prisoners. Most officers regarded such labour as beneath their dignity and preferred to pay a substitute to carry out any manual tasks assigned to them. The going rate was one sou or ten ounces of bread from the day's rations.

Hawkwood had no such qualms, having served in the Rifles, where every man was expected to pitch in. And even before that, as a captain, it had always been Hawkwood's contention that he would never assign a task to one of his soldiers that he wasn't prepared to do himself. It had been a good way to garner loyalty and in the heat of battle it had served him and the men he'd led very well. So Hawkwood had willingly lent his back to hoisting supplies on board and swilling down the foredeck and the Park after supper. Better the smell of honest sweat in his nostrils than the all-pervading stench of the hulk's lower deck.

Lasseur, too, had done his share of manual graft, working alongside Hawkwood at the hoist and in the ship's hold. The temperature within the ship was such that jackets and shirts were soon discarded. The prisoners' backs ran wet with sweat and it was easy to tell whether an inmate was new on board or a regular member of a work party: the irregulars were the ones whose flesh was as pale as paper.

Lasseur's hide carried the healthy sheen of a seaman whose voyages had taken him to warmer, far-flung climes. His torso was well formed without being muscular, and evenly tanned – in contrast to some of the men, whose forearms and faces were the only areas of their bodies that showed the effects of exposure to the sun. The rest of their skin, normally covered by a shirt, looked bleached white in comparison.

What also set Lasseur apart were the marks of the lash across his spine. Hawkwood had passed no comment on the scars. He'd enough of his own, including the ring of bruising around his throat, which had drawn a few curious looks both when he'd taken the bath prior to his registration and when he removed his shirt during the work details.

Lasseur had noticed Hawkwood's passing glance at his back and had made only one comment: "I wasn't always a captain."

"Me neither," Hawkwood had told him, and that had been enough. The rest of the men, whose quizzical looks might have indicated a desire for explanation, they ignored.

When he wasn't labouring in a work party or talking with Hawkwood or Fouchet, or sometimes with the boy, Lasseur spent most of his time pacing the deck and gazing restlessly across the estuary, locked within his own thoughts. With so many bodies crammed in one place, physical solitude was but a dream. Hawkwood knew there wasn't a man on board who wouldn't try and seek solace in the privacy of his own mind. He sought it himself when he could, and took advantage of the opportunities it offered to observe shipboard routine at close quarters. And in the course of his observations Hawkwood had seen enough to know that making a successful escape from the hulk looked well nigh impossible. Moored a stone's throw from the middle of a busy estuary; surrounded by inhospitable marshland; heavily guarded by its contingent of militia and a commander who was fully prepared to use deadly force against the slightest infraction, the ship was too well sealed.

According to Ludd's reckoning, four men had made it off the hulk in recent weeks. In the short time he'd been on board, Hawkwood had yet to uncover a single clue as to how they might have done it. He'd tried to pin Fouchet and the others down, but to his frustration they had been of no more help than Lieutenant Murat.

With the exception of those who'd retreated into their own little world and the denizens of the orlop deck, most of the prisoners seemed content to co-exist in small social groups centred round their messes. Many would probably have no idea there'd been an escape, let alone have any knowledge of how it had been accomplished; their first inkling that something untoward had taken place would come with the increased activity of the hulk's commander and his crew, and the heavy-handed actions of the guards as they inspected and emptied the deck to take an unexpected body count. Someone as well informed as Fouchet would know more, but the teacher was too cautious to discuss such matters with a new arrival, particularly in the light of Murat's reference to informers. Hawkwood had operated clandestinely before and, though patience did not come easily to him, he'd learned that a subtle approach would achieve better results than barging around asking too many pertinent questions.

Ludd's suspicion that there was organization behind the escapes had been confirmed by Murat. Yet Hawkwood was still no wiser as to who was behind it. He wondered how long it would be before the translator got back to them. A week? Two? Or would it be a month? Or longer? The thought made his blood run cold. His rendezvous with Ludd was in three days. Would he have *anything* positive to report? It didn't seem likely. Unless a man could change himself into something the size of a rat and slip between the grilles like Hawkwood's scaly-tailed friend the other night, the only way off the hulk seemed to be as a corpse wrapped inside a burial cloth. Even then you wouldn't get very far.

There had been seven deaths in the time Hawkwood had been aboard. The cause was marsh fever. During the summer months the fever claimed many victims among the weak and undernourished. Age was an inevitable contributing factor, though in the close-knit squalor of a prison ship, fever, typhus, pox and depression showed no favouritism. Two of the dead men had been in their twenties.

There had been no ceremony in the removal of the deceased. Wrapped in filthy sacks of hastily sewn sailcloth, the corpses had been lowered into a waiting boat using a winch and net. Then, accompanied by a burial detail of prisoners and a quartet of militia, the sorry cargo had been rowed to a bank of shingle half a mile off the hulk's stern. Hawkwood and Lasseur had watched in sombre silence as the bodies had been carried up the foreshore and thrown into a pit dug at the back of the beach. From what they'd been able to see, no words were spoken over the burial before the boat made its return journey.

What had been noticeable to Hawkwood was that, aside from himself, Lasseur and a few of the newer prisoners, no one had taken any interest in the proceedings. On *Rapacious,* death and burial were commonplace.

Mid-afternoon of his fifth day on the hulk, Hawkwood was leaning on the forecastle rail, taking a rest after three hours spent hauling barrels of dried herring and sacks of onions on board. The work had been hard, but there had been a sense of purpose to the task, and, more importantly, it had made the time pass quicker. Now the sun was warm on his back and the estuary wàs calm. If he closed his eyes and nostrils, a man could, for a moment or two, imagine he was a thousand miles away.

Lasseur was standing next to him. The privateer captain had pulled the cheroot out of his jacket for what must have been the hundredth time and was staring at it with all the concentration of a drunkard eyeing a bottle of grog.

Hawkwood sensed a presence at his shoulder.

It was the teacher, Fouchet, his face frozen in an expression that struck Hawkwood with a sense of impending dread.

"Sébastien?" Lasseur enquired cautiously.

Fouchet stared at them, as if he didn't know where to begin. Sorrow exuded from every pore.

"Sébastien?" Lasseur said again.

The teacher's face crumpled. "They've taken the boy."

Hawkwood frowned. "Who have? The guards?"

Fouchet shook his head. "The Romans."

Lasseur gasped in shock, his cheroot forgotten. "What? How?"

"I sent him to the galley after his lessons to help Samuel prepare for supper. He didn't arrive. I only found that out when I went to sort out the rations for the mess." The teacher began to wring his hands. "I should have gone with him. It's my fault."

At Lasseur's request, Fouchet had secured the boy a job as assistant to one of the galley cooks.

"How do you know the Romans have him?" Hawkwood said. "He could be with one of the other boys."

The dwellers from the orlop had kept a low profile since their lightning raid on the Park – collectively, at any rate. Individually, they still made forays on to the forecastle in search of galley scrapings or the chance to barter, though they were usually given short shrift by the non-Roman captives. En masse, however, their presence on board, only a deck below, continued to cast a dark shadow in the minds of all the other prisoners. They reminded Hawkwood of the untouchables he'd seen in India: hated and feared, but impossible to ignore.

Fouchet shook his head. "I spoke with Millet and Charbonneau. They asked around. Lucien was seen with Juvert."

"Who's Juvert?" Hawkwood asked.

"I know him," Lasseur said quickly. "Damned pederast! I caught him talking to Lucien on the first day. I warned him to leave the boy alone."

Hawkwood's mind went back to the prisoner he'd seen crouched beside the boy, slender fingers caressing Lucien's back. "He's a Roman?"

"He's one of Matisse's acolytes," Fouchet said.

"Matisse?"

"A vile creature; calls himself king of the Romans. He rules the lower levels. A Corsican, too, if you can believe that," the teacher added sourly.

"There's a leader?" Lasseur couldn't hide his disbelief.

"What about the guards?" Hawkwood asked, wondering why Matisse had adopted the title of king. The Romans of old had been ruled by an emperor, hadn't they? Though on second thoughts, one Corsican emperor at a time was probably enough. His mind went back to the comment he'd overheard between the two militia men when he'd arrived on board:

Wait till His Majesty gets a look at that!

A sick feeling began to worm its way into Hawkwood's stomach.

Fouchet shook his head. "They'll do nothing. No crime

has been committed. In any case, they won't dare to venture that far below deck."

Hawkwood stared hard at the teacher. "It's a British ship! You're telling me the British Navy has no rights on one of its own vessels?"

Fouchet spread his hands. "It has the *right.* It's the will that's lacking, especially where the Romans are concerned. If you want the truth, I think the commander and his men are more wary of Matisse and his courtiers than we are."

"But the British are armed. They have guns!" Lasseur protested.

"True, but you saw for yourselves the other day: they'll not use them unless one of their own is threatened."

Lasseur gazed at the teacher in horror. Fouchet wilted under the scrutiny.

"This is what you meant, wasn't it?" Lasseur said finally. "This is why you told me to watch him. Matisse has done this before. He's taken other boys. My God, what sort of place is this?"

"If I told you the half of it," Fouchet replied softly, "you'd say I was mad."

"What about the tribunal? Doesn't that have influence?"

Fouchet shook his head. "Not over Matisse, it doesn't. Besides, tribunal is just another word for committee. When was the last time a committee did anything constructive? And by the time the tribunal's convened it would be too late. We have to do something now!"

Dear God! Hawkwood thought wildly. "All right, Charbonneau told us anything that happens below deck stays below deck. We'll take care of it ourselves."

"How?" Fouchet's head jerked up. "Wait, you're going down there?"

"Unless you can think of another way," Hawkwood said. He waited for an answer.

Fouchet looked at them helplessly.

"This Matisse, can *you* take us to him?" Lasseur asked.

Fouchet paled. He took a step back, nearly overbalancing in the process.

Anger flared briefly in Lasseur's eyes and his expression hardened. But as he stared at Fouchet, he saw the fear in the teacher's face.

"We're wasting time," Hawkwood said.

"I'm so sorry," Fouchet whispered. His face sagged. He looked suddenly very old and very frail.

Lasseur gave the teacher a reassuring smile. "We'll get him back, Sébastien, I give you my word." He turned to Hawkwood. "Perhaps we should be armed?"

Hawkwood looked at Fouchet. "Will they have weapons down there?"

Fouchet gave an unhappy nod. "It's possible."

"Wonderful," Lasseur said. "What should we do about that?"

"I can't see Hellard giving us the key to the armoury," Hawkwood said drily. "And we don't have time to go searching. We'll just have to improvise." He turned to Fouchet. "Where's Juvert? Have you seen him since the boy went missing?"

A spark of hope brightened the teacher's eyes. He nodded and pointed.

Claude Juvert was savouring the moment. He was on the beak deck, in the forward heads, enjoying a piss. There was a splendid view of the river from the pissdales, if you kept your eyes front and ignored the unsightly sterns of the prison ships moored over the bow. There was the gross stench, of course, but it was impossible to avoid that, even with the deck exposed to the elements. There were only six seats of ease on the hulk and with over eight hundred prisoners on board it was rare not to find most of them occupied at any one time. Four prisoners were seated behind Juvert, trousers bunched around their ankles, contemplating their future. Conversation was desultory.

Had *Rapacious* been at sea and under sail, the smell would have been barely noticeable. The constant deluge of salt and spray cascading over the forward netting would have ensured that the deck received a regular sluicing. The shit and piss stains that accumulated around the holes in the gratings would have been washed away without any bother. With the ship moored in the middle of a river in almost flat calm water with only an occasional choppiness to break the monotony, the sanitary arrangements weren't anywhere near as effective. It was decidedly moist and treacherous underfoot.

Juvert shook himself dry, buttoned his trousers and wiped his hands on his jacket. Emitting a small sigh of satisfaction, he turned to go.

The blow from Lasseur's boot took Juvert in the small of the back, propelling him head first against the netting stanchion. There was a dull crunch as Juvert's thin nose took the brunt of the impact. He let out a yelp. Blood spurted. Lasseur stepped in, took Juvert by the throat and squeezed. Blood from Juvert's broken nose dripped over the privateer's wrist.

"Remember me?" Lasseur said. His eyes burned with rage.

Juvert's eyes opened wide, first with shock and then in fear. He moaned and tried to jerk free, but Lasseur's grip held him fast.

Hawkwood took Juvert's left arm. Lasseur took the right. They hauled him to his feet.

"Any trouble," Lasseur hissed, "and it won't be just your nose – I'll break your neck."

Hawkwood smiled grimly at the row of squatting, slack-jawed prisoners who didn't know whether to remain where they were or try to make a strategic and ungainly withdrawal. "As you were, gentlemen. We're just leaving."

They left the heads, escorting the whimpering Juvert between them. Their emergence drew curious looks. A few frowned at the froth of blood on Juvert's face as he was bundled unceremoniously along the deck, but one look at Lasseur's steely grimace was enough to warn them it would be a mistake to interfere.

Lasseur placed his lips close to Juvert's ear. "Did I or did I not warn you to stay away from the boy?"

"W-what boy?" Juvert spluttered. The collision with the post had split his lip and loosened what remained of his yellowing front teeth.

It was the wrong answer. Lasseur spun Juvert round and slammed him against the curved bulkhead. Then he slapped Juvert sharply across the face. "Don't play games with me! I'm not in the mood."

"What have I done?" The words emerged weakly from between Juvert's bloodied lips.

Lasseur hit him again, harder and very fast.

Juvert let go another high-pitched squawk. Blood dripped from his nose and down his chin.

"You took the boy, Lucien, didn't you?" Lasseur pressed.

Hand over his nose, Juvert mumbled something unintelligible. Tears of pain misted his eyes.

"What?" Lasseur cupped a palm to his ear. "Speak up. We can't hear you."

Juvert, anticipating another blow, threw up his hands. "I had to do it." The words bubbled from his broken nose and split lip.

"Had to?" Hawkwood said.

Juvert spat out a thick gobbet of blood. "It was Matisse!

He made me. I was in debt after losing a w-wager. He said if I delivered the boy to him, he'd consider the debt paid."

"You gutless piece of shit," Lasseur snarled. He drew back his balled fist.

Juvert cringed and shut his eyes. "Please –"

"*Please?* You dare to beg? Did Lucien Ballard beg? Did *any* of the boys beg when you delivered them to him?"

Juvert shrank back.

Concerned that Lasseur would do Juvert permanent damage before they'd achieved their objective, Hawkwood put out a restraining hand.

"You're taking us to Matisse," Hawkwood said. "And then Captain Lasseur and I are going to point out to His Majesty the error of his ways."

"You can't," Juvert pleaded, trying to pull away. His frightened gaze moved first to Hawkwood then to Lasseur and then back again. "You don't know him. Matisse will kill me."

Hawkwood nodded towards Lasseur. "He'll kill you if you don't. And if he doesn't, I will. So move yourself."

There should have been an inscription carved into the overhead beam, Hawkwood thought, as he looked down the darkened stairwell: *Abandon hope, all ye who enter.* He'd heard the phrase somewhere, but he couldn't recall when or where.

Lasseur had purloined one of the lanterns from the gun deck. He held it over the hatchway. The opening was small compared to most of the others on board. The stairs leading down looked narrower and a lot steeper, too. Poised on the rim, Hawkwood could just make out the bottom step. It lay in shadow, barely visible. There were no signs of life, though he thought he could hear vague sounds rising from deep within the well; faint whisperings, like tiny wings fluttering. There were muted rustlings too, and growls of laughter, and a rattling noise, as if tiny claws were skittering across a table top.

Juvert looked like a man about to be thrust into a pit full of vipers. Blood from his broken nose had congealed along the crease of his upper lip and both cheeks carried thin vertical scars where the sweat and tears had forged tracks through the dirt on his face.

"Move," Hawkwood said brusquely.

Pushing the reluctant Juvert ahead of them, Hawkwood and Lasseur stepped down through the hatch.

It was like plunging into an oven. Hawkwood felt as if the air was being drawn from his lungs with each step he took. He recalled Murat's description of the orlop and its lack of headroom compared to the gun deck. Even so, when he reached the bottom of the stairway, he was unprepared for just how low the deckhead was; at least another six inches lower than that of the gun deck. His ears picked up a dull thump. The lantern light wavered and he heard Lasseur curse; proof that even an experienced seaman could be caught unawares.

Hawkwood suspected the word had been passed the moment Juvert's heel hit the top step. The whispering he thought he'd heard earlier had intensified as news of their descent spread through the deck. It sounded like leaves soughing in the wind.

Had the ship still been seaworthy, the orlop would have been below the waterline, with no access to natural light or ventilation. But, as Hawkwood had seen from the longboat, scuttles had been cut into the hull along the line of the deck. Smaller than the gun-deck ports, square cut, and blocked by metal bars, they were nevertheless of sufficient size to allow daylight in, much to Hawkwood's relief. He hadn't relished negotiating the dark with the lantern as their only source of illumination.

If the gun deck resembled a cellar, the orlop was more like a catacomb. He heard Lasseur mutter another oath under his breath and remembered the privateer's comment about boarding a blackbirder off the African coast. It sounded as if Lasseur was reliving the experience. The heat would have been enough to trigger memory. It was stifling; more so than on the gun deck, and the humidity was intense. Hawkwood's shirt was damp with sweat. His skin prickled uncomfortably.

According to Charbonneau, the Romans craved the darkness. The statement wasn't strictly true: the open scuttles proved that and Hawkwood could also see the flicker of lantern light. It made him wonder if it wasn't the Romans and the Rafalés' fear of outsiders that governed their near nocturnal existence rather than their supposed predilection for perpetual twilight.

Peering into the orlop's murky interior, he could make out crude benches and rows of sleeping racks. Many of the men on the racks were naked. Huddled together like spoons, their skins as grey as cadavers. Others, clad in what remained of their uniforms, resembled scarecrows, while the ones dressed only in their blanket togas looked more like moths as they melted in and out of the shadows or hovered around the guttering candles, gripping their cards with spindle-thin fingers.

Hawkwood, shirt moulded to his flesh, was beginning to envy the men who were without clothes. It was becoming harder to draw breath. The cause of the faint rattling noise that he'd detected earlier was now clear and he chided himself for not recognizing it as dice being rolled across table tops. Even naked and starving, the Rafalés were prepared to gamble their lives away. The darkness couldn't conceal the wild expressions on the faces of the wretches hunched around even the dimmest candle flame. Each tumble of the die was accompanied by cries of excitement or gales of manic laughter. It was like walking through the corridors of Bedlam.

Heads turned towards the intruders. Some faces showed open hostility. Others reflected fear at seeing their sanctuary violated. Some of the men on the sleeping racks, who in the midst of all the wretchedness had still managed to retain a small sliver of dignity, hunkered down in a desperate bid to conceal themselves beneath their meagre scraps of blanket. The remainder turned their faces away and tried to merge into the shadows.

Charbonneau had referred to the orlop-dwellers as animals. Even allowing for prejudice, the description had seemed harsh, but looking around it wasn't hard to see the truth in it. As he made his way along the deck, Hawkwood's stomach heaved at the sight and stench of prisoners lying in their own filth.

"I would not keep dogs in a place like this," Lasseur whispered, horrified.

It seemed impossible to believe that men could allow themselves to be subjected to such degradation. It made Hawkwood wonder about British prisoners held in French gaols. He didn't know if the French used hulks. There were prison fortresses, he knew that; many of them in the north, at Verdun, Quimper and Arras. Were the conditions there as bad as this? It was more than likely any French prisoner who did manage to escape would waste no time in reporting the brutal manner in which they'd been kept. It wasn't inconceivable that, in retaliation, the French authorities would make it their duty to display the same lack of compassion as their British counterparts.

Like many soldiers, Hawkwood had always viewed a quick death in battle as infinitely preferable to being cut and probed by the regimental surgeon and slowly dying, crippled and in agony. Now, bent almost double and surrounded by such abject misery, it was only too clear there were fates far worse than the surgeon's knife. Being captured and held in a place like this – that was death of a kind; a slow, lingering death. And no man, no matter in which army he served, deserved that.

As Hawkwood crabbed his way beneath the beams, trying to avoid the stares, several dark objects tacked to the support struts caught his eye. He paused, curious. Lasseur held up the lantern. Hawkwood found he was looking at a row of rat pelts, with the ears and tails still attached. What had Charbonneau told them? *Even the rats aren't safe.* Hawkwood wondered what rat meat tasted like. He turned away, sickened.

They were almost at the bow. Ahead of them, the base of the foremast rose solidly out of the deck. The press of bodies wasn't so bad here, Hawkwood noticed, which was curious. It was as though the mast was some sort of totem, beyond which the mass of the Rafalés were not prepared to venture.

Hawkwood was acutely aware of the ache at the base of his spine; the effect of being bent double. He tried to ease the discomfort by straightening, suspecting it would be a futile exercise, but discovered to his relief that the height of the deckhead between the crossbeams had become a little more generous. He still wasn't able to stand upright, but there was a definite improvement over the miserly head-room at the bottom of the hatchway.

Juvert paused. He looked suddenly apprehensive. Hawkwood peered ahead cautiously. He could hear voices, but forward of the mast the bow section of the orlop lay in near impenetrable darkness and he couldn't see a thing. Then he heard a bray of harsh laughter and he looked again. It took a second for him to see there was in fact a thick layer of blankets in the form of a curtain suspended from the overhead beam, effectively sealing off the main part of the orlop from the fore platform. From the darkness beyond the heavy veil came the hollow rattle of dice and the murmur of conversation.

Lasseur raised the lantern. He nodded. Hawkwood took Juvert's arm and drew back the edge of the curtain.

During his time in the army Hawkwood had endured a good many sea voyages. The majority of them, almost without exception, had been miserable. But he still held memories of the transport ships and had a vague idea of their layout below deck. In the hulk's previous life, the fore platform had probably housed the boatswain's and carpenter's quarters and workshop, along with the gunner's storeroom, and the area would have been separated from the main orlop by a concave bulkhead. On *Rapacious* the bulkhead had been removed. The cabins and storerooms had been transformed into gloomy, lantern-lit alcoves, some of which were partially concealed behind hanging blankets. Hawkwood saw that scraps of cloth had also been hung over the scuttles, reducing the daylight coming in through the grilles.

There were perhaps ten or twelve men present, seated at the tables or sprawled on sleeping racks; most were clad in the drab yellow prison garb. Some, however, were wearing blanket togas. A couple were engaged in a dice game. At another table a foursome was playing cards – drogue, from the looks of one pair, who had wooden pegs clipped over their nostrils while they awaited the outcome of the next hand.

Hawkwood was struck by the strong resemblance to a rookery drinking den. The only difference between this section of the orlop and a rookery were the half-dozen hammocks suspended from the beams.

At Hawkwood's and Lasseur's entrance, conversation

ceased abruptly. At the card table, the losing pair sat up straight and surreptitiously removed their nose pegs.

Hawkwood broke the silence. "We're looking for Matisse."

No one answered. Several men exchanged wary looks.

"Cat got your tongues?" Hawkwood gripped Juvert's elbow. "Point him out."

Juvert winced. His mouth formed an O. He looked petrified, but before he could reply, several men stood up. They weren't empty-handed. Each was armed with what looked like a heavy metal blade, about eighteen inches in length.

Well, Fouchet did warn us, Hawkwood thought. *But swords?* He heard Lasseur mutter an obscenity.

Benches slid back noisily. Dice and cards lay forgotten.

One of the armed men shuffled forward. He was heavy set with bowed legs and a low brow. "What's your business here?"

Lantern light played across the speaker's face. A large, pear-shaped birthmark, as dark as a gravy stain, covered his right cheek and jaw. His nose had been broken at some time in the past.

Hawkwood took a surreptitious glance at the blade in the man's hand. It looked like an iron barrel hoop that had been hammered flat. The edge was a long way from honed, but it looked as if it could still do considerable damage.

"You're Matisse?"

The man looked anything but regal.

"I'm Dupin."

"Then you're only the monkey. It's the organ grinder we want."

Close to, Hawkwood noticed there was something different about Dupin's uniform. As well as the arrows and the letters on the sleeves and thighs, the yellow jacket and trousers were covered in an uneven pattern of small black dots. Some of the dots were moving. Dupin's clothes were alive with lice. Hawkwood's skin crawled. He resisted the urge to scratch and bit down on the sour taste that had risen unbidden into the back of his throat.

Lasseur had seen the infestation, too. The lantern illuminated his disgust. He shuddered.

Hawkwood said, "Tell His Majesty that Captains Hooper and Lasseur are here. He'll know what it's concerning."

"Best do it quickly," Lasseur said. "Otherwise stand aside."

Dupin stared hard at the marks on Juvert's face. Then he turned. He jerked his head at the men over his shoulder and as they moved apart another table came into view at the back of the compartment. Five people were seated around it. There was no throne, as far as Hawkwood could see; only benches. No crown or robes of state, either. Bottles and jugs sat on the table alongside platters of half-consumed bread and cheese.

The figure at the centre of the table leaned forward, revealing a closely shaven, oval-shaped head and a face empty of hue.

Lasseur gasped. The privateer's reaction had come not from seeing the man's bald pate but from his eyes. They had no discernible pupils. The centre of each eye was not dark but shell pink, as if a thimbleful of blood had been emptied into a saucer of milk. Even odder was the way the head appeared to be disembodied, for the rest of the seated figure, from the neck down, looked to be swathed entirely in black, save for one pale, slender arm which rested languorously over the shoulders of the small, blond boy seated beside him.

"*Matisse.*" Lasseur made the name sound like a whispered obscenity. He went to take a step forward only to find his path blocked.

The thin, bloodless lips split in two.

"It's all right, Dupin. You can let them by. We've been expecting them."

7

Hawkwood stared at the pink eyes and the shaven scalp and wondered about the colour of Matisse's hair. There was a name given to people whose hair was so blond it was almost white and whose red-rimmed eyes looked as if they were leaching blood. Whiteface, some called it, though that wasn't its only name. Spain was where Hawkwood had come across the phenomenon, for the first and only other time, in the person of a small boy in an orphanage run by priests outside Astariz. The boy had been abandoned in the confessional as a baby, wrapped in a blanket, his only possession a small silver crucifix strung on a bootlace around his neck. The child had been seven years old when Hawkwood had met him and something of a miracle, for no one had expected him to live beyond his fourth birthday. The boy's eyes had been sensitive to light, Hawkwood recalled, forcing him to spend most of his waking hours in a darkened room. It was one of the brothers who'd told Hawkwood that the word used to describe the boy's condition had been borrowed from Portuguese traders. It was the name they gave to the white Negroes they'd encountered on the coast of Africa. They called them albinos.

The colour of Matisse's eyes suggested he might be a victim of the same abnormality. Maybe that was how the

Romans' alleged preference for the dark had got started. Maybe the stories were based purely on a distorted understanding of the Roman leader's affliction.

Hawkwood's thoughts were interrupted.

"Captain Lasseur! This is an honour! It's not often we get to meet one of the republic's naval heroes. Why, I was regaling my friends here only yesterday with tales of your exploits. Very impressed they were, too; especially with your taking of the British brig. *Justice*. Where was it now? Off the coast at Oran? I heard you were severely outgunned. That must have taken some courage. We admire a man with backbone, don't we, boys?"

There was a curious rough yet sibilant quality to the voice. The mocking words were heavily accented and didn't so much emerge as slither from the tip of the man's tongue. Hawkwood presumed that was due to the speaker's Corsican heritage. There was no response from the other men lounging at the table, who looked as dissolute as their leader and decidedly unenthused by the prospect of receiving visitors, irrespective of their reputation.

"And you'll be our gallant American ally, Captain Hooper! I regret to say, due to an oversight no doubt, Captain Hooper's reputation has failed to precede him. My commiserations, nevertheless, on your capture, sir. The Emperor needs all the help he can get. My spies tell me you're newly arrived from Spain; a bloody battleground, by all accounts. The newspapers here say that Wellington's giving us a roasting. Is that true? Or are they pamphleteering, I wonder?"

Hawkwood ignored the question. He stuck out his boot and shoved Juvert forward. "I'm told this belongs to you."

Surprise and gravity did the rest. The trip sent Juvert flying. Forced to put out his hands to save himself, he let out an undignified splutter as he slewed across the deck, forcing several of the onlookers to scramble back from his line of trajectory. The boy jumped nervously, his eyes wide. Shaken out of their insouciance, the men on either side of him sat up. Shock lanced across their faces.

The shaven-headed man's pose did not change. It was hard to read the expression in his eyes as he stared down at Juvert's prostrate body. Only the contraction of his jaw muscles indicated the essence of his thoughts. He looked up, his arm still draped across the boy's shoulders.

"You've a flair for the dramatic, Captain Hooper, I'll grant you that. From the look of him, I'd say Claude doesn't quite share your enthusiasm. It's true, he performs errands for me now and again. Not always to my complete satisfaction, it has to be said." There was an undeniable hint of menace in the last statement.

Juvert got to his knees and winced. From the pallor in his cheeks, his ears had obviously picked up the nuance in his master's voice. He looked like a man trying to decide between advance or retreat, knowing in his heart and from the mutterings and the looks he was attracting that, whichever path he took, he was unlikely to recruit much sympathy.

The shaven-headed man gave a jerk of his head. "Take him away."

Juvert was afforded no opportunity to protest. Hauled unceremoniously to his feet, he barely had time to throw Hawkwood and Lasseur a backward glance before he was bundled through the curtain. No one looked sorry to see him go. A muffled grunt came from outside and then there was the sound of an object being dragged away. Then silence.

Matisse sat back. He looked composed, at ease with his surroundings. His spidery fingers played idly with the hair on the back of the boy's neck. "You'll forgive us for not rising. We're not used to company. I apologize for the inadequacy of the illumination, by the way. My eyes have an aversion to light; daylight in particular. Even candle flames cause me some discomfort. An inconvenient ailment, but I've grown used to it."

The words confirmed Hawkwood's suspicions. They also explained the rags draped over the scuttles.

"We don't give a shit for your health," Lasseur snapped. "We're here for the boy."

The backs of the men seated around the table stiffened at this. The shaven head tilted. Lucien Ballard sat unmoving; he looked terrified. The hand on his neck stilled but did not relinquish possession.

Hawkwood tensed.

"He doesn't belong down here," Lasseur said.

"Is that right? Who says?"

The fingers resumed their fondling. It reminded Hawkwood of a cat being stroked. Lucien Ballard was not purring, however. He looked mesmerized.

"I warned Juvert what would happen if he showed his face again," Lasseur said. "He disobeyed me – on *your* orders."

The Corsican's hand froze once more. His chin came up sharply.

"Diso-*beyed* you? Juvert is not yours to command, Captain Lasseur. He's my emissary. In case you've forgotten, you're not on your quarterdeck now. This is *my* dominion. You're the trespasser here."

"Commander Hellard might have something to say about that," Hawkwood said softly. It wasn't only the man's gaze that was disconcerting, he realized. Matisse hardly ever seemed to blink.

"Hellard?" the bald man sneered. "Hellard's a weakling. He's commander in name only. I hold sway here, not him."

"*King* Matisse?" Hawkwood said, and wondered if that was the reason Hellard hadn't given the order to fire on the well deck.

The pink eyes shifted so that they were trained directly at Hawkwood. It was an unsettling feeling. But from the exchanges so far, Hawkwood sensed that, behind the grotesque façade, there was a dark, manipulative intelligence at play.

"Some call me that. Though, to tell the truth, I can't even remember how it started. Some would think it an indulgence, but why should I discourage it? It serves its purpose, helping keep the lower orders in check."

The words were spoken dismissively. Hawkwood wondered whether Matisse included the men around him as part of the "lower orders", and what they thought of it. There was no suggestion that any of them had taken umbrage. Maybe they weren't sure what it meant, or else they assumed it meant the rest of the Rafalés.

A thin smile played along the bald man's lips. "Personally, I like to think of myself more as a pastor, a shepherd administering to the welfare of his flock." His fingers resumed toying with the boy's collar.

Not again, Hawkwood thought. A cold shiver passed along his spine. *I had my fill of pastors and parsons the last time.*

Maybe that was why Matisse was dressed in black; to perpetuate the illusion, or perhaps in some strange way to accentuate the ghostly complexion and make him appear more striking. Matisse's attire was remarkably similar to a priest's. There were no superfluous frills or finery or affectation, save for one: a tiny tear-shaped object that occasionally caught the lantern light. Hawkwood hadn't noticed it before. It was a pearl pendant earring that dangled delicately from Matisse's left ear.

Lasseur growled, "For the last time. Hand the boy over."

The earring danced as Matisse turned. "You know, when Juvert told me you'd taken an interest in him, I confess I was rather intrigued. What were we supposed to make of that? Perhaps you've designs on him yourself, Captain Lasseur – is that why you're here?"

"I'm here to keep him from harm."

"Harm?" Matisse slid his hand from the boy's neck and placed it, palm flat, over his heart. His nails were long and discoloured; their tips sharp, like talons. "You think *I'd* harm a child? How could you suggest such a thing? You wound me, Captain."

"Don't play games," Lasseur said.

"Games?"

"Fouchet warned us."

"Ah, yes, the teacher. And what exactly did he warn you about?"

"He warned us about you," Lasseur said. The disgust in his voice sounded like gravel at the back of his throat. "He told us about the others."

"Others?"

"The other boys you've brought down here."

"Did he now?" The Corsican pursed his lips. "That old man's become rather belligerent of late. I shall have to have words with him." The maggot-white face lifted. "He needs to be reminded of his place."

"You don't deny it?"

"Why should I?" Matisse stroked the boy's cheek and turned Lucien Ballard's face towards him. The boy's lower lip began to tremble. "Have you ever seen anything so precious?"

"He's a child."

"Yes, he is. He's a sweet child, but you make it all sound so sordid, Captain. You think we're all apprentices of Sodom? You couldn't be further from the truth, I assure you. If we weren't shut away in this foul place, do you really think we'd be having this conversation? We're a long way from home; from our wives and sweethearts. What's a man to do? All we crave is a small measure of comfort. There's nothing wrong with that, surely? A man's not meant to be on his own. A man has needs. What's so bad in trying to find companionship and affection to see us through these dark days? Would you deny us that? What right have you to judge?"

"*Affection?*"

"Yes, affection. Tell them, boy. Tell the captain. Has Matisse hurt you? No. There, you see? Not a hair spoiled. He's perfectly safe."

"Safe?" Lasseur stared at Matisse. "You'd take him into your bed; you'd turn him into one of your catamites? You'd share him among these scum – and you call that *safe*?"

Chairs scraped back as the men at the table rose around their leader.

A nerve flickered along Matisse's jawline. "D'you hear that? He called you scum; and queer scum at that. I'd take care, if I were you, Captain. The navy may hold you in high esteem, but you'd do well to remember where you are. As for this particular boy, who elected *you* his guardian? You've no legitimate claim on him, have you?" There was a pause. "After all, it's not as though he's your son, now, is it?"

"God damn you!" Lasseur swore. He took a pace forward. His face was rigid.

A warning growl sounded from deep inside Dupin's throat. He raised the hoop blade.

Quickly, Hawkwood put a restraining hand on Lasseur's sleeve. The muscles along the privateer's arm were as taught as knotted rope. Hawkwood's hold was enough to restrain Lasseur, but only for as long as it took for the Frenchman to shrug his hand away angrily. "I demand you hand the boy over, now!"

The deck went deathly quiet.

The black-clad figure placed both palms on the table and

pushed himself to his feet. The movement was effortlessly sinuous. The Corsican didn't so much rise from his seat as uncoil.

"*Demand?* You dare to come here and demand of *me*? Look around you, Captain. This is *my* kingdom. *I* reign here; no one else. You're newly arrived, so you're not yet acquainted with the order of things. Go back to your gun deck and take Captain Hooper with you. And if you're thinking of summoning assistance, think again. Do you really believe the British control the lives on this hulk? Oh, they may have the uniforms and their fine muskets. They may even have the authority, but do you think for one moment that they hold the power? There are more than eight hundred of us imprisoned on this stinking barge. What do you think would happen if there was a full-scale rebellion? The British don't keep the inmates in check here; *I* do. Matisse! Commander Hellard may despise me. He may even fear me. But you can be certain that he and the rest of his crew thanked God the day I came on board!"

"You utter filth!" Lasseur hissed.

For one heart-stopping moment, despite Dupin's proximity, Hawkwood thought the privateer was about to hurl himself across the table. The moment he did that, they were both dead. But then, as quickly as he had let it slip, Lasseur seemed to recover his equilibrium. He looked Matisse straight in the eye. "Very well, name your price."

"My *price*?" The bald head swivelled. The movement was performed so fluidly, it reminded Hawkwood of a cobra winding itself up for the strike.

"You heard. How much?"

"You offer me money?" The mocking tone was still there.

"We want the boy. We're not going back without him."

"Brave words, Captain. Have you considered the possibility that you might not be going back at all?"

"You think you can stop us?" Lasseur said.

"Of course I can stop you. I need only click my fingers. How far do you think you'd get? This time, you really are outgunned."

Looking around, Hawkwood knew the man was right. Despite Lasseur's attempt at bravado, neither of them had a hope of taking on Matisse's crew. They'd be fools even to contemplate it. It had been a mistake to have come so unprepared. They'd underestimated the hold that Matisse had over the lower deck; and indeed, if his boast was to be believed, the rest of the ship.

"We need to settle this," Hawkwood said. "We need to settle this now."

Matisse shook his head, though whether this was an expression of bafflement or merely amusement was hard to decipher. "You really want him that badly?" The earring jiggled again. Matisse looked to his lieutenants, who were gazing back at him in renewed, bright-eyed anticipation. They had scented blood. He turned back slowly, a shrewd look on his face. He pouted. "All right, perhaps there is a way."

"How?" Lasseur said.

Matisse paused. "A contest."

A murmur ran around the compartment.

Lasseur looked nonplussed. "You mean a wager? You'd decide the boy's future by the throw of a dice?"

"Not dice."

"The turn of a card? I'll still have no part of it!"

"There are more ways of proving a man's mettle than by having him win a hand of whist, Captain."

"Like what?" Lasseur enquired cautiously.

"A trial."

"Prisoner's tribunal?" Lasseur looked sceptical. "You want us to plead our case?"

"Not that kind of trial."

"Then what kind do you mean?"

"I mean trial by combat."

The deck erupted in excited chatter. It took several seconds before it grew still again.

"He wants you to fight for him," Hawkwood said, not quite believing it himself.

Matisse gave a short, harsh, humourless laugh. "You make it sound so vulgar, Captain. As if I was suggesting some kind of brawl. I prefer to think of it as a contest of arms. 'To the victor the spoils' – isn't that what they say?"

Lasseur stared at Matisse in horror. "I'm not going to fight you!"

"Fight me? You misunderstand, Captain. I was referring to the old-fashioned way of settling a dispute, when kings did not cross swords themselves. They nominated a champion; a valiant knight to fight on their behalf, someone versed in the art of war – a warrior." Matisse looked directly at Hawkwood. "You, Captain Hooper; you're a warrior. You've the scars to prove it. I nominate you as Captain Lasseur's champion."

"What?" Lasseur said disbelievingly.

"It's your only chance of getting him back. What do *you* say, Captain Hooper?"

"I think you've been down here too long. It's addled your brain. You want the boy's fate to be decided by the outcome of a bout?"

As he spoke the words, Hawkwood's brain began to spin. What the hell was happening here? What had Lasseur been thinking? This wasn't part of the plan. How in the name of all that was holy had he allowed himself to be dragged into Lasseur's private war?

"Adds piquancy to the broth, doesn't it?" Matisse said, grinning. "And it's been a while since our last diversion.

When was that? Does anyone remember?" He regarded the ring of faces expectantly. "No? Ah well, that's the trouble; you lose track of time on the lower levels. Each day just seems to merge into the next. Anyway, there it is, Captain Lasseur. A sporting chance. If my man wins, the boy stays with us. If Captain Hooper emerges victorious, I'll set him free. What do you say to that?"

"Leave Captain Hooper out of this," Lasseur said. He looked at Hawkwood. His face was ashen.

"Too late for that," Matisse said.

Hawkwood saw the excitement in the eyes of the other men around them. Lasseur was still staring back at him in disbelief.

"Who's *your* man?" Hawkwood asked. "Dupin?"

"Dupin?" Matisse expressed surprise. His chin came up. "Oh no, not Dupin. While Corporal Dupin is a true and faithful lieutenant, I can see he'd be no match for a veteran of your calibre. No, do not protest, Corporal. You know I speak the truth. Captain Hooper is an experienced soldier, whereas you are merely a courtier with a stick. You wouldn't last five minutes, and where's the sport in that? No, Captain, I choose another; a much more worthy opponent. Call it royal prerogative."

Matisse turned. Several of the men at the table exchanged knowing grins.

"Kemel Bey!" Matisse called.

A pale wedge of light appeared in the wall of darkness behind the table. For the first time, Hawkwood saw the opening in the bulkhead over Matisse's shoulder, indicating there were yet more compartments further forward.

Lasseur drew in a breath. Hawkwood saw why.

An apparition stepped into the lantern glow. The man's skin was so dark it looked as if he might have been carved from the hulk's timbers. He was not as tall as Hawkwood, but neither was he small of stature. His face was broad. His nose was wide and flared. Below it there grew an extravagant, raven-black moustache. His hair was long and oily and curled away from the base of his neck in tight ringlets. Each ear was pierced with a golden ring, which gleamed brightly in the lantern light. His eyes, in contrast to those of Matisse, were as black as olive pits.

His striking looks were offset by the incongruity of his dress. He wore a yellow prison jacket stretched tight across a compact, muscular torso. His legs were encased in a pair of voluminous maroon pantaloons. His feet were bare. He looked, Hawkwood thought, as if he'd stepped out of the illustration in a children's book or from the ranks of a theatrical masquerade.

Hawkwood had heard reports of Bonaparte's Mamelukes from guerrilla fighters in Spain, but he'd never seen them in action. They enjoyed a fearsome reputation. It was said that the Emperor, despite having defeated them in battle, had been so taken with their fighting skills during his Egyptian campaign that he'd authorized two squadrons to accompany him on his return to France. A plea from their commanding officer and a vow that they'd defend France to the death had been enough to justify their immediate incorporation into the ranks of the Imperial Guard. Mameluke cavalry had played a decisive role in Murat's brutal suppression of the Madrid uprising.

It was also patently obvious that, compared to the majority of the hulk's population, the Mameluke was in good physical shape. But the same could be said for the rest of Matisse's crew. It was clear they weren't suffering the same privations as the others. On the hulk, Matisse and his court were like a wolf pack, where the dominant animals took the richest morsels. In fact, Matisse appeared the most undernourished of the lot, which meant that he used brain not brawn to stamp his authority, and that, Hawkwood knew, made him more dangerous than any of them.

"Colourful, isn't he?" Matisse said. "Kemel Bey's a prince of the blood. Leastways, that's what we think he told us. He doesn't speak our language very well. He was taken captive on board a transport off Tangier a year back. Did you know the Emperor still has a Mameluke bodyguard? Helps His Majesty shave every morning; a steady hand with a razor, they say." The side of Matisse's mouth lifted. Several of his minions responded in kind; a private joke shared.

"They also say a Mameluke's training starts from birth. I dare say that's an exaggeration, but they do possess a wonderful abundance of skills: swordsmanship, spear-work, archery, the use of firearms . . . Fine wrestlers, too. They're completely fearless. I choose Kemel Bey as my champion, Captain Hooper." The red-rimmed eyes threw out the challenge. "So, what's it to be? Will you stand, or will you run? Do we have our contest?"

Lasseur stepped close and gripped Hawkwood's arm. When he spoke his voice was low and urgent. "This is not your quarrel."

Hawkwood looked around at the ring of grinning faces, at the sardonic smile on the bald man's lips, at the haunted expression and the dried tear-tracks on the boy's face.

"It is now," he said.

"But it's my fault we're here. I should be the one to fight, not you!"

"It isn't a fight," Hawkwood said. "It's a contest of arms."

"I forbid you!" Lasseur hissed. His hold on Hawkwood's arm intensified.

"You can't forbid me," Hawkwood said evenly. "It's not your quarterdeck, remember? Besides, it has to be me. If you take on Matisse's man and you lose, the boy will have no one in his corner. I'm not a father. I don't have the same bond with him as you do. If anything happens to me, you'll still be here."

"And yet you'd fight for him?"

"It's not a fight," Hawkwood said. "It's –"

"I know," Lasseur said wearily. Reluctantly, he let go of Hawkwood's arm. "Well, at least you're honest, my friend. I can't deny that. A little strange, too, I think."

"And practical," Hawkwood said softly. "You're financing my way off this bloody ship. I don't want anything happening to you. If I lose, it won't matter much, the chances are you'll still make it."

Lasseur's mouth opened and closed again quickly.

"In your own time, Captain," Matisse called sarcastically.

Hawkwood stared at Lasseur. "You hadn't thought about that, had you? About what would happen to him once you were gone?"

Lasseur looked suddenly contrite.

"Dear God!" Hawkwood swore. "Tell me you weren't thinking of taking him with us. You know that's impossible!"

"I'll think of something," Lasseur said, though his expression suggested he wasn't too sure.

Hawkwood watched the doubt creep across the privateer's face. Things had just moved from bad to worse and they had run out of time. He searched for options. From what he could see, there weren't any, save one, if he was to keep to his agenda and maintain the charade. He looked at Matisse and sighed.

"All right, where do we do this?"

"Excellent! Spoken like a true officer and gentleman." Matisse pointed to the deck. "Down there."

The pink eyes finally blinked. They alighted on the hovering Dupin.

"Bring the boy."

8

Entry was through the floor of the gunner's storeroom.

At the Corsican's signal, the men bent down and began to remove boards from the deck. They did so quickly and in silence, setting the boards against the bulkhead. It was clearly a well-rehearsed routine.

"There used to be a hatchway," Matisse said in a conversational tone. "It was sealed when they converted the ship into a hulk. We found it and opened it up again. The old magazine rooms are directly below us. They used the hatch to pass cartridge boxes to and from the gun decks during battle. We guessed it was here. They modelled these ships on the design of our seventies. There's not that much difference between theirs and ours. We know the inside of this one like the backs of our hands. After lights out, we have the run of the place. Not that we need lights. We can find our way in the dark. Some of us don't have any choice."

The last board was laid aside. A steep stairway was revealed.

Matisse's men led the way down, carrying lanterns. Most of them also carried beaten barrel hoops. It was a deliberate display of force, Hawkwood knew, intended for his and Lasseur's benefit. It was to let them know there was nowhere for them to run. They were not shackled or bound and no one had hold of them, but it was Matisse's way of telling them they were there at his whim, prisoners within a prison.

Entering the hold after the constraints of the orlop, Hawkwood felt as if he was walking into a cathedral. For the first time since leaving the top deck, he found he could stand upright. The relief was exquisite. They were deep inside the belly of the ship. Broad wooden ribs curved high around them. Shingle ballast cracked as loudly as eggshells beneath their heels. Matisse picked his way between the deck joists like a spider crossing the strands of a web.

Provision casks, including the water barrels, were embedded in the shingle and stacked in tiers about them, with the larger casks at the bottom to take the load. Wedges had been driven under the stacks for additional stability.

A mixture of strong odours dominated the hold's interior: leakage from the casks, stagnant water and rotten food, along with tar and cordage. There were other pungent smells, too. The whiff of vinegar and sulphur, a legacy from the last time the hold had been fumigated, did little to mask the smell of the rats. With a ready-made food source at their whisker-tips, the rodents had grown numerous and bold. Dust from their droppings drifted in the air like dandelion spores, accumulating at the back of the throat, while at every turn a swift flash of sleek, silken fur would catch the eye as the animals scampered away from the approaching glimmer of the lanterns.

"Top hatches are closed," Matisse said. "Next delivery boats aren't due till morning. We've got the place to ourselves."

At a signal from Matisse his men strung the lanterns from the beams. As the darkness withdrew and the candleglow grew stronger, Matisse reached into an inner pocket and withdrew a pair of spectacles. He placed them carefully on his nose and made great play of securing them behind the backs of his ears. At once, his face was transformed, for the spectacle lenses were round and dark and matched almost exactly the circumference of his eye sockets. When the pale face was viewed full on, the resemblance to a naked skull was uncanny and disturbing.

"When you're ready, Dupin!" Matisse said. He looked at Hawkwood. "My apologies, Captain; we're a little short of pistols and foils. We've had to turn to our own devices; as you'll see."

Lasseur frowned.

Hawkwood looked around at the flattened barrel hoops. An uneasy feeling began to spread through him.

Dupin walked into the circle.

"Catch," he said.

Hawkwood had barely time to react. As he snatched the object out of the air, he saw what it was. It looked the same as the sticks the fencing class had been using the day the well deck was invaded, with one noticeable augmentation. Bound tightly by twine to the end of the stick was an open razor.

"What's this?" Lasseur demanded.

Matisse tipped his head to one side. The spectacle lenses were like black holes in his face. "What did you think 'trial by combat' meant, Captain? A boxing match?"

"British law forbids duelling," Hawkwood said. "Even on the hulks."

"British law doesn't apply here, Captain. We make our own law – Matisse's law."

Hawkwood gazed down at the weapon. It was remarkably light and almost as flexible as a real foil. There was a momentary gleam as lantern light glanced off the six-inch blade.

Matisse grinned. "A shade crude, perhaps, but in the right hands it's very effective. It was Corporal Sarazin over there who came up with the idea. He saw them used to settle disputes when he was a prisoner on Cabrera."

Hawkwood recognized the name. Cabrera was a tiny island, ten miles to the south of Majorca. From what he'd heard, the prison there made *Rapacious* look like paradise. It had achieved its notoriety following the French defeat at Baylen, when the Comte de l'Étang surrendered his entire corps of eighteen thousand men to the Spanish. The senior staff officers were repatriated. The rank and file were sentenced first to the Cadiz hulks and then to the island. Some had later been transferred to England. It occurred to Hawkwood it had probably been some of those men who'd been cast into Portsmouth Harbour by the crew of the *Vengeance*.

"Sarazin was at Millbay for a time, too. They used compass points there instead of blades, but we found they're not quite as effective. Not so readily available, either. I put it down to your friend Fouchet's geometry and navigation classes." The Corsican gave a dry chuckle.

Hawkwood stared at the blade then at Matisse. "And if I choose not to fight?" he asked.

"Then you forfeit. The boy remains with us. His future's in your hands, Captain."

"And if I win, you'll give the boy up?"

"I told you: in the event of that happening, the boy will be set free. You have my word."

"What are the rules?"

"There are no rules," Matisse said.

Several of the men laughed.

Lasseur frowned. "Then what determines the outcome of the contest? Is it the first to draw blood?"

"No, it's when one of them stops breathing."

The interior of the hold went still. Only the creaking of the hulk's timbers broke the silence.

The blood drained from Lasseur's face. "This is madness!"

"No, it's how we maintain order. There has to be order. You see that, don't you? You're military men. You understand the need for discipline. Without it, there'd be anarchy. Can't have that. It would upset the balance."

"No!" Lasseur said. "You cannot do this!" He threw Hawkwood a despairing look.

"Oh, but I can. Down here I can do anything I like."

He stared at Hawkwood. It was a blatant challenge.

A voice spoke softly inside Hawkwood's head. *Walk away now!*

"At least take the boy outside," Hawkwood said. "He doesn't need to see this."

Matisse shook his head. "On the contrary, I think it will do him the world of good. His first blooding. It could be the making of him. If Kemel Bey does his work, it might even be his first time for experiencing other pleasures, too." Matisse chuckled softly and squeezed the boy's shoulders. "How's your Latin, Captain? You strike me as an educated man. Do you know the phrase: *Jus primae noctis*? It means the law of the first night. We call it the lord's right in French. *My* right. I can't tell you how much I've been looking forward to it. Our evening entertainments have been lamentably dull of late. It's why we look forward to fresh arrivals. It gives us a chance to meet new . . . friends."

There was movement behind Dupin. The putrid air prickled with tension as the Mameluke emerged from the ring of men and stepped into the light. He'd removed his jacket. His torso was bare. Dressed only in the pantaloons, he stood as still and as silent as a statue, arms loose by his sides, looking neither right nor left.

Lasseur leant close and whispered nervously. "Please tell me you can best him."

Hawkwood studied the Mameluke. He wondered what

was going through the man's mind. There was no change of expression, no show of concern in the eyes or anything in the face to imply that the man had heard or understood any of the conversation. Hawkwood had been shown an automaton once, a wondrous mechanical device that had consisted of a small, perfectly made manikin in the figure of a Turk. By a remarkable system of levers, rods and pulleys, the automaton had sprung to life, folding its arms and bowing its head, even smoking a tiny hookah pipe. Kemel Bey looked like a life-sized version of the toy; a mechanical man awaiting instructions.

"I was hoping for a quicker response," Lasseur murmured.

Hawkwood wasn't listening. He was looking at the Mameluke's scars. Back on the orlop, they had been concealed by the darkness and the prison coat. Now, with coat discarded, they were plainly visible within the ring of lantern light. There was no symmetry to them. They formed a tapestry up his right arm from wrist to shoulder like a pattern of twigs cast haphazardly on to the ground. There were more scars across the firm flesh of his abdomen and along the ridges of his upper chest. The latter, however, looked quite old and showed as pale, raised streaks against his dark skin. The ones along his arm appeared more recent.

Matisse's voice broke into his thoughts. "Don't let the scars fool you, Captain Hooper. Kemel Bey's quite an expert with the razor, but then he's had the practice. How many have there been, Dupin? Is it four or five?"

"Six," Dupin muttered. "You're forgetting the Swiss."

"Ah, yes, the Swiss. I always forget the Swiss. Mind you, it's easily done. They're a forgettable race, like their tedious little country. It's so small I'm surprised anyone knows where it is from one day to the next."

Hawkwood presumed the most recent scars were from previous razor duels and the remainder legacies of the

Mameluke's skirmishes on the battlefield. Whatever their cause, it was clear that Kemel Bey's expertise with weapons had not been achieved without personal cost and, presumably, a good deal of pain. Hawkwood had more than enough scars of his own, but they were few in number compared to Matisse's champion.

Matisse snapped his fingers. Hawkwood removed his jacket and passed it to Lasseur, who received it half-heartedly. The men backed away, pulling Lasseur with them, extending the radius. Some took up positions between the deck struts. Others found seats on the tops of barrels. A small amphitheatre formed in the centre of the hold.

Hawkwood could feel warm beads of moisture gathering uncomfortably in the small of his back. Strange, he thought, considering the back of his throat was as dry as sand. He glanced towards Lasseur. Even in the half light he could see that the privateer's face was pale.

Dupin tossed the Mameluke the second razor stick.

"Begin," Matisse said.

The Mameluke attacked.

Hawkwood sucked in air as the razor curved towards his belly, brought his own stick down against the outside of the Mameluke's stave and exhaled as he parried the blade away. The thwack of wood on wood was as loud as a pistol shot.

Hawkwood had seen the attack coming. The microscopic widening of the eyes, the tensing of the shoulders and the subtle shifting of weight on to the right leg had telegraphed his opponent's intention. Even so, the Mameluke's speed was impressive. So, too, was his strength. The shock from the collision shuddered through Hawkwood's arm, jarring nerve endings from wrist to shoulder.

Then the Mameluke was turning, bringing his blade around in a reverse strike towards the back of Hawkwood's sword hand. Hawkwood rotated his wrist, slanted away, and felt the bite of the Mameluke's blade as it scored across his knuckles.

Hawkwood stepped back quickly, adjusting his hold on the stick, extending his thumb in a rapier grip, testing the balance and the flexibility in the shaft. It wasn't a lot different to a duelling foil; slightly thicker but the length was about the same. The main difference was the sharp blade instead of a point. This was a weapon meant to sever and cleave, not pierce. There was no guard to protect the hand either. It explained the scarring across the Mameluke's wrist and forearm, and the cut in Hawkwood's flesh that was already welling blood.

The Mameluke advanced again, the thin blade swooping in from on high, cutting down and across. Hawkwood brought his stick round to block the stroke, anticipated and absorbed the impact, transferred his weight and aimed a backhand slash towards the Mameluke's throat. The Mameluke twisted violently and Hawkwood felt the almost imperceptible tug as his blade ripped across his opponent's ribcage. There was a collective intake of breath from the men watching.

"Bravo, Captain!" Matisse's voice, lightly taunting.

But the move had left Hawkwood exposed. The Mameluke grunted, checked, and whipped his blade towards Hawkwood's left flank. Hawkwood jerked back, but he was too late. There was no pain; not at first. Only when he straightened did he feel the tightening of skin at the point of the incision. There was no time to check for blood, because the Mameluke was coming in again.

The Turk's movements seemed unhurried; almost nonchalant. There was no sign of elation on the ebony face, no quiet smirk of satisfaction at having drawn blood. Neither did he appear out of breath, despite the bright sheen of sweat that coated his brow, shoulders and upper chest.

Another swing, this time towards Hawkwood's undefended left shoulder. Hawkwood spun towards the attack, slashing down, going for the tendon running up the inside of the Mameluke's right wrist.

He felt his heel slip in the shingle and knew he'd missed his target by a mile. For the first time, he saw the light of opportunity in his opponent's eyes. Fighting for traction, Hawkwood tried to fling himself aside. The Mameluke's blade arced towards him.

Had he found his feet and braced himself, the Turk's razor would have caught him full square. But Hawkwood was still falling backwards. The blade raked across his breastbone, paring shirt and skin in equal measure. This time he felt it: a sharp burning sensation searing across his chest.

He heard someone swear and thought it must have been Lasseur, and then he was pushing himself upright, bringing his stick round, more in a wild flail than any sort of coordinated riposte, but when he felt the steel bite, he knew he'd made contact.

Hawkwood's blade had taken the Mameluke across the back of his right forearm two inches below the elbow, slicing through flesh and clipping bone. The Turk bellowed in pain and turned. Hawkwood started to scramble clear, saw the threat homing in, parried the counterstrike more by luck than judgement, and swung his blade at the Turk's carotid.

It should have ended there and then. How the Mameluke evaded the cut, Hawkwood would never know. Whatever the reason, the blade missed by a hair's breadth. In that split second, Hawkwood tried to pull the strike but he was already committed. The razor struck the deck support with the full force of Hawkwood's body behind it, and snapped cleanly in two.

There was a gasp from the men around.

Blood dripped down the Mameluke's arm and belly. He was breathing harder now. The corners of his mouth lifted. He stepped forward eagerly, his blade raised.

But Hawkwood was already moving. His right hand shot out. The fistful of shingle struck the Mameluke's face like a flurry of hailstones. The Mameluke threw up his left hand to protect his eyes. Using the floor joist behind him as a fulcrum, Hawkwood launched himself towards his temporarily unsighted foe.

Hawkwood's shoulder charge lifted the Mameluke off his feet. Locked together, the two men crashed through the ring of watchers, who broke apart in alarm.

Hawkwood's left hand gripped the Mameluke's sword arm. The Turk drove his other fist into Hawkwood's gut. Air exploded from Hawkwood's lungs. The Turk clamped his left hand around Hawkwood's neck and began to squeeze.

The Mameluke's smell was overpowering; a combination of musk, sweat and blood. Hawkwood felt his throat start to close. A red mist began to descend. He rammed his knee into the Turk's crotch and brought his free hand up. He heard a brief exhalation, felt the grip around his neck loosen, bent back the Turk's wrist and slammed his forehead against the exposed nose. The Mameluke's head rocked back. Hawkwood side-stepped to his left, transferred his right hand to the Mameluke's sword arm and as he rotated and locked the Mameluke's wrist, let go with his left hand and drove the heel of it against the elbow joint. There was a dull crack. A spasm shook the Turk. His hand opened and the razor fell to the shingle. Hawkwood increased pressure on the injured arm. The Mameluke dropped to his knees. A keening wail broke from his lips. Blood from his broken nose was running down his chin. His face twisted in pain and he sank to the deck.

Hawkwood straightened and Lasseur yelled a warning.

Hawkwood turned. The Mameluke had retrieved the fallen razor. He was crouched on one knee. His right arm hung uselessly by his side. His left hand was drawn back. The razor blade glinted. There was a renewed look of savagery on his face.

Hawkwood's right foot lashed out. The edge of his heel caught the Mameluke on the side of his jaw. The dark eyes rolled back into his skull. His body slumped across the deck and lay still.

There was a stunned silence.

Dupin was the first to break ranks. He bent down and lifted the Mameluke's head. Letting it fall back, he stared hard at Hawkwood then turned to Matisse. "His neck's broke."

"Satisfied?" Hawkwood said coldly.

"Very impressive," Matisse said softly. "Not quite the result I was expecting. You've done for my champion, and so decisively, too. Who'd have thought it? You may be an officer, Captain Hooper, but my bones tell me you're no gentleman." The dark lenses glittered in the lantern light.

"I'll take that as a compliment," Hawkwood said. He felt suddenly tired and experienced an overwhelming urge for a strong drink.

Lasseur broke away from the cordon. "You left it a little late, my friend. You had me worried."

"You weren't the only one," Hawkwood said wearily, and winced. He waved away Lasseur's extended arm and lifted the edge of blood-soaked shirt to examine his injuries, noting the blood across his knuckles. The gash along his side didn't look too deep, but it would probably benefit from a stitch or two. As for the cut across his chest, the resulting scar would more than likely make it appear worse than it was. More war wounds, Hawkwood thought. He knew he'd been lucky. He looked down at the Mameluke's corpse. It could so easily have gone the other way.

Lasseur followed his gaze and his face clouded. He turned to where Matisse was standing with his arm around Lucien Ballard's shoulder. "It's over. Your man lost. Give us the boy."

Matisse said, "I'm sorry, Captain. I'm not with you. Why should I do that?"

Hawkwood went cold.

Lasseur nodded towards the Turk's prostrate body. "Our agreement. You said if Captain Hooper defeated your champion, you'd hand the boy over."

"You're mistaken, Captain. I said no such thing."

"What?" Lasseur said, his voice dripping venom.

A half smile played across the Corsican's lips. His hand rested lightly across the back of Lucien Ballard's neck. The boy was staring at the Mameluke's corpse.

Hawkwood looked around. Had a pin dropped, the whisper of it hitting the ballast would have sounded like cannon fire.

"The thing is, Captain," Matisse said, "the more I think about it, the more it occurs to me that it wouldn't be right. I've a reputation to maintain. I can't have newcomers coming down here and dictating terms. If I allow that to happen, what's to stop every other worm crawling out of the woodwork and questioning my authority? How would it look if I handed the boy over to you? It would make me seem weak. It'd give every other poor wretch on this ship ideas above his station. Where would it end? More to the point, where's the profit?"

"Did it occur to you that you might actually gain some respect?" Lasseur said.

"Respect?" The Corsican gave a coarse laugh. "That's my point, Captain. I don't want respect. I want them to *fear* me.

If they fear me, they'll obey me. That's how I bring order out of chaos. You think I'd let one small boy jeopardize my standing here?"

"If you'd no intention of keeping your word, then what was the point of *that*?" Lasseur pointed angrily at the Turk's dead body.

The Corsican shrugged. "We all have to make sacrifices. But then, who says I'm breaking my word? Not me, Captain. You merely misinterpreted the terms. I never said I'd hand the boy over. What I said was, I would set him free."

"I don't understand," Lasseur said. "What's the difference?"

Matisse reached down and cupped the boy's face. He stroked the smooth cheek lovingly and in one swift move wrenched his hands sideways. There was a sharp crack and Lucien Ballard's body went limp. With a dismissive shrug, Matisse pushed the body away and dusted his hands. "There, it's done. I've freed him. The problem is solved." He jerked his head at Dupin. "Kill them both."

Lasseur's scream of rage reverberated around the hold. Before anyone could stop him, he leapt forward, scooped up the Mameluke's discarded razor and scythed it towards the Corsican's throat.

If there was a look of shock in Matisse's eyes, it was eclipsed by the dark lenses. Only his mouth showed animation, opening and closing soundlessly as he tried clasping his hands about his neck in a futile attempt to staunch the jet of blood that spurted like a fountain from his severed artery.

As the Corsican collapsed in a bloody heap across Lucien Ballard's still body, Lasseur swung round, the razor still in his fist. Teeth bared, he had the look of a berserker, his appearance made all the more extreme by the crimson splashes on his face and clothes. He stepped quickly to Hawkwood's side and they turned back to back.

"Who's next?" Lasseur roared.

A curse sounded from Hawkwood's right. One of Matisse's men came out of the shadows, barrel hoop raised. Hawkwood ducked and drove his elbow into the attacker's belly. The man faltered. Hawkwood slammed his boot against a knee and as the man went down Hawkwood wrested the hoop out of his grip and drove it across the back of his attacker's skull.

Behind him, Lasseur, wild-eyed and blood-splattered, wielded the razor like a man possessed. Another of Matisse's crew reeled away, shrieking, his cheek ripped through to the gums. "Come on, God damn you!" Lasseur yelled. "I'll take you all with me!"

Hawkwood felt warm liquid flowing down his left side and knew his brief exchange with the last attacker had aggravated the wound made by the Turk's razor. His right hand was also slick with blood. He adjusted his grip on the barrel hoop. Small beads of blood bubbled out from the cut across his knuckles and dribbled between the cracks in his folded fingers.

Hawkwood wondered about the irony of dying with a Frenchman defending his back. Nathaniel Jago would have thought that funny. In fact, he'd have thought it bloody hilarious.

He wondered too why Matisse's men were still willing to wage war with their leader dead. It didn't seem to make sense, unless they thought that he and Lasseur had designs on Matisse's kingdom. No time to debate the matter now, though.

Lasseur swore suddenly and Hawkwood had a half-formed view of a hoop sweeping towards the privateer's head. He sensed that Lasseur had widened the distance between them to give himself room to manoeuvre. There was the sound of a blow, metal on wood, followed by a cry and then he was turning to fight his own corner as two more of Matisse's men waded in. Hawkwood swung the hoop to block the strikes. He managed to evade one, but the second attacker's home-made blade caught him high on the shoulder. His left arm went numb.

Lasseur was still trading blows when there came a splintering sound and the noise of a body hitting the shingle, followed by a cackle of glee which could only have come from one of Matisse's henchmen. He heard Lasseur call out; the words unintelligible. Then, too late, from the corner of his eye he saw Dupin. The Corsican's lieutenant was behind him, swinging the hoop-like club above his head.

Hawkwood felt a massive impact across his back and something hard caught him a glancing blow at the base of his skull and he was falling. He tried to keep hold of the barrel hoop, knowing it was his only means of defence, but he couldn't feel his fingers. They'd gone numb, too.

He crashed to the deck and looked up through pain-filled eyes.

"Nice boots." Dupin grinned above him. He raised the hoop.

Hawkwood watched, helpless, as the hoop began its descent. Then there was a sharp report and the back of Dupin's head exploded.

More detonations followed, then a mass of surging bodies, as suddenly the hold was filled with scarlet uniforms. He looked for Lasseur and tried to sit up, but the task proved beyond him. His head felt as though it was about to burst. It was a lot less painful just to lie back and let himself drift. The strategy seemed to work. Sensation in his limbs was slipping away. It was rather a pleasant feeling. Suddenly, out of nowhere, a hand touched his forehead and he jerked back. The movement sent pain shooting through his skull and into his chest. Then he felt an arm under his shoulder and a face came into view. It was bearded and looked vaguely familiar.

He was still thinking that as the darkness rose up to claim him.

9

Hawkwood realized his mistake when he tried to move. Opening his eyes hadn't been a problem. In fact, that had been the easy part; no real expertise involved: a quick flicker of the eyelids and, presto, he was back in the land of the living. But when he tried to raise himself on to his elbows to find out where he was, it was like getting hit across the back of the head and shoulders all over again, only a lot more painful.

He lay back down, lowered his eyelids, and waited for the hammering inside his skull to abate. The seconds, or it could well have been hours, ticked by. Hawkwood was more than content to wait, feeling no obligation to repeat the experiment until he was sure he could cope with the immediate after-effects.

When the pounding had eventually dwindled to a dull ache, he took a deep breath and tried again, cautiously.

His second attempt was more successful; though not by much. His head still felt as if it was being skewered by a hot poker, and when he saw what lay around him, he wondered if the view had been worth the effort.

As usual there wasn't much illumination. A couple of lanterns hung from the beams and there was a square grating set in the deckhead at the far end of the compartment through which light was slanting, enough to inform him that dusk had yet to fall – though it was probably not far off – and that he was in a part of the ship he'd not been in before. He was lying on a cot, surrounded by other cots. Most, as far as he could tell, were occupied. It was too gloomy to see by whom, but from the sniffling, coughing, wheezing and retching noises it wasn't hard to guess.

The fact that he could still smell vinegar confirmed his suspicions.

He looked down. Just the dipping of his chin sent a bolt of agony screeching across the back of his eyeballs. His shirt had been removed. Dressings and bandages had been applied to his wounds. Several dark spots of blood were visible on the gauze. A single, none-too-clean linen sheet covered him below the waist. Movement caught his eye, just in time for him to see a trio of shiny carapaces disappearing at speed over the edge of his cot; cockroaches on the run.

His gaze moved out beyond his feet. There was an open hatchway leading through to a smaller, similarly dim-lit compartment. He could make out part of a table and the edge of a chair. A jacket sleeve could just be seen draped over the chair back. Cabinets and shelves were set against the bulkhead. The shelves held an impressive selection of corked and labelled bottles in a variety of hues. Some were the size of gin bottles, others looked as if they might once have contained perfume. On the table, more bottles were arrayed next to a pestle and mortar and writing materials.

Allied to the noises around him and the vinegary smell, these items told Hawkwood all he needed to know about his location. The vinegar, he knew, would have been swabbed into the deck in a vain attempt to cover the stench of the vomit and the piss and all the other excretions made by the bedridden men around him. He was in the hulk's sick berth.

"Welcome back."

The greeting came from the next cot, which lay in semi-gloom.

Hawkwood turned his head, slowly, to be on the safe side.

Lasseur had bruises and cuts on his face and a dressing on his left shoulder. He regarded Hawkwood's bandages with a laconic eye. "Looks as if we'll both live to fight another day, my friend. How are you feeling?"

"Like shit," Hawkwood said truthfully, and discovered that talking was only marginally less painful than trying to sit up.

"Me, too, but they say it's better than being dead." A shadow flitted across Lasseur's face suggesting he wasn't a firm believer in the statement.

"I thought I saw Fouchet," Hawkwood said. "Or did I imagine it?"

The privateer did not respond immediately. He still looked preoccupied. Hawkwood presumed he was reliving the boy's death and the subsequent debacle in the hold. Finally Lasseur nodded. "Our teacher friend had an attack of conscience. He alerted the guards."

"I thought they didn't like to venture below deck."

"They don't usually. Sébastien was very persuasive."

"They killed Dupin," Hawkwood said.

"Shot him dead – luckily for you. Though, if you ask me, I'd say whoever did it was probably waiting for an excuse."

"Were there others?"

"You mean apart from Lucien and the Turk and that Corsican filth?" Lasseur screwed up his mouth and nodded towards a point over Hawkwood's shoulder. "Ask him. He'll know the full count."

Hawkwood was debating whether or not to try and turn his head when he sensed a presence behind him. He risked an upward glance. The man standing over Hawkwood's cot was young and dark complexioned, with soulful brown eyes. He was in frayed civilian dress, his sleeves rolled up to his elbows. A severely stained once-white apron was tied around his waist. He spoke in English.

"I see you're awake, Captain Hooper." The brown eyes crinkled. "We've not met. My name is Girard."

"Ship's surgeon?" Hawkwood asked.

The answer was a brisk shake of the head and what might have passed for a self-deprecating smile. "Officially, no. That distinction falls to Dr Pellow. Regrettably, Dr Pellow's other duties tend to keep him ashore, which prevents him from making regular visits. I have the honour to supervise the sick berth in his absence."

From what he'd seen, Hawkwood doubted it was much of an honour.

"He means the son of a bitch has got a very profitable private practice," Lasseur said contemptuously. "He's more interested in the money he earns from his rich English lords and ladies than he is in the likes of us."

Ignoring Lasseur, the surgeon lifted the edge of the dressing on Hawkwood's side and peered at the wound beneath. "I suggest you try and keep your exertions to the minimum. We don't want to disturb the sutures."

Hawkwood suspected the youthful-looking medic was being waggish.

The surgeon clicked his tongue. "You were lucky, Captain. Your wounds should heal well, providing you keep them clean, which in a place like this won't be easy, but I urge you to try. They'll make fine additions to the rest of your collection, which, I have to say, is quite impressive." The brown eyes ranged across Hawkwood's chest, narrowing slightly when they took in the ring of faded bruising around his neck.

"Don't worry," Lasseur said in a mock whisper. "He might

look as though he's just started shaving, but he knows what he's doing. Or so he says."

Girard gave a rueful grin. "I was an assistant surgeon to the garrison at Procida before I was taken prisoner. The British thought I'd be better employed here than whittling bones on the gun deck."

"Lucky for us," Lasseur said. "Seeing as they can't even persuade their own man to make house calls."

The surgeon shook his head. "On the contrary, Dr Pellow's last inspection was only a few days ago. In fact, you probably just missed him. No, wait; it would have been the day of your arrival. You may even have arrived in time to witness an example of his bedside manner." There was an abrasive edge to the surgeon's voice.

Hawkwood and Lasseur looked blank. Then Lasseur swore. "The longboat set adrift! That was Pellow?"

Girard nodded. His mouth was set in a grim line. "They were transferees from Cadiz. When he saw the state of them, it was Pellow's contention they were suffering from some contagious disease and that they should be sent to the hospital ship. The poor devils weren't diseased, they were just badly dealt with by the Spanish. Mind you, the British aren't much better. They treat their damned house pets better than they do their prisoners, especially if they're French. Fortunately, we only see Pellow once a week, if that."

"Whore's son!" Lasseur spat.

It was clear Lasseur's anger was still close to boiling point. The privateer's face had been cleansed of blood, but the savage expression that had contorted his features when he'd sliced open the Corsican's throat was still vivid in Hawkwood's memory. Hawkwood felt a sharp stab of pain cut across his forehead. It was as if the effort of remembering had triggered the hurt.

Something must have shown in his expression, he realized, for a look of concern flashed across the surgeon's face.

"You ought to see the other one," Hawkwood said, without thinking.

The surgeon's expression grew serious. "Oh, but I have, Captain Hooper. I've seen all of them. You left quite a lot of damage behind, you and Captain Lasseur." The surgeon threw a look towards the next cot.

Hawkwood sank back on to the mattress. "How many?"

Girard's eyes flickered back. "Five dead, including the boy."

"Five!" Hawkwood tried to recall the sequence of events. He remembered relieving Matisse's man of the metal hoop, but it was all a bit hazy after that, and his head was still throbbing away merrily so it was easier to give up.

"There were also a couple of wounded men, with lacerations similar to your own, which was interesting. It's not the first time I've treated such wounds. Razors are a common weapon on board the hulks, particularly in settling disputes. Captain Lasseur was noticeably reticent, however, when I pressed him for details."

Hawkwood said nothing.

The surgeon shrugged. "Very well, so be it. Though it's not me you'll have to answer to. I'm under instruction from Lieutenant Hellard to inform him the second either of you awakens. It was my intention to delay that moment, but I suspect one of the guards outside may have taken it upon himself to send word. It would not surprise me if the lieutenant has already dispatched an escort to deliver you to him."

"You mean he'll not come to visit us in our sickbeds?" Lasseur said in mock indignation. "I'm shocked and offended."

"Lieutenant Hellard is not inclined to make house calls. It's a characteristic he shares with the ship's surgeon," Girard added witheringly.

"Captain Hooper has barely recovered from the blow to his head," Lasseur said.

"I think you'll find Lieutenant Hellard of the opinion that, unless either of you has lost the use of your legs, you're required to attend him under an armed guard – which, unless I'm mistaken, is here already."

A heavy tramp of military boots sounded from the stairs.

"They didn't waste any time," Lasseur muttered.

Hawkwood looked and saw a quartet of militia making their way between the cots towards them. They were experiencing some difficulty. The confined space didn't leave a lot of room for brandishing muskets.

The surgeon bent low and said quickly, "Just so you know, I may have exaggerated the nature of your wounds and the length of time needed for your recuperation. It would be best if you were to go along with that minor deceit for the time being."

Hawkwood and Lasseur exchanged glances.

"Why?" Hawkwood asked.

But the surgeon was already turning away.

"Sergeant Hook! It's always a pleasure," Girard announced.

The sergeant halted his guards. He paid no heed to the surgeon's sardonic greeting but stared coldly at the two men in the cots. "On your feet! Commander's orders!"

"These officers are not returned to full strength, Sergeant," Girard said. "Perhaps you could advise Lieutenant Hell—"

"They're breathin', ain't they?" Hook glared at the surgeon.

"Clearly," the surgeon said. "However . . ."

"Then they're to get their arses out of their cots and come

with us. Or else we'll drag 'em. It's their choice, *Doctor*. Don't matter to me either way."

The surgeon bit back a retort, turned and addressed Hawkwood and Lasseur in French. "The sergeant is distraught to find you so incapacitated and asks you if you'd both be so kind as to vacate your cots and accompany him to the commander's quarters."

"But of course," Lasseur said, folding back his sheet. "Please advise Sergeant Hook that it's a pleasure to find him in such rude health and that Captain Hooper and I would be only too delighted to attend him. You may also inform him that I couldn't help noticing that his face is remarkably reminiscent of a cow's arse."

A nerve moved in the surgeon's cheek.

"What did he say?" Hook demanded; his tone suspicious.

"He asked if your men could point their muskets somewhere else. They're making him nervous."

"Did he indeed?" Hook said. He launched a kick at the base of Hawkwood's cot. "I said, on your feet!"

"What a tiresome little man," Lasseur said. "I hope his balls shrivel to the size of currants."

"Unless someone cuts them off first," Hawkwood said.

"May God grant us another one of Sébastien's miracles," Lasseur said, reaching for his boots.

"You'll want this," Girard said, and passed Hawkwood his jacket. "Your shirt was beyond salvage, I'm afraid."

A lot like my bloody assignment, Hawkwood thought.

"I'll not have prisoners waging a private war on my ship!" Lieutenant Hellard fixed Hawkwood and Lasseur with a Medusa stare. "Even if it is scum fighting scum." He turned to Murat. "D'you hear?"

The interpreter nodded uncomfortably. "Yes, sir."

"Then tell *him,*" Hellard said, indicating Lasseur.

"That will not be necessary, Commander," Lasseur said. "I speak English."

Hellard glared at the privateer. Lasseur stared back at him, his expression impassive. The lieutenant turned his attention to Hawkwood. His eyes took in the bandages and the blood. His gaze lifted and he frowned. Hawkwood wondered if the commander was recalling the moment on the quarterdeck when he had scanned the line of prisoners to see whose eyes were upon him. Hawkwood held the lieutenant's eyes for the appropriate amount of time before switching his gaze to a point over Hellard's shoulder, thus giving the impression it had been he who'd weakened and broken eye contact.

They were in the commander's day cabin, which on the hulk, as in any ship of the line, doubled as an office. Two militia men guarded the door. Hellard was seated behind the main desk with his back to the inward-slanting stern windows. An open ledger lay before him, along with several sheets of paper. Outside, sunset was starting to fall over the western marshes, bathing the wetlands and the estuary in a vivid red glow. There was still plenty of movement on the river, with vessels taking final advantage of the early evening tide to navigate their way upstream to an anchorage or downstream towards the open sea.

Out of the corner of his eye, Hawkwood saw that Lasseur's gaze was fixed on the view beyond the commander's shoulders. It wasn't hard to guess what he was thinking.

The cabin was sparsely furnished. On active duty, it was usual for a vessel's commander to equip his quarters to his own specifications, depending on the depth of his pockets; everything from desks to dining tables, sideboards to wine coolers and carpets to cutlery were shipped aboard at a captain's expense.

From what could be seen, the furniture on *Rapacious*

suggested that Hellard was either a man of very limited means – not unlikely, given his rank and the circumstances governing his appointment – or else the items had been provided by the Transport Board with the emphasis on practicality rather than personal comfort. In other words, Lieutenant Hellard had been forced to make do with what he'd been given; which wasn't much. The few sticks of furniture looked as drab and as distressed as the hulk that housed them, as if they had been salvaged from a long-forgotten storeroom in some abandoned dockyard warehouse, and taken on board as an afterthought.

Aside from the desk, there was a mirrored dressing cabinet, which Hawkwood suspected was campaign furniture; an elderly writing slope which stood in one corner; a four-drawer sideboard; and a small round table bracketed by four plain-backed hall chairs. Dark red drapes framed the windows. A layer of dust lay along the top rail. There appeared to be no personal possessions on display; no watercolour portraits on the bulkheads, no miniature likenesses of a wife or sweetheart on the cabinet or sideboard; no books. The left-hand wall was partitioned. Hawkwood guessed that Hellard's bed lay behind it. All in all, the commander's quarters were as austere as the man himself.

Up close, Hellard was more gaunt than he'd appeared on deck. Until now, Hawkwood had only seen him from a distance; a lone figure stalking the quarterdeck, hands behind his back. Close to, his cheeks were more sharply defined, his eyes more melancholic. There were flakes of dandruff on the collar and shoulders of his coat.

"Do either of you know the penalty for duelling?"

"There was no duel," Lasseur said, drawing himself up. "It was self-defence."

"Then how do you explain the razor sticks we found in the hold?" Hellard said curtly.

"Matisse's men attacked us with them," Lasseur said. "We were forced to defend ourselves."

Hellard grunted and said, "Lieutenant Thynne informs me it was a disagreement over one of the child prisoners that led to the killings. What's your story, Hooper?"

Thynne, his features made angular by the rays of the fading sun coming in through the big windows, was standing behind and a little to one side of Hellard's chair, worrying a nail. Hellard half turned to acknowledge his fellow officer's presence, then looked towards the privateer.

"The lieutenant's correct," Hawkwood said. "Matisse took the boy against his will, for his own perverted amusement and that of his men. Captain Lasseur and I took it upon ourselves to confront Matisse in the hope of returning the boy to the upper deck."

Hellard said immediately, "Why did you not inform the guards of the boy's abduction?"

"We didn't think there was any need. We didn't know the situation would turn violent."

"A touch naïve of you, I'd have thought," Hellard said. "Given Matisse's reputation."

Lasseur cut in quickly. "With respect, Commander, we are only recently arrived on board. We knew nothing of Matisse or his reputation."

Hellard consulted the ledger in front of him. "So I see. You didn't waste any time finding trouble though, did you? Either of you."

The lieutenant moved his eyes to the papers. He picked up a pen and made a note on one of the sheets. "Which one of you killed Matisse?" He did not look up, but continued writing.

The question was followed by an extended silence, broken only by the pedantic scratch of nib on paper.

"I did," Lasseur said.

Hellard paused in his scribbling. He raised his head sharply and his eyes narrowed. "Then perhaps, Captain Lasseur, you would describe to us *your* version of events? If you find your English inadequate, Lieutenant Murat will decipher."

He stared hard at Hawkwood. Hawkwood half expected Hellard to say, "I'm not sure I like the cut of your jib" and was almost disappointed when the words didn't materialize.

Hellard glanced away, "Well, Captain Lasseur?"

"Matisse killed the boy. He did it in cold blood, in front of our eyes."

"Why would he do that?"

"To prove he could," Hawkwood said. "Captain Lasseur and I tried to stop him. That was when he ordered his men to attack us."

"You appear to have given a good account of yourselves, in spite of the odds. You were severely outnumbered."

Lasseur's chin came up. "Captain Hooper and I are professionals. Matisse's men were a rabble."

Hellard sighed heavily. He put his pen down and leaned back. "I'm not sure I believe a word of it, frankly. Contrary to belief, my officers and I are not totally ignorant of what goes on below deck. You think we care a fig if you fight amongst yourselves? That is one of the reasons we choose not to interfere with your internal squabbling. We knew fine well that Matisse used the Turk to enforce his authority and intimidate his rivals. We're also aware of the use to which razor sticks are put. Interesting, by the way, that the wounds on the Turk's body should be similar to those suffered by Captain Hooper," Hellard added pointedly. "This leads me to suspect that something more was going on beyond a tug of war over the boy's virtue."

"It was the Turk who had the weapon," Hawkwood said. "I took it off him." Which was close enough to the truth anyway, he thought.

Hellard waved a quieting hand. "Yes, well, that was very enterprising of you, Captain Hooper. That is how you new Americans like to think of yourselves, isn't it? Enterprising pioneers forging a new nation? I suppose you know the word pioneer comes from the French? *Peonier* – it means foot soldier. A shade ironic, wouldn't you say, given your circumstances?"

Hawkwood said nothing. He suspected Hellard was trying to bait him.

"You're a renegade, Hooper, you and the rest of your countrymen. I have no truck with you or your kind, except perhaps to pity your poor choice of causes. There can't be many men who've aligned themselves with two flags and found they've made the wrong choice both times."

"The war's not over yet, Lieutenant," Hawkwood said.

"It is for you," Hellard snapped. "On that you can depend." The commander's eyes narrowed. "I'm intrigued by those bruises around your throat, though. How did you come by them?"

Hawkwood looked straight back. "None of your damned business."

Murat drew a sharp breath.

Hellard fixed Hawkwood with a raptor stare. After several seconds, which seemed to stretch for an eternity, he nodded his acceptance at Hawkwood's defiance, leant forward and closed the ledger with a thud. "I'll confess, the loss of the boy is unfortunate. However, you won't find me sacrificing a moment's sleep over the death of the Corsican or the Turk or any of the other men who lived in his shadow." Hellard paused for effect. "That said, I cannot ignore events."

"Duelling's a hanging offence," Thynne said, almost lazily, looking at Hawkwood. "Says so in the Regulations."

"Indeed it does, Lieutenant," Hellard said. "Thank you for reminding me."

Thynne coloured.

"There was no duel," Lasseur repeated stubbornly.

"Yes, Captain. So you say." Hellard threw the privateer a sour look. "The injuries sustained by the Turk and Captain Hooper here suggest otherwise. Either way, men have died today, in a most barbaric fashion, which means I am required to take action. The Admiralty demands it. I am further mindful that an example needs to be set, both to penalize and more importantly to deter. With Matisse gone to meet his maker, or in his case more likely the Devil, the prisoners need to be reminded who is in charge here, should anyone have a hankering to assume the Corsican's crown. You get my meaning?" Hellard sat back.

"What about the rest of Matisse's crew?" Hawkwood asked.

Instantly the atmosphere in the cabin changed, as if the air had been charged with an electrical current. Hellard glanced towards his fellow lieutenant.

Thynne took his finger out of his mouth. There was a significant pause then he said, "We're going to hang the bastards. Every man jack of them; God rot their black souls." The lieutenant clenched his fists.

"For duelling?" Lasseur said. He stared at the hulk's commander.

No, Hawkwood thought, watching the exchange, it was something else. He remembered the words Fouchet had spoken: *If I told you the half of it, you would think me mad.*

"What is it?" Hawkwood asked. His head was starting to throb again, not that it had ever really stopped.

"Tell me, Hooper," Hellard said curtly, "did you ever stop to consider what would have become of your bodies if Matisse's men had killed you both?"

"We were too busy trying to stay alive."

"Then why don't I let Lieutenant Murat tell you what would have been your fate, had you failed," Hellard said.

"Go on, Lieutenant; tell them what Matisse did with the bodies of the men who fought in previous duels against the Turk and lost."

Murat swallowed nervously.

"I'm sure they'd like to know," Hellard said, "before I pass sentence."

Hawkwood waited.

"Tell us," Lasseur said.

Murat took a deep breath. "It seems the usual method was for the loser's body to be . . . disposed of."

"How?" Hawkwood asked.

"The corpses were cut into pieces and dropped through the latrines into the sea. That way the evidence was removed and the victor was saved a hanging."

Hawkwood and Lasseur stared at the interpreter.

Hellard, watching Hawkwood's and Lasseur's response, said: "Well, go on, tell them the rest of it."

Murat paled.

"What does he mean?" Lasseur asked.

"There was another method." The interpreter threw a look of mute appeal towards Hellard, who returned the look with a stony glare.

"Sarazin says it has happened once that he knows of. He said that he heard of it being done when he was at Portsmouth . . ." Murat hesitated, an odd catch in his voice.

"Go on," Lasseur said.

"He said that on one occasion the body was cut up but was not dropped into the sea. Sarazin said the corpse was jointed and fed to the Rafalés."

Lasseur went white. He turned to Hellard in horror. "Is this true?"

Hellard shrugged. "It may only be a story. The creature tried to save his own skin by informing on his comrades. He'll hang from the yard with the rest of them."

Sarazin, Hawkwood remembered, was the one who'd been on Cabrera and in Millbay.

"So," Hellard said into the pregnant silence, "that leaves us with the question: what am I to do with the two of you?"

"Plenty of room left on the yard," Thynne said, and then muttered, "though, if you ask me, hanging's too good for the buggers."

Hellard stood up.

As the lieutenant moved out from behind the desk a knot formed in Hawkwood's stomach. Aligning himself with Lasseur had seemed like a good idea. Now, because of the privateer's crusade to rescue some wet-behind-the-ears cabin boy and his own irrational sense of obligation, Hawkwood's assignment was unravelling at a rate of knots. In fact, it was probably safe to say it was beyond unravelling. It was lying in tatters around him.

Hellard pursed his lips. It looked worryingly as if he was giving Thynne's suggestion serious consideration.

Thynne, from the window, intoned, "Regulations –"

"Thank you, Lieutenant," Hellard interrupted tartly without turning. "I'm aware of the Regulations."

Thynne flushed. Hawkwood watched as the lieutenant's expression changed. There was no mistaking the acrimonious look that Thynne directed towards his commanding officer's back. Hawkwood sensed it wasn't only because of Hellard's acerbic put-down. The animosity ran deeper than that and, judging from Hellard's demeanour, the resentment was mutual. Hawkwood wondered why that was. There could have been any number of reasons, though, from the needling reference to the Regulations, it was clear that Thynne considered himself to be the better man and therefore more suited to be in charge.

Hawkwood wondered about Thynne's background. Like the army, the navy needed its best men at the war front.

It didn't assign competent officers to oversee the running of decrepit prison ships in remote backwaters if it could be helped. Somewhere along the line Thynne, like Hellard, must have blotted his copybook. Either that or Thynne had sought to avoid the heat of battle by securing a lieutenancy as far away from the fighting as possible, only to find his bid for command of the hulk usurped by a disgraced officer of equal rank but seniority in years. Hawkwood had to admit to himself that the latter scenario seemed unlikely. Whatever the reason, there didn't appear to be much love lost between the two lieutenants.

Hellard said, "From prisoner Fouchet's statement and by your own admissions, I'm inclined to give you both the benefit of the doubt that your actions were out of concern for the boy's welfare. You will be spared the attention of the hangman."

"Sir?" Thynne went to take a step forward.

"However," Hellard said, holding up a hand, halting Thynne in his tracks, "the deaths of Matisse and his men cannot – indeed, will not – go unpunished. That *would* go against Regulations, and it would be remiss of me if I did not render chastisement commensurate to your crimes. The Admiralty will expect it. My decision is also governed by the fact that there is little doubt your actions have bestowed upon you a deal of notoriety. I suspect there are those who'd have you assume the Corsican's mantle. I would deem that singularly unacceptable. You will both, therefore, be transferred to the prison ship *Sampson,* currently moored in Gillingham."

Lasseur gave a sharp intake of breath.

The privateer's reaction was understandable. Every prisoner on *Rapacious* had heard of the *Sampson,* no matter how long he had been on board. It was the ship set aside for the prisoners considered to be trouble-makers. Rumour had it that conditions on *Sampson* were so harsh they made the regime on *Rapacious* look like a church fête.

"You'd rather I hang you with the rest of them, Captain?" Hellard said.

A smug smile broke out across Thynne's face.

Lasseur did not reply. His face remained carved in stone.

"Regrettably, you will not be making the transfer immediately," Hellard said. "I've received word there's been an incident on board the *Sampson*. Some prisoners have led an insurrection to protest at their rations. The commander ordered his men to fire on the demonstrators and a number have been killed. There will be a delay while things calm down. I am not an inhumane man. Until your transfer, therefore, as the punishment cells are now full and it would be unwise to incarcerate you with what remain of Matisse's cohorts, you will both reside in the sick berth under armed guard, where at least your wounds can be attended by the surgeon. I suggest you use the opportunity as a period for reflection. Naturally, Captain Hooper, your participation in this debacle means that your eligibility for parole has been revoked. I understand you're due to appear before an assessment board. That has been postponed indefinitely, pending subsequent reports on your behaviour. I venture it will be some considerable time before either of you see your homeland again, a state of affairs for which you only have yourselves to blame." Hellard nodded to the guards. "That's all. Take them down."

10

"It would have been better," Lasseur said despondently, "if we had been cut up and fed to the crabs."

"Better than being fed to the Rafalés," Hawkwood said. He felt a warm dampness on his side. His wound had begun weeping again.

"Do you really think what Murat told us was true?" Lasseur asked. The muscles around his mouth tightened.

"Maybe," Hawkwood said. "They say eating human flesh turns you mad. There's certainly madness in this place."

Lasseur went quiet. Then he said softly, "Many years ago, I was third mate on a schooner in the South China Seas when we came across an open boat. There were four men on board. Three were barely alive. The fourth was dead. His body was badly mutilated. Two of the survivors died, the third lived. He said that seabirds were responsible for the wounds on the fourth body, but he was not believed. It was thought that he and the others had feasted upon the dead man to save their own lives. Otherwise why had they not rid themselves of the corpse at the time of death? When the last survivor was finally able to walk, he tied himself to a length of chain and threw himself overboard. We assumed he was overcome with remorse at having consumed human meat. Either that or the act had driven him insane." There was a pause, then Lasseur said joylessly, "I hear it tastes like chicken."

"I heard it was pork," Hawkwood said.

Lasseur shuddered and fell silent. A short time passed and then he said, "How did Matisse and the rest of them cover up the loss? The discrepancy would have showed up at roll call. How did they get past the head count?"

Hawkwood had been wondering the same thing. He said heavily, "Maybe they didn't."

Lasseur shifted on his cot. "Then how would they explain the missing men?"

"By letting Hellard and the guards think there'd been an escape." Hawkwood waited for the implication to sink in.

It took a while before Lasseur said, "Oh God."

The half-formed thought had been nagging away at Hawkwood since they'd left Hellard's cabin. It was only after he was back in his cot that it had become whole.

"If there have been no genuine escapes," Lasseur said, "it means Murat deceived us from the beginning."

Hawkwood said nothing.

"If I find it to be so, I'll kill the two-faced bastard," Lasseur said, eyes blazing.

"They *will* hang you, then," Hawkwood said. "Maybe you should stop while you're ahead."

"Christ's blood!" Lasseur cursed. "We've been played for fools!"

The privateer sank back in despair.

Could that be true? Hawkwood wondered. Perhaps Ludd had got it all wrong and there had been no genuine escapes, only disputes and the settling of arguments, with the dead men's remains disposed of through the ship's heads or in the Rafalés' mess tins.

But that wouldn't have accounted for *all* the missing men, surely?

What was it Matisse had said? That it had been a while since they'd enjoyed a diversion, implying it had been some time since the last duel. And Ludd had told Hawkwood and James Read that escapes had occurred quite recently. Perhaps men had actually made it off the ship after all, alive and whole, rather than in pieces through the heads.

But the counts still had to be manipulated. How easy would that be? From what he'd seen, the roll call procedure left a lot to be desired. The discrepancy only had to be concealed for the time it took an escaper to flee the ship and gain a head start once he'd made it ashore.

Not that this speculation was getting them anywhere, Hawkwood reflected. It was academic. His assignment wasn't just lying in tatters. It was dead in the water. Literally.

And how was he going to extricate himself from the mire this time? He had to get word to Ludd, but Hellard had put the lid on that. When he failed to keep his rendezvous, Ludd would surely make enquiries. He'd discover Hawkwood's fate soon enough and would take steps to retrieve him. The Admiralty would have to devise another means of investigating the prisoner escape routes and the fate of its two officers. What a bloody disaster. As Hawkwood cursed his stupidity, he realized the pounding drumbeat inside his head had, miraculously, all but dissolved. At least that was one less thing to worry about.

A series of hacking coughs from a prisoner half a dozen cots away interrupted his thoughts. The coughing intensified until it seemed as if the patient's guts were about to spew from between his lips in bloody lumps. Within seconds of the outburst a chorus of similar coughs and throat-clearing rattles had risen to a crescendo throughout the compartment until the noise was rebounding off the bulkheads. It was accompanied by the sounds of violent retching and heaving. The stench of fresh vomit and excrement began to spread through the sick berth. In the gloom Hawkwood could see orderlies moving between the cots, rags and leather buckets in their hands. There was no sign of the militia guards. Hawkwood presumed they had removed themselves outside to the comparative sanctuary of the stairwell and companionway.

Gradually the coughing died down; exhaustion having claimed most of the afflicted. Hawkwood spotted the surgeon, Girard. He was bending over patients with a concerned eye. Three times, Hawkwood saw the surgeon pause, touch the side of a patient's throat and shake his head wearily. He continued to watch as the sheets were pulled up over the faces of the dead. In the dim light, the surgeon's features looked drained of colour. As each patient's condition was confirmed, the orderlies wrapped the sheet around the body until it resembled a large cocoon. With a nod from the surgeon, each wrapped corpse was lifted from its cot and lugged unceremoniously through to a compartment at the aft end of the sick berth. Hawkwood could just see the inside of the hatchway. There were at least ten shrouded bundles laid out on the deck. He presumed they included the bodies of Matisse and the boy and the others killed in the hold.

Most of the linen wrapped around the corpses carried dark stains. It was hard to tell the colour in the dim light. It looked black, like tar. Hawkwood knew it wasn't. It was blood hacked up from the patients' lungs.

"Perhaps we'll die of fever before they transfer us," Lasseur said morosely, watching over Hawkwood's shoulder.

"If I've got a choice," Hawkwood said, staring at the filthy, gore-matted sheets, "I'll take the *Sampson*."

"You mean where there's life, there's hope?" Lasseur said. The privateer was unable to keep the cynicism out of his voice.

For me, perhaps, Hawkwood thought. *At least I have a lifeline, a way out.*

Lasseur had only a boat ride and an uncertain future in another floating hell-hole to look forward to. Hawkwood was intrigued at how much Lasseur's fate was starting to bother him.

He looked to where the orderlies were wiping down the decks around the recently emptied cots. A familiar tang began to waft through the compartment.

"We call it haemoptysis."

The surgeon was standing at the end of Hawkwood's cot. He was wiping his hands with a damp cloth which smelled strongly of vinegar. His hair hung limply over his forehead. He looked tired and drawn.

"Most of them have it. It's caused by congestion, brought on by consumption and fever and a dozen other diseases. I tried to persuade Dr Pellow to ship some of the more critical patients to the *Sussex,* but he told me there was no room. There's no hospital in the dockyard, so we must make do. As you can see, we've precious little space as it is. We'll be burying the poor devils in the morning, along with the rest of them." Girard tucked the soiled rag into his waistband.

"Rest of them?" Lasseur said, frowning.

"Matisse's men. The ones you killed and the ones that are going to hang."

"They're carrying out the sentence on board?" Hawkwood said.

The surgeon nodded grimly.

"I thought they'd do it ashore."

"It seems Commander Hellard wants it over and done with quickly."

"I'd have thought the British Admiralty would have something to say about that," Hawkwood said. "They'll want them punished, but it sounds as if the lieutenant's taking the law into his own hands."

"On his own ship, a commander is judge, jury and executioner. I'd say our Lieutenant Hellard's marking his territory. Besides, you think that anyone in the British Admiralty will lose sleep over a handful of foreign murderers? I think not." There was a pause, then Girard said, "There's a rumour that some of the prisoners have volunteered to draw on the ropes."

"My God!" Lasseur said, and then added reflectively, "Not that I'd hold it against them. I doubt there's any that'll mourn the bastards."

The surgeon sucked in his cheeks. "They say you and Captain Hooper have been nominated for sainthood."

"No wonder the lieutenant wants to get rid of us," Lasseur snorted. "When do the hangings take place?"

"Dawn."

"Then I'll pray for fine weather," Lasseur said. His face lit up suddenly. "Sébastien!"

Hawkwood and Girard turned.

The teacher was limping towards them. In his hands were two mess tins and two spoons. "I saved you a little something from supper. I thought you might be hungry."

"As long as it's not herring," Lasseur said, grimacing. "Or I may throw up like those other poor devils."

"Bread, potatoes and a bit of pork." Fouchet passed the mess tins over. "It's not much."

Lasseur studied the contents. "You're sure it's pork?" He glanced at Hawkwood.

"It could be mutton," Fouchet said, frowning. "What day is it?"

"Maybe I'll just eat the potatoes," Lasseur said.

"I think it's safe," Fouchet said. "Matisse hasn't killed anyone for a while, that we know of."

"You heard?" Hawkwood said.

Fouchet nodded. "It's all round the ship."

Lasseur continued to stare bleakly into his mess tin. "What about Juvert?"

"He's in the black hole with the rats, licking his wounds. A week in there and he'll be eating his own shit." Without a trace of sympathy, the teacher nodded at the food. "What you don't eat now, you can save for later."

Lasseur placed the mess tin to one side.

"I'll leave you to it," Girard said. "I've patients to see to. And you should eat. It will keep your strength up." He nodded to Fouchet, fished the vinegar-soaked rag from his waist and walked away through the cots.

Fouchet watched him go then laid a hand on Hawkwood's arm. "Tell me the boy did not suffer."

"It was quick," Hawkwood said. "That's about the only thing good you could say about it."

The teacher's face sagged. "He would still be alive if I'd kept watch over him," he said forlornly.

"The boy died at Matisse's hands, Sébastien," Lasseur said gently. "Not yours."

Fouchet eyed Hawkwood's and Lasseur's bloodstained bandages. "I would have liked to have seen you kill the swine."

"If you had, we wouldn't be here," Hawkwood said. "If it wasn't for you bringing the guards, they'd have been delivering us to the heads in buckets . . . or worse."

"And now they're sending you to the *Sampson,*" Fouchet said unhappily.

"Better than to the yard," Lasseur said.

"You might not think so when you get there."

I think I've had this conversation before, Hawkwood thought.

"I heard there was a fight to the death on the *Sampson* only a month back," Fouchet said. "Two men went into the black hole. Only one came out."

"I wonder where they got that idea from," Lasseur smiled thinly.

Fouchet leaned close. "Charbonneau heard two of the militia talking. The British believe the revolt on the *Sampson* is part of a plot to foment a rising of all foreign prisoners in England."

Lasseur gnawed at the inside of his cheek. "That must have put the fear of God up them."

Fouchet shrugged. "One can understand their quandary. While their Admiralty believes there's a benefit to containing all the instigators of the revolt in the one location, by the same token, they're mindful of the dangers in placing so many trouble-makers in close proximity. Clashes between prisoners don't bother them; they regard it as one way of culling the herd. But to have so many malcontents under one roof could place British lives at unnecessary risk."

"The last thing they need is another two joining them," Lasseur said. "No wonder they're delaying our arrival. I'm beginning to wonder why Commander Hellard didn't sentence us to the noose."

"Because that's what his second-in-command wanted him to do," Hawkwood said. "Lieutenant Thynne believes his commander isn't fit for the purpose. Hellard thinks Thynne is after his command. I'd say we owe our lives to Commander Hellard's contrariness."

"Lucky for us it wasn't the other way round then," Lasseur said, "and it wasn't Thynne suggesting clemency."

"Amen to that," Hawkwood said.

There was a shout from outside. A bell began to clang.

"Curfew," Fouchet said. "I have to go."

Hawkwood looked towards the grating. The last of the daylight had disappeared. The only illumination left came from the lanterns suspended from the deckhead.

The teacher shook their hands solemnly. "I am very glad

you are alive, my friends. I'll gather up your belongings and make sure no one helps themselves." He gave a smile. "Not that they'd dare. You've both gained quite a reputation."

"I doubt that'll stop Murat from selling our spaces to the next lot of new arrivals," Lasseur said moodily. "What's the betting he'll even try and turn our reputation to his advantage? 'Captains Lasseur and Hooper slept here. That'll be ten francs extra, thank you very much.'"

Hawkwood couldn't help but grin.

"You shouldn't judge the lieutenant too harshly, Captain," Fouchet said seriously. "In this place, all of us make do as best we can."

"And some of us make do better than others," Lasseur said.

Fouchet wagged an admonishing finger. "I'm off before they put me in the hole for breaking curfew. If I were you, I'd try and get some sleep. We've an early start tomorrow morning."

"We have?" Lasseur said. "How come?"

"Hadn't you heard?" Fouchet said drily. "There's going to be a hanging."

There was no scaffold.

Bisected by the stub of the main mast, the yard was outlined against the dawn sky like the arms of a scarecrow. Suspended from the yard's port and starboard quarters were three wooden blocks. A rope was threaded through each block. One end formed a noose. The free end of each rope was secured to a cleat at the ship's corresponding port and starboard bulwarks.

A line of militia guarded the ship's rails, bayonets fixed. The rest of the ship's complement was drawn up on the quarterdeck. An unsmiling Lieutenant Hellard was standing with the equally stern Thynne on his right and the interpreter Murat on his left, their backs to the newly risen sun. Both officers were in full uniform. Opposite them, on the port side of the deck, a row of prisoners stood in line abreast, some in prison uniform; some in civilian dress. At first glance, Hawkwood had taken them for the men under sentence until he took a closer look and did a count and realized how cleverly Hellard had played his hand. They were the eight members of the prisoners' tribunal.

You convened quickly enough to see Matisse's crew swing, Hawkwood thought.

He'd witnessed punishment on board ship before, on a voyage taking him back to England after the ignominy of Corunna. It had been a flogging; a seaman had been found guilty of disobeying an order while drunk. He had been tied to a grating on deck where he had received twenty-four lashes administered by the boatswain's mate. The ship's crew had been assembled to witness the event, with marines standing by, muskets at the ready.

Squeezed against the forecastle rail with Lasseur at his shoulder and the two militia escorts from the sick berth at their backs, Hawkwood was struck by the similarity. But while the scene was almost identical, the mood was not. The flogging of the seaman had been greeted by an almost sullen silence, whereas the atmosphere on the deck of *Rapacious* was more reminiscent of a public execution outside any London gaol.

It had been Commander Hellard's directive that all prisoners, as well as the ship's complement, were required to view the punishment, excluding those too ill to leave the sick berth, but the sheer number of prisoners housed on the hulk rendered the order impractical. In the end, the summons had been amended to the requirement that at least two delegates from each mess were to be present, including Rafalés. As a result, the decks were full. Hawkwood didn't think he'd ever seen such a woebegone, ragbag gathering of human beings in his life.

Down on the Park the air, sour with the stench of the befouled, prickled with a sense of anticipation bordering on excitement. So much so that Hawkwood was half expecting the ship's pedlars to come crawling out of the woodwork and start touting for business like the pie and sweetmeat sellers that played the crowds outside Newgate.

As he looked on, Hawkwood tried to ignore the compression that was forming inexorably at the back of his throat and the sweat that was leaking from between his shoulder blades.

A murmur ran through the watchers as the condemned were brought out on deck, hands tied behind their backs and flanked by a militia guard. Two of the men were wearing togas, the rest were dressed in the yellow uniform. Half the men had cuts and bruises on their faces. The pair wearing the togas also had wounds on their arms and legs. Hawkwood wondered how many of the injuries had been inflicted during the fight in the hold and how many were due to the militia's late intervention.

Someone yelled an obscenity from the Park, which encouraged a cacophony of catcalls. The condemned men were white-eyed with terror and visibly shaking.

"Silence!" Sergeant Hook's voice boomed across the deck.

As the militia began to place nooses about the men's necks, two of the condemned collapsed weeping on to the deck. A jeer went up as they were lifted to their feet. Both swayed precariously as the ropes were finally slipped around their throats. When all the nooses had been made fast, hoods were placed over the men's heads.

Lieutenant Hellard stepped forward, accompanied by Murat. He raised his arm and the deck fell quiet.

Hellard spoke. Murat translated.

Hawkwood wondered about the other nationalities on board. Who translated for them?

"Let it be known that the ship's company and prisoners are gathered here this day to see justice done. The men you see standing before you have been found guilty of the most heinous crimes. It is upon the order of the Admiralty of His Britannic Majesty that each man is hereby sentenced to death, to hang suspended by his neck until dead. May God have mercy on their souls."

Abruptly, as if embarrassed by the brevity of his pronouncement, Hellard stepped back and nodded towards the members of the tribunal.

The surgeon was right! Hawkwood thought.

He watched as twelve men dressed in yellow prison uniforms stepped forward. The twelve broke into three teams of four. Each team retrieved a rope end from the cleat by the port bulwark. Turning their backs on the condemned men, the three teams stood in silence, each man holding a section of rope over his right shoulder.

"Carry on, Sergeant Hook," Hellard said.

The sergeant nodded towards a pair of militia guards, one of whom pointed his musket into the sky. The men on the ropes took up the strain. The militia escort stepped away.

Hawkwood's fists clenched. The guard fired his musket.

At the instant the shot rang out, the men holding the ropes sprinted hard towards the ship's stern. Behind them, three hooded bodies shot into the air, heading for the yard. As the ropes were pulled tight, and with the musket report still echoing around the deck, the rope ends were made fast. Only then did the members of the teams look up at their handiwork. High above them the three corpses, still spiralling from the momentum of the hoist, dangled below the yard like grotesque ornaments.

The teams moved to the starboard ropes. The militia escorts stepped aside.

At another nod from Hook, the second guard discharged his musket and the hangmen repeated their charge. Three more bodies ascended rapidly into the warm air.

A sigh, like a small wind, went around the deck.

One of the militia let out a curse as a shower of urine and a splatter of faecal matter released from one of the slow-swinging cadavers missed his shoulder by inches and hit the deck at his feet. Casting startled looks skywards, his companions jumped back to avoid the flow of piss and shit raining down from on high as the bladders and sphincter muscles of the hanged men relaxed. A ripple of laughter broke from the mass of prisoners. The tension in the air began to dissipate.

"Silence!" Another roar from Hook.

"A surgeon once told me it's a quick way to die." Lasseur stared up at the bodies.

Hawkwood said nothing. He had known that already. The fact that there had been no kicking or pedalling from the victims' legs after the bodies had left the ground confirmed the anonymous surgeon's statement. Death had occurred the second the ropes were pulled taut, from a swiftly broken neck rather than protracted asphyxiation. He looked down at his hands, to the redness in his palms where his nails had bitten into the skin.

He heard Lasseur mutter something sharp under his breath and turned to find the privateer regarding him with a mortified expression on his face. Lasseur's mouth opened.

"It's all right, Captain," Hawkwood said. "It was a long time ago."

For a moment Lasseur looked as if he was about to respond. His eyes flickered to Hawkwood's throat and the weals on his palms and he nodded silently.

Hawkwood turned away and looked towards the quarterdeck where Hellard and Murat were in consultation with the tribunal, while above them the six bodies, their lower limbs wet and stained with excreta, continued to sway gently in the morning breeze. His eyes moved over the water to some of the other hulks. Figures, both prisoners and crew, were lining the rails; all eyes focused upon *Rapacious*. Hawkwood wondered how quickly it had taken for word of the impending executions to spread around the estuary. Not long, if navy rumour mills were as effective as the army ones he'd known.

Slowly the prisoners started to disperse. The mood was subdued. It was as if the full reality of all that had just happened was finally sinking in. There were a lot of baleful glances up towards the yard. Hawkwood recognized the signs. The collective euphoria that had greeted the hangings was giving way to doubt and the realization that, in the guise of the tribunal, every prisoner on board *Rapacious* had just, in effect, given support to the enemy.

Hawkwood had also been aware for a while that his and Lasseur's presence on deck was becoming the focus of some attention. They were drawing glances, both overt and surreptitious, some respectful, some wary, and the sick-berth guards were getting twitchy. Hawkwood allowed himself to be led back below deck.

He glanced over towards the quarterdeck. The planking below the yard was being swabbed and the militia were letting out the ropes and lowering the bodies. It was tradition, Hawkwood knew, for the corpses of hanged men to remain suspended from the yard sometimes for an hour or two, as a potent warning. He suspected Hellard wanted the latest victims brought down, either as a gesture to the tribunal or, more likely, because the smell of the bodies in the heat of the morning would be too much to bear.

The surgeon, Girard, was watching the proceedings. Hawkwood presumed he was there to pronounce the men dead; not that there was likely to be any doubt. If there was one skill in which the navy enjoyed mastery, it was the tying of knots.

Hawkwood and Lasseur returned to their cots. Even with the smell of sickness seeping from every pore of the compartment it was a relief to be back in the sick berth after the overcrowded topside.

"When do you think they'll transfer us?" Lasseur looked pensive.

Hawkwood shrugged, glancing towards the guards who'd resumed their positions over by the hatchway. "It could be any time. As soon as the commander receives authorization, would be my guess. It was never going to be before the hangings. We were always going to be present for that. Hellard and the Admiralty wouldn't want to miss the opportunity to use us to warn the prisoners on the *Sampson* what will happen to anyone who breaks the rules. I wouldn't put it past the bastards to have shown the two of us leniency just so that we can spread the word and put the fear of God up any other would-be insurrectionists."

Lasseur threw Hawkwood a sideways glance. "Did anyone ever tell you, my friend, that you've a very suspicious mind?"

"All the time," Hawkwood said. "It's a curse."

Lasseur forced a grin, stroked his goatee, lay back and placed his arm over his eyes.

It was odd, Hawkwood thought, how easy it had become to align himself with the plight of the prisoners and how quickly the Admiralty had become the villain of the piece.

The sound of weighted footsteps and an outpouring of profanities interrupted his ruminations. Two prisoners were stepping off the bottom tread of the stairway. Slung awkwardly between them was a body. Lasseur let go an exclamation of disgust. The dead men that Hawkwood had seen being removed from the yard were starting to arrive.

Hawkwood and Lasseur watched as one by one the corpses of the hanged prisoners were delivered into the hands of the orderlies. Millet and Charbonneau were among those delegated with the task of toting the dead. They caught Hawkwood's eye and nodded imperceptibly. The surgeon Girard brought up the rear.

Hawkwood wondered who had come up with the suggestion that prisoners should play such an active role in carrying out the sentence. If it had been Hellard, in many respects it had been a master stroke. Matisse and his Romans had waged their war of intimidation on their fellow prisoners. If Hellard, having taken full advantage of the loathing felt by all the prisoners for the Corsican's crimes, had, by some subtle stroke, put the idea in the heads of the tribunal, in one fell swoop he'd not only adhered himself to the prisoner hierarchy, he'd also partly absolved himself of what could have been seen as implementing a draconian sentence on foreign nationals.

It was inconceivable that the Admiralty would have sanctioned prisoner involvement or, quite possibly, even the hangings themselves, particularly on board the ship; officially, at any rate. Unofficially, Hawkwood began to wonder. He suspected that the Admiralty, like the army, politicians and the judiciary, was perfectly capable of nefarious dealings when it suited its purpose. The tribunal's participation had lent an air of legitimacy to the sentencing and method of execution. If there were repercussions, the Admiralty could lay the blame squarely on Hellard's already blackened shoulders by accusing him of acting of his own volition.

As for Hellard, it could be construed that he was exerting his authority, both to the prisoners and his superiors as well as an audience closer to home, namely Lieutenant Thynne and the rest of the ship's company. By setting up the hangings, Hellard had established himself as a force to be reckoned with. Perhaps, in some bizarre way, he'd even seen it as a means of restoring himself in the eyes of the Admiralty.

Hearing Lasseur grunt, Hawkwood looked up to see a familiar figure limping towards them, carrying two knapsacks held high.

"I received permission to bring you these. Thought you might need them," Fouchet said. "And we can't have you going hungry." Handing over the knapsacks, the teacher fumbled in his pockets.

"Please tell me it's not pork again," Lasseur pleaded.

"Breakfast – the usual. Don't eat it all at once."

Hawkwood looked down at the hunk of dry bread Fouchet was pushing into his hand. It would keep the hunger pangs at bay for a short while.

"You'd have made someone a lovely wife, Sébastien," Lasseur said.

Fouchet chuckled. "Someone's got to look out for you." The smile slipped suddenly. "Remember what I said; you might want to save that for later."

Lasseur stiffened, the bread paused halfway to his lips.

"You've heard when they're shipping us out?" Hawkwood reached into his sack and extracted his one spare shirt. It wasn't much cleaner than the one the surgeon had cut off him. He put it on, taking care not to dislodge the dressings covering his wounds.

The teacher turned to look towards the aft compartment where, through the open hatchway, the orderlies could be seen sewing the bodies of the hanged men into sailcloth burial sacks and where Millet and the others, under the bored eyes of the two militia guards, were awaiting instructions.

As Lasseur and Hawkwood followed the teacher's gaze, two more men appeared at the bottom of the stairs. One wore a militia uniform; the other caused Lasseur's face to cloud over. It was the interpreter, Murat.

The guard nodded towards the orderlies. "Tell the buggers the burial boat's 'ere and that Lieutenant Hellard wants the bodies off the ship in double-quick time. This bleedin' tar bucket stinks bad enough as it is." With a grimace at the smell in the sick berth, and after throwing a look of sympathy at his two colleagues, the guard retreated back up the stairs.

Murat relayed the information in French to the orderlies and the waiting men. "You can start taking them out."

Hawkwood, Lasseur and Fouchet watched as the first body-bag was picked up by the head and feet and carried out towards the stairs. It was a laborious business. The men carrying it were nearly bent double, both by a combination of the corpse's dead weight and the space in which they had to manoeuvre, which included the restricting height of the deckhead. There was no sense of reverence. The team's curses were as vociferous as they had been when the bodies of the hanged men had been brought down for wrapping.

As the first of the dead began their journey up the stairs under the supervision of Murat and the surgeon, inside the compartment the orderlies continued sealing up the rest of the sailcloth burial sacks.

Watching the procedure, Hawkwood wondered how many times the surgeon had carried out this particular duty.

It was as the seventh or eighth bundle was being hefted up the stairway that the calamity occurred. There was a clattering sound and a cry of woe, followed by a loud thump and barrage of invective as the man supporting the corpse's head and shoulders lost his footing and his grip. As man and cadaver slid down the stairs, careering into the pair coming up behind, a second sack slid from its handlers' clutches. Within seconds the stairs were a tangle of tumbling bodies, both alive and dead.

Alerted by the commotion, the two sick-berth guards turned quickly. With insults and accusations flying around their ears as to which imbecile had lost his footing, the militia men waded in to restore order.

The moment the guards' attention was distracted, Fouchet grabbed Lasseur's sleeve. "Come with me now," he hissed urgently. Leave your knapsacks." Reaching out, the teacher extinguished the lantern strung from the nearby deckhead.

Instinctively, Hawkwood looked towards the rumpus. Another lantern blinked out, but there was just enough light remaining for him to see two men – prisoners – hurrying towards them through the cots; Millet and Charbonneau. Each of them had a body slung over his shoulder.

Hawkwood rose to his feet. "Do it," he snapped, quickly seizing his jacket.

Lasseur looked beyond Hawkwood, to where a third man was standing by the aft compartment hatchway. Murat, beckoning furiously.

The guards' backs were still turned.

Lasseur sprang to his feet. Keeping his head low, he dodged under the beams and, half stumbling in his haste, followed Hawkwood and Fouchet towards the aft compartment.

Hawkwood knew, as sure as night followed day, the guards were going to turn round. He was still thinking that as he ducked through the hatchway and realized to his astonishment that he'd made it. Twisting, he saw that Millet and Charbonneau were placing the bodies in the vacated cots and covering them with the sheets. Then Murat was pushing him towards two half-sewn, blood-splattered sailcloth cocoons laid out side by side on the deck.

Murat pointed to the sheets. "Get inside. Cross your wrists over your stomachs. Try to remain still. Quickly!"

Hurriedly, Hawkwood and Lasseur did as they were told. As soon as their feet were at the foot of the sacks, the orderlies pulled the two lapels of the cloth around them, tight enough to prevent displacement of their bodies, yet just loose enough to still allow movement in their limbs.

At a nod from Murat, the orderlies took up their needles.

"Wait! Out of the way!" Thrusting Murat and the orderlies aside, the surgeon bent down next to Hawkwood, a wooden bowl in his hands. "Close your mouth."

"Hurry!" Fouchet hissed from the hatchway. "We haven't much time."

Hawkwood clamped his jaws shut. His eyes widened as the surgeon lifted a blood-soaked rag from the bowl and hastily squeezed it out over his lips, chin and jowls. The surgeon repeated the process with Lasseur.

"It won't fool a close examination, but it's the best I can do under the circumstances." The surgeon started as two shadows appeared in the hatchway behind Fouchet. Relief flooded across his face when he saw it was Millet and Charbonneau.

"It's done," Millet said.

Murat glanced through the hatch. "All right, the excitement's over. Get ready to start passing out the rest of the bodies." He nodded towards the two orderlies. "Sew them up." He paused. "And don't forget to piss on them."

He looked down at Hawkwood and Lasseur, at the horror on their faces. "Would you want to look inside something that was bloodstained and reeking of piss? No, me neither. And remember, you're supposed to be dead men. Not a sound. It will seem like a lifetime and the smell will be terrible. Try to keep your breathing steady. I'm sorry we had no time to warn you earlier. We received word that your passage has been agreed. We thought we had another day, but I overheard the commander and Lieutenant Thynne talking. You're due to be transferred to the *Sampson* tomorrow. This was our only chance to get you off the ship. We've managed to signal to our contact ashore. No matter what happens, remain calm. Millet and Charbonneau are part of the burial party. Trust them. They both know what to do. God speed."

"Hellard will know you helped us," Hawkwood said.

Fouchet shrugged. "What can he do to us that's any worse than what we have to endure now?"

"I hope you get a good price for our sleeping spaces," Lasseur said.

"Sold them already." Murat grinned. He snapped his fingers at the orderlies. "Come on! We need to get them out of here."

"They could put you in the hole," Hawkwood said.

Fouchet smiled. "They'll have to move Juvert out first. Though I could do with some peace and quiet."

"Be careful what you wish for," Hawkwood said. He looked up at Murat. "Is this how the others got out?"

Murat's face darkened. "No."

Despite the heat, Hawkwood felt a chill. "Matisse?"

Murat nodded unhappily.

"How many?"

"Two, according to Sarazin. One through the heads, the other –"

Christ! Hawkwood thought.

"We managed to get two off," Fouchet said.

"How?"

Fouchet glanced at Murat, who somehow managed a weak smile as he said, "You expect us to reveal all our little secrets, do you, Captain?"

"Give them our regards, if you see them," Fouchet said. "Lieutenant Masson and Captain Bonnefoux."

"I'll do that," Hawkwood said.

Lasseur looked up at Murat. "I might have misjudged you, Lieutenant. I'm sorry."

"You're not free yet, Captain."

Lasseur glared at the orderly who was sealing him in. "Put that stitch through my nose and I'll have your guts. And your piss had better smell of roses."

The orderly said nothing, but as he secured the final suture in the cloth, his hands shook. Lasseur's blood-smeared features disappeared from view.

Hawkwood's last sight was of Fouchet staring down at him. The teacher's mouth formed the whisper, *"Vive la France!"*

Not the words I want to hear going to my grave, Hawkwood thought as the needle punctured the cloth over his face for the last time.

Murat had been right. The smell inside the sack was truly appalling. The tang of urine filled his nostrils while the coppery taste of blood lingered unpleasantly at the back of his throat. He wondered what other body fluids the cloth had been subjected to. It was probably best not to think about that. He assumed Lasseur was suffering the same discomfort. A perverse part of him hoped so.

Suddenly, the hands under his shoulders shifted their grip and then his legs dropped. They were ascending the stairway. At least they were bearing him up head first, he thought.

It was a strange sensation, being carried and sightless at the same time. It was too dark below deck for him to make out anything through the cloth, other than subtle changes in the density of shadows, but his other senses had already started to compensate. Every footfall, every groan of timber, every thump, every vocal emission, from a shout to a whisper, began to take on a new resonance. When he'd climbed into the burial sack, his first instinct had been to let his body relax so as to mimic dead weight. Now, with his senses heightened, there was not a muscle, tendon, nerve or sinew in his entire body that wasn't drawn as tight as a bowstring. The fear of discovery had become all-consuming. So when he heard Charbonneau murmur throatily, "We're coming on deck," he felt the sweat burst from his palms.

The transformation from gloom to daylight was instantly noticeable. Hawkwood still couldn't discern anything specific through the cloth, but the mere fact that there was light beyond the confines of the material made the inside of the sack seem marginally less claustrophobic.

His mind shifted back to the day he and Lasseur had been witness to the burial barge's previous voyage. On that occasion there had been seven corpses requiring passage. This time there was more than double that number. Pray to God, Hawkwood thought, they wouldn't have to make two trips.

"Belay there!" The shout came from somewhere close.

The men carrying Hawkwood froze. Hawkwood felt sure they would be able to hear his heart thudding like a drum against his chest.

The same voice came again. "All right, shift your arses, then! Toss the bloody thing! Lively, now! He ain't goin' to feel anythin'. He's bleedin' dead already!"

The order was greeted by a cascade of laughter.

They moved off. Hawkwood exhaled and heard Charbonneau swear under his breath. He tried to recall how many corpses had been removed from the sick berth before him. He had a vision of being placed into the net and smothered by the pile of bodies being tossed in after him, and fought to quell the rising tide of panic.

And then he was being lowered. He felt the strands of the net through the cloth and the pressure of another burial sack against his flank. He allowed himself to take several slow and cautious breaths. The blood the surgeon had daubed around his jaw had dried and he ran his tongue along his lips to moisten them. He wondered if it was his imagination or if it really was piss he could taste.

The sounds of the hulk enveloped him on all sides: the clatter of wheels in their blocks, the flap of lines against the yards, voices conversing – in a variety of accents, both muted and strident – gulls protesting from the mastheads, the tramp of boots across the decking.

He wondered if the body next to him was Lasseur. Pulse pounding, despite his attempt to breathe evenly, he waited for the cry of alarm that would indicate their disappearance from the sick berth had been discovered. How long would the surgeon and Murat and the orderlies be able to conceal their absence? Was this how prisoners before them had made their escape?

Another shout rang out and the sack next to him moved.

Hawkwood felt his breath catch.

Was it Lasseur easing a cramp, or a suspicious guard making an inspection? Then something rolled against his other thigh. He heard the rattle of a winch and realized the net was being hauled into the air. The movement had been caused by gravity settling the bodies. He had a flash of memory, mackerel in a basket, heads and tails jumbled, and wondered if that was what the net-ful of burial sacks looked like to an observer.

Murat hadn't only been right about the smell. Hawkwood knew it couldn't have been much more than ten minutes since the orderlies had applied their final stitch, yet it seemed a lifetime ago. His nerves were stretching with each passing second.

He detected another shift in the net's trim. A sixth sense told him to brace himself. He did so just in time. The net landed with a thump. It was more of a collision than a grounding – no sympathy for the dead from the man on the winch – and the motion beneath him told Hawkwood that they had been deposited in the thwarts of the boat. He felt the craft rock as the burial party and the militia escort arranged themselves. Then came the command to cast off and wear away, followed by the unmistakable sound of oars turning in rowlocks as the boat was edged out from the side of the ship.

It was warm inside the sack and the squeaking of the oars and the gentle pitching of the boat were starting to have an hypnotic effect. Hawkwood was deeply conscious not only of the stench in his own burial bag but the aroma of the bodies around him, all of them caked in either piss, blood or shit, or in some cases all three. The accumulated smells would become worse as the sun continued to rise, which was why Hellard had wanted the bodies removed. There were too many for them to remain on board. Hygiene was difficult to maintain at the best of times. Conditions would have become untenable, particularly in the already tainted sick berth, had the remains of the dead been kept on board.

Hawkwood knew they were close to their destination when he heard the order to boat oars. A brief silence, followed by a shudder as the boat's keel grated against the shingle, confirmed it.

Hawkwood could hear digging sounds as he was carried up the foreshore. A strong, sickly bouquet began to infiltrate the sack the closer they drew to the crunch of the spades, so cloying it even masked his own scent. Hawkwood knew what it was. He'd come across it before, in field hospitals and mortuaries. It was the smell of putrefying bodies. Lying on the ground, pebbles digging into his back, nose pressed against the rancid cloth, it was all he could do to prevent himself from retching.

"All right, toss the buggers in!"

The order, Hawkwood realized, had come from several paces away. He suspected the escort were trying to remain upwind and some distance from the burial pit.

A voice came close to his ear and he recognized Charbonneau's whisper. "Not long now, Captain. It's nearly over."

Hands slid under his shoulders again, dragging him across the mud. He felt the sharp edge of a stone rake his shoulder blade, and then the ground dipped sharply and he had the sensation of being deposited atop what felt, from the lumps and bumps and other, sharper protrusions, as if it might be a stack of logs. The stench of rotting corpses was suddenly far worse than anything that had come before.

His ears picked up the dull clunk of a blade being driven into the ground.

Hawkwood gasped as the first spadeful of mud and pebbles landed across his legs. His heart lurched as the second load was deposited over his chest. The mud was damp and heavy. He tried to move his arms, but he was prevented from doing so by another fusillade of stones that rattled against the outside of the cloth like rain striking the side of a tent.

He heard a voice call softly. "Goodbye, Captain."

And then the earth closed over his face and the world went dark.

11

Hawkwood uncrossed his wrists and brought his right arm down by his side. He flexed his fingers and tried bending his knees and experienced a wave of relief when he found he was able to accomplish both tasks, albeit with some difficulty. He couldn't bend his knees to any great angle, but he knew there was probably enough leeway, despite the weight of the earth, for him to achieve his objective.

He could still make out tiny patches of daylight through the cloth, which meant the filling in of the burial pit had either been half-hearted or deliberately slipshod, with just enough dirt having been cast over the newly interred burial sacks to deceive the militia.

He could no longer hear voices. They had faded as the burial detail returned to the boat. He could hear seabirds in the distance and the lap of waves along the shoreline. He could also hear sheep bleating. It was a sound the prisoners had grown used to, for when the wind was in the right direction the animals' plaintive cries could be heard clear across the marshes, even as far as the hulks.

He drew his right knee towards him, extended his right arm, stretched his fingers and began inching his hand down his thigh. It wasn't as easy as he'd hoped. There wasn't enough room in the sack to allow him the flexibility he was looking for while laying on his back. He paused, muscles straining. Then, taking a deep breath, he twisted on to his left side. Immediately, he felt the corpse beneath him move. A wave of putrescence enveloped him. He bit down on the sour taste and tried the manoeuvre again. This time, he almost made it. His fingertips moved beyond his kneecap. Hunching his shoulders, he reached down once more. The muscles in his shoulder shrieked as his thumb and forefinger drew the knife out from the inside of his boot.

He rested, chest heaving, and waited for his shoulder to stop protesting. Then he turned on to his back once more and brought his arm up. With the knife less than a hand's breadth from his face, he infiltrated the razor-sharp blade into the gap between the stitches in the sailcloth and began cutting.

He was on the second stitch when his ears picked up a sound that hadn't been there before. His skin prickled. Slowly, he withdrew the knife blade down into the bag.

He heard the noise again; someone was approaching cautiously. Hawkwood went rigid. There was a soft scraping sound followed by a brief silence. Then he thought he heard voices talking softly. The words were indistinct. It had to be the militia, come back to check, trying to be quiet about it, and failing. Carefully, Hawkwood reversed the knife and held it flat against his chest beneath his arm. The scraping noises resumed. Suddenly the light showing through the cloth was blotted out. A figure was kneeling over him. Without warning, a knife blade, larger than his own, stabbed through the vent in the cloth inches from his face, sliced effortlessly through the next dozen stitches and the edges of the sailcloth were peeled apart.

"You smell almost as bad as me." Lasseur wrinkled his nose, chuckled softly and jerked his head. "He says we've to hurry and we're to keep our heads down, which seems sensible advice."

Hawkwood looked beyond Lasseur's shoulder to where a man of indeterminate age was crouched, holding a short-handled spade. He was dressed in a long-sleeved grey shirt and a pair of dirty brown breeches. Other than a pair of narrowed dark eyes, it was hard to make out his features, for his mouth and nose were covered by a triangular folded scarf. Hawkwood presumed it was as a guard against the smell from the pit rather than an attempt at disguise. Curly black hair peeked from beneath a soft felt cap.

"Does he have a name?" Hawkwood asked.

"He says we're to call him Isaac." Lasseur was about to hand Hawkwood the knife when he caught sight of the blade concealed beneath Hawkwood's arm. "I see you started without me."

Lasseur tossed the knife to the man behind him and watched with approval as Hawkwood used his own blade to cut himself free before returning the weapon to its place of concealment.

Lasseur grinned. "Maybe I should be calling you the sly boots instead of Murat."

"Quit talking and move your arses!" The man calling himself Isaac slid the knife into his belt. "And don't forget the bloody sacks. You do parlez English, yes?"

"I told you," Lasseur said. "We both do." He looked at Hawkwood and rolled his eyes.

"Right, well, keep your bleedin' heads down! We ain't out of the woods yet."

"Woods?" Lasseur frowned. "I see no trees." He looked about him.

"Jesus," the man muttered, waving his hand. "Bleedin' Frogs. Come on, get behind me."

Hawkwood and Lasseur did as they were told as the guide began shovelling mud back across the top of the burial pit, filling in the depressions where Hawkwood and Lasseur had lain, restoring the disturbed surface. When he'd completed the task to his satisfaction, he turned and pushed past them, still keeping low. "Follow me. Stay close."

Hawkwood risked a glance seaward and saw why they'd been instructed to keep their heads down. Between the burial pit and the beach there was a slight rise in the ground. On the other side of the rise, the shingle sloped down to the water. At ground level, where they lay, the slope was just high enough to block the view of the hulks. A clear worm's-eye view of the estuary was also hampered by clumps of sea-grass which crested the shingle bank for several yards in either direction.

A throaty mutter came from behind. "I'd stop admirin' the bloody view, if I were you. Signal said we had to get you away sharpish, so unless you're plannin' on hangin' around for the militia, we'd best get goin'. We ain't got all day!"

Hawkwood felt his arm tugged. Turning his back on the water, he tucked the sailcloth bundle under his arm and followed Lasseur and the guide on all fours, away from the pit and its gruesome contents.

It was a laborious crawl. Hawkwood estimated they had probably covered close to fifty yards on their bellies before the ground suddenly opened up in front of them, revealing a steep-sided ditch, some six paces in width. At the bottom of the ditch a three-foot-wide ribbon of murky brown water was bordered by rushes and tall, thin-bladed reeds.

Isaac removed the scarf from his face, passed it to Hawkwood and nodded towards the water. "Ain't sweet enough to drink, but you might want to think about cleanin' yourselves up a bit. Be quick about it, though."

Hawkwood soaked the scarf in the water and rinsed the blood from his face before handing the cloth to Lasseur. The water was warm and smelled of peat and more than a hint of dung. Hawkwood didn't like to think what else might be lying under the surface, but anything was better than the stench of the pit.

"You said you had a signal," Hawkwood said, remembering that Murat had used the word, too. "What signal?"

He saw that the man was giving him a strange look.

"You don't sound like a Frog," Isaac said.

"That's because I'm not."

"Your English is bloody good. What are you then? A Dutchman?

"American."

"A Yankee?" Isaac's eyes widened. "Bloody hell, you're a long way from home."

"So everyone keeps telling me," Hawkwood said. "What signal?"

Isaac's expression shifted from surprise to disbelief that anyone with half a brain would ask such a question. He glanced towards Lasseur as if seeking reassurance that his opinion of Hawkwood's ignorance was well founded, and looked surprised to be confronted by the same quizzical expression.

He turned back. "Your bleedin' washing lines, of course! What did you think it was?"

"Washing lines?" Lasseur said, mystified. Suddenly he glanced down at the rag in his hand and his eyes opened wide. "Flags! My God, they used the laundry as signalling flags!" He swung back to Hawkwood and grinned wildly.

"All right, that's enough," Isaac said impatiently. He stared hard at the blood spots on Hawkwood's shirt and at the marks on Lasseur's face and waved the scarf away when Lasseur tried to return it. "Let's go. *Allez!*"

Without waiting for a reply, their guide broke into a run along the edge of the watercourse. Still carrying their sailcloth burial bags, Hawkwood and Lasseur set off in stumbling pursuit.

Hawkwood watched Lasseur stuff the piece of rag into his pocket and had a mental image of shirts and breeches twitching in the breeze like lines of bunting. He wondered how the system worked and guessed the messages were hidden in the sequence of the washed garments. A shirt followed by a pair of stockings followed by two sets of breeches and so on. It was, he was forced to admit, brilliant in its simplicity and – unless you were privy to the secret – totally undetectable.

The land around them was flat and featureless; a mixture of bog and clumpy pasture, crisscrossed with ditches that twisted through the marshland like drunken adders. There were no trees in the immediate vicinity, though further east the land rose towards a series of copse-dotted hills that rolled away gently towards the centre of the island.

Trailing Isaac along the ditch was like following a hound. Every twenty paces or so, their guide would lift his nose in the air as though searching for a scent, before turning to make sure they were still following.

They had travelled a further half-mile before they halted for the second time. They were still only a little over a mile from the ship, Hawkwood estimated. Slightly less as the crow flew; and not nearly far enough away for comfort. Their guide was evidently of the same opinion, for he peered over the rim of the dyke, back towards the way they had come, as if searching for pursuers. Satisfied that the coast was clear, he ducked back down and they set off once more.

Even though it was not the most direct path to safety, Hawkwood knew that using the ditch as cover was the sensible thing to do. The land along this stretch of coast was so low lying that if they stood up they risked being seen by anyone aboard the hulks with a half-decent spyglass. Isaac's strategy prevented their heads from breaking the skyline. Better to be safe than sorry, Hawkwood reasoned. With good fortune looking over their shoulders, they'd be able to make up the time before too long.

The day was turning warm. He could hear Lasseur breathing hard and wondered how fit the man was and whether he could keep up the pace. In the army, Hawkwood had been used to route marches; and as a Rifleman he'd led his men on skirmishes over moor and mountain trails that would have defeated regular troops. Since returning to England and joining Bow Street, however, he was the first to admit that some muscles had grown soft through disuse. Runner by name, perhaps, but the number of times he'd had to pursue criminals for long distances over heath and hedgerow had been few and far between, which was to say never at all, as far as he could remember.

Ten paces ahead of them, Isaac held up his hand and laid a finger to his lips. When Hawkwood and Lasseur caught up with him, their guide raised his eyes above the edge of the dyke. Hawkwood and Lasseur followed suit.

"*Merde!*" Lasseur whispered.

The sheep were less than twenty paces away, hemmed inside a wicker pen. It was a small flock; perhaps thirty animals in total, black faced and long tailed. Some had small curved horns. It wasn't the sheep, however, that had caused Lasseur alarm. Tied to the pen's gatepost were two wire-haired black-and-white dogs. At the sight of the men, both dogs stood, tongues lolling. Their ears were pricked. Their eyes were bright and alert.

Lasseur laid a warning hand on Hawkwood's arm.

"It's all right," Isaac said. "They know better than to bark. They do and they'll get a taste of my belt."

Isaac climbed out of the ditch and trotted towards the dogs. He gave a curt word of command and the animals dropped to their bellies.

"You can come out now," he said and waited for

Hawkwood and Lasseur to join him. The dogs watched their approach with interest.

Isaac unhitched the dogs and swung the gate open. Immediately the dogs raced round to the back of the flock and began herding the sheep out of the gate into the open pasture.

Walking into the pen, Isaac dropped to his knees and used the edge of the spade to lift out a section of turf, exposing a knotted rope handle. Hooking his fingers under the rope, he leaned back and pulled. A larger section of turf came with him. The turf was bedded on top of a wooden trapdoor. Isaac pulled the trapdoor aside and Hawkwood found himself staring down into another pit.

The chamber had been well constructed. The floor was clay. The walls were lined with wooden slats. Half a dozen wooden kegs – half-ankers, Hawkwood guessed; each one capable of holding four gallons of spirits – were stacked against the wall. On the floor next to the kegs were several oilskin bags and a muslin sack. Isaac climbed into the hole and passed the sack out. "There's some bread and cheese and apples and a little something to wet the whistle." He mimed a drinking motion when Lasseur frowned. Then he held out his hand. "Give me the body sacks. Take these and put them on." He deposited the spade and the body sacks into the pit and passed out two coarse linen bundles.

Hawkwood and Lasseur opened them up. They were shepherds' smocks folded around two soft, wide-brimmed hats.

"These, too," Isaac said and held out two short hazelwood crooks. Retrieving a third, longer, crook for himself, he closed the trap and replaced the turf over the rope handle. Then he tamped down the edges of the turf and, collecting up a handful of sheep droppings, scattered them over the area. Satisfied that the entrance to the underground chamber was again concealed, he looked up and indicated the smocks. "I said put them on. Time we were leavin'."

Hawkwood and Lasseur stared at him.

Even the dogs, who had returned to Isaac's side, looked doubtful.

Isaac gave an exasperated sigh. "They'll be lookin' for two men on the run, not three shepherds movin' their flock to fresh pasture. But if you think you know better, then be my guest. Ferry's that way." Isaac pointed a stubby finger towards the south. "Make your bloody minds up."

At that moment, a sharp report, not unlike a distant roll of thunder cut short, came from the direction of the estuary. It was followed by the faint ringing of a bell. The dogs' ears and muzzles flicked towards the sounds. Isaac's head swivelled. "Shite!"

"That doesn't sound good," Lasseur said.

Hawkwood laid the walking stick down, slipped his arms through the smock's sleeves and pulled the garment over his head. It occurred to him that it was like climbing into the burial sack from the opposite direction. He jammed the hat on his head and picked up the stick.

Isaac nodded his approval. Hawkwood had the feeling he'd just transformed himself into the village idiot.

Lasseur put on his smock and hat and threw Hawkwood a lop-sided grin.

The grin made it worse. Hawkwood wondered what the chances were of one village having two idiots. He picked up the muslin sack and slung it over his shoulder.

Isaac let out a series of short, sharp whistles. Obediently, the dogs hurtled off and in a pincer movement began to drive the sheep towards a wooden gate at the far corner of the field. Isaac pointed towards the nearest tree-topped crest. "We'll take them round Furze Hill towards the East Church Road."

Lasseur followed the pointing stick and then stared back towards the coast. Hawkwood knew the privateer was gauging the time factor.

"If they've let off the cannon it means they've searched the ship and found us gone," Hawkwood said. "They're bound to send a detail to check the burial pit. That'll take them a while."

Retaining the burial sacks and filling in the pit had been a shrewd ploy. With obvious signs of disinterment removed, the only way to prove Hawkwood and Lasseur had been carried ashore would be to open the pit, exhume the full body bags and count the corpses, all of which would, hopefully, add to the confusion. Hawkwood didn't envy any of the men assigned to *that* task.

The dogs were enjoying themselves; zig-zagging back and forth under Isaac's watchful eye. The sheep were obviously well used to the imposition, so much so that it looked as if they were the ones who were obeying Isaac's short sharp whistles rather than the dogs. Reaching the gate, the animals waited patiently for the men to catch up. Isaac pointed past the gate to a small wooden bridge that lay beyond it. "The road's yonder."

When they got there, it wasn't much of a road; more like a fifteen-foot-wide bridle path; narrow and pitted and rutted with cart and animal tracks. On the other side of the path, the land lifted in a gentle incline.

"This here's the Minster Road," Isaac said. "We want the one over the 'ill – it runs right the way across the Isle. We'll stay off it, but if we follow alongside it'll take us where we want to go. As long as we keep our eyes peeled, the dogs'll do all the work. You spot anyone comin', you sing out. Remember, all they'll see is three locals drivin' sheep, so no need to go runnin' off. Keep your 'ats on and your 'eads down and, whatever you do, don't open your bloody mouths.

You can spit on their boots if you like. Militia are used to that. They stands for authority an' Sheppey folk ain't too partial to folk in authority – don't like being told what to do; goes against the grain." Isaac grinned. He looked at Lasseur. "You understand, Monsewer?"

Lasseur nodded. "I think so."

"Right then, gentlemen," Isaac said. "Let's take a walk, shall we?"

Sheep were not fast walkers, especially up hills, and as a disguise and an aid to flight, their steady perambulations didn't exactly instil confidence. Though it was, Hawkwood conceded inwardly, a pleasant enough way to travel if you didn't have a care in the world or the possibility of armed militia snapping at your heels.

Even allowing for the fact that pursuit could be drawing ever nearer, the sheer joy of being anywhere other than on board the hulk was a wondrous feeling. No wooden walls, no men crammed on top of one another in stinking darkness. There was only the wide blue sky and grass beneath their feet. The smell of the marshes didn't seem so pervasive out here in the fields. And there was, of course, a birdsong accompaniment; not the raucous, incessant complaining of gulls, but the melodious twittering of song thrush, blackbird and hedge sparrow. Hawkwood had followed the drum through Spain, Portugal, South America and a host of foreign climes, but there was nothing he'd seen that could compare to the English countryside on a bright summer morning.

Even Lasseur looked entranced. Hawkwood had caught the privateer lifting his face to the sun on several occasions. For the Frenchman it was probably the next best thing to being on the deck of his ship.

They were moving steadily and were on the brow of a hill, about to descend into the valley, when Hawkwood saw

Isaac stiffen. The guide was peering over Hawkwood's shoulder, down towards the west.

Hawkwood turned.

There were horsemen in the distance. At first glance they appeared to be heading towards them. Hawkwood's heart skipped several beats but, as he continued to watch, the riders suddenly veered away to the south.

"They'll be headin' for the Swale," Isaac said confidently. "Probably come from the Queenborough Road or Mile Town. They ain't no threat. They've likely enlisted the garrison's help, but it'll take them a while to get organized. They don't 'ave too many mounted troopers out here. Long as we take it nice an' easy and keep movin', we'll be fine. Better than runnin' around lookin' like chickens with our 'eads chopped off. And we don't 'ave that far to go. Be like strollin' to church for Sunday sermon."

They dined while they walked. The simple pleasure of biting into a hunk of bread they hadn't had to soak first in order to swallow was impossible to put into words. The cheese was full of flavour, the apples sharp and crisp. The cider, kept cool in the underground chamber and sipped straight from the jug, was as refreshing on the palate as water from a mountain spring.

They'd been going for more than two hours, resting the flock at intervals, when it occurred to Hawkwood that, with the exception of the mounted patrol glimpsed earlier, they hadn't spied another soul all morning. The same thing had struck Lasseur.

"That's why we came this way," Isaac said when Lasseur mentioned the fact to him. "Most folk live to the north, along the top road and the coast. Down south, towards Elmley and Harty, it's mostly fever and swamp land. Some folk say it's the last place God made. That's why they call Sheppey folk Swampies."

"Swamp-ies?" Lasseur had trouble with the pronunciation.

"What you might call a term of affection," Isaac said, adding wryly, "Same reason we call you lot Frogs."

Lasseur raised a cynical eyebrow. Hawkwood kept his face straight, albeit with some difficulty.

"Where are you taking us?" Lasseur asked.

"Well, it ain't all the way home, that's for certain. My part's played as far as Warden. After that you're someone else's problem."

A tingle moved up Hawkwood's spine. If further proof was required that there was an apparatus in place to assist escapers, it had just been provided.

"This place, Warden – how long will it take us to get there?" Lasseur asked.

"Two shakes of a lamb's tail," Isaac said, without breaking stride.

It took the rest of the day.

They bypassed East Church. There wasn't a great deal to the place; a small, sleepy hamlet straddling a crossroads, comprising a dozen or so cottages huddled around a squat, grey church with crenellated walls and a square tower. There were a few people about, but they were a good distance away and, other than responding in kind to Isaac's friendly wave, paid no mind to the sheep, dogs or counterfeit shepherds.

The village occupied one of the highest points on the island. The land rolled away in a series of gentle undulations revealing spectacular views in every direction, particularly to the south, all the way to the Swale and across to the mainland.

A short way past the village, Isaac pointed towards a gentle incline. "Warden's about a mile further, at the top of the 'ill, other side of them trees."

It was about then that Lasseur began to grow restless. The excitement in his eyes was palpable. Watching the privateer catch his first smell and sight of the sea through an unexpected fold in the hills reminded Hawkwood of a thirsty horse scenting water. He suspected that even if Lasseur had been deaf and blindfolded he'd still have found his way to the coast.

They approached the village from the south, the dogs driving the sheep up the slope in a tight wedge before them.

There wasn't a lot to Warden, from the little Hawkwood could see of it through the woods. It looked to be just another row of miserly cottages and a church, all clinging like limpets to a small coastal outcrop stuck on the arse end of the back of beyond.

Isaac hadn't lied when he'd told them it would be like strolling to church on a Sunday morning, because that was precisely what they were doing, give or take a day. The church was located at the seaward end of the village, less than a stone's toss from the cliff edge. They emerged from the spinney with the late afternoon sun shining across the stonework and the coo of wood pigeons in their ears, to find the graveyard barring their way. Isaac opened the gate and the dogs did the rest. As the flock spread out between the tombstones and began to graze, Isaac secured the latch behind them, tethered the dogs to one of the gate bars, and led the way through the stones towards a heavily studded side door. Passing the stones, Hawkwood saw they were severely weathered. Most of the names were indecipherable, worn smooth by the passage of weather and time. It was easy to imagine how desolate and inhospitable the place was likely to be in the depths of winter.

Isaac knelt by the door. Removing a brick from the wall of the church, he reached in and extracted a key from the cavity behind. He caught Hawkwood and Lasseur eyeing him. "Vicar's out." He replaced the stone, adding, "Vicar's always out when there's a run on."

They entered the vestry and Isaac locked the door behind them and led the way into the nave. The interior of the church was cool and dry and smelled of stone and wood, candle grease and dust. The late afternoon sunlight shone through the stained-glass windows, casting intricate rainbow patterns on to the walls and stone floor.

"You won't be needin' them any more." Isaac indicated the smocks and the hats. "Leave 'em on the pew, there; the crooks, too. Now, give me an 'and with this." Isaac walked to the side of the nave where a row of inscribed flagstones were set into the floor. They were old, Hawkwood saw, and very worn, the names faded with time and, like the tombstones outside, barely legible, though many of them bore what looked like the name Sawbridge. Some local high-born family, Hawkwood deduced, though the village didn't look substantial enough to support anyone with aristocratic blood.

Isaac bent down and levered his knife into a crack alongside one of the flagstones. The stone looked thick and solid, but prising it up was remarkably easy. Hawkwood saw that it was a lot thinner than the stones that bordered it. Like the trapdoor out on the marsh, it had been designed to deceive; either ground down or fashioned from a lighter stone and carved with the same inscription and artificially aged so that it blended in with its companions.

Isaac descended first and told them to wait. There was a sound of flint striking steel and a second or two later the glow of a lantern bloomed in the darkness below. "Down you come," Isaac called.

He waited until they had joined him, then handed Hawkwood the lantern before reaching up and replacing the stone over the hole.

Beneath the church, Hawkwood was struck with a sudden

vision of another crypt a world away from the Kent marshes. The bone vault under St Mary's, where he'd hunted the killer, Titus Hyde. A shiver ran through him, unseen by the other two.

The tunnel was just wide enough for two men to walk abreast, but it was easier in single file. Isaac took the lead with the light. Lasseur and then Hawkwood followed behind. The air was damp and smelled heavily of clay.

Where the hell is he taking us? Hawkwood wondered.

They had travelled about a hundred paces before the floor of the tunnel began to slope upwards, ending abruptly in front of a crude black wooden door. Isaac lifted the latch. Opening the door, he raised the lantern. They were in a smaller tunnel, its sides almost perfectly round. Hawkwood frowned. He tapped the walls. They were wooden and sounded curiously hollow. A loud click came from a few feet ahead of him as another latch was lifted and the entire end of the tunnel, like a ship's porthole, swung open before them.

The first objects Hawkwood saw when he clambered through the opening were the liquor tubs. The walls were lined with them: all sizes, from half-ankers to hogsheads. He heard Lasseur click his tongue in what sounded like admiration and turned, just in time to see Isaac closing the tunnel entrance behind them. Lasseur's reaction was fully justified. The end of the tunnel was formed from a huge cask, one of several stacked on their sides. Hawkwood could only guess at the volume of spirits each one might have contained – several hundred gallons at least. Each cask head had a wooden spigot driven into it. Curious, Hawkwood turned the tap in the cask from which they'd just emerged and watched as a trickle of dark liquid splashed on to the floor. He cupped his hand beneath the tap and raised it to his lips. It was wine. He turned and saw Isaac regarding him with a sly grin. "Pays to have an escape route in case the Revenue decides to drop in."

"What is this place?" Hawkwood asked.

"Cellar room of the Smack." Isaac indicated the casks. "Local inn; figured it was best bringin' you this way rather than parade you down the 'igh street. Like I said before, folks hereabouts don't 'ave much liking for the authorities, but you can't be too careful."

Sounds came from above: a dull thud as though someone was moving furniture, and muffled voices.

"Wait 'ere," Isaac instructed. He placed the lantern on the top of a nearby tub and headed for the cellar door. Before he left the room, he turned. "An' don't bleedin' touch anythin'." The door closed behind him.

Lasseur stared around him. "Well, at least we won't die of thirst." He indicated the muslin sack that Hawkwood was still carrying. "I could eat a horse. Is there anything left?"

Hawkwood tossed Lasseur an apple and shook the earthenware jug. He was rewarded with a faint sloshing sound. He held out the jug to Lasseur, who wrinkled his nose and walked over to the false cask. He turned the tap, cupped his palm, and took a swallow. His face contorted. He turned the tap off hastily and threw Hawkwood a look of disgust. "How can they drink this piss?"

"They probably don't," Hawkwood said. "I doubt they'd put the good stuff in there. It's only in case the authorities decide to search the place."

Lasseur took in the other barrels. Hawkwood could tell he was debating whether or not to try their contents.

There were footsteps outside. The door opened and Isaac entered with another man. The newcomer was stoutly built with a florid face, impressive side whiskers and small, piercing eyes. He was wiping his hands on a dirty apron.

"This is Abraham," Isaac said. "He owns the place."

Lasseur bowed. "Honoured. I'm Captain –"

"Don't need names," the whiskered man cut in. "You ain't stoppin'."

"You're leavin' tonight," Isaac said. "There's a run on."

"Run?" Lasseur said. "Where are we running?"

Isaac and the landlord exchanged glances. The landlord shrugged.

"It means a delivery," Isaac said. "Contraband; brandy and tobacco. Same boat as brings the stuff in will be takin' you out. It'll be after dark, so we've got a couple of hours to kill. Might as well make yourselves comfortable." He eyed the muslin sack and the cider jug. "I'll bring you some food."

"Bandages, too," Hawkwood said.

The landlord swung round. He stared at Hawkwood, his eyes hard.

"He's a Yankee," Isaac said.

"He's a long way –"

"Everybody tells him that," Isaac said.

The landlord took in Hawkwood's scarred face, matted hair and the blood on the front of his shirt. He turned to Isaac. "Thought you said you had no trouble."

"We didn't," Isaac said. "He was bleedin' already."

The landlord's gaze moved towards the bruises on Lasseur's face and his brow furrowed. "Either of you need a doctor?"

Hawkwood shook his head. "Just the bandages."

What might have been relief showed in the landlord's eyes. He nodded brusquely. "I'll see what I can do."

The victuals and bandages were delivered a short time later. The food consisted of two bowls of mutton stew, a loaf of bread and a pitcher of ale. The stew was very tasty, with solid chunks of meat and thick gravy. Even Lasseur was impressed, though after the prison fare Hawkwood knew both of them would probably have eaten toad pie and pronounced it exquisite. But then, if a Sheppey cook couldn't provide a decent mutton stew, who could?

Isaac had also provided a kettle of hot water from the inn's kitchen, a bowl and a towel. Hawkwood and Lasseur cleansed the rest of the blood from their faces.

"How are you feeling?" Lasseur asked.

"Better than I've a right to," Hawkwood said. He was aware of a faint throbbing behind his eyes and was glad he was in the relative dark of the inn's cellar rather than in the open with the sun beating down. The hats provided by Isaac might have given the two of them an oafish look, but they had been a godsend.

Lasseur watched as Hawkwood unwound the used dressing from his side. He hesitated and then said, "In the hold, before you broke the Mameluke's neck . . . when you turned away; you knew he was going to attack, didn't you?"

Hawkwood didn't reply immediately. He examined his wounds by lantern light. Contrary to his concern, the cut across his side had not reopened. Surgeon Girard's sutures remained intact. He wound the fresh bandage around his belly. "I thought it likely."

Lasseur frowned. "That sounds as though you were inviting him to attack you."

Hawkwood shrugged. "You think if I'd been on my knees, my arm broken, he wouldn't have finished the job quickly? He wouldn't have thought twice."

"You're not telling me you were giving him a chance?"

Hawkwood shook his head. "That's one thing he never had."

Lasseur's eyes narrowed and then widened again as he gasped, "My God, that was your intention! You lured him into the attack! You killed him for the effect it would have. You were toying with him."

Hawkwood tucked in the end of the bandage.

An expression of disquiet moved across Lasseur's face. He shook his head sorrowfully. "I see a darkness in you, my friend. I saw it in your eyes in the hold when we were fighting. I think I see a measure of it now. It saddens me greatly. I'm glad we're on the same side."

Hawkwood buttoned his shirt over his wounds. "You take advantage of an opponent when you can. You might only get the one chance. Nine times out of ten, it's not pretty."

Lasseur put his head on one side and said, "There was a Malay I sailed with many years ago who got into a fight with a fellow crew member, a Sicilian. The Sicilian had a knife and yet the Malay disarmed him using only his bare hands. It was one of the strangest things I ever saw. The Malay moved as if he were dancing. It was like watching water flow. There was something similar in the way you broke the Mameluke's arm after you lost your razor. It was as if you had anticipated what you were going to do even before you struck him. Where did you learn such skills? Or did I imagine it?"

Hawkwood rinsed his hands in the rest of the water from the kettle. "I knew a soldier once. He'd travelled in the east, selling his services to any army that would pay him. There was a nawab he fought for, a prince of the Mogul empire who had a Chinoise bodyguard. The soldier said that the Chinoise used to be a priest and that there was a rebellion and priests were forbidden to carry swords and knives. So they learned to make their own weapons from farm tools and to fight with their hands and feet. He said it took years of training. He learnt a few of the skills from the bodyguard. He taught some of them to me. It isn't always effective. I'd rather use a pistol."

Or a rifle, Hawkwood thought.

The soldier in question had in fact been a Portuguese guerrilla named Rodriguez, a small but energetic man who looked as though a stiff breeze would have knocked him off his feet. Hawkwood had taught him how to fire a Baker rifle. In turn, Rodriguez had taught Hawkwood how to defend himself, unarmed, against knife and sword attacks. The guerrilla had been quick to tell Hawkwood the techniques didn't always work. If in doubt, and if you had one, use a pistol. It was a lot more effective.

"These men bringing the brandy and tobacco," Lasseur said. "You think they'll take us all the way to France?"

Hawkwood considered the question. "They're more likely to ferry us to the mainland and send us overland to one of their southern ports, then across to Ostend, or Flushing. We'll find out soon enough."

As if on cue, the cellar door opened. Isaac stepped through. "Time to go," he said briskly. "Abraham's just received word. Boat's on its way in."

They left the cellar and made their way upstairs to the taproom to find they had acquired company. Hawkwood counted at least fifteen men; all dressed in dark clothing, seated around the candlelit tables. They looked up, but no one spoke. Hawkwood recognized their kind immediately. The London rookeries were full of them: hard men with no allegiance to the law, loyal to their own kind and instantly suspicious of any stranger who wandered uninvited into their protectorate.

Abraham, minus his apron, emerged from a door at the back of the counter, tucking a pistol into his belt. "All right, let's do it." He moved to a table and picked up an unlit lantern. Three sides of the lantern, Hawkwood noticed, were blacked out.

The landlord looked towards Hawkwood and Lasseur. "Keep close and keep quiet. Once we get the goods ashore, you'll be shipping out."

The men at the tables rose to their feet. They were well

armed, Hawkwood saw as he followed them out of the door. Every man carried a pistol in his belt, and some had wooden clubs. Curiously, they were also wearing what appeared to be a leather harness across their chests and shoulders.

Down in the cellar, Hawkwood had lost all track of time and, although Isaac had warned them, it was still an odd sensation walking outside and finding it was night.

Abraham led them in single file past the church and towards the end of the village. Isaac had talked about parading down the high street. Once again the description was a misnomer. The Strand and the Haymarket were high streets. Warden's main thoroughfare was a country lane bordered by darkened cottages, woods and brambles. Aside from the men emerging from the pub there were no other signs of life.

When they reached the edge of the cliff, the view in the moonlight was extraordinary. It was like standing on the edge of the world. To the north, isolated points of light that might have been taken for stars had they been at a higher elevation twinkled distantly along a dark finger of coastline. Hawkwood tried to recall his geography and decided it was Foulness. Further west, but not as far, another faint, bobbing speck indicated the Nore Light, moored at the mouth of the Thames estuary. Hawkwood followed the panorama around. As far as the horizon, the masthead and deck lanterns of ships scattered across the water shone like tiny fireflies. To the south, on the mainland, some lights glowed with a greater intensity. One cluster indicated a substantial number of dwellings. Hawkwood guessed it was probably Whitstable, six miles across the bay.

"There!" one of the men whispered. An arm pointed.

Hawkwood saw it at the same time. Half a second later and the sight would not have registered. It was a blue powder flash. Hawkwood recognized what it was. He'd employed the same signalling method himself in the field, using a barrel-less flintlock pistol. Charging the pan with powder and pulling the trigger produced the vivid blue light – highly visible, if you knew where to look.

Hawkwood concentrated his attention on the area where the flash had originated and caught sight of a blunted shape heading towards the shore. Out beyond it, he thought he could see another, larger, shadow but as there were no lights showing he couldn't be sure if it was a vessel or not. It could just as easily have been a trick of the eye or the movement of the waves, though there didn't appear to be much of a swell.

Swiftly, Abraham raised the lantern. Turning the open side towards the direction of the powder flash, he lit the candle. He was rewarded with another blue spark.

He extinguished the lantern quickly. "Let's go."

With the moon guiding their steps, the landlord led the way down the cliff. The path was steep and in parts crumbly underfoot. Three minutes later they were on the beach, the shingle crackling under their boot heels. The wash of the waves against the shore sounded like distant applause.

The men stood still and listened. From the darkness beyond the surf came the rhythmic scraping of oars. Hawkwood's eyes caught a ripple of quicksilver as water broke against a half-turned blade. Suddenly, the scraping ceased, and as the rowing boat scudded towards them the men on the beach stepped back. The oarsmen were out of the boat before it had grounded. Whispered greetings were exchanged and the unloading got under way.

The men worked without speaking. Moonglow played over their tense faces. Hawkwood and Lasseur stood well back up the beach so as not to impede the operation, watching as the tubs were taken off the boat and placed on the shingle. The reason for the leather harnesses soon became clear. They were for carrying the tubs; one on the chest, a second slung between the shoulder blades. Hawkwood was impressed by the weight each man was carrying: it had to be close to one hundred pounds. Lugging the contraband back up to the inn was going to be hard on the legs and lungs.

The moment the tubs were secured in the rigs, the men set off across the shingle towards the cliff path. It took a while to get all the tubs out of the boat and pile them on the beach. When the last one had been unloaded, the boat crew began to pass out large oilskin bags. Hawkwood assumed it was tobacco.

When the line of weighted men was strung across the width of the beach, the tiller man waved urgently.

Isaac grabbed Hawkwood's sleeve. "Right, on your way."

At that moment, from the direction of the church, there came the plaintive cry of an owl.

Isaac went rigid. "Aw, Christ!"

And the night erupted in a rattle of musket fire.

12

Powder flashes and lights bloomed along the clifftop, sending the men on the shingle scattering for cover.

Isaac dragged a brace of pistols from his belt and drew back the hammers with his thumbs.

From both ends of the beach came the crunching clatter of hooves and Hawkwood turned and saw the swiftly moving shapes of horsemen outlined against the surf.

"Head for the boat!" Isaac yelled. A pistol cracked in his hand.

Hawkwood looked towards the edge of the beach, where the oarsmen were pushing the boat off the shingle and into the water.

"Move yourselves!" Isaac's voice again.

Hawkwood could see Abraham's men trying to run, their gait hampered by the weight of the tubs at front and back. They looked like drunken turkey cocks waddling in the darkness.

Shots rang out.

Hawkwood heard a grunt and saw Isaac stagger and go down.

Instinctively, Hawkwood reached towards Isaac's unfired pistol and felt his arm grabbed.

"Leave it!" Lasseur cried, pulling him back. "They're not going to wait!"

The horses were drawing closer. Riding officers, Hawkwood guessed, or possibly cavalry, brought in to assist. He could see them clearly now, silhouetted against the sky. Some of the headgear looked like dragoon helmets. He ducked as a ball whickered past his ear, looked for Lasseur, who had let go of his arm, and saw the Frenchman ducking as he ran for the retreating boat.

Isaac's body showed no sign of movement. Across the beach, more bright flashes and explosions showed where gunfire was being exchanged.

Following Lasseur's lead, Hawkwood abandoned the unused pistol and stumbled towards the water. In front of him, the privateer had almost reached the surf. Hawkwood picked up speed. The clatter of hooves was growing louder. He could hear jangling bridle sounds, too. The horsemen were gaining, rapidly.

Then Lasseur went down.

Hawkwood's first thought was that the privateer had been hit, and then he saw that the culprit had not been a pistol ball but one of the oilskin bundles that had been inadvertently left behind in the panic by both the boat crew and the shore party. Lasseur had fallen over it.

Hawkwood heard a sharp cry, thought it was Lasseur and then realized it was one of the horsemen who had seen the Frenchman go sprawling.

Lasseur got to his knees with a curse and looked for the boat. There was another yell, a warning this time, from one of the boat crew. The noise of hooves on the beach sounded like rolling thunder. Shouts and gunshots continued to ring out behind them.

Hawkwood glanced to the side and saw a silver glint. One of the riders had drawn his sabre; a dragoon. Moonlight flickered along the blade.

Lasseur was getting to his feet but the horsemen were

coming in fast. The leader was closing at a remarkable speed, sabre raised high. Hawkwood threw himself towards the sea.

Lasseur was still floundering as the horseman put spurs to his horse. Hawkwood knew the Frenchman was never going to make it. The boat was still out of reach and the horseman was almost on top of him. As if hearing the hoofbeats for the first time, Lasseur turned and saw death bearing down.

Hawkwood reached the edge of the shingle less than ten yards ahead of the horse and rider. He had a vision of a dark mass blotting out the moon, as he hooked his arm around Lasseur's shoulder and hauled the Frenchman towards the water, knowing they didn't stand a hope in hell of reaching the boat alive.

He felt the pressure of displaced air pushing against his spine as the horse reared and he braced himself for the blow.

Then there was a crisp report from the boat and a cry from over Hawkwood's shoulder as the ball took the dragoon in the chest. A second shot rang out. Hawkwood heard the horse whinny, followed by the colossal crash of a huge and heavy body slamming down into the surf. A tidal wave surged over him. He did not dare to look around but continued to propel himself onward, pushing Lasseur ahead of him.

Sensing more mayhem, he looked over his shoulder; both mount *and* rider had gone down, forming a barrier between himself and the other horsemen. It was the last chance he was going to get. He turned again and saw that the water was up to Lasseur's thighs but that he had made it to the boat. Arms were already reaching for him. Hawkwood struck out into the waves and threw himself forward. As his feet lifted off the bottom he felt a hand grab his collar and made a desperate lunge. His fingers curled around the gunwale.

Feet kicking, he hauled himself aboard. Another shot rang out, closer to his ear, and he felt the heat of the ignited powder, abrasive against his cheek. He turned, gasping for breath, and watched as another of the riders tumbled back over the rump of his horse.

"Glad you could join us," a voice said, as the tiller man let fly with a stream of profanity and threw his weight against the rudder.

As the bow churned towards the open sea, the crew slammed their oars into the water and the vessel started to pick up momentum.

"Pull, you buggers, pull!"

On shore, the beach reverberated with the sound of conflict. Lights dipped as the lantern bearers continued their descent of the cliff path, still firing. On the beach below, dark shapes were running in all directions. Hawkwood thought about the odds of any of the smugglers making an escape while carrying kegs two-thirds the weight of a man strapped over their shoulders. Abraham and his men would have to dump the contraband in order to avoid capture. They wouldn't have a choice.

There was still a danger, Hawkwood knew, of someone on the boat being hit, but the odds were lengthening with each stroke of the oars. Even so, the men kept their heads down.

And then, from the direction of the cliff path, there came more reports. Not muskets this time, Hawkwood could tell, but pistols. Reinforcements had come to Abraham's aid. The sounds of battle intensified.

"Bastards!" someone behind Hawkwood hissed.

Gunshots continued to echo along the foreshore. Hawkwood could see from the convergence of the lights that the lantern bearers were now congregated in one spot and seemed not to have progressed beyond the base of the cliff. It looked as if they were pinned down between Abraham's men and the reinforcements. Gradually, the rate of fire began to diminish.

Finally, the reports ceased altogether. Hawkwood continued to stare shoreward and watched as, one by one, the lights at the base of the cliff blinked out. He strained his ears. Another sound reached him that might have been the faint ring of sword blades and the scream of a horse, but they were deeply muted. Eventually, the noises faded away completely and the only sound was the splash of the oars.

Hawkwood found his heart was beating fast.

"Jesus!" someone muttered in relief at having survived.

"After us, you think?" Lasseur said softly.

Hawkwood shook his head. "More likely the Revenue Service, but from the look of things they were out-numbered."

"We live to fight again," Lasseur murmured.

Only just, Hawkwood thought. He turned away in time to see a hull materializing out of the darkness ahead of them. The larger craft's appearance did not come as a shock. The surprise was its proximity. It wasn't hard to work out why the craft had remained invisible for so long. Dark painted and with no running lights, even in the moonlight the vessel had been just another patch of shadow on the sea.

The rowing boat bumped against the pitch-black hull and a line of pale faces appeared at the rail. Helping hands reached down. At a signal from the tiller man, Hawkwood and Lasseur climbed aboard. It took only a matter of minutes for the boat to be winched up after them and for its crew to take up their stations.

"Welcome aboard the *Starling,* gentlemen." The greeting was voiced in passable but poorly accented French. "If you'd both stand aside while we get under way, I'd be obliged."

Hawkwood and Lasseur turned. Facing them was a stocky man with a wind-weathered face, a flattened nose and jowls in need of a shave.

"Captain?" Lasseur said.

"At your service, sir. You can call me Gideon."

Giving Hawkwood and Lasseur no time to respond, the seaman turned away and gave the signal to raise sail.

Within minutes, the main was up, the bowsprit was pointing towards open water and the jib was unfurling. It had been a very smooth transition; no berating, no barked orders. Lasseur, watching the crew in action, nodded his head in appreciation, a gesture that did not go unnoticed by *Starling*'s skipper.

"You're men of the sea, gentlemen?"

"*I* am," Lasseur said. "My friend is more at home on dry land."

"I'll not hold that against you, sir; each to his own."

"I am Captain Lasseur. My friend is Captain Hooper."

"Is that right? Well everyone needs a name. Now, may I offer you something to ease the chill? I've some fine brandy on board."

"I'd be sorely disappointed if you hadn't, Captain." Lasseur grinned as he and Hawkwood followed the vessel's skipper down below. The cabin was small and cramped and smelled of damp clothing, sweat and tobacco. Not as confining as the hulk, but still claustrophobic after the rolling fields and the open boat and the endless expanse of the night sky.

The bottle uncorked and the brandy poured, Lasseur raised his mug. "Your very good health, Captain."

Gideon gave a nod of acknowledgement. "And confusion to the enemy . . . whoever they may be."

They drank.

The world's gone raving mad, Hawkwood thought. *I'm in the middle of a bloody war, and I've a French privateer and an*

English smuggler, who've never clapped eyes on each other before tonight, toasting each other's health as if they hadn't a care in the world. Why the hell do we bother to even listen to the politicians and the generals?

And Gideon hadn't lied about the quality of the spirit.

"My compliments, sir." Lasseur licked his lips in appreciation. "You have excellent taste."

Taking another swig, Gideon smacked his lips and winked. "Perks of the job. That and putting one over on the Revenue." The weather-worn face suddenly clouded.

"What do you think happened back there?" Hawkwood asked, reading the captain's mind.

The question was met with a shrug. "Looks as if some bugger tipped them off. We can count ourselves lucky there wasn't a cutter around, too. If they did for the goods, we'll make it up on the next run. The advantage is with our side. So much coastline and not enough Revenue men."

"You think Abraham and his men got away?"

"Probably. Abraham's a smart one. If anyone was done for, it was the Revenue. My experience, they couldn't hit a barn door if it was six inches in front of them. And even if Abraham and his crew were arrested, naught'll come of it. Never does."

"Why not?" Hawkwood asked.

"Because the local magistrate's one of us."

Lasseur blinked.

"How do you think Abraham knew we were on our way?" Gideon said.

"We saw you signal," Hawkwood said.

Gideon shook his head. "That was to let him know our position. He knew we were coming before that. A little bird told him."

Hawkwood and Lasseur waited.

"The local squire's house is just along the lane from the inn. He's got a pigeon loft in his smoking room. We release the bird a couple of miles off shore. Soon as it arrives, he knows we've got the goods aboard. He passes Abraham the word."

"And the squire just happens to be –"

"The magistrate. A sweet arrangement all round."

Bloody hell, Hawkwood thought. No wonder the free traders ruled the coast.

Lasseur was grinning like a loon. Hawkwood wasn't at all surprised. As the captain of a privateer, a breed of men not exactly renowned for staying within the law – maritime or otherwise – the Frenchman was clearly of the opinion he was sharing drinks with a kindred spirit.

"Where did you learn your French?" Lasseur asked.

"Whoring and trading, mostly," Gideon chuckled. "It's amazing the vocabulary you can pick up. Nothing like commerce and copulation for broadening the mind."

"You've no qualms about helping people like us? Our countries are at war."

Gideon shook his head dismissively. "Men have been running goods around these shores for the past five hundred years; a lot earlier, probably. War's never stopped it before. It won't do now. And this war won't last for ever. My apologies, Captain, but a blind man can see your Emperor's losing the fight. I'm not a betting man, but even I'd wager a year's cargo of tubs that there'll be another war along after this one and likely more after that. There'll still be men like me doing business long after I'm cold in my grave. Fact of life. Might as well try and stop breathing. You two are just another cargo, far as I'm concerned."

"A friend once told me the first rule of commerce was never to let political differences get in the way of business," Hawkwood said.

"Did he? Well, he's a wise man, your friend," Gideon said. "In the Trade, is he?"

If you only knew, Hawkwood thought. "He's dabbled a time or two."

"Then I raise my glass to him."

"I, too," Lasseur said. He threw Hawkwood a sideways glance. "Well, it is uncommonly fine brandy and I haven't had a decent drink since I don't know how long."

Lasseur proffered Hawkwood a silent toast and drained his glass.

"How far are you taking us?" Hawkwood asked.

Gideon helped himself to another drink. "Not far."

A noncommittal answer if ever there was one, Hawkwood thought, and wondered if that was a half smile he'd seen touch the edge of the captain's lips.

The deck tilted. Lasseur frowned. He put his drink down and gave Gideon a wary look. "We're coming about?"

"That we are. Time I was on deck." The captain placed the stopper back in the bottle. "Here, you might want to keep a hold of this. It'll be a while before you can get ashore and the sun isn't due to show for a while. I'll see to it you've a couple of warm jackets to hand. Sharply now."

The captain vacated his berth and led the way topsides. Mystified, Hawkwood and Lasseur had no option but to follow.

On deck, Gideon called to a crewman: "Couple of coats out of the slop chest, Willy. Smartly does it!"

Frowning, Lasseur made his way to the rail. The breeze had freshened and the boat was running under full sail but there was little lateral movement as the keel cut through the water. Hawkwood hung on to a rope and stared over the Frenchman's shoulder at two light clusters an arm's span apart. The collection of lights over the port bow was noticeably brighter than the group over the starboard rail, indicating a larger number of buildings.

"Chandelier's Whitstable; the candle's Seasalter," Gideon said from behind them. He held out two pea-jackets. "Well, you didn't think we were taking you all the way up the Seine, did you?"

Hawkwood looked back over the stern, recalling the view from the clifftop.

"I don't understand," Lasseur said.

Hawkwood didn't, either.

"We don't have a choice," Gideon grunted. "Tide's on the ebb. I haven't enough draught under the keel to take you on to the beach, not even with the rowboat, and we can't stay; we've more deliveries to make. There's a platform offshore. Fishing boats use it to unload and pack their catches. We'll be leaving you there. While the tide's out, the mud's firm enough. You'll be able to walk ashore."

Lasseur stared at him.

"Don't worry. You'll be safe. There'll be a mess of people conducting business. It'll be like Billingsgate Market: fisher folk, gutters, shrimpers and the like. No one'll pay you heed. Once ashore, you make for the church. There'll be a gravedigger plying his trade; name of Asa Higgs. He'll be there from sun up. He'll see you right. You can't miss him. He's lacking the middle finger on his right hand." Gideon held up his own digit to demonstrate. "You got that?"

Lasseur nodded hesitantly.

"Yes," Hawkwood said.

"Grand." Gideon rubbed his hands together. "It's a fine night. Bit of a breeze, but you've got coats and my best brandy. You won't freeze."

"And the exercise will do us good," Hawkwood said.

Gideon grinned. "That's the spirit!"

It took another two hours. When they reached the platform it was bigger than Hawkwood had expected; with a jetty long enough to accommodate several boats. The timber pilings were encrusted with barnacles and seaweed, and the structure looked as if it had been there for centuries – which it probably had, give or take a replacement strut or two, though it seemed solid enough when they stepped on to it. There were open-sided shelters and lines of wooden tables, with baskets stacked alongside.

"You'd best take these, too," Gideon said. "You know how to gut fish?"

Before either Hawkwood or Lasseur could reply, two baskets of mackerel were passed over the boat's rail, along with two gutting knives.

"They're not the freshest catch of the day, but when the first folk start arriving, be they on the boats or from over the sand, it'd be best if you were looking busy. They'll just think you were early risers, which you are. That way, you won't have to talk to anyone. It'll help you blend in, make it look like you're part of the scenery. Anyone does try and strike up a conversation, say you're Belgian fishermen. We get them here looking for oysters. And don't forget," Gideon called as the boat slid away, "Asa Higgs; missing a finger!" He gave a final wave.

They watched the boat disappear into the night. Then Hawkwood took stock. The lights from the towns beckoned invitingly. They still seemed a long way off. The moon showed the tide had a way to travel before it would recede as far as the platform. Hawkwood wondered when the first fishing boats would show up to offload. Not until first light, he suspected, though that was likely to be early.

There was indeed a cool breeze coming off the sea, and he was thankful for the coat. He gave silent thanks, too, that Ludd hadn't asked for Bow Street's help in the dead of winter.

Lasseur passed him the brandy bottle after taking a swig. "That's another thing that'll have my crew pissing themselves," he said mournfully.

"What's that?" Hawkwood asked.

"Me having to tell them I was marooned."

Hawkwood shook his head and raised the bottle to his lips. "There's a difference."

"There is?"

"I heard marooned men were given a loaded pistol for when it got too bad to bear."

"Damn," Lasseur said. "We should have asked."

"We'll have to make do with this," Hawkwood said, passing the bottle.

"Better make it last," Lasseur said, eyeing the fish and the knives. "It could be a long night."

The farm was bounded by woods. There wasn't a great deal to it; a half-stone, half-brick farmhouse, a couple of outhouses, a barn, a henhouse, a sty, a wooden-fenced sheep enclosure similar to the one back on Sheppey and containing six sheep, and a small paddock, in which a pair of horses grazed contentedly. An apple orchard framed one side of the house. At the rear there was a well-tended garden containing vegetables and herbs. To the front lay a meadow of short grass, dotted with wild flowers, through which ran a small, gently flowing stream.

Approaching the farm, Hawkwood thought it one of the most tranquil places he'd ever seen. It was also one of the best concealed. The locals obviously knew the location, but anyone not of the district would only have happened upon the valley by chance. He presumed that was why it had been chosen. As a place to hide, it was ideal.

They had left the fishing platform shortly after dawn, carrying their baskets of mackerel, just as the first of the boats and the early rising townsfolk had begun to arrive. Many of the latter had been women, who weren't averse to calling out lewd suggestions to any male within hailing distance. Other than suffering the crude but good-natured banter, Hawkwood and Lasseur had negotiated the mile and a half tramp across the mud without incident.

The church had been a five-minute walk from the shingle beach. They had found the gravedigger, a small man with a nut-brown complexion, bow legs and three fingers and a thumb on his right hand, contemplating a newly filled clay pipe and a freshly dug example of his handiwork.

He had looked up, viewing Hawkwood and Lasseur's unshaven faces and mud-caked boots with a wry eye. "You'll be the two Frenchies I'm expectin'."

Lasseur nodded. Hawkwood didn't bother to contradict him. It seemed easier than having someone else tell him he was a long way from home.

"Speak English? All right, best come with me. Leave the fish."

Leading them out of the graveyard to where a horse and cart were tethered, the gravedigger pointed to the back of the cart and the two cheap wooden coffins, partially covered with sacking.

"We'd normally be travellin' at night when there's less folk about, but I don't reckon it's wise to have the both of you hangin' round here all day. We'd best be on our way. You'll be comfortable enough and I ain't goin' to nail you in. We don't have far to go. I'll let you out soon as we're off the road." He jerked his head. "In you get."

Hawkwood and Lasseur exchanged disbelieving looks and Hawkwood wondered if Lasseur had understood all that the gravedigger had told them. Not that it mattered. Both of them had been too weary to argue. And the gravedigger had been proved right. It was a comfortable way to travel. Hawkwood had come close to dozing off a couple of times.

They were out of the coffins and sitting on the back of the cart, feet dangling over the tail board, when they emerged from the trees to find the farmhouse nestling in the dip before them.

The gravedigger clicked his tongue and coaxed the horse down the track. "Welcome to the widow's."

Lasseur frowned while Hawkwood stared at the house and the wispy tendrils of wood smoke drifting from the chimney. Whoever had lit the fire had used apple logs. The smell was unmistakable and strangely comforting and reminded Hawkwood of autumn rather than summer.

"It's what folks call her." There was a slight pause. "Among other things."

"Other things?" Lasseur said.

"There's some folk round about think she's a witch."

Lasseur looked at Hawkwood and said in French, "He says it is the house of a witch."

"Perhaps she'll make us disappear," Hawkwood replied in the same language. "And we'll wake up in France."

He wondered how he'd explain that to James Read.

I've found out how they do it, sir. They smuggle them off the ships in body bags and then they deliver them to this old woman who has warts and a cat, and she turns them into blackbirds and they fly away home.

There was no cat, but there was a dog. It was lying by the open door of the barn. It raised itself as the cart drew near and looked over its shoulder. Then it padded forward hesitantly. It was a big dog, with shaggy brown hair and eyes hidden behind a fringe. It wasn't young, Hawkwood saw. There was grey around its muzzle and it was walking like an old man suffering the first stages of arthritis. Giving a brief wag of its tail, it emitted a single bark and then lay down as if exhausted by its efforts.

The bark had been not so much a warning as a summons.

A woman walked out of the barn, a pail in her hands. Hawkwood's first thought was that she didn't look like any witch he might have imagined.

Hawkwood heard Lasseur catch his breath.

Thick black hair, drawn back and tied with a ribbon at the base of her neck, framed a pair of deep brown eyes and a strong face warmed by the sun. She was dressed in a long grey skirt, a white blouse open at the throat and a faded blue waistcoat. The clothes that covered her slender figure showed evidence of repair, with patches at knee and hem. The opening at the top of the blouse showed a V of freckled skin. A smudge of dirt marked her right jaw. A strand of hair hung down her left cheek and flirted with the corner of her mouth. She brushed it away and tucked it behind her ear. A bright sheen of perspiration lay along her top lip.

She watched the cart's approach.

The cart halted. The horse lowered its head to crop the grass.

"Morning, Jess." The gravedigger touched his cap.

"Asa."

The woman shielded her eyes from the sun and made no attempt to approach.

"You were expectin' us." The gravedigger gestured to Hawkwood and Lasseur to get down from the cart.

The woman looked Hawkwood and Lasseur up and down and said nothing.

Hawkwood knew what both of them must have looked like: bedraggled and unshaven, breeches and boots mud-stained and still damp from their recent soaking.

"Madame," Lasseur said, inclining his head.

She bestowed Lasseur with a frank look but did not

acknowledge his gesture. Her gaze moved to Hawkwood, settled for a second and then moved on back to the gravedigger. Then she nodded.

"How long is it for?"

"They didn't say."

A flash of irritation touched the woman's eyes and then died. She gave a resigned nod. "Do they speak English?"

"We both do, madame." Lasseur smiled. "My name is Lasseur; Captain Paul Lasseur. This is my friend, Captain Matthew Hooper."

The woman looked at him but did not return the smile. She stared at Hawkwood then turned to the gravedigger, who was giving Hawkwood a funny look. "Tell Morgan I'm still holding those tubs. I'd prefer it if they were gone."

"He knows. I'll be along to pick them up in a day or two."

"Good."

The gravedigger nodded. "Right, then, they're all yours. I'll be off."

"How's Megan?" the woman asked.

Higgs climbed back on the cart. "She's doin' well. That magic potion you gave me 'as done wonders."

The woman gave an exasperated sigh. "It wasn't magic, Asa. Just an infusion of herbs. You could grow them in your own garden, if you'd a mind to."

Higgs shook his head hurriedly. "Lord, no. More than my life's worth. I do that an' she'd never let me leave the 'ouse." He grinned.

A smile touched the woman's face. All at once her features were transformed. She was beautiful, Hawkwood thought. "I've some elderflower cordial. You could take Megan some."

"If you're offerin'."

"Wait here." The woman set down the pail and walked into the house.

The dog tracked her progress through its fringe, trying to

decide whether to follow or remain on guard, eventually concluding that vigilance in the face of strangers required marginally less effort.

The woman returned with a small earthenware jug, which she handed to the gravedigger. Placing the jug between his feet, Higgs picked up the reins, nodded briefly to Hawkwood and Lasseur, and set the cart in motion with a click of his tongue.

They watched as it trundled back towards the woods.

The woman turned. "This way. Come with me." She led the way to the barn. The dog got up and followed in a slow, lumbering jog.

It was cool in the barn. There was a corn bin and two stalls, one of which contained a milking cow. The place smelled of fresh manure and chickens. Several hens were pecking around for food.

"It's dry and there's plenty of room. I will provide you with blankets. You'll be comfortable enough, I think."

She led them to a corner. Several straw bales were stacked against the wall. Taking hold of one of the bottom bales, she pulled it out to reveal a dark opening. In the space behind, Hawkwood made out a bucket and some tubs stacked against the barn wall. "If anyone comes, you are to hide in here." She indicated the dog. "This is Rab. He's getting on in years, but he is a good dog and he will warn me of strangers."

Hearing his name, the dog looked up. His tail wagged.

"There is a man who comes in to help me. His name is Thomas. You will know him for he has a bad leg and a scar here." The woman ran the point of her finger across her right eye and cheek. "You do not have to hide from him." As she spoke, she glanced at the scars on Hawkwood's face. "Hooper, did you say?"

"That's right," Hawkwood said.

"You're English?"

"American."

She studied him for several seconds before nodding silently. Then she said, "When it's time, I will bring you something to eat and drink."

"Thank you," Lasseur said, subdued by the uncompromising gaze. "What do we call you?"

"*Madame.*"

She turned before they could reply, heading for the farmhouse in purposeful strides, the dog following closely in her wake. She picked up the pail as she passed.

Both men watched her go.

Lasseur turned to Hawkwood and grinned. "I think she likes me."

13

Hawkwood's eyes were closed. It was odd, he thought, how he could still smell the hulk. Common sense told him it was impossible for the reek from the prison ships to have carried all the way to the farm, and yet he could swear the odour was there, coagulating at the back of his nostrils.

Though he knew it was ridiculous, he opened his eyes to reassure himself he wasn't back on the gun deck. An irrational wave of relief rushed through him at the sight of the meadow and the stream and the surrounding woods. He was seated on a log, his back against the wall of the barn.

He sniffed and the hairs along the back of his neck lifted. It was then he realized it wasn't his imagination. The smell *was* there, and the source was a lot closer to home. It was his own odour he could smell. He was carrying the taint of the hulk with him. It was in his clothes and it was in his sweat. He sat up, held his sleeve to his nose, and reeled. He could even smell the mackerel. No wonder the gravedigger had made them sit at the back of the cart and no wonder the woman had regarded them with disdain and told them to stay clear of the house. A wild thought crossed his mind. Was that why everyone had been so eager to pass them down the line? Was it because each participant in the escape route had only been able to stand the smell for so long? He sat up quickly.

Lasseur, who had been dozing beside him, sensed movement and snapped awake fast. "What is it?" The privateer's eyes flicked towards the tree line.

Hawkwood stood. "I'm going to take a bath." He walked into the barn and retrieved his blanket and headed for the stream.

Lasseur watched him go, a look of bewilderment on his face. He raised his sleeve to expose his own armpit, inhaled, and recoiled.

The privateer had always considered himself to be a fastidious man. Maintaining personal cleanliness at sea wasn't difficult when one was surrounded by water. Taking care of one's laundry in those circumstances was no great hardship either. The facilities were certainly better than those of a soldier on the battlefield. Since his capture by the British, however, all that had changed.

There had been washing facilities on the hulk but they had been totally inadequate given the number of prisoners there had been on board. Soap had never been in great supply. Often there had been none at all. Lasseur's last immersion had been on the day of his registration, when he and Hawkwood and the rest of them had been forced into the water barrels on the quarterdeck. Since then soap had been as much a rarity as fresh fruit.

It was curious and not a little disturbing how easy it had been to let his standards slip, to the point that both he and Hooper had become so immune to the smell of the ships, as prophesied by Murat, that neither of them had noticed their own rank state.

Lasseur looked down at his clothes. There was no denying they were filthy and in need of a scrubbing, too. Deciding that just rinsing them in water wouldn't do, he got up and made his way towards the farmhouse.

The dog was lying by the door. It stood as Lasseur approached and barked once.

The woman came around the side of the house, a wicker basket in her arms. There were clothes in the basket and, behind her, Lasseur could see a washing line strung between two of the apple trees.

The dog, its guard duty performed, moved to the woman's side and sat down. Lasseur assumed it was watching him. It was difficult to make out the animal's eyes behind all the hair.

The woman's eyes, in contrast, were perfectly visible. They reflected neither fear nor friendliness at his presence. She did not speak, but looked at him, one hand holding the basket, the other resting lightly, almost protectively, on the dog's head.

Lasseur stopped ten paces from her. The hair was again hanging loose alongside her cheek, he noticed. He wondered about her age. There were lines around her eyes. They were not deeply etched but, without them, Lasseur decided, her face would not have possessed the same strength of character. She was about thirty, he guessed, and it occurred to him that his late wife, Marie, had she lived, would have been the same age. Lasseur was suddenly struck by an overwhelming sense of loss and longing. He swallowed quickly, wondering if the woman had sensed his momentary waver.

"Forgive me, madame. I wonder if you might have some soap. My friend and I would like to bathe and wash the dirt from our clothes."

He tugged at his shirt as if to hold it to his nose, and decided to risk a smile.

She did not respond but continued to gaze at him without

speaking. Lasseur was surprised by how intimidated he felt. Self-consciously, he buttoned his jacket and ran a hand through his unkempt hair. He wondered just how bad he smelled. He was glad he hadn't drawn closer.

"Wait here," she said abruptly. She put down the basket and went into the house.

Lasseur and the dog regarded each other in silence. All Lasseur could see was a pink tongue protruding through brown foliage.

Lasseur squatted. "Hello, Rab. Good dog."

The dog's tail twitched.

Lasseur snapped his fingers softly.

A definite wag this time and what might have been a slight rising of the ears.

Two more snaps.

The dog walked forward and licked the back of Lasseur's proffered hand. The animal was obviously not offended by the smell.

Lasseur stood as the woman came out of the house.

"Here –" She held out a small bar of soap at arm's length. There was a short pause. "It's about time."

She stepped away and picked up the basket.

Lasseur felt himself redden. "Thank you, madame. I will see it is returned." Lasseur took the soap and attempted another smile. "He is a fine dog."

"And easily distracted." The woman looked down. What could have been taken as a flicker of affection passed briefly across her face, or it could have been Lasseur's imagination.

The dog looked up at her.

"I have often found dogs to be excellent judges of character," Lasseur said.

"He's old. Sometimes he gets confused."

"I know the feeling," Lasseur said. He gave a brief bow. "Thank you again for the soap."

The woman nodded but her gaze remained neutral. Deflated, Lasseur turned away.

The woman and the dog watched him go. She walked towards the apple trees. Suddenly, she stopped and looked over her shoulder at the dog, which had not moved. It was still staring after Lasseur.

"Rab."

The dog wagged its tail and padded towards her.

"Come on, you," she said.

She looked beyond the dog and her eyes followed Lasseur as he disappeared around the back of the barn.

Hawkwood was checking his dressings when Lasseur reappeared.

Lasseur grinned and tossed him the soap.

Hawkwood stared at him.

"She definitely likes me," Lasseur said.

"I could pass away now and die a happy man," Lasseur announced contentedly.

Both men, blankets around their waists, shirts, undergarments and breeches drying in the sun, were seated on the bank, ankles submerged in the cool water.

Lasseur reached over into his jacket and with an exhalation of pleasure drew out his last cheroot. "I was saving this for a special occasion. I'd say cleaning the stench of the hulk from my clothes qualifies. What do you think?"

"I think you should cover yourself up," Hawkwood said. "Your blanket's slipping."

Lasseur adjusted the offending item. "I feel as if I'm wearing one of those damned togas." Realizing he had no means of lighting the cheroot, he stuck it between his lips and sucked on it pensively. "I wonder how her husband died. The war, perhaps?" He looked back towards the house, but the barn was blocking the view.

"If that was the case," Hawkwood said, "I'd have thought the last people she'd want around the place would be enemy prisoners of war."

Lasseur took the cheroot out of his mouth. "You're right. I am an idiot." He looked around at the barn behind them and the other buildings.

"You could always ask her," Hawkwood said. "Seeing as she likes you so much."

"I might have exaggerated slightly on that score," Lasseur said. He stuck the cheroot back in his mouth, sucked on it for several seconds before removing it and rolling it contemplatively between his fingers. "I was thinking, this farm is not large. It's smaller than the one my wife was brought up on. Nevertheless, a place like this takes work. It cannot be an easy life for a woman alone."

It never was, Hawkwood thought, though, from what he'd seen, things could have been a lot worse. She could have been alone in the city, for one thing. Here, it appeared she had the essentials to hand, a roof over her head and, with the animals and the produce in the garden, a means of feeding herself that didn't involve stealing or selling her body on the nearest street corner, wherever that was.

There had been no sign of the man called Thomas. Hawkwood wondered about that.

In the time they had been on the farm, she had barely spoken to them, even when delivering their meals, which she carried to the barn in a basket. He considered her attitude. From the beginning, it had not been exactly welcoming. She'd treated their arrival as an imposition. He had the impression that would have been the case even if she'd taken the two of them for Englishmen. The others who had helped them – the shepherd, the innkeeper, the sea captain and the gravedigger – had been considerably less reticent; probably because all of them earned a living from operating outside the law and had, if not a hatred for authority, then certainly ambivalence towards it. As the seaman, Gideon, had said, they were just another unlawful cargo.

But why would a woman involve herself in the business of helping repatriate enemies of her country? She had sounded a reluctant hoarder of contraband, too, judging by her exchange with the gravedigger.

He wondered who Morgan was. Mention of the tubs implied he was part of the smuggling fraternity, but of what rank? Was he someone of importance or merely the next man down the line?

Either way, Ludd's conviction that free traders were aiding escaped prisoners had been proved correct, but even Ludd couldn't have envisaged the degree of planning that must be involved. There were obviously keen brains working behind the scenes. But whose?

Hawkwood reached for his shirt and breeches. They were already dry. He put them on. Lasseur followed suit.

"I wonder what happens next," Lasseur said as he pulled on his boots. "How long are we likely to be here, do you think?"

"It might be for some time. The British have the Sleeve sewn up pretty tight with their blockade." The nickname had come easily to him though Hawkwood had never understood why the French name for the Channel had come from an article of clothing.

"But the smugglers come and go," Lasseur pointed out.

"The penalty for helping escapers is probably greater," Hawkwood said. "It's close to treason. They wouldn't want to risk it unless they were sure."

Hawkwood knew that a physically fit seaman caught during the seizure of a smuggling vessel faced impressment into the navy. The penalty for helping prisoners to escape was transportation, possibly for life. No smuggler would risk a dash across the Channel with escaped prisoners in tow unless he was confident of success.

Lasseur nodded glumly.

"Don't look so downhearted," Hawkwood said. "It's only been a couple of days and anywhere's better than that stinking ship."

Lasseur sucked on his cheroot. Then he clapped Hawkwood on the shoulder. "You're right, my friend. We have the fresh air, the sky above our heads and moderately clean shirts on our backs. If I was on the deck of my ship, life would almost be perfect."

Hawkwood closed his eyes and let the afternoon sun play across his face.

"I dreamt about Lucien," Lasseur said.

Hawkwood opened his eyes.

He'd known there was something preying on Lasseur's mind. The Frenchman had been restless all night. Hawkwood knew that because his own sleep had been fitful and, in the silence of the barn, in the gaps between waking and sleeping he had listened to Lasseur toss and turn through most of the early hours.

"He saw his father die," Lasseur said. "It was why he was on his own. He was a cabin boy on his father's fishing boat. They were surprised by an English cutter. They lowered sail, but for some reason the cutter captain decided to have some sport. He turned his guns on them and blew them out of the water. Lucien's father was killed by a flying splinter. One crew member went down with the boat, the other man was taken, but they got separated. I suspect he was transferred to a different prison ship." Lasseur fell silent and then said, "If we hadn't interfered, he'd still be alive."

"As a plaything for Matisse and his crew," Hawkwood said. "They'd have used him and discarded him when the next pretty boy came along."

"He didn't deserve to die."

"No, he didn't. But *we* didn't kill him."

Lasseur sighed. "You reckon that absolves us of responsibility? I think not. You know, I once heard an old proverb that says the road to Hell is paved with good intentions. I'm not sure I understood what that meant, until now." He stared at Hawkwood, dampness misting the corner of his eye. "I miss my son, Matthew. I want to go home and hold him close and tell him that I love him. This bloody war . . ."

"Wars don't start by themselves," Hawkwood said. "You want to blame anyone, blame the bastard politicians."

"And to whom do *they* answer? God? I'm not sure He even exists any more." With a gesture of frustration, Lasseur got to his feet and tucked the cheroot back in his pocket. "Enough of this; I need to clear my mind. I'm going for a walk. And before you say anything, don't worry; I'm not going to run away. I won't go beyond the woods. I'll stick to the farm." He patted Hawkwood on the shoulder. "You're a good friend, Matthew Hooper. I'm glad we're together."

Hawkwood said nothing. He watched Lasseur walk away, head down. As a father, it was inevitable that Lasseur should have been hit harder by the boy's murder. Hawkwood thought about his own reaction to Lucien Ballard's death. He'd felt anger but, unlike Lasseur, he'd felt no guilt. He wondered what that said about him. Hawkwood had never wanted the responsibility of fatherhood. Was that something he could live with? Yes, it was. He wondered why he was even asking himself the question, especially when he had more pressing matters on his mind; like how to get a message to Bow Street, for one.

But what information did he have for James Read anyway? Ludd would have been told about the escape by now. He'd know Hawkwood was on the run. Hawkwood's own store of knowledge didn't extend much beyond that.

He still needed to find out who was behind the escape organization. Until he had that information, all he could do was maintain his deception and see where the road led him. With luck and application, he'd be able to pick up information further down the line.

As he walked, Lasseur could see that more than a few areas of the farm were in need of repair. There were gaps in the walls of the barn. A corner of the cow stall was falling down. There were gate-posts that needed replacing, and the meadow grass close to the house and a number of trees at the sides and rear needed chopping back. They were small jobs, but Lasseur knew from his wife's parents' farm that, if small jobs were not tackled, they grew into bigger jobs. It was the same on board ship.

The woman had told them that there was a man who helped out, but so far there had been no sign of him. Lasseur glanced over towards the house and caught sight of the stack of logs by the back door, and next to it the axe stuck blade-deep in a chopping block with a birch broom propped up against it. Weren't witches supposed to ride on broomsticks? Lasseur grinned to himself.

Then he saw the dog.

He stopped, uncertain. The animal was behaving strangely; padding to and fro outside the door, breaking off to scratch on the wood, as if it wanted to be let in. There was no sign of the woman. The dog continued its pawing. Lasseur could hear it whining. He drew closer.

The dog saw him coming. He could tell it was unsure, as if it didn't recognize him. He waited for the bark, but it didn't come. Instead, the dog returned to the door and scratched again. Then it turned and came slowly towards Lasseur, head low. It looked as if it couldn't decide whether to wag its tail or not.

"Here, Rab," Lasseur said softly, crouching down and ruffling the dog's ears. "What's the matter, boy?"

He realized he was addressing the dog in French. He switched to English. "Good boy."

The dog squirmed away from him and headed back towards the door.

At first Lasseur thought it was the dog whining, but the sounds were coming from inside the house. Curious, he walked forward. The closer he got to the door, the more it sounded as though someone was in distress. The dog looked back at him and made a snuffling noise. It obviously wanted to be let in.

Lasseur bent and looked through the window into the kitchen. A large table dominated the centre of the room. The base of the woman's spine was pressed against it. Her skirt hem was raised high upon her bare hips. A lank-haired man was leaning forward over her, his legs between her parted thighs. Lasseur could not see his face and his back obstructed Lasseur's view of the woman's features. The man was reaching down between his legs. Lasseur couldn't tell if he was fumbling with his own clothes or the woman's. He saw a hand reach out and clasp the man's shoulder.

Lasseur stepped back hurriedly, fearful that they might have sensed his shadow at the glass. The sounds he'd taken for whimpers from someone under duress had in fact been cries of passion. He looked down at the dog, which was still watching him expectantly, and smiled ruefully. "Sorry, my friend, but I'm not sure your mistress would appreciate the interruption."

Lasseur tried to cast his mind back. Had the dog barked earlier? He couldn't remember. More than likely, he'd been too busy rinsing the grime of the hulk out of his ears.

The woman's lover was probably the man she'd mentioned earlier. He tried to quell the irrational feeling of envy that rose in his chest.

He was turning away from the house when the sound of a blow stopped him in his tracks. This time, there could be no mistake. The utterance that accompanied it was guttural and unmistakably male while the responding cry came from a woman in distress, not the throes of ecstasy.

Lasseur returned quickly to the window and peered into the room. The positions of the two figures had hardly altered. The woman's back was still arched. The man had not moved from between her legs. But this time Lasseur could see it all. The man's left hand was clamped over her mouth, while his right fumbled with the front flap of his breeches. Her hand was still on his shoulder but as Lasseur could now see, she was not trying to pull the man to her but to thrust him away. As he took in the scene, the woman's head turned towards him and Lasseur found himself staring into her face. The woman's eyes widened. Lasseur saw that her blouse was ripped, enough that her left breast was almost fully exposed. He saw then the track of a tear on her cheek.

The dog was already thrusting past him as Lasseur slammed the door back against its hinges.

The man turned, his hand poised over his half-unbuttoned crotch flap. Shock flooded his face. There was no scar. It was not the man Jess had described to them as her helper.

The dog leapt forward with a growl. For its age, it showed unexpected agility.

Instinctively, the man lashed out with his foot. There was a shrill yelp as his boot made contact with the dog's ribs. The woman cried out as Lasseur sprang forward and scythed the back of his hand against the man's jaw. There was a satisfying sound of knuckles striking flesh and bone. The man grunted and jerked away, but not before Lasseur had caught the whiff of alcohol on his breath. Following through, Lasseur took hold of an arm and a fistful of hair. As he hurled the man across the room, the woman pushed herself away from the table and began rearranging her dress. The dog was barking furiously at the man, who twisted free and staggered backwards through the open door. Lasseur, eyes dark with anger, stormed after him. The man dabbed a hand to his lip. It came away stained crimson. He stared at the blood, then at Lasseur and finally at the woman. "You bitch! You wanted it! Don't tell me you didn't!"

Clutching the torn half of her blouse to her body, she stood in the doorway, her face burning, her breasts rising and falling. "Not with you, Seth! Never with you. Hell would freeze over before that."

The man's gaze moved to Lasseur, then flickered sideways.

Lasseur's heart turned over when he saw what had caught the man's attention.

They both moved at the same time, but Lasseur knew he wasn't going to make it, he was too far away. The woman's attacker jerked the axe out of the chopping block. His mouth split in a crooked grin. "First I'm going to deal with you; then I'll take care of her."

Lasseur looked for a weapon. He grabbed a log and held it before him like a club. It seemed spectacularly inadequate.

There was a bark. The dog, its courage restored, had made a lumbering dash for the open door. The woman grabbed for the dog's neck and missed. Her blouse slipped, revealing her nakedness once more. "Rab, no!"

The man swung the axe. The dog jinked aside as the blade missed its skull by inches. It continued to bark, growing more excited.

Lasseur moved forward, brandishing the log.

The axe man sneered, revealing stained and uneven teeth. His hair hung in greasy fronds around his pockmarked face. He wasn't big, about Lasseur's height, but his frame was solid and muscular. "That the best you can do?" He curved the axe towards Lasseur's skull. Lasseur swung the log in an attempt to parry the blow. The axe blade thudded into the wood, wrenching it out of Lasseur's hand.

Lasseur heard the woman cry out, "No, Seth!" as the attacker moved in, axe held high.

And a tall dark shape detached itself from the corner of the wall.

"Hey!"

The axe man turned.

Hawkwood whipped the broom through the air.

The scream that erupted from the axe man's throat as the broom head raked across his face was so intense it reduced even the dog to silence. Lasseur could only guess at the number of birch twigs that formed the broom head, but the end of each one had flayed the attacker's skin like a sharpened claw. Dropping the blade, the axe wielder stumbled away and lifted his hands to his ruined flesh. Blood oozed from between his fingers.

Lasseur picked up the axe. His unshaven face was a savage mask. Before Hawkwood could stop him, he ran forward and kicked the attacker to the ground. The man raised his arms to protect himself. His face looked as if it had been lashed with a scourge.

"Not so brave now, are you?" Lasseur grated. *"Lâche!"*

Through the bloody runnels, he saw the man's expression change. Instantly, Lasseur knew his accent had betrayed him. He raised the axe. The man cringed.

A hand fell across his arm. Lasseur heard the woman say, "Don't!"

Lasseur shook his head. "He forced himself on you. Don't you want him punished?"

"Not like that." She looked down at her attacker. Her eyes flashed. "But if you show your face here again, Seth, I'll take the gun to you. I swear it."

Lasseur glared down at the blood-streaked face.

"If you kill him, Paul," Hawkwood said, his hand sliding from Lasseur's arm to the axe handle, "and they catch us, they'll hang us for certain."

"He needs to know that I *will* kill him if he comes near her again."

"He knows," Hawkwood said. "Believe me, he knows."

Slowly, Lasseur relinquished his hold, allowing Hawkwood to take possession of the axe.

"Go home, Seth," the woman said. Her face was still highlighted with colour. "Go now, while you still can."

Lasseur backed away, his eyes afire, and the man rose unsteadily to his feet. With a final glare of defiance he turned and stumbled towards the woods. Only when he had been swallowed by the trees did Hawkwood place the axe back in the chopping block.

Lasseur picked up the broom and leant it against the wall. "A very under-rated weapon, the broom; especially in the hands of an expert." He threw Hawkwood a look before turning to the woman. "Are you hurt, madame?"

Still staring towards the trees, she shook her head and then shivered. "I am unharmed."

"But you're cold. Here, take my coat."

Lasseur removed his jacket. She did not protest as he placed it over her shoulders. Suddenly, she looked around, her face anxious. "Rab?"

"He's here," Lasseur said as the dog loped towards her, tail wagging.

She ruffled the dog's hair, her face softening with relief.

"Come," Lasseur said gently.

There was only a slight pause, then, gathering the jacket about her and holding the torn halves of her blouse to her breast, she nodded and turned towards the house.

Hawkwood and Lasseur fell into step beside her. The dog followed close behind. When they reached the threshold, she paused and gave a small gasp, as if seeing the disorder for the first time. The floor, Hawkwood saw over her shoulder, was in disarray and littered with dirt and debris; shards of earthenware lay strewn among a scattering of twigs and leaves that had been crushed underfoot, presumably during the assault. More plants and herbs hung from the beams. The room was more like an apothecary's herbarium than a kitchen.

She took a breath, gathered herself and said, "Forgive me, Captain Lasseur. I neglected to thank you for your intervention; you, too, Captain Hooper."

"You're most welcome, madame," Lasseur gave a small bow.

"I did not want you to think I was ungrateful."

The redness she had sustained from the slap to her cheek was fading.

"Nothing was further from our minds," Lasseur said. "You are safe. That is all that matters."

She nodded. "Nevertheless, it was remiss of me. You put yourselves at risk."

"You called him by his name," Lasseur said. "You knew him?"

There was a pause. "He is my sister's husband."

Lasseur hesitated, taken aback by the response. "This has happened before?"

She pulled Lasseur's coat about her and shook her head. "No."

There was an awkward silence.

"We should leave you to recover," Lasseur said gently. "Unless there is anything we can do . . . ?"

She drew herself up with an effort. "Thank you, no. You have been very kind."

"It was nothing, madame. Anyone would have done the same."

She looked at him. "It was not *nothing*, Captain. And no, they would not."

Turning, she stepped inside the house, called the dog, and closed the door behind her.

Finding themselves left on the step, there seemed little else to do except leave.

Heading back to the barn, Lasseur said, "I think I might have killed him if you hadn't taken the axe from me."

"I think you would have, too," Hawkwood said.

Lasseur shook his head. "But you were right. It would have been madness."

"Yes it would."

"Even though he might yet tell someone he saw us here?"

"You think so? He tried to rape a woman. I'd say he has as much to hide as we do."

"He might see it as a way of getting his own back on her for refusing his advances and on us for intervening."

"It's possible," Hawkwood said. "Though with those scratches on his face, I suspect he may want to lie low for a while, by which time we'll likely be on our way."

"It won't hurt to keep an eye out though," Lasseur said.

"No," Hawkwood agreed. "It won't."

They entered the barn.

"Ah," Lasseur said. "It's good to be home."

It was dusk when the dog came to them. It went to Lasseur first, wagging its tail. Then it moved to Hawkwood. It was the first time the animal had shown itself to be comfortable in his company. Hawkwood felt curiously honoured.

The dog had not come alone. A shadow fell across the straw. Hawkwood and Lasseur stood.

She had changed clothes and was looking more composed than when they had left her at the house, though she had still not found a way of keeping the wayward lock of hair in place. She carried a basket in one hand and a cloth bundle in the other. She set the basket down.

"Your coat, Captain," she said, holding out the neatly folded bundle. A nerve moved in her cheek. "I noticed there was a tear in the sleeve. I've darned it for you. I would not call myself a seamstress, but it is an improvement, I think."

Lasseur took the proffered garment. "That was most thoughtful, madame. Thank you."

She nodded. "Yes, well, it was the least I could do." She brushed the errant hair behind her ear.

"You are recovered?" Lasseur asked gently.

"Yes, thank you." Self-consciously, she smoothed down the front of her skirt and indicated the basket. "I've brought your supper. There's bread and some sausage, and a gooseberry pie. I hope it is to your taste."

She turned as if to leave, then hesitated. "I brought you this. I thought that you and Captain Hooper might make use of it . . . that is, if you do not think it impertinent of me." She reached into the pocket of her dress and took out a small item wrapped in a square of towel. She passed it to Lasseur and stepped back. Lasseur unfolded the towel and a smile lit up his face. He held up the razor and ran a palm over his dark stubble. "Thank you, madame. We shall put it to excellent use." He showed it to Hawkwood and, unseen by the woman, lifted one eyebrow in a laconic slant.

"It belonged to my late husband. I had quite forgotten I had it. You have the soap still?"

"Forgive me," Lasseur said. "I meant to return it to you."

"That will not be necessary. Please keep it."

"Thank you."

She nodded, hesitated, and then, as if coming to a decision, said, "Seth Tyler . . . the man who was here earlier . . ." She took a deep breath. "Since my husband passed away, he has made known his . . . feelings . . . towards me. At no time, despite what he said, have I ever given him cause to think that I might be receptive to his advances . . ."

A faint flush had crept across her neck.

She brushed an imaginary hair from her cheek. "And so you should know, I am called Jess. My husband's name was Jack – Jack Flynn. I have been widowed for three years. I have worked this farm on my own since my husband died and, as may have become apparent, I am unused to company. There, it is said."

Her hands formed themselves into fists.

"We are pleased to meet you, Jess Flynn," Lasseur said.

Her jaw tightened. "Thank you, Captain. I hope the supper is to your satisfaction. You'll find wine in the jug. It is French, I believe." She unclenched her fists and spun abruptly. "Come, Rab!"

With the dog by her side, she headed for the door.

"Madame Flynn?" Lasseur called.

She paused, and turned back to face him. "Captain?"

"If this man, Seth, were to return; what then?"

Hawkwood knew what Lasseur was getting at. He knew the woman did too. Next time, there might not be anyone around to help. A nerve pulsed in her throat.

"He will not return."

"He heard Captain Lasseur speak," Hawkwood said. "He'll guess what we are. He may tell someone."

"He won't do that either."

"How can you be so sure?"

"When he's sober, he'll remember that I have protection. He'll know what will happen to him next time."

Hawkwood remembered her threat to use the gun.

"You mean you'd arm yourself?"

"That, too."

She turned away, leaving the words hanging in the air.

Lasseur stared after her. He recovered his wits as she reached the door.

"There is one other thing, madame. Before, I could not help noticing that parts of the farm are in need of repair. Captain Hooper and I would like to offer our services in exchange for your hospitality. If you have the tools to hand, we could make ourselves useful and it will help us pass the time. That is, if you find the idea . . . acceptable."

She halted and looked back, surprise crossing her face. "Thank you, Captain. That is a most generous offer. However, as I told you, I have a man who comes . . ."

"Yes . . . well, as we have not seen him, we thought perhaps . . ." Lasseur's voice trailed off.

Her head lifted. "You thought that he was an invention . . . to deter you from trespass?" There was an edge to her voice.

"We thought that a possibility, yes."

"I see. Well, I assure you Thomas *does* exist. Though his visits can be . . ." the corners of her mouth lifted ". . . infrequent."

"Ah . . ." Lasseur said, nodding.

"However . . ." She held his gaze.

Lasseur waited.

"I expect him here tomorrow. He can show you where things are kept. He will, I think, welcome your help." With a final nod, she turned away. "He keeps telling me he's not getting any younger."

The two men watched her go. Registering the expression on the privateer's face, Hawkwood hoped Lasseur wasn't about to make a fool of himself.

14

"This is Thomas . . . Tom," Jess Flynn said. "As you can see, he is flesh and blood."

Thomas Gadd was sixty if he was a day; a short, wiry man with powdery grey hair secured in a plait at the nape of his neck. His leathery brown complexion and labourer's hands spoke of a life spent outdoors. His limp was noticeable but not severe and despite the injury he appeared sprightly for his age. The scar, on the other hand, was a lot more livid than Hawkwood had envisaged from Jess's description. It looked as if it had been made by a blade. It was a miracle the man had not lost his eye.

Gadd had seaman written all over him. His grizzled countenance and braided queue were a dead giveaway, as was the tattoo of an anchor emblazoned on his right forearm.

"Tom, this is Captain Hooper, and Captain Lasseur."

Gadd's face betrayed no surprise, as if being confronted by prisoners of war on the run was an everyday occurrence.

"These gentlemen would like to earn their keep, Tom," Jess Flynn said.

Hawkwood and Lasseur felt themselves perused in turn.

"Been tellin' you I could do with some help," Gadd said. He stared hard at Hawkwood. "Jessie tells me you're a Yankee, Captain."

"That's right."

Gadd nodded. "Won't hold that against you. Met a fair few in my time. Liked most of 'em." In the same breath, Gadd said, "You'll be a soldier, too, Captain Hooper, and your friend's a seafaring man, I'm thinking."

Lasseur blinked in surprise.

Gadd sniffed. He regarded Hawkwood levelly. "You walk straighter. I saw you and I said to myself, now there's a man who's done some marching and carried a pack or two in his time." He turned to Lasseur. "You, though, Captain, you've the mark of a man who's used to the wind and spray on his face. You only get that look on the deck of a ship. Am I right?"

"You are right, my friend," Lasseur replied, impressed and not a little bemused.

"Then you and me have got something in common. Reckon I've sailed on just about every kind of rig there is, and then some. Did time with John Company *and* the Dutch navy before I joined the King's service. Got the wounds at the Nile, in case you were wondering, but don't worry, I ain't a man who holds a grudge; leastways, not for that long."

"I'm very glad," Lasseur said.

"Speak your lingo, an' all." He favoured Hawkwood with a grin. "Enough to get by, anyways. Picked up a bit of Spanish, too; an' I can curse in Portuguese if I've a mind."

"Tom was in the navy with my husband," Jess Flynn said.

"Served together on *Orion,*" Gadd said. "Jack was an able seaman. I was a quartergunner. Got paid off in '02."

When the peace had been signed at Amiens, Hawkwood recalled. Though it had not lasted long. Hostilities had broken out again just over a year later. He wondered why Gadd and his friend Jack Flynn had not returned to sea. Gadd's wounds wouldn't have prevented him from joining a ship.

Maybe he'd just had enough of the life. As for Flynn, perhaps it had been because he'd acquired a wife. He wondered when the Flynns had taken their vows.

"Crew mates look after each other," Gadd said. "That's how it works. They see their mates' families are all right, too. Isn't that so, Captain?" He looked to Lasseur.

Lasseur nodded soberly. Hawkwood wondered if he was thinking of his dead wife and son.

"Right then," Gadd said briskly. "Can't stand here chin-wagging all day. Why don't you leave these gentlemen to me, Jessie? I'll find something for them to do. Reckon we'll have this place lookin' shipshape in no time!"

They rested at midday when the woman took them a basket of food and a jug of cider, which they placed in the stream to keep cool. By that time the gate to the sheep pasture had been mended, the meadow grass had been cut back and the slats on the barn nailed into place. The woman had left the food and returned to the house, leaving the three men to fend for themselves.

Hawkwood took a sip of cider and passed Gadd the jug. The seaman was puffing contentedly at a short-stemmed clay pipe. He put the pipe down and raised the jug to his lips. When he had drunk he wiped his mouth on his sleeve, put the jug to one side, leant back on his elbow and took up his pipe once more. With his eyes half closed against the sun he looked like a man satisfied with his lot.

"Is Madame Flynn a smuggler?" Lasseur asked.

Gadd opened his eyes at the unexpected question. Then he removed the pipe from his mouth and tapped the bowl against his boot. "Not everyone in the trade works the boats. There's some folk who just store the goods till they can be moved up the line to the buyer."

Shepherds, innkeepers and widows, Hawkwood thought. "Are there many like that?"

"A whole army. Someone offers you a keg for the use of your byre for a few nights or they need a couple of ponies for a run; you're not going to turn them down. You take someone like Morgan, for instance; he's got people all over the county."

"Who's Morgan?"

It was the second time the name had cropped up.

"Ezekiel Morgan. He controls most of the coast around here. Took over when the old gangs died out. There's not much goes on that he doesn't know about."

"Did he arrange our stay here?"

Gadd nodded.

"Will we get to shake his hand?" Lasseur asked.

"If you do, best count your fingers afterwards."

Gadd paused as if suddenly aware that he might have given out a little too much information. He reached over and placed the stopper back in the jug. "Anyways, you don't need to bother your heads about that. We've chores to finish. And we'd best get a move on. Jessie'll have our hides if she sees us sitting here gossiping like three old fishwives."

Hawkwood wondered if Morgan was the other form of protection Jess Flynn had mentioned the previous evening. He mulled over the possibility as they returned to work.

It was late afternoon when they halted for the day, by which time a pleasant ache had settled across Hawkwood's back and shoulders.

Lasseur drew a hand across his brow. "I shall sleep well tonight, I think."

"You'll eat first," Jess Flynn told them.

She had prepared food, which they ate seated at the table in the kitchen, while the dog kept watch outside the open door.

"How many others have there been before us?" Hawkwood asked.

"A few," Jess Flynn acknowledged. "But not for a while."

"This man, Morgan; did he arrange their passage, too?"

"Morgan?" Jess Flynn looked up, her face suddenly still.

"Thomas mentioned the name. He told us Morgan rules the free-trade business and that he'll have been the one who arranged our escape."

Jess Flynn looked towards Gadd, who returned her stare with an apologetic shrug before tearing off a hunk of bread and using it to mop the gravy from his plate.

"We were just curious, that's all," Hawkwood said. "We wanted to know who to thank for our freedom."

"I doubt your thanks would interest Ezekiel Morgan," Jess Flynn said tartly. "His only interest will have been in counting the money he's been paid for your passage."

"Sounds as if you don't care for him much," Hawkwood said.

"Can you blame her?" Gadd said.

"Tom," Jess Flynn said warningly.

Gadd threw her a look that said, *You might as well tell them.*

Jess Flynn hesitated, then said, "My husband worked for Morgan. It was after we were wed, when Jack was signed off the *Orion*. There wasn't much work around."

"Lots of ships lying in ordinary," Gadd cut in. "Too many men; too few jobs."

The price of peace, Hawkwood thought. It was ever thus. An end to hostilities meant ships were placed on reserve and their crews laid off, creating a glut of idle bodies in search of employment.

"He was always good with his hands, though." She smiled at the memory. "He could make anything."

"Built the barn out there." Gadd jerked a thumb and his lips tightened. "For Morgan."

"Ezekiel Morgan's my landlord," Jess Flynn explained. "He owns a lot of land hereabouts. That's the honest side of his business. Well, honest in comparison to his other interests. When we came here, the farm didn't pay for itself. We'd sell eggs and milk, but it wasn't enough. Jack would do all sorts of odd jobs to make ends meet: mending carts, shoeing horses, fixing gates – everything. He even made coffins. It was hard, but we got by. Then Morgan increased the rent. The first time we were unable to pay, he asked for the use of our horses for one of his runs. The next time, he needed some tubs stored for a few days. Then it was tobacco. Before long, we were hiding something away every week."

"You don't say no to Morgan," Gadd interjected. "Not if you know what's good for you. Anyone who does is soon put right. You'll find a couple of your pigs have died overnight or a hay rick's caught fire or a dead lamb's been tossed down your well. It's a lot safer to go along with whatever it is Morgan wants. If you're lucky and it all goes well, there'll be a keg of brandy on your doorstep the next morning."

Jess Flynn continued. "After a while, Jack began going out on runs. It was good money. He started off as a tub carrier, then a bat man and lookout. Eventually, he became one of Morgan's lieutenants." She stopped and her voice faltered. "And then one night he didn't come back." She fell silent.

Gadd took up the story. "There was a landing up at White Ness; a big consignment, two hundred tubs plus tobacco; seventy ponies. They were carrying the kegs up from the beach. A Revenue patrol was waiting for them at the top of Kemp's Stairs. Ten of Morgan's men were taken; six were injured; three were shot, including Jack, but he and a couple of men managed to get away. They made it as far as Reading Street. The Revenue searched the houses. The others were found. Jack managed to hide out. Morgan got the doctor to him, but it was too late; he was gone."

Jess Flynn said, "I thought I'd have to leave the farm, but Morgan let me stay on. In return, he has the use of the horses when he wants and I still hide tubs from the Revenue. Once in a while I'll get a message that he needs a special favour, and I end up taking in strays like you."

"What would happen if you told him about Seth?" Hawkwood asked.

"Seth?" Tom Gadd said, puzzled. "What's that bugger got to do with anything?"

"It would depend," Jess Flynn said.

"On what?"

"On Morgan deciding whether or not Seth bothering me was a threat to his business."

"Has he been here?" Gadd stared at her.

"And if he did consider him a threat?" Hawkwood said.

"Then I'd be lending my sister my mourning dress."

"What's the bugger done now, Jessie?" Gadd asked.

"It's all right, Tom. Nothing happened."

"He tried to force himself on her," Lasseur said. "Captain Hooper and I saw him off."

"Bloody hell, Jess!" Gadd said.

"He was drunk, Tom."

"He's always bloody drunk," Gadd muttered.

"And if Morgan decided that Seth bothering you wasn't a risk to his business, what then?" Hawkwood asked.

"I'd spend my days worrying about Annie and her boy."

"Annie?" Hawkwood said. "Your sister?"

Jess Flynn nodded. "Seth threatened to hurt them if I didn't give myself to him. I don't know whether he really would, but if I went to Morgan and he didn't do anything, and Seth found out, he could take it out on them to spite me."

Lasseur turned to Hawkwood. "You should have let me kill him."

Hawkwood did not respond to that. He studied Jess for a moment. "So you've no idea whether Morgan will take your side or Seth's?"

"No. But Seth can't be sure either. He's one of Morgan's bat men, but he knows that won't save him if Morgan decides he's stepped out of line."

"And you're hoping that the mere threat of going to Morgan will be enough to keep Seth at bay?"

"That's a dangerous game you're playing, Jess," Gadd said.

"I know, Tom. You don't have to tell me."

"Bloody Morgan," Gadd said.

Outside, the dog let out a single bark.

"Shite!" Gadd spat, swinging round in alarm.

"Stay here," Jess Flynn said. She stood up quickly and walked out into the yard, closing the door behind her.

They should have stayed in the barn, Hawkwood knew, close to the hiding space behind the bales. They had grown careless.

"There's a cellar," Gadd said urgently. "Entrance is in the pantry, under the mat." He nodded towards a door in the corner.

Hawkwood and Lasseur were already moving as the latch lifted on the back door.

Too bloody late, Hawkwood thought.

The door opened.

"It's Asa," Jess Flynn said. "He's come to pick up the tubs."

"God save us," Tom Gadd said, relief flooding across his seamed face.

Hawkwood and Lasseur helped with the loading. There were six tubs in total. It didn't take long to remove them from the hiding place behind the bales.

The gravedigger had brought two empty coffins with him

on the back of the cart. Hawkwood wondered if they were new or the same ones as before. They placed three tubs in each coffin. Laid on their sides, end to end, they were a snug fit. Once the tubs had been secured, Higgs used thin nails to keep the lids in place.

"What if you're stopped?" Hawkwood asked, stepping back. "Won't it seem an odd time of day to be transporting coffins?"

The gravedigger shook his head. "Dead don't know what time it is. It ain't as though they keep regular hours. Leastways, not round here. Besides we'll be stickin' to the back lanes."

"But what if you're stopped and someone wants to take a look?"

"I'll tell 'em I'm carryin' a couple of pox victims. See if they want to take a look then. God's sakes, you ask a lot of bleedin' questions for a Frenchie." Higgs's eyes narrowed. "But then, you ain't a Frenchie, are you?"

"You were misinformed," Hawkwood said.

Tom Gadd rolled his eyes.

"Aye, well, it wouldn't be the first time," Higgs said morbidly. "Not that it makes any bleedin' difference. I just does what I'm told. Now, you ready or not?"

"For what?" Hawkwood said.

"Tubs ain't the only things I came for," Higgs said. "You got any belongings you want to take with you, best grab them now. We've a ways to go."

"Go?" Lasseur said.

"You didn't think you'd be stayin' here permanent, did you? Time you was movin' on."

"Where to?" Hawkwood asked.

"A little place in the country; nice and secluded, no pryin' eyes."

"I thought this *was* the country," Hawkwood said, thinking, *If this isn't secluded, what is?*

"There's other parts."

"Asa?" Jess Flynn said.

"Come on, Jess, you know you're not supposed to ask. I deliver 'em and I take 'em off your hands when I'm told. You don't need to know the rest."

"Bollocks, Asa," Gadd said. "Don't give me that. Where are you taking them?"

Higgs sighed, bit the inside of his lip, and said, "All right, I'm takin' them to the Haunt. Satisfied?"

Gadd frowned. "Why there?"

"God's sake, Tom, I'd have thought that was bleedin' obvious."

"What's at the Haunt?" Hawkwood asked.

"It ain't what," Gadd said, an edge to his voice. "It's who."

Hawkwood waited.

It was the gravedigger who finally answered: "Mr Morgan wants to meet you."

Well, this should be interesting, Hawkwood thought.

The sun was hanging low over the end of the valley as the gravedigger steered the coffin-laden cart up the track towards the trees. It was a strange feeling, leaving the place that had been their home for the past three days. Hawkwood had never been one for looking back over his shoulder but, on this occasion, even though he was impatient to move on, he couldn't help himself. Sunset was probably less than an hour away; at the edge of the woods, shadows were already lengthening and the house and barn were suffused in a warm russet glow. Hawkwood glanced to his side. Lasseur was staring back too, but there was a distant look in his eye that suggested he was seeing something far beyond his immediate view.

There had been no protracted farewells.

Shaking their hands in turn, Tom Gadd had wished them

a fair wind and then looked vaguely embarrassed by his verbosity.

Jess Flynn had hung back, only stepping forward to press a folded napkin into Lasseur's hands. "Some food for the journey. It's not much; just some bread and cheese."

As she stepped away, Hawkwood saw her fingers make contact with the back of Lasseur's wrist. The gesture had been so subtle, he wondered if he might have imagined it; yet he knew instinctively he had not and that more had been said in that fleeting touch and in the look on Jess Flynn's face than could have been expressed in a thousand words.

She had turned to Hawkwood then. "Safe passage, Captain Hooper."

"Madame," Hawkwood said.

With a brief nod and a final glance towards Lasseur, she turned and, straight-backed, head held high, made her way back to the house, a shaggy, four-legged shape padding obediently in her wake.

Lasseur had watched her walk away, his face still.

"Time to go, Captain," Tom Gadd murmured beside him.

Lasseur nodded.

The seaman lingered as Hawkwood and Lasseur climbed on to the cart. At the last minute, Lasseur turned to him. "Watch over her, Thomas," he said quietly. "Try and keep her safe."

Gadd nodded. "I'll do my best, Captain." He watched as Lasseur settled himself down and waited until Asa Higgs had set the horse in motion before turning to follow the woman and dog towards the house.

"So, if you ain't a Frenchie, what the hell are you?"

Asa Higgs winkled a clot of ash from his pipe and tapped the bowl against the side of his boot.

"American," Hawkwood said.

"Is that right?" The gravedigger considered Hawkwood's response. "An' that's why you'd rather be fighting for Boney than for the King?"

"He's not *my* king," Hawkwood said. "That's why we had a revolution."

The gravedigger sucked on his pipe stem. "Emperors pay well, do they?"

"Better than kings," Hawkwood said.

The gravedigger grinned and adjusted his gnarled grip on the reins. "Got a cousin over Rochester way tells me they've got hundreds of your lot behind bars. Said the Crown Prince at Chatham is full to the gunwales with pressed Yankee sailors who've refused to fight for Farmer George."

Which was why Hawkwood had been sent to *Rapacious,* further downriver, where there had been less risk of his false identity being discovered.

The gravedigger went on: "Heard tell the army's been sendin' recruitin' sergeants aboard offerin' sixteen guineas to any American willing to switch sides. From what I knows of the hulks, you'd have thought they'd be queuin' up, but they ain't had any takers. You was lucky you got away."

It had been some time since they'd left the farm. Sunset had given way to dusk, which in turn had darkened into an indigo-hued twilight. It was now night time. There were no clouds to mask the moon. The sky was bright and clear; the stars strewn across the night sky like diamonds on black velvet.

From what Hawkwood had been able to deduce, Asa Higgs had been true to his word, keeping them well away from anything resembling an established road. Most of the journey had taken them down narrow cart tracks and drovers' trails; hidden byways which, over the centuries, had been used by generations of farmers to herd stock across country to market. Some of the trails were so overshadowed by trees it was like passing through a series of tunnels. On these occasions, Higgs had been content to let the horse take the lead, which it had done without any notable deviation. The animal was obviously as familiar with the ground as its driver, which was fortunate, for even in daylight the most eagle-eyed person might have found himself teetering on the rim of the trail, or plunging into the steep-sided gulley below.

On one occasion they had crossed a river. As the cart rattled over the old stone bridge, Hawkwood had seen the moon reflecting on the dark water flowing beneath them.

Signs of habitation were few and far between. Occasionally a distant light would catch the eye, indicating an isolated cottage or farmstead. There had been no sign of any other travellers. Hawkwood, Lasseur and the gravedigger might well have been the only people abroad.

"Your friend don't have a lot to say for himself," the gravedigger murmured.

"Been a long day," Hawkwood said. "He's feeling a bit weary."

The gravedigger was right, though. Lasseur had been noticeably quiet since they'd left the farm. It was obvious he was thinking about Jess Flynn.

Just as well we left when we did, Hawkwood concluded. It was patently obvious that Lasseur's feelings for the woman went beyond mere sympathy for the loss of her husband and her solitary status. The manner of their leaving had suggested the attraction was mutual, though Hawkwood knew it was equally possible that the widow's parting gesture had not been a sign of some deep-seated feeling but a tactile expression of gratitude for Lasseur's intervention when she had been attacked. A gut instinct, however, told him that wasn't the case. And therein, he knew, lay the problem. The privateer's concern for the underdog, while admirable, had already cost them dear, nearly compromising their escape plan, and Hawkwood's assignment in the process. The last thing Hawkwood needed was for Lasseur to lose his objectivity over a woman with whom he had no possible future. Sooner or later the Frenchman would have to be reminded that he couldn't save all the lost and disaffected souls, no matter how hard he tried.

The land rose before them. They were no longer travelling in the dips and the hollows but had emerged on to a broader track bordered on both sides by tangled thickets. The night was full of eerie feral sounds: owls hooting, frogs croaking, animals foraging and leaves rustling. Somewhere deep within the wood a fox barked. The noise rose like a scream into the night like a soul in torment. Even though he recognized the sound, the short hairs prickled along the back of Hawkwood's neck.

Suddenly the bark was cut short.

The evening seemed suddenly unnaturally still. Asa Higgs urged the horse on and looked about him warily.

Hawkwood tensed. There had been a movement to his right; a vague, shadowy shape at the corner of his vision, flitting through a break in the trees; moonlight glancing off . . . something; he wasn't sure what.

He felt Lasseur stir beside him and was reassured. Despite the distractions, the privateer's senses were still fully alert.

Even so, neither of them was prepared for the wild, nerve-jarring screech of laughter that exploded from the trees, or the ghastly apparitions that vaulted without warning on to the track ahead of them.

The startled gravedigger yanked back on the reins and the cart slewed sideways.

There were two of them; a matching pair. They were

dressed like monks, in black habits and hoods. But it was not the nature of their attire, which was torn and streaked with dirt, or the pistol that each of them brandished that drew the eye and set the heart beating; it was what lay within the cowls. For the black-clad priors had no faces, only bare skulls that gleamed like white-hot coals in the darkness.

15

Hawkwood wrinkled his nose. Piss; there was no mistaking the pungent odour. It was there, souring the inside of his nostrils every time he inhaled. Holding his breath wasn't a viable option, so there was little he could do except try and ignore it, which was difficult for the smell was coming off the man seated beside him in waves. It was strange, Hawkwood thought; before he'd washed the stench of the hulks from him, he doubted the smell would even have registered. Now, it was all he could do not to clamp his hand over his face.

Sensing Hawkwood's aversion, the black-clad figure turned his head. "Ain't me. It's the bleedin' paint. An' if you think I smell bad, you're lucky it's me keepin' you company and not Billy back there." The figure jerked a thumb. "Now, *'e* does bloody stink!"

Lasseur, who had given up his seat and shifted into the back of the cart with the coffins, grimaced.

Hawkwood's knowledge of alchemy bordered on the non-existent. He had no idea what made the paint – if that was the catalyst – glow in the dark, and could have cared even less, though he had to admit the effect was quite dramatic, especially if you weren't expecting it. Presumably Asa Higgs had been anticipating some kind of ghostly manifestation, but even he'd nearly jumped out of his skin, much to the amusement of the spectral duo when they'd seen who was driving the cart.

The skull images had been painted in some kind of waxy substance on to close-fitting black cloth hoods, similar to those used by executioners. When framed by the folds of a cowl and lit by moonlight, the result was spectacular and, to the uninitiated, quite terrifying. It was certainly an effective way of persuading unwelcome visitors of an inquisitive disposition to keep their distance.

But from what?

The track continued its steady ascent. It was then that Hawkwood saw a light through a gap in the trees. There was some kind of man-made structure ahead, too, but its outline was indistinct. It was only as they rounded the final bend and the gradient flattened out that he realized what he'd been looking at.

The turreted gatehouse looked old, as did the high, grey-stone wall that flanked it. Set into the gatehouse was a Norman archway. Two men dressed in work-day clothes and armed with clubs and pistols guarded the entrance. The malodorous friar gave a nod and the pickets parted to let them through.

The gravedigger clicked his tongue and guided the horse forward. "Welcome to the Haunt."

"Haunt?" Lasseur echoed from behind.

"Monk's Haunt. Leastways, that's what we call it now. Used to be St Anselm's Priory; most of it fell into ruin, but there's a fair bit still standin'. You'll see for yourself. Place has seen a few owners since them days. One of the local squires moved in and built himself a house. It was run as a farm for a while after he died, and then Mr Morgan took it on. It was him who gave it the name, 'cause of all the stories 'bout how the place was haunted. That's how he stops nosey parkers from gettin' too close and learnin' 'is business; on nights when we're moving goods around, he gets the likes of Del here to play silly buggers and scare 'em away."

The mock friar grinned then. He had an unruly mop of curly hair, a thin weasel face, and teeth like a mule. It was on the tip of Hawkwood's tongue to suggest he probably didn't need the mask.

The friar threw the gravedigger an admonishing look. "It's no good sniggerin', Asa Higgs. It works and don't you deny it. I've seen people piss their breeches when we've leapt out on 'em. There's even been a few who've passed away with the fright of it."

"With the bleedin' smell, more like," Higgs muttered under his breath.

"I told you," Del's voice rose in indignant protest, "it ain't me, it's the bloody paint."

While Del and the gravedigger discussed the phosphorescent properties of piss and pigment, Hawkwood and Lasseur exchanged wary glances. Each knew the other was thinking back to their conversation with Jess Flynn and Tom Gadd.

A building came into view. It was hard to make out specific details in the darkness. Hawkwood assumed he was looking at the main house. The impression was of stout walls, gabled windows and high chimneys. He could see the silhouettes of other buildings behind it. Some looked to be whole, while others stood in obvious ruin; from their imposing size, he presumed they were part of the original priory. He thought about the gatehouse and the adjoining wall and how far it might extend. That in turn made him wonder how many other guards were roaming the woods, for while the place may well have started life as a retreat devoted to prayer and meditation, this was clearly no longer the case. From what he'd seen so far, the Haunt had all the hallmarks of an armed compound.

The gravedigger drove them into a gravelled stable yard, bringing the cart to a halt outside a set of large wooden doors. The doors were open. Light from within the building spilled out. The smell of compacted straw and animal dung hung in the air.

Del climbed down from the cart, nearly tripping over the hem of his habit in the process. "The boss wanted me to bring you to 'im. We'll try in 'ere first. One of the mares is in foal. He's expectin' 'er to deliver tonight. Best wait here, Asa." He beckoned to Hawkwood and Lasseur. "You two, come with me."

Del led the way into the stables. Two men were standing by the opening to the stall furthest from the entrance doors. At the sound of footsteps, they looked round. One was hunched, with thinning hair and short bandy legs. He wore a dark waistcoat and a worn leather apron and was holding a lantern. His companion was taller and leaner; his swept-back hair was silvery grey. So, too, was his beard, which was short and neatly trimmed. With his blue eyes and lined features, he could have passed for a distinguished lawyer or a benevolent uncle, had it not been for his shortened left arm, which ended in a leather cup just below his elbow.

Del's gaze shifted to the grey-bearded man. "Mr Pepper." His tone was immediately deferential.

"Del," Pepper said. There was no warmth in the response.

Not so benevolent, after all, Hawkwood thought, and wondered who Pepper was and whether the severed limb indicated that he'd served in the wars.

"Asa brought them," Del said, jerking a thumb over his shoulder.

A spark of interest showed in Pepper's blue eyes. He looked Hawkwood and Lasseur over. "And the tubs?"

"They're outside on the cart," Del responded nervously.

"Good, go and help Asa unload. You can store them in the usual place."

Del nodded. He still looked, Hawkwood thought, a little cowed. Studying Pepper, it wasn't hard to see why. The man exuded menace, even though he'd barely moved a muscle. With a look of relief and a sideways nod towards Hawkwood and Lasseur, Del departed, robes flapping.

"Where's that damned lantern, Thaddeus?"

The question came from behind Pepper's back.

The mare was standing, legs straddled, in the centre of the stall, flanks glistening with sweat. The distended belly told its own story. A stocky, broad-shouldered man with close-cropped black hair and a dark beard, shirt rolled back to his elbows, was gently stroking the mare's neck. He made no acknowledgement of Hawkwood or Lasseur's presence.

The man with Pepper stepped back into the stall and held the lantern high. The mare looked around. Her soft brown eyes, caught by the candle flame, gleamed brightly. She shifted restlessly, pawing the straw.

"She's close," the dark-haired man said. He stepped away quickly. "Let's give her some room."

Suddenly, as if on cue, the mare braced herself and whickered softly as a stream of fluid gushed from her rear opening and flowed down her hind legs, dampening the bed of straw beneath. Abdominal muscles quivering and with her waters still breaking, the mare sank heavily to her knees and rolled on to her side. The rush of fluid seemed endless. Eventually, after what must have been the release of several gallons, the flood ceased and the mare recovered her breath. Her belly continued to undulate.

"The foal's turning," the bearded man said.

The mare laid her head on the straw, as if gathering strength. Then she raised her head and whinnied softly. Her hindquarters roiled and a small bulge of white mucus ballooned from beneath her tail. As the men watched, the balloon increased in size, becoming elongated in the process. Within the expanding membrane a pair of dark, stick-like objects could be seen. Hawkwood realized he was looking at a pair of forelegs. The mare quietened, belly heaving. She pushed again. A triangular shape appeared, resting on top of the legs. It was the foal's head. The veined birth sac continued to stretch until, without warning, it ruptured and a small hoof poked into view. The mare paused and then gave another heavy push. Nothing happened. She tried again. There was still no movement.

"Come on, girl," the dark-bearded man said coaxingly.

The mare strained again. The foal's head and feet remained resolutely in place. The dark-bearded man cursed under his breath.

"Looks like she's stuck, Mr Morgan," the man holding the lantern said. "Should we give her a hand?"

Morgan stared down at the horse. His lips moved soundlessly. Hawkwood wondered if he was praying.

The mare's hind legs thrust weakly against the straw as she tried again to expel the foal. She gave a small snuffle of distress and laid her head down.

Morgan stepped into the stall. "Hold the light up."

As the lantern was raised, Morgan squatted down and positioned himself behind the mare's hindquarters. Moving the tail out of the way, he took hold of the foal's forelegs, just above the fetlock joints. "All right, girl, let's give it another try." Bracing himself, he pulled gently on the foal's legs.

As if sensing that assistance was at hand, the mare, head still lowered, pushed again. Morgan increased his grip and angled the foal's legs towards the mare's hocks. The mare strained once more. Morgan's arm muscles tightened.

Suddenly, the mare's flanks rippled. Morgan continued his steady pull. A pair of narrow shoulders eased into view. The mare heaved again and Morgan let go. Seconds later, the foal lay in a glistening wet heap.

Tenderly, Morgan cleared the membrane away from the foal's mouth and nostrils. The foal's head lifted and Morgan grunted with satisfaction. Taking care not to sever the umbilical cord, Morgan eased the foal around to where the mare could see it. He stood up and, by the time he'd moved out of the way, the foal had rolled upright. The mare got to her knees and then to her feet and nuzzled her newborn, licking away the rest of the birth sac.

Morgan wiped his hands with some dry straw and looked round. "Captains Hooper and Lasseur, I presume? Welcome, gentlemen; good to meet you. I'm Ezekiel Morgan."

Hawkwood guessed that Morgan and Pepper were of similar age. From Pepper's grey hair and the light dusting down the laughter lines either side of Morgan's jaw, he doubted either of them would see fifty again, though they did not have the deportment of old men. When they stood side by side, the difference in height was even more apparent. Morgan's head was level with Pepper's shoulders. In the lantern light, Morgan's eyes – dark, deep set, intelligent and watchful – were the brightest.

Morgan tossed the used straw aside. "My apologies for not giving your arrival my full attention. As you see, I'd a rather pressing matter to attend to." Morgan held out his hand. His grip was firm and still slightly damp. Hawkwood could feel the calluses. "You've met my associate, Cephus Pepper?" Morgan indicated the grey-haired man.

Pepper did not extend his hand but instead held Hawkwood's gaze for several seconds before giving a curt nod.

Morgan cocked his head. "You've had quite a journey.

The Warden incident gave us some concern. We weren't expecting an affray."

"Neither were we," Hawkwood said. "How many men did you lose?"

"None, fortunately; though we had three wounded."

"We saw Isaac go down," Lasseur said.

Morgan nodded. "He was lucky. The ball took him in the shoulder, but there's no permanent damage."

"And the attackers?" Hawkwood said. "Were they after us or the contraband?"

Morgan threw Hawkwood a wry look. "It's all right, Captain. You can rest easy. It was the goods they were after, not you. Someone tipped them the nod. My people are making enquiries. When we find out who it was, they'll be dealt with." Morgan cocked his head on one side. "Gideon said it was a close-run thing. You only just made it into the boat."

Hawkwood shrugged. "Better to be damp than dead. What about the Revenue? Did they lose anyone? There was a lot of shooting. There looked to be some dragoons with them."

Morgan frowned. "Three Revenue men wounded and one dragoon dead. There was a horse killed, too, which was a bloody shame." He glanced over to the stall. "Good mounts are hard to come by."

So are good dragoons, Hawkwood thought. "You had reinforcements on the cliff."

"We always have reinforcements. It pays to be cautious. Jessie Flynn looked after you all right?"

Hawkwood nodded. "No complaints there. We could have done without the ambush on the way here, though. It nearly gave your man Higgs a heart attack."

A flicker of alarm moved across the bearded face and then understanding dawned. "Ah, you mean our phantom friars.

I'll admit they're a mite crude, but they do the trick. Gave you a bit of a fright, did they?"

"Only the smell of them."

"That'll be our Del. Fragrant, ain't he?"

"Not the paint, then," Hawkwood said.

The corner of Morgan's mouth lifted. "No. The paint's made with putrefied horse piss. It's what makes it glow. But it doesn't hold the smell. That was all Del. It's why we like to keep him out in the fresh air, away from the house."

"You make paint from horse piss?" Lasseur said.

Another wry smile formed between the bearded lips. "Not personally. I employ people for that. Don't ask me how they do it. Some kind of fancy chymical process." Morgan fell silent and then said, "I understand the two of you caused quite a rumpus before you left."

Lasseur's head came up.

He knows about Seth Tyler was the thought that speared its way into Hawkwood's brain. Lasseur, he knew, would be thinking the same thing, though the privateer's face betrayed no outward emotion.

How had the man found out? Had Tyler told him?

And then he heard Morgan say, "Lucky we got you out before they transferred you," and realized that Morgan was referring to the events aboard *Rapacious*.

Hawkwood let out a slow, inaudible breath. As he did so he wondered how Morgan knew what had occurred on the hulk. The man obviously had a good intelligence system in place.

"You shouldn't believe all you hear," Lasseur said, his expression neutral.

Morgan's head lifted. "Oh, I don't, Captain, but you really mustn't underestimate yourself." He looked at Hawkwood. "I've a mind to offer you the same advice, Captain Hooper, but, if you'll forgive the impertinence, modesty's not a trait

I'd associate with you Americans, judging by the ones I've come across."

"Met many of us, have you?" Hawkwood asked.

"There've been a few. And I have to say I've always found them refreshingly honest in the promotion of their own abilities. Not sure if it's self-confidence or sheer bloody arrogance, but it's a damned powerful quality either way. Won you your revolution *and* forged a damned country. Can't argue with that."

"We just don't like anyone else telling us what to do," Hawkwood said.

Morgan's dark eyes flashed. "Ha! Did you hear that, Cephus? We'll make a free trader out of him yet!"

Pepper said nothing. It was becoming clear that Morgan's lieutenant was a man of few words.

"How's our new arrival doing, Thaddeus?" Morgan addressed his groom, who was still watching over the mare and her foal, seemingly oblivious to the exchange going on behind his back.

"Very nicely, Mr Morgan. Afterbirth's on its way."

"Good. Keep your eye on her." Morgan turned back.

"Why are we here?" Hawkwood asked.

The question seemed to catch Morgan off guard. Pepper's eyes narrowed.

Morgan showed his teeth again. "By God, there's no beating about the bush with you, Captain Hooper, is there? No matter, I like a straight talker. You're here because I've a proposition for you."

Lasseur frowned. "What sort of proposition?"

"If all goes well, a damned profitable one."

"What about our passage to France?" Hawkwood asked.

"Don't worry, you'll both be delivered safe and sound as promised, only with a little extra something to remember us by."

"And what might that be?"

Morgan looked as if he was still mildly amused by Hawkwood's directness. "All in good time, Captain." He drew a watch from his waistcoat pocket and consulted the dial. "It's too late to go into details now. I still have work to do here and I'm sure you've both had a long day. Why don't I let you get some rest and we can talk again in the morning? I'll explain everything then; saves me having to do it twice. How does that sit with you?"

Do we have a choice in the matter? Hawkwood thought and wondered what Morgan had meant by the comment about doing it twice.

Before either of them had a chance to reply, Morgan gave a satisfied nod. "Then it's settled. Cephus'll show you to your cell. It's all right, Captain," Morgan added, chuckling at Lasseur's expression of alarm. "Just my little jest. You're quite safe. You'll find no gaolers here." Morgan turned away and then paused, as if he'd just remembered something. "I'd advise you, however, while you're at liberty to move around, it'd be best if you didn't stray too far. As you saw earlier, I do have men patrolling the outer walls and, having gone to all the trouble of getting you this far, it'd be a damned shame if you wandered off and one of my lads put a ball through your brain because he thought you were trespassing."

Morgan smiled at Lasseur's expression, though his eyes remained dark. "Stranger things have happened, Captain. Trust me."

They emerged from the stables to find the cart had gone. Hawkwood assumed it meant Asa Higgs and Del were away unloading the liquor tubs; either that or the gravedigger was already making his return to the coast while Del was back frolicking in the woods with his equally odorous pal, Billy.

A taciturn Pepper, lantern in hand, led the way across

the yard and around a series of corners, emerging eventually into a cloistered quadrangle. The cloisters were clearly very old, a remnant of the original priory. Beneath the arches, the flagstones, worn smooth over the centuries, reflected the moonlight like the dark surface of a pond. It wasn't hard to imagine black-robed friars stalking the shaded walkway, wrapped in silent contemplation and wearing away the stones with each pious footstep.

Pepper did not dawdle but took them through a stone archway in the corner of the building. Entering a dark corridor, they arrived at a low wooden door. When Pepper pushed the door open and stood back, Morgan's little joke was explained.

The cell, for that had undoubtedly been the room's former rolé, was plainly furnished with just enough room for two narrow cots, a chair and a small table on which stood a candle-holder containing a stub of wax and tapers. Opposite the door, high in the stone wall, a tiny window, barely worthy of the name, admitted a thin shaft of moonlight. The only thing missing was a crucifix on the wall.

Pepper used one of the tapers to transfer a flame from the lantern to the candle stub. "Dormitory's full, so you're in here. You'll be comfortable enough. Mind what you were told. Stay close to the house. It's for your own safety. There's a washroom and privy down the passage."

Without waiting for a response, Pepper backed out and closed the door behind him. Hawkwood and Lasseur stood in silence. The thickness of the door prevented them from hearing whether Pepper had retraced his path or if he was still outside with his ear pressed against the wood.

Hawkwood tried the handle. Although there had been no sound of a key turning he'd half expected the door to be locked, but it opened without opposition. The passage outside was dark, empty and silent.

"So," Lasseur said, testing the cot and wincing at the lack of spring in the thin palliasse. "The adventure continues. What do you think of our Monsieur Morgan?"

"I think anyone who surrounds himself with a cordon of armed men deserves to be taken seriously."

Lasseur smiled. Candlelight played across his aristocratic face. "And Pepper?"

"Pepper's dangerous," Hawkwood said, without hesitation.

Lasseur considered that for a moment. "This proposition Morgan talked about; what do you think he meant?"

"It won't be something for nothing," Hawkwood said. "It never is."

Lasseur looked around the room. "So, we sleep on it."

Hawkwood stretched out on the second cot and laced his hands behind his head.

"For now," he said.

Dawn.

Hawkwood pushed aside his blanket, sat up and pulled on his boots. He looked over at Lasseur's cot. The Frenchman gave no sign that he was awake. His face was turned to the wall.

Picking up his coat, Hawkwood let himself out of the cell and made his way to the privy, where he took a piss before sluicing his face with cold water in one of the large stone washroom sinks. His fingertips brushed stubble. He ran a hand along his jaw and wondered idly about growing a beard. Then he pictured the look on Maddie Teague's face when he turned up at her door sporting whiskers. Not such a good idea after all, he decided.

He shrugged on the jacket. Time to take a walk.

Retracing his path to the cloisters, Hawkwood left the shelter of the arches, cut away from the main buildings and headed towards open ground. Jacket collar turned up, hands in pockets, he walked in plain sight. Mindful of the maxim that it was unwise to send a terrier down a rat hole without there being at least one viable way out, Hawkwood knew his first task was to gauge the layout of the Haunt and the efficiency of its outer defences.

Hawkwood had no watch. He guessed it was a couple of hours past sunrise. The morning had all the makings of another fine day. A watery sun had burned away most of the early haze. Misty vapours still hung low above the dew-soaked grass. Wood pigeons fluttered and cooed in the nearby woods while, beyond the trees, from meadows further down the hill, the sound of lowing cattle rose plaintively in the still air. In such a peaceful setting, it wasn't hard to see why a religious order had found the site so appealing. The elevation and isolation would certainly have given the holy fathers the illusion they were closer to God.

Hawkwood doubted the current landowner harboured the same spiritual sentiment. Ezekiel Morgan's appreciation of the location would be governed purely by logistics. It would have taken a blind man not to see the strategic advantage of occupying a position with such commanding views over the surrounding countryside. Even allowing for the encroaching woodland, the chances of a substantial force scaling the Haunt unseen were, Hawkwood judged, exceedingly remote.

He looked back over his shoulder. Daylight revealed the extent of Ezekiel Morgan's domain. Jess Flynn's smallholding could probably have fitted into the Haunt several times over. If the size of the estate was anything to go by, the profits from running contraband were manifestly greater than anything Hawkwood could have envisaged. Small wonder the man put so much effort into protecting his privacy.

In addition to the house and the stable block, Hawkwood

could see a number of outhouses and a large barn. There were several paddocks, with a handful of horses in each. The remains of the original priory buildings were easily identifiable by their age and architecture. The walls were all that were left of the chapel, the roof having long since collapsed, leaving the nave exposed to the elements. The tall windows, which would once have been monuments to the art of stained glass, looked like sightless eye sockets in a line of grey skulls. Dark-fleeced sheep grazed among the stones.

Hawkwood took a deep breath. The air was fresh and scented with grass and pollen and a world away from the pervading stench of London's crowded streets. The smell of the hulk seemed a distant memory.

The nine-foot perimeter wall looked, at first sight, to be intact, but as he continued walking, Hawkwood noticed shading in the stonework where repairs had been undertaken. Further on, he saw where parts of the wall had fallen down. Set in the breaches were lengths of palisade. The palisades didn't look that strong. It was clear they were intended purely as a holding measure, for at the base of each were assorted tools, buckets, a large pile of loose stones, and sacks of sand and lime; the main ingredients for making mortar.

Stretches of the wall disappeared behind trees, but Hawkwood was confident they would be undamaged or, if they had fallen into disrepair, stop-gapped and awaiting full restoration. He'd seen enough to be certain that Morgan, like a good general, would make sure his perimeter was protected above all else. Hawkwood was reminded of the fortified villages he'd seen in Spain, another place where churches dominated the high ground.

The appearance of other early risers came as no great surprise. The presence of livestock had guaranteed some kind of on-site work force. A couple of figures were making their way between one of the barns and the stable block. It hadn't been hard to spot Morgan's pickets either, as they patrolled the outer edges of the grounds. They were some distance away, but close enough for him to see the cudgels in their hands and the pistols in their belts. They'd issued no challenge. Hawkwood assumed it was because he was in plain sight and therefore had not been perceived as a threat. Lifting a hand in feigned recognition, he proceeded on his circuit without interruption. The lack of interest in his presence suggested the pickets weren't as conscientious as their employer supposed, which in turn meant that the Haunt wasn't quite as watertight as Morgan thought it was. It was possible that the men had grown lax after a night's patrol, but Hawkwood filed the information away for future reference.

Ahead of him, the walls of an ancient outbuilding rose out of the sheep-cropped grass. Empty doorways gaped like open jaws. Weeds sprouted around the bases of the moss-covered stones. He was about to pass by the ruin when a dark, four-legged shape appeared through one of the gaps in the wall. When it saw Hawkwood it stopped dead.

Hawkwood froze.

The dog was huge, with a brindle coat. Powerful shoulders supported a head that was at least three feet off the ground. When the second dog, which was just as large, padded round the corner of the wall to his right, Hawkwood's stomach turned over. This one had a fawn pelt and a black face and muzzle.

The brindle-coated dog growled. It was possibly one of the most chilling sounds Hawkwood had ever heard. It came from deep within the animal's throat and it felt as if the air was vibrating.

The dogs took a pace forward. Their paws made no noise on the still damp grass.

Behind them, two more shapes materialized into view.

One tall and grey-bearded, the other short and bull-necked and carrying a stout blackthorn walking stick.

"Captain Hooper!" Ezekiel Morgan called cheerily. "Good morning to you. You're out and about early. I trust the accommodation is to your satisfaction?"

Hawkwood realized he'd been holding his breath. He let it out slowly. He made a point not to look at the dogs, which wasn't easy, given the way they were eyeing him and the size of their teeth.

"New billet, strange bed. It takes a while to settle. Thought I'd get some fresh air. You know how it is."

He hadn't had to lie. His sleep *had* been intermittent for the reasons he had given. Lasseur's heavy breathing hadn't helped much either.

Morgan stretched out his arms and inhaled a lungful of air. "A morning constitutional? Splendid idea! Who could blame you on a day like this? Makes a man glad to be alive. Captain Lasseur's not with you?"

Hawkwood wondered if the man standing at Morgan's shoulder was glad to be alive. It was difficult to tell. Cephus Pepper's face was a model of taciturnity.

"Still in his pit. How's the new arrival?"

Morgan lowered his arms and tapped the stick against the side of his boot. "The foal? He's in fine fettle. The mare's a good mother. They'll do very nicely, I think."

Morgan was making no attempt to call the dogs to heel. Hawkwood knew the man was confirming who was in charge: Morgan's house, Morgan's rules.

"Fine-looking animals," Hawkwood said, conscious that it was probably wise to remain still and not make any sudden moves.

"Thor and Odin," Morgan said. "Thor's the brindle." He regarded the dogs with affection. "It was the Phoenicians who brought mastiffs to Europe. Did you know that?"

At the mention of their names, the dogs' ears pricked up. They switched their gaze to Morgan, as if awaiting instructions. It was the first time they'd taken their eyes off Hawkwood.

"Can't say I've given it a lot of thought," Hawkwood said.

"They were here before Julius Caesar," Morgan went on, unconcerned by Hawkwood's less than ecstatic response. "The Romans took them home and trained them to fight in the arenas. They used to match them against bears. Used them in battle, too. They say there was a mastiff on the first ship to make landfall in the New World. Interesting it was the Phoenicians, though, don't you think? They were traders too, like me. Could be I've inherited some of their blood along the way. That'd be something, eh?"

Hawkwood looked at the dogs. The mastiffs gazed back at him, unflinching, eyes bright, tongues hanging from their impressive jaws.

Morgan smiled. "Would you care to walk with us, Captain? Cephus and I often take a stroll around the grounds at this time. It gives us a chance to exercise the dogs and put the world to rights."

Hawkwood nodded and wondered briefly if Morgan had extended the invitation to prevent him wandering around on his own.

Morgan snapped his fingers and, with a wave of his arm, sent the dogs running effortlessly ahead, noses pressed to the ground. Hawkwood fell into step alongside him. Pepper walked several paces ahead, as if on point.

"We were told you control all the Trade along the coast," Hawkwood said. He thought he saw the back of Pepper's head twitch.

Morgan did not alter his stride but kept walking, hands behind him, holding the stick horizontally across the base of his spine. "Were you now?"

"Is it true?"

Morgan smiled. "Take a look around, Captain. What do you think?"

"I think that I'm in the wrong business."

Morgan maintained his smile. "Then I'd say you've just answered your own question. It's all a matter of supply and demand. If the bloody government wasn't so determined to tax us all to within an inch of our lives, do you think we'd be having this conversation?"

"Governments use taxes to pay for their wars," Hawkwood said. "It's the only way they can raise the money. Doesn't make any difference if you're English, French or American, you have to pay to make your country safe. It's why taxes were invented in the first place."

Morgan shook his head. "It's not the principle I object to, it's the percentage and the fact they only tax the pleasures, never the pain. Damn it, they even tax playing cards! Can you believe that? That's almost as stupid as the tax on bloody windows! A man works hard in the fields all day; it strikes me he's a right to enjoy a pipe, a hand of whist and a swig of brandy without having to pay the bloody exchequer over the odds for the privilege. The way I see it, if I can make his life a bit more bearable, then that's no crime. And if it means I can shove two fingers up to the government at the same time, that's all right, too."

Morgan kicked aside a stone. "Don't get me wrong, Captain. I'm not running a charity here. You said earlier that you thought you were in the wrong business. Well, that's exactly what this is – a business. I saw an opportunity to invest and I seized it. I've been in it a long time now, and the returns have been excellent – like most of my other enterprises, I'm happy to say."

"You must have substantial outlays," Hawkwood said.

Without breaking stride, Morgan shrugged. "Wages,

transport and distribution, warehousing; no different to any other business. I've got a few more palms to grease, that's all."

More than a few, Hawkwood thought. He turned and found Morgan was giving him a quizzical look.

"What were you expecting, Captain? This is the nineteenth century; or had you forgotten? If you thought the Trade was made up of a couple of fishermen and a rowboat, you can think again. Those days are long gone. Oh, I'll not deny that still goes on, but it's not where the big money comes from. Buy in bulk and make sure you've got a good accountant – that's where the profit lies."

"You mean like the other night at . . ." Hawkwood feigned memory loss ". . . where was it?"

"Warden." Morgan called out to Pepper: "How many tubs was that, Cephus?"

"Twenty-five," Pepper said, without looking back. "Plus six bales of tobacco."

Morgan nodded. "Twenty-five tubs. That's not bulk, Captain Hooper. That's small change. I've had runs where we needed eighty ponies to transport the goods. A week ago I had two hundred and fifty men on a job; fifty to carry the goods ashore, the rest to guard the flanks."

"You're not telling me you've got that many men *here*?" Hawkwood nodded towards the house and outbuildings and the cloisters, where he and Lasseur had spent the night.

Morgan shook his head. "I hire in. If there's one thing I'm not short of, it's manpower. And I pay well. A labouring man'll earn a shilling a day, if he's lucky. I pay tub carriers four times that for one night's work. I pay my scouts ten times that amount. They know I'll look after them. I've a surgeon on call in case of mishap and, if the worst happens, I make sure their families are taken care of. I've got a firm of lawyers who'll arrange bail if they're picked up and brought before a magistrate. No one serves gaol time working for me, Captain. You can take that as gospel."

"Accountants, surgeons *and* lawyers?" Hawkwood said. "I'm impressed."

"So you should be." Morgan stopped walking, leant on his stick, and gazed towards the house and the priory ruins, as if admiring their worth for the first time.

"Well, you can't argue with the evidence, I'll grant you that," Hawkwood said, following Morgan's stare. "It's a fine place."

Morgan turned and gave a mock bow. "Why, thank you, Captain. Though, I'm afraid I can't claim all the credit. Most of the hard work was done for me. I did think about having all the ruins pulled down and clearing the rest of the land, but the local vicar objected. Said I'd be consigned to everlasting damnation if I removed a single stone. Mind you, he was in his cups at the time, courtesy of a keg of my best brandy, so he might not have meant it."

"But you decided not to risk it, just in case?" Hawkwood said.

"It'd be a foolish man who tried to second guess the Almighty, Captain Hooper."

"Not to mention the clergy," Hawkwood said.

"Indeed. Especially Reverend Starkweather. His Sunday sermons are particularly well attended." Morgan paused and then grinned. "Not that he should complain, considering I am at least carrying on the St Anselm tradition."

"How's that?"

"I'm still taking in pilgrims."

"Pilgrims?"

"They used to shelter here on their way to Canterbury, until King Henry had the monks all thrown out. Now we provide sanctuary for the likes of you. Curious how things come to pass, isn't it?"

"There've been other prisoners brought here?"

Morgan smiled. "Only those that have shown promise."

"Were they offered a proposition as well?"

Hawkwood sensed Pepper, who had halted up ahead, stiffen. Morgan's smile did not falter, though his laughter lines may have shortened a little. Hawkwood saw that the dogs had paused too. The brindle ran across to the grass to sniff energetically at its companion's rear end.

"How did you know about the fight on the ship?" Hawkwood asked.

"I have my sources."

"The guards?"

"They're useful for looking the other way or passing messages, but any number of people are involved in maintaining the ships, and I can afford to employ a wide net – ashore and on the water. Money talks."

At that moment a hand bell rang somewhere in the cloisters.

The dogs' heads swivelled.

Matins? Hawkwood thought wildly. *Don't tell me Morgan holds prayers as well.*

"Ah," Morgan said cheerfully, resting the walking stick across his right shoulder. "Time we were heading back." He gave a whistle that sent the dogs running towards him, then started walking towards the house. "We'll leave you to rouse Captain Lasseur. You can tell him breakfast will be provided in the refectory. It'll be our first chance to introduce you to the others."

"Others?" Hawkwood said.

Morgan smiled. "Your fellow pilgrims."

16

"And this is Lieutenant Gilles Denard," Rousseau said, his eyes blinking earnestly behind a pair of wire-framed spectacles.

Denard, a pleasant-looking, balding man in his late thirties, extended his hand across the table. "An honour, Captain."

"And for me," Lasseur said. "Allow me to present Captain Matthew Hooper, one of our American allies. His French is excellent, by the way."

Denard shook Hawkwood's hand. "Welcome, Captain. I've a great liking for your country. I've sailed into Boston a number of times. Do you know the city? It has some splendid inns. A particular favourite of mine was on Washington Street. The Lion, run by a Colonel Doty, I think his name was. Are you familiar with it?"

"I think you'll find that was the Lamb," Hawkwood said. "The Lion was further north."

Denard frowned and then laughed. "Why, I do believe you're right! Well, it's been a while since my last visit."

"Gilles served with Surcouf," Rousseau said.

"When were you taken?" Lasseur asked.

Denard pursed his lips. "June '08. I was in Cadiz, then transferred to the *Prudent* in Portsmouth for a year before I wound up on the *Poseidon*. That's where I met Rousseau, here."

With the exception of the *Poseidon,* the names of the ships meant nothing to Hawkwood. He knew of the *Poseidon* because it was another Chatham hulk and one of several Medway-moored ships mentioned by Ludd during his briefing at Bow Street.

They were in the refectory which was situated on the opposite side of the cloister garth from the wing housing Hawkwood and Lasseur's cell. It was long and rectangular in shape, with a low, black-beamed ceiling. Two heavy oaken tables – one long and one short – formed a T which occupied the centre and ran almost the full length of the room. There was food on the tables: fresh baked bread, eggs, ham, sausages and coffee. Morgan had not stinted on the victuals.

"The two of you escaped together?" Lasseur asked, reaching out and pouring himself a mug of coffee. He looked at Hawkwood. Hawkwood nodded and Lasseur poured a second mug.

Rousseau nodded. "We behaved ourselves until they granted us parole and then we went for a walk one day and never went back. You?"

"We died," Lasseur said, grinning, and explained.

Denard looked at Lasseur in awe.

Hawkwood took a swig of coffee. It was very strong with a bitter aftertaste. It reminded him of the camp-fire brews he'd had to endure.

One by one, Rousseau introduced the men around the table. There were eight in total.

"Lieutenants Souville and Le Jeune from the *Bristol.* Leberte is from the *Buckingham.* Louis Beaudouin, there, made it off the *Brunswick* and Masson and Bonnefoux at the end, there, you may know or have heard of. They're from your ship, *Rapacious.*" Rousseau chuckled. "I wouldn't like to be in her commander's shoes, not with the number of prisoners he's had that have made a run for it."

"Lieutenant Hellard sends his regards," Lasseur said. "He wanted me to tell you that he's missing you and to hurry back."

While Lasseur joked, Hawkwood took another sip from his mug and mentally ticked off the names from the list that Ludd had given him. Including the two men who'd been murdered and disposed of on the hulk, the number tallied. With all Ludd's escapers accounted for, that was one mystery solved at least.

He wondered if Masson and Bonnefoux knew about the murdered men. There was nothing to be gained by telling them, he decided.

"How did you get off the ship?" Hawkwood asked the former *Rapacious* prisoners.

It was Masson, a thin-faced man with a prominent Adam's apple, who replied. "We hid out in a couple of empty water casks. What's so funny?" he asked, perplexed by the expression on Lasseur's face.

Lasseur shook his head.

"How did they cover your escape?"

"They'd have disrupted the count," Bonnefoux replied without hesitation. "You don't know?"

Hawkwood shook his head. "Our departure was . . . hurried. We never found out."

Bonnefoux grinned. His teeth were surprisingly clean and even.

Over a period of time, using augers filched during work-party duties and a saw fashioned from a barrel hoop, bevel-edged holes had been cut in the deck planking between the upper, gun and orlop decks. As prisoners were counted down into the lower decks, a designated number returned to the upper deck through the holes and rejoined the men waiting to be counted. When the count was complete, the holes were sealed to await the next departure.

So damned simple, Hawkwood thought. And as long as the prisoners kept their nerve and the guards didn't discover the trick, there was no reason it couldn't be used time and time again.

Hawkwood presumed Murat and the others had planned to conceal his and Lasseur's escape using the same method, after transferring the two substitute bodies from their bunks back into the side cabin to await the next burial party. Then he realized the ruse would only have worked if the militia guards failed to notice their absence for a while, which didn't seem a likely scenario, given Hellard's decision to transfer Hawkwood and Lasseur to the *Sampson*. In fact, the early discovery of their escape had prevented the miscounting ruse from being used, which was probably a good thing in the long run, lessening the risk of the holes in the decks being discovered, at least until after the next successful escape.

Souville and Le Jeune had employed almost the same method to escape from the *Bristol*. Using similar tools they had cut a hole in the side of the hulk close to the water-line, below the level of the sentry walkway. It had taken them four weeks to fashion and stain a square of timber to place over the hole to hide their handiwork and to cut through the hull. They'd jumped ship under the cover of darkness then made their way to shore and a pre-arranged rendezvous with one of Morgan's intermediaries.

"By the way," Rousseau said, addressing Lasseur. "If you want funny, ask Louis how he escaped."

Beaudouin looked about seventeen but was probably in his mid twenties. A thin moustache that left the impression it had been drawn on with a pencil was stuck precariously to his upper lip.

"How *did* you get away?" Lasseur asked.

Beaudouin grinned. "In a very fetching blue bonnet."

To Hawkwood and Lasseur's amazement, Beaudouin told them that the *Brunswick* had become one of Chatham's main attractions. For a small charge, local boatmen, in collusion with the hulk's commander, would row visitors out to the ship at regular intervals. They would be escorted up to the quarter-deck and from this vantage point, they could look upon the prisoners in the well deck below. Even more astonishing was the fact that many of the sightseers were female, which had given Beaudouin his idea.

Desperate to find ways of occupying time on board the hulk, the *Brunswick*'s prisoners had formed a theatre group, performing short plays, written by themselves, for the pleasure of their fellow inmates. The culmination of their efforts had been the staging of a swashbuckling melodrama involving a pirate and his lady.

"I played the lady," Beaudouin said, "because of my angelic looks. Of course, I didn't have the moustache at the time," he added seriously.

The acting troupe had made its own costumes. The manufacture of female attire, however, had proved difficult, so an appeal had gone out to the ladies of Chatham. Donations had arrived by the sackload. Thus Beaudouin had his disguise; all he'd needed was an opportunity.

Picking his moment on the day of a visit, Beaudouin had secreted himself close to a stairway and hatch leading to the quarterdeck, merging with the departing visitors, petticoat rustling, with a handkerchief to his face as if overcome by the smell of the ship and the misery he had just witnessed. The most nerve-racking moment had been fending off the advances of one of the militia guards, who'd mistaken Beaudouin's attempt to hide his face for coquettish flirting.

"I wouldn't have minded so much," Beaudouin said, with

a smile, "but the oaf had a face like a shovel." He turned to Leberte, a trim man with well-tended side whiskers and a flamboyant moustache that put Beaudouin's effort to shame. "Pierre – why don't you tell them how *you* did it?"

The others grinned.

Leberte's escape had been spectacular for several reasons. He had achieved his freedom from the *Buckingham* after watching the movement of the sentries on the outside gangway. Leberte had timed how long the sentry took to march the length of the gantry and how long his back was turned. His next task had been to "accidentally" drop a cabbage from the ship's rail and time its fall. Then he waited for high tide. When the sentry turned to retrace his steps along the walkway, Leberte made his dive for freedom.

It had been late afternoon and Leberte's plunge over the side of the forecastle had taken everyone by surprise, even his fellow prisoners. By the time the militia had recovered from the shock and collected their wits, Leberte had swum under the hull of the ship to the bow, where, using a breathing tube fashioned from a hollowed-out length of sheep bone he'd procured from one of the galley cooks under the pretence that he was making himself a bone flute, he had remained submerged until the search for his body had moved away from the hulk into the further reaches of the river. After which, at dusk, he had made his way ashore and into hiding.

"Tell them the best bit," Beaudouin grinned.

It hadn't been the cold water or sucking in air through the narrow tube that had taxed Leberte's resolve, it had been the awful knowledge that he'd taken shelter directly below the ship's heads.

Lasseur held up his hand and said hastily, "Thank you, my friend. There's no need to elaborate."

Leberte was a lieutenant in the 93rd Régiment d'Infanterie

de Ligne and the only other non seaman present. Unlike the British, the French Navy didn't have marines. That function was performed by regular infantry units acting under the auspices of the Ministère de la Marine. Leberte had been in charge of a unit on a frigate, the *Navarre,* when he'd been taken prisoner in a skirmish off Ushant.

He'd been on the run for two weeks prior to arriving at the Haunt, living in thickets and under hedges, stealing food from fields and orchards before taking shelter in a barn, where his presence had finally been discovered. A weary Leberte had thrown himself upon the mercy of the farmer. Fearful that a search of his property would reveal the two dozen tubs of brandy and three bales of tobacco hidden in his cellar, the farmer had run not to the authorities but to Ezekiel Morgan, who, true to his reputation as a businessman, had informed Leberte that the only obstacle confronting his safe return to France was the fee for his transport.

Fortunately, Leberte's wife's family had money. The transaction had been brokered through Fector's Bank in Dover with, Hawkwood assumed, the assistance of Morgan's tame accountant.

It was fortunate, Hawkwood thought, that Leberte had had the means to pay for his passage home. He wondered what the lieutenant's fate might have been had that not been the case.

Leberte shrugged philosophically when Hawkwood posed the question. "Then I would have had to make my own way, wouldn't I?" he said.

The other seven had been Morgan's guests for differing lengths of time. Rousseau and Denard had been at the Haunt the longest, nearly five weeks, which fitted in, Hawkwood calculated, with Ludd's own records. All of them had been given refuge by farmers in the area, though

Hawkwood and Lasseur were the only ones that had stayed with Jess Flynn.

As Hawkwood listened to the men's accounts, the extent of Morgan's reach became clear. With the exception of Leberte, who'd acted on his own initiative, all the other escapers from the hulks had had their route to freedom pre-arranged by prisoners' committee and Morgan's network of informers.

Rousseau and Denard, who had had the advantage of being ashore already, had engineered their flight following a direct approach by the landlord of their lodging house, further evidence of Morgan's sphere of influence.

"Why haven't you been moved on to the coast?" Hawkwood asked. He threw a look at Lasseur as he said this.

"Too dangerous." It was Denard who answered. "The British have been increasing their coastal patrols. We've been waiting for the right time." He shrugged. "Leastways, that's what they told us up until a couple of days ago."

"What do you mean?" Hawkwood asked.

Denard exchanged glances with the men around him. He turned back. "We were told our passage home had finally been arranged and that it was only a few days away, but there was something they wanted our help with first. When we asked our friend Morgan what sort of help, he laughed and told us he had something up his sleeve that would bring the colour back to our cheeks."

"He didn't tell you what it was?"

Denard shook his head. "Still, things could have been a lot worse. At least here we've been given food and shelter, so it's comfortable enough. Better than those bloody ships, I can tell you that."

"But it's not home," Souville said. "We're tired of waiting. We've all paid our fee. We just want to go home."

There was a collective nodding of heads.

"What about you and Captain Lasseur?" Rousseau asked.

"We think we're going to be offered the same proposal," Hawkwood said.

"And you don't know what it is either?"

And then the door opened and Morgan and Pepper walked in. Leberte said, sotto voce, "I think we may be about to find out."

The men looked on expectantly as Ezekiel Morgan strode briskly to the head of the table and viewed the room, Pepper at his shoulder.

Morgan spoke in French. "Good morning, gentlemen." He glanced towards Hawkwood. "I trust you've no objections, Captain Hooper? I know you have a command of the language, whereas some of your fellow travellers have no English. It will make it easier for all of us."

Morgan's accent was very good; acquired, Hawkwood presumed, from a lifetime's trading with the other side of the Channel. Looking at Pepper's face and the calm way he was surveying the room, Hawkwood suspected Morgan's lieutenant was just as fluent.

"Thank you, Captain." Morgan scanned the men seated at the table. "So, gentlemen, to business. I know that it hasn't been easy being separated from your loved ones and, though you've all shown great patience, you've been wondering about the delay in sending you home. My apologies for that. I think it's about time I explained myself, don't you?"

Morgan turned to Pepper and held out his hand. Pepper reached inside his coat and extracted a small bag. He handed it to Morgan.

"Thank you, Cephus."

Morgan hefted the bag in his hand. There was the unmistakable chink of loose coin. Morgan loosened the drawstring, turned the bag upside down and let the contents fall.

A shower of gold cascaded across the table top.

As Morgan tossed the bag aside, the men gasped and craned forward.

The coins were small, a little less than an inch in diameter. The ones that had landed face up carried the portrait of what looked like a Roman emperor complete with flowing hair and a crown of laurels. The moon face and the pendulous jowls, however, were not those of a Roman. The inscription that framed the head – GEORGIVS III DEI GRATIA – and the spade-shaped shield on the reverse side confirmed the bust's identity. Hawkwood knew immediately what he was looking at. He said nothing, presuming the others around the table did too.

"Gentlemen," Morgan said, "let me tell you about the guinea boats."

Lasseur's head came up sharply.

Morgan caught his eye. "You're familiar with the term, Captain Lasseur?"

Lasseur nodded. "I saw one once." He reached over, picked up one of the coins and studied it carefully. "It was off Grand Fort-Philippe. A galley; low in the water, moving very fast."

"Why don't you tell your compatriots and Captain Hooper what they're used for," Morgan said.

Lasseur turned the coin over in his hand. "They're given the name because smugglers use them to carry English guineas across the Sleeve to France."

Masson frowned. "What do we French need with English guineas?"

"It's not the guineas," Lasseur said, replacing the coin on the table. "It's the gold."

Masson's frown remained in place.

"The Emperor needs it to pay our troops," Lasseur said.

The room went quiet.

After a moment Denard said, "*Our* troops?"

Lasseur nodded.

Hawkwood said, "You're telling us the British smuggle English guineas across the Channel to pay *Bonaparte's* army?"

"I told you, it's the gold that matters. It just happens to come in the form of guineas."

"And they *pay* them in guineas?"

"Occasionally, I believe. Otherwise, they're melted down and re-minted."

Beaudouin turned to Leberte. "Were you ever paid in guineas, Pierre?"

"I can't even remember the last time I *got* paid," Leberte said. He stared at the coins with a wistful expression.

"What about you, Captain Hooper?"

Hawkwood shook his head.

Denard stared at Morgan. His expression mirrored the questions that were obviously racing through his mind.

Morgan nodded. "It's perfectly true, gentlemen, I assure you, and it's been going on for years. It's all part of the Trade."

"It doesn't make sense," Souville said, looking equally puzzled. "Why would the English do such a thing? Surely they realize they could be adding to the length of the war, which means more of their men will die." He stared at Morgan. "Do you really hate your country that much?"

Morgan gave a dismissive shrug. "I don't judge it in those terms, Lieutenant. It's not personal. It's purely a business arrangement."

Souville shook his head in wonderment. "Then it is a very strange business indeed."

First rule of commerce, Hawkwood thought, and was it any stranger than helping enemy combatants get back home so that they could rejoin the fight?

Morgan rewarded Souville with what could have been a sympathetic smile. "I can see how you would think that.

It would be interesting to put the same point to your Emperor."

"What do you mean?" Bonnefoux asked, his brow furrowing.

"Do you think it's only free traders who are running goods, my friend?"

Before Bonnefoux could reply, Morgan smiled thinly and said, "Because if you did, you'd be wrong."

"I don't understand," Bonnefoux said warily.

Morgan leant forward and fixed Bonnefoux with a piercing gaze. "What if I were to tell you that, while you've been locked away on that stinking hulk and while your comrades were lying dead on the field or being maimed by broadsides, English and French merchants have been doing business with each other and making money with the collusion and blessing of both our governments?"

Bonnefoux stared blankly back at him, as did everyone else.

"And I don't mean people like me, Captain. I'm not talking about free traders. I mean legitimate men of business."

"What are you saying?" It was Le Jeune who cut in.

Morgan straightened. His gaze took in all the seated men. "Let me ask you this: aside from defeating her armies on the field, what's the best way to bring an enemy to its knees?"

"Attack her trading routes," Lasseur's reply was instantaneous.

"Ha! Got it in one, Captain. And you should know, eh?" Morgan raised a hand and knotted his fist. "It's like laying siege to a fortress while poisoning the well. Do that and you'll squeeze your enemy dry. More than that; you'll stop them from generating income. Bonaparte knows our strength lies with our Royal Navy. He also knows that we maintain it with profits from our overseas trade. That's why he issued his decree forbidding France's allies from trading with us. It was his plan to bring us to our knees. Trouble is, we did for most of *his* navy at Trafalgar. We also stopped him getting his hands on the Danish fleet in Copenhagen, which is why he's had to rely on privateers like Captain Lasseur here. Worked for a while, too; your privateers were damned effective. But then our government decided to exchange fire with fire by issuing orders-in-council that all neutral ships bound for France must divert to British ports. The result was that both sides ended up suffering, which wasn't good because we both still had men at sea and on the battlefield and equipping them is expensive. Soldiers need muskets and musket balls and the navy needs ships and cannon. What's to be done?"

Morgan smiled knowingly. "Come on, gentlemen. Just because we're at war doesn't mean we can't be civilized. You didn't really think a thousand years of trade would end just because our generals are in a paddy, did you? Of course not; which is why our governments, in a gesture of mutual co-operation, agreed to issue special licences allowing some of *our* merchants to trade with some of *your* merchants, even though we're at war. It's been going on for the past three years. You send us grain and brandy and fine wines, and we send you wool, cotton and tin. While your friends have been fighting and dying, British and French merchants have been growing fat on the profits – and it's all been perfectly legal."

The room had fallen silent. The food lay forgotten and untouched.

Morgan spread his hands. "So, ask yourselves: who's the real villain here? At least I don't deny who I am or what I do. In fact, we free traders operate with Bonaparte's blessing as well. Why? Because he needs us, because he's after as many markets as possible for his goods, same as our merchants. That's why he's allowed our vessels free access to French ports. He knows free traders have the contacts and customers legitimate merchants can only dream of."

"And gold's the key?" Hawkwood said.

Morgan turned and jabbed a finger. "That's right, Captain Hooper. Gold *is* the key. It's not brandy or cotton that keeps the world turning, it's gold. The value of a country's gold reserves determines its wealth. You probably didn't know it, but back in '97 there was a heavy run on our banks. The government was so afraid the country was going to run out of gold it stopped all exports. Ordered the Bank of England to stop issuing it too. The Bank Restrictions Act, they called it; a fancy little title. Damned fools thought they could rely on paper money." Morgan shook his head. "But we all know what that's worth when there's a war on, don't we? Which is bad news when you've an army and a navy to fund.

"So, British merchants started settling their accounts in gold. But they couldn't export English gold, so they started buying in foreign. When that started to run out, they dipped into our reserves, and that sent the price up, which was when everything changed."

Morgan's gaze grew more intense as he warmed to his subject. "Y'see, it didn't take long for some bright bugger to realize that, if you buy gold in London with British bank notes and sell it for British bank notes on the Continent where gold fetches a better price, you're going to make money. And when we learned that Bonaparte needed gold to pay his armies, we couldn't believe our luck. With the help of our contacts in London, we started shipping him our English guineas. Who cares if they're going to the enemy, so long as we're making money?

"And it's been doubly good for us free traders because, as long as we keep him in guineas, Bonaparte'll keep his ports open for us so we can make him even more money by stocking up on his brandy and his silks and all manner of fancy goods. Everybody's happy." Morgan's face clouded. "Or at least we were, until the bastard Excise stuck their oar in."

Morgan, incensed, had forgotten his audience and had vented the last sentence in English.

"Oar?" Lasseur said, confused by the sudden switch.

"Only stole our bloody boats, didn't they?"

Morgan paused, realizing his slip. With a gesture of apology, he reverted to French. "Government orders; all galleys in the south-east to be seized and destroyed. Dover, Folkestone, Sandgate, Hythe – there isn't a town that hasn't been hit. They confiscated nearly twenty vessels at Deal. That's the second time the place has borne the brunt. I was there in '84 when Pitt sent the troops in. He wanted to teach the town a lesson on account of its involvement in the Trade. They set fire to its entire fleet. Burnt all the boats in one night."

Morgan shook his head in disdain. "And they wonder why Deal folk have a tendency for rebellion. You'd be rebellious, too, if you'd seen *your* livelihood going up in flames. By God, the government was keen enough to accept the help of Deal men to bring the Danish fleet back to England back in '08 and to use their galleys at Walcheren, and it doesn't object when we pass it word of what we've seen and heard as regards Boney's activities. But if some poor bloody foot soldier or fisherman tries to put food on his table by bringing in a few tubs, that's a different matter. And do you think there's mention of compensation for seizing and burning a man's boat? Like hell there is!"

Morgan picked up the coins and replaced them in the bag. Despite his display of anger, his movements were calm and unhurried.

When the last coin had been put away, he looked up and

sighed. When he spoke, his voice was steady. "I told you earlier it wasn't personal, it was business. That's not strictly true. Those were *my* galleys they seized. I use them because they're not subject to the whim of the breeze. They're swift and they're manoeuvrable and they don't need a lot of men to crew them. A good team can cross the Channel in a couple of hours. Not having the galleys increases the chances of the guinea runs being intercepted. And if I can't deliver, Bonaparte will close off his ports, which means I'll lose business. I've got customers, people who rely on me. I have responsibilities; investors, who won't take kindly to being short-changed. My reputation's at stake. *That* makes it personal." Morgan paused and then said, "Which is why you're here, gentlemen. To hell with those bastards in the government; with your help I'm going to teach them a lesson they'll never forget."

"How?" Lasseur asked.

"By giving them a taste of their own medicine. They've taken from me, so I'm going to take from them. They think they've stopped the gold runs. I'm going to prove them wrong. I'm going to get Bonaparte his gold."

Hawkwood said, "And you're going to do that, how . . . ?"

"I'm going to steal it."

"From the *government?*"

"Not exactly."

"Who then?"

Morgan smiled. "Wellington."

"*Lord* Wellington?" Hawkwood said cautiously.

Morgan tossed the bag of coin to Pepper, who caught it nimbly with his good hand. "You know of another one?"

Hawkwood ignored the riposte. "The last I heard, Wellington was still in Spain. How are you going to steal *his* gold?"

"Well, strictly speaking, it's the army's gold. It's to pay Old Nosey's troops."

"You want us to help you steal gold from the British Army?" Rousseau blinked behind his spectacles.

Hawkwood flicked a glance at the faces around the table. Everyone was looking equally stunned.

Finally, after several seconds' consideration, Souville enquired tentatively, "How much gold?"

Morgan placed his palms on the table and leant forward. "Five hundred thousand pounds' worth."

Beaudouin, his eyes as wide as saucers, was the first to break the silence. "What's that in francs?"

"About twelve million," Rousseau said, sitting back in his seat and polishing his spectacles with the hem of his shirt.

"God Almighty!" Leberte breathed.

Morgan surveyed the room. "I take it your interest has been piqued, gentlemen?"

You could say that, Hawkwood thought, his brain spinning.

"This gold," Lasseur said cautiously, "where is it?"

"At the moment, that's not important; it's where it's going to be in four days' time."

"And where's that?"

"Deal."

"*Deal?*" Lasseur stared at Morgan in disbelief.

"They've been using the place as a transit point for bullion for years." Morgan smiled wryly. "You've got to admit, it does have a certain irony."

"Where in Deal?" Le Jeune's tone was instantly suspicious.

"There's a castle," Lasseur said, looking at Morgan for confirmation.

"There is indeed, but that's not where they're storing it, Captain. That's the beauty."

Lasseur's features took on a dubious frown. "Where then?"

"The Port Admiral's residency."

"Why in the name of God would they be storing it there?"

"Because that's where they put all the bullion that goes through the town. Before the government bought the house, it belonged to a banker. It still has a strong room. All specie and bullion passing through Deal is kept there. It's either landed from a ship to be forwarded by escorted wagon to London or it's transported from the London banks to Deal for shipment abroad, usually to Spain to pay the army."

"And how do you plan to remove this gold? Knock on the front door and ask them to hand it over?" Lasseur looked sceptical.

"I was thinking of something a little more persuasive."

Hawkwood realized that no one had asked the pertinent question. It looked as if it was up to him.

"Why us? What about your own crew? You told me if there was one thing you weren't short of, it was men."

Morgan nodded. "That I did, Captain, and it's no word of a lie. But there's no harm in recruiting extra bodies, especially men who've proved they're not afraid of a challenge and who are willing to take risks to achieve their objective. In my book, you all fit the bill. You've endured hell on the prison ships and yet you've not been cowed by capture. You've escaped using ingenuity and lived to tell the tale. That proves to me you have the character. You're all experienced seamen and soldiers. That tells me you're used to discipline and can work as a unit. More importantly, you've no allegiance to King George, so I doubt you'll consider betraying our intention to the authorities. In short, gentlemen, my proposition is this: I'm offering you a chance to get your own back on the country that's treated you worse than rats in a cage. They say revenge is sweet. What do you say? Do you fancy a taste?"

Morgan's eyes flashed. "Think of the glory. Instead of returning home with your tails between your legs as prisoners captured on the field, you'll be going back as free men, laden with treasure. By God, gentlemen, you'll be given a heroes' welcome! When your Emperor sees what you've done for him, there's nothing you will want for!"

"And you're doing this because your boats have been confiscated?" Lasseur said, staring hard at Morgan.

"I'm doing it for two reasons, Captain. The first is payback for what they've stolen from me and from the men of Deal. As for the second; the way I see it, twelve million francs will buy me a lot of favours with your Emperor. He'll keep his ports open and I can carry on trading; hopefully build more galleys. The last thing I need is a breakdown in supply. I don't want to give the edge to my competitors."

"I didn't think you had any competitors," Hawkwood said.

Morgan gave Hawkwood a sharp look. "There's always someone who thinks they should be top dog. Right now, that's me. I intend to keep it that way. Look upon this as a special delivery. A gesture of good faith on my part."

"You mentioned an escort," Hawkwood said.

"Nothing we can't handle," Morgan said confidently.

"Perhaps you should let us be the judge of that," Lasseur said drily.

Morgan looked towards Pepper.

Pepper came out of his state of repose. "A small detachment of marines."

"Is that all?" Lasseur said. "You had me worried for a moment. I thought it was going to be difficult."

"How small?" Hawkwood asked.

"Shouldn't be more than thirty men. They won't be a problem, though."

"Why not?"

"Because they won't be watching the gold all the time."

"How so?"

It was Morgan who replied: "Because Admiralty House doesn't have the facilities to accommodate troops. It's too small and, in any case, it's a residence. While the gold is in the strong room, the guards will be quartered in the castle."

"I thought Deal had a barracks," Lasseur said.

"There are troops stationed in the town as well?" Le Jeune said quickly.

"A token force. There used to be two companies of volunteers, but they were disbanded. Plans to raise a militia never came to anything because the townsfolk raised a stink. The barracks are mostly used as a way station for transients. In any event, they're almost closer to Walmer than they are to Deal. There's a company of Bombardiers at the castle to man the guns. Other than –"

"Guns?" Hawkwood interjected. "You mean cannon?"

"Nine 36-pounders, but they're all facing seawards. They're not expecting an attack from the land."

"So no more troops?"

"Other than the ones in the castle, the nearest are a couple of miles to the north. There's a shore battery on the Sandwich Road, but they won't be a threat. They'll be kept occupied."

"What about those castle troops?" Le Jeune asked.

"They and the marines will be occupied. I've a diversion planned to keep them bottled up."

"How do you expect to get away?" Hawkwood asked.

"There'll be a ship lying off the beach, ready to transport us across the Channel."

"Right in front of those Bombardiers with their 36-pounders," Hawkwood pointed out.

Morgan shook his head. "They'll be too busy watching their backs, and even if they aren't, they won't see us."

"Why not?"

"We'll be carrying out the raid at night. The darkness will give us the cover we need. It will be easier to spread confusion, and we'll be able to take advantage of the tide."

"What about the weight?" Lasseur asked.

"Four tons, give or take. A couple of stout wagons, specially strengthened, will be sufficient."

"Still a devil to move, though." Lasseur pursed his lips as he considered the implications.

"We won't be moving it far. It's less than four hundred yards from the front door of the residency to the shore. It's a straight run with no obstacles. Even if we only manage to shift half the damned stuff, we'll still be in profit."

"How do you plan to get into the strong room?" Hawkwood asked.

"That won't be a problem."

Morgan did not expand on his statement. Evidently, he wasn't inclined to give away too much information at this stage.

He's baited the hook well, Hawkwood thought. He looked around at the flushed faces. Flattery had helped.

Rousseau took off his spectacles. There was a mischievous glint in his eyes. "And our commission; what did you have in mind for that?" He held Morgan's gaze. "Because you won't be *giving* the Emperor the gold, will you? Even though you haven't actually *paid* for it, you'll be selling it to him, the same as with the other deliveries you've made."

All heads turned towards the head of the table.

Morgan smiled. "I wondered how long it would take you."

Backs straightened as the significance of Morgan's response permeated the minds of the men gathered around the table.

Rousseau breathed on his lenses, polished them with his sleeve and slipped the spectacles back over his nose.

"What's the usual profit on a guinea run?" Masson asked, trying to appear nonchalant but failing comprehensively.

Morgan glanced towards Pepper, but his lieutenant's countenance remained as inscrutable as ever. Morgan turned back: "Ten per cent."

"In that case," Rousseau said, "let's not be greedy. Why don't we make it fifteen per cent of the final profit?"

"It's going to be all profit," Masson said. "Remember?"

"Sounds fair," Le Jeune said, fixing Morgan with a speculative expression.

Hawkwood tried to calculate the amounts in his head. Fifteen per cent of twelve million francs – nearer fourteen, if Morgan realized his usual advantageous exchange rate – was a fortune, whether in francs or sterling.

Morgan stared at Pepper. Again Pepper said nothing, but this time a look passed between them.

Morgan nodded slowly. "Very well; fifteen it is."

A sequence of widening grins ran around the table.

"So, gentlemen, that's settled. Now, are you with me?"

Hawkwood looked round the room. There wasn't a man present who didn't look like the cat about to swallow the cream, except Pepper, of course. Did anything disturb that grey-bearded countenance?

Le Jeune was the first to voice his response. He nodded and laughed. "I'm up for it, by God!"

"Me, too!" Bonnefoux said eagerly. "If it means I can get my own back on those bastards!"

Morgan's eyes swept the room. "What about the rest of you?"

"Damned right, we're with you!" Masson clapped Souville on the shoulder. "Wouldn't miss it, would we, lads?"

Hawkwood wondered why Morgan bothered to ask the question, for the light of greed in their faces should have been enough to persuade him he already had them in the palm of his hand. Any lingering resentment caused by the delay in returning home had been eclipsed the moment the gold coins had hit the table top. Hawkwood caught Lasseur's eye. The privateer lifted an eyebrow in silent enquiry.

"Captain Lasseur," Morgan said amiably. "We've not heard from you."

Lasseur broke eye contact with Hawkwood and turned. "You put your case very well, my friend. I'm almost persuaded." The privateer smiled. It was the first time he'd shown any spark of humour since leaving the widow's. "But for a twenty per cent share I could be convinced beyond all doubt."

Pepper's head swivelled.

The chatter ceased.

Morgan stared at Lasseur. His expression was impenetrable.

The world revolved slowly.

Then Morgan nodded. "Agreed." He turned to Hawkwood. "Looks like you're the only one left, Captain Hooper. Are you in or out?"

This is bloody madness, Hawkwood thought. This went way beyond anything foreseen by Ludd or James Read. He looked at Lasseur. The privateer winked back at him.

Christ, Hawkwood thought.

Brain spinning, he turned to Morgan and grinned.

"Wouldn't miss it. I'm in."

17

Hawkwood and Lasseur were in the cloisters.

Morgan and Pepper had departed the refectory leaving the room abuzz with excitement. Any despondency at the lack of home comforts had evaporated as quickly as the early morning haze. Uppermost in everyone's mind was the final instalment of Morgan's plan, which he had promised would soon be forthcoming.

Hawkwood had tried to imagine what £500,000 would look like accumulated in one place and had given up. The idea of four tons of bullion heaped on to the back of a wagon – most of which, according to Morgan, would probably be in ingots – hadn't proved any easier to digest. His head was spinning with the enormity of it. He needed to think. After a suitable period of listening to the others planning their futures – which seemed to consist entirely of country estates, fine wines and, for the ones who weren't married, and even for a couple who were, a supply of pliant women – he had left the refectory and walked into the open air.

Footsteps sounded behind him and he cursed under his breath.

"You have to admit," Lasseur murmured, "it's a devil of a proposition."

"There'll be a price to pay," Hawkwood said.

"Undoubtedly. Though I notice it didn't prevent *you* from accepting our host's offer," Lasseur commented wryly. He patted his pockets, as if looking for the last of his cheroots.

"Four tons of gold's a fearsome incentive," Hawkwood said.

"You think it's possible?" Lasseur asked. His hands gave up their search.

"Anything's possible," Hawkwood said and then thought, *Well, maybe not anything,* because alerting the authorities was now his first priority and so far he hadn't come up with a single feasible idea on how to do that. In the meantime, he reasoned, there was more chance of his foiling Morgan's insane plan by remaining inside the tent pissing out than outside the tent pissing in.

"Our host seems to have addressed all the likely hindrances."

"He thinks he has."

"You don't agree with his strategy?"

"He was a little short on specifics. I don't have enough information to hand to make a judgement."

Lasseur looked sceptical.

"I'm just weighing the odds," Hawkwood said. "The moment you put a plan into action, what's the first thing that usually goes wrong?"

Lasseur thought about it. The corners of his mouth lifted. "The rest of the plan. So?"

Hawkwood nodded. "So remember what Tom Gadd told us? If we ever shook hands with Morgan we were to count our fingers afterwards."

"In other words, we watch our backs."

"And everything else," Hawkwood said.

"The others don't seem to share our concerns," Lasseur pointed out.

"They haven't had the benefit of Tom Gadd's opinion or

the Widow Flynn's experience of dealing with the man. All they see is the gold at the end of the rainbow and the thanks of a grateful Emperor."

"Some might think that was sufficient," Lasseur said.

"Not me," Hawkwood said. "But, as you once pointed out, I'm a suspicious bastard. I've been around long enough to know that you don't get anything for nothing."

Morgan's warning about keeping within the grounds and the presence of pickets had suddenly taken on a new meaning. Now that Morgan had revealed his grand plan, it was clear those precautions were intended not only to keep unwanted visitors at bay, but to ensure that information did not escape from the compound. It occurred to Hawkwood that one form of prison had been replaced with another. Admittedly, as Denard had stated, there was a deal more comfort, but it was still a gaol of sorts. And one from which Hawkwood had to find a way out.

"You seem well informed about Deal," he said to Lasseur.

The privateer laughed. "Never walked the streets, but British merchantmen use the Downs as an anchorage and there are rich pickings along that stretch of coast for a crew with enough nerve and a fast ship."

"And the *Scorpion*'s a fast ship," Hawkwood said.

"That she is, and the fortress makes a good landmark for navigation. Mind you, I've felt the breeze from those thirty-six-pounders a few times, too. Had my run-ins with the locals as well. They're fine seamen. There's more than one privateer that's been chased away from its target by a pack of sharp-sighted Deal boatmen."

"They're well armed?"

"Pistols and swords, usually, but their boats are . . . were . . . so damned fast. They'd be on you and under your guns before you'd have a chance to disengage. They've no shortage of courage, I'll give them that."

"That's what makes them such good free traders," Hawkwood said. "It'll be a family business for most, I expect, and there's no greater bond than family."

Save a man's regiment, where comrades in arms were often as close as brothers; closer, sometimes, Hawkwood thought, remembering.

"Stealing a wagonload of gold isn't the same as hefting two dozen tubs of brandy up a beach," Lasseur pointed out.

"No, it isn't," Hawkwood agreed. "But it's a bloody sight more profitable."

"Damned right!" Lasseur said, his eyes lighting up. "I've taken some prizes in my time, but nothing like this. By God, Matthew, say what you like about Morgan, he doesn't do things by halves!"

Lasseur was right about that, Hawkwood conceded. It sounded as though the privateer was warming to the man. But then, why wouldn't he be? Morgan was providing him with a roof over his head, victuals and a passage home, not to mention a share of the profit from a strike against a hated enemy, something at which Lasseur excelled anyway. From Lasseur's point of view, and indeed from that of Masson and Le Jeune and the rest of them, it was their sworn duty to harass and inflict damage on the enemies of France. For them, Morgan's mission was a golden opportunity.

Literally.

Watching the thrill of the chase expand across Lasseur's face and hearing the excitement in his voice, Hawkwood knew a primeval change was taking place. He was reminded of a wolf scenting blood and knew that Lasseur was reverting from prisoner back to privateer, his true character. Hawkwood recalled the story of the scorpion that asked the frog to carry him across a stream, promising the frog it would not be stung. And yet when they were halfway across, the scorpion reneged on its promise and stung the frog to death, thus precipitating its own demise. When the frog had asked why, the scorpion replied, "Because I'm a scorpion. It's my nature."

Lasseur's nature was to sail the oceans in search of prey, using every means at his disposal. Perhaps the name of his ship was just a coincidence, Hawkwood thought. With a growing sense of disquiet, he realized that once again Lasseur had become his enemy.

Which meant he was on his own.

He saw that Lasseur was looking over his shoulder.

Hawkwood tensed as he turned. It was the groom, Thaddeus.

The groom jerked a thumb in the direction of the main house.

"Mr Morgan wants to see you," he said.

Morgan was seated at his desk when Hawkwood and Lasseur entered the room. He was dressed as he had been during his morning walk, in dark breeches and jacket and a navy waistcoat. Hawkwood looked for the two mastiffs and was relieved to see they were nowhere in sight. The blackthorn stick, however, was propped against the side of the desk.

Morgan nodded at the groom, who backed away and closed the door behind him. Pepper, who was standing behind Morgan, looking out of the window, turned, his good arm held behind his back.

Morgan moved out from the desk and walked to a circular table upon which stood a bottle and four glass goblets. "Drink, gentlemen?" He did not wait for a reply but reached for the bottle.

"I think this will be to Captain Lasseur's liking. It's from the Bertin vineyard. I'm told it's Emperor Bonaparte's favourite tipple." He glanced towards his lieutenant. "Cephus?"

Pepper stalked over. Morgan passed out the drinks and raised his glass. "Here's to profit!"

The four men drank. Hawkwood took stock of the room. There was a marked lack of frills, making it undeniably masculine in style. Apart from a comfortable-looking settee facing the fireplace, it was more of an office than a sitting room. On first impression, it reminded Hawkwood a little of Hellard's quarters back on *Rapacious*. On closer inspection, however, he saw that the furnishings, although plain, were of a superior quality. And in contrast to Hellard's cabin, there were a clutch of paintings on the walls, mostly equine in character. He wondered if Morgan had a family. With the goblet in his hand, the smuggler looked every inch the prosperous gentleman farmer, while Pepper, dressed in grey, had the veneer of an efficient, albeit intimidating, estate manager.

Morgan addressed Lasseur. "You slept well, Captain? Captain Hooper tells me that new surroundings make it hard for him to settle."

"Not me," Lasseur said. "Though I'm more used to beds that sway."

"Ah, of course. And they have hammocks on the hulks, don't they? By the way, did I mention that you and Cephus here have something in common? Cephus was at sea, too, before we joined forces. Weren't you, old friend?"

Lasseur regarded Pepper with renewed interest. "You were in the navy, Mr Pepper?"

"It was a long time ago," Pepper said.

There was no attempt to elaborate. Lasseur glanced at the remains of Pepper's left arm but made no comment. Whether it was out of politeness or in deference to Pepper's demeanour, Hawkwood couldn't tell.

"That was before he found a more lucrative line of work," Morgan added.

"The Trade?" Lasseur said.

"That's right." Morgan smiled. "The wine's to your liking, Captain?"

"I'm happy to report that His Majesty has excellent taste," Lasseur said.

"And what's the point of being in the business if you can't sample the goods, eh?" Morgan took a sip from his glass and compressed his lips in appreciation. "Find a seat. Make yourselves comfortable."

Hawkwood took a chair. Lasseur moved to the settee.

Morgan put down his glass and held open a veneered wooden box. "Manila?"

Lasseur, with an exclamation of pleasure, helped himself to a cheroot. He held the roll of tightly wrapped tobacco leaf under his nose and sniffed appreciatively.

Hawkwood declined. Morgan took a cheroot for himself and offered the box to Pepper, who shook his head.

This is all very civilized, Hawkwood thought warily, and wondered what it was leading up to. Morgan didn't seem the sort to indulge in social chitchat, and Pepper looked as if he'd rather chew his good arm off than engage in conversation, polite or otherwise.

As Lasseur lit up and drew on his cheroot, Morgan said, "That was an interesting stroke you pulled back there, Captain."

Lasseur leant back on the cushions and expelled smoke. "But fair, I think, considering the return, especially when you're expecting men to risk their lives." Lasseur raised his goblet, flicking a glance towards Hawkwood as he took a sip. "In any case, I think you would have gone to twenty-five."

Morgan's eyes widened. Then the wrinkles at the corners of his eyes deepened as he jabbed his unlit cheroot towards Lasseur's face. "I might have, at that." He turned to Hawkwood. "What about you, Captain Hooper? You haven't had much to say for yourself so far. Something tells me there's more going on in here than you let on." Morgan tapped the side of his head. "I'll wager those scars of yours could tell some tales. Am I right?"

"They just mean I was slow getting out of the way," Hawkwood said. "And all soldiers carry scars."

He took a sip of wine. Lasseur was right. The taste was exceptional.

"That's true, but some run deeper than others, eh?" Morgan said.

Hawkwood did not reply and watched as a shadow moved across Morgan's face.

"We have a situation, gentlemen."

"Situation?" Hawkwood said guardedly.

Morgan paused to light his cheroot. Hawkwood suspected it was to give him time to think.

When the leaf was glowing to his satisfaction, Morgan continued. "We've been having some problems with the Revenue. An occupational hazard, I know, but there's a particular Riding Officer who's been sniffing at our heels. He's developing into something of a nuisance."

Hawkwood wondered how Morgan was expecting them to respond. It didn't seem the moment for platitudes. He took another sip of wine, and waited. Lasseur was obviously of the same mind. The privateer expelled a thin plume of tobacco smoke and made a play of looking unconcerned while picking a shred of leaf from his bottom lip.

Morgan continued. "He was only appointed a few months back and he's been trying to make a name for himself ever since. Probably thinks we haven't been taking inventory, but we have. Thing is, he's not from round here. Usually, the Revenue recruits from the local area. It's not like the militia: that lot reckon there's less chance of someone perverting the course of justice if there are no family connections to the immediate district. That's why Kent lads have been freezing their balls off in Dumfries, poor sods, and Dungeness had to put up with a company from Flintshire."

Morgan took a pull on his cheroot before removing it from his lips and rolling it between his fingers. He studied the end and looked up.

"As I was saying, he was brought in from another county. His name's Jilks, by the way, and he's proving rather more . . . conscientious than we were led to expect."

"I take it you've tried inducements?" Hawkwood said.

Morgan nodded. "They haven't worked. Prides himself on keeping to the straight and narrow. Anyway, over the last month or so, a number of our runs have been intercepted. There was a landing at Sandwich a couple of weeks back; we lost a hundred kegs and two men wounded. We've discovered he was behind the Warden ambush. The last thing we need is for him to find out about the Deal job and pass the word. That happens and we're all buggered. That means you, me, Bonaparte's ability to pay his troops, future landings – the whole damned trade. We can't risk that." Morgan paused. "We need to neuter the son of a bitch before it's too late."

"Neuter?" Lasseur said.

Hawkwood felt an uncomfortable prickling sensation worm its way down his spine.

"Remove," Morgan said, taking a long draw on his cheroot and letting the smoke fill his lungs.

The word hung ominously in the air.

"You want him dead," Lasseur said flatly.

"That would be the preferred option."

Lasseur sat up slowly as the light dawned.

The pins and needles invading Hawkwood's spine suddenly felt more like chips of ice.

There'll be a price to pay.

"And you want *us* to take care of it," Hawkwood said.

Morgan jabbed towards Hawkwood with the now glowing tip of his cheroot. "You, sir, are as perceptive as your friend here." He turned to Pepper. "Didn't I say they'd be a pair to be reckoned with?"

Lasseur lowered his glass. "Why us?"

Morgan put his head on one side. "Delivering the gold to Bonaparte is my gesture of good faith. This would be yours."

"I don't follow," Lasseur said. Unseen by Morgan, he threw Hawkwood another sideways glance.

"No?" Morgan sucked on his cheroot stem, making a play of savouring the taste. "Well, y'see, back in the refectory, when I was outlining my little plan, I got it into my head that somehow you and Captain Hooper weren't warming to the notion quite as quickly as the others. Which is a pity, because Cephus and I took the two of you for a cut above the rest and we'd hate to think we might have made a mistake in judgement.

"That's not to say it hasn't happened before, mind. You know how it is; you hold out the hand of friendship to someone, only to find they don't quite measure up to expectations. Creates all sorts of regrets and recriminations. Bottom line is, Cephus and I need to know who we can depend on. Which is why I don't think it's unreasonable to ask for proof of your commitment, do you?"

"By asking us to kill a Revenue man?"

"To prove you're fully on board." Morgan smiled engagingly. "I mean, it's not as though the pair of you are choirboys, is it? There's the matter of that incident back on the hulk. How many were killed? Five, wasn't it? That's a very impressive total. One might even say *excessive*. That drew our attention right away, didn't it, Cephus?"

"Certainly did," Pepper said. It was the first time Morgan's lieutenant had employed emphasis.

"All we're asking is that you put your expertise to good use," Morgan said.

"You take us for assassins?" Lasseur said.

Morgan shook his head. "The thought never entered my head. But you *are* still at war, aren't you? Which means Riding Officer Jilks *is* the enemy and, given what's at stake, I'd say that makes him as much a threat as a Royal Navy frigate or a regiment of dragoons. Wouldn't you?"

"The man's got a point," Hawkwood said.

"And there's nothing to connect him with either you or Captain Hooper," Morgan said. "Complete the job and in a few days you'll be on your way home, considerably richer."

"You're implying that we have an obligation?" Lasseur said.

"I'm suggesting you're both supremely practical men who are about to embark on a vital mission. What's the life of one man when weighed against the future of France?"

"And your investments." Lasseur played with the stem of his glass. "Let's not forget those."

"Without which your Emperor will be considerably poorer and your army less well equipped." If Morgan felt any rancour at Lasseur's reply, he gave no sign. "It's your duty to turn that fortune around, Captain."

Lasseur looked at Hawkwood.

"He's right, my friend," Hawkwood sighed. "If we were on the *Scorpion* and we spied a fat merchantman lying at anchor off the Downs, we wouldn't be having this conversation. We'd be sanding the decks and running out the guns and Devil take the hindmost. I say if this Jilks is the only thing standing between me and a Goddamned fortune, the bastard's fair game." Hawkwood lifted his glass. "And you know it."

He turned to Morgan. "You want him taken care of? Consider it done."

* * *

Chief Magistrate James Read stood by his window, looking down on to the scene below. Bow Street echoed with the sounds of a city going about its daily toil. The clatter of hooves mingled with the rumble of carriage wheels while the wavering cries of the street vendors rose into the air in a discordant chorus of strangulated vowels.

Read's eyes were drawn to the opposite side of the road and the exterior of the Brown Bear public house. A small boy, one of the countless street urchins that roamed the area, had just attempted to fleece a passing pedestrian of his pocket watch and was being beaten roundly about the head by his intended victim. The boy was struggling like a minnow on a hook. Read couldn't help but admire the young pick-pocket's nerve, plying his trade only strides from the entrance to the Public Office. He shook his head despairingly as the boy kicked his aggressor in the shins and ran off through the crowds. It took only a matter of yards before he had vanished from view. It was interesting, Read thought, that no one from downstairs had seen the altercation and thought to intervene. He would have to make enquiries. Perhaps a constable stationed permanently by the front entrance would rectify the situation.

Read made a mental note and returned to his desk. As he sat down, there was a knock at the door. It opened and Ezra Twigg entered.

"A communication from the Admiralty, sir. Just delivered by courier. I've told him to wait in case there's a reply."

"Thank you, Mr Twigg."

Read slit open the seal while Twigg hovered. His eyes skipped unerringly to the signature at the bottom of the page. The message was from Ludd.

Ezra Twigg watched as the magistrate's brow darkened.

"I take it there's been no word, sir?" Twigg said.

Read did not reply. He laid the letter on his desk and said

in a subdued tone, "You may tell the courier he can go. There is no reply."

Twigg nodded and headed for the door. He hesitated and turned. "Is everything in order, sir?"

Read looked at his clerk. "You were correct in your assumption, Mr Twigg. Captain Ludd informs me that there has been no word from Officer Hawkwood since he escaped from his confinement. Nor has there been any word *of* him."

Twigg blinked behind his spectacles as he regarded the Chief Magistrate's solemn expression. The clerk had worked for James Read long enough to know that look. Read's appearance, from the swept-back silver hair and aquiline face to his dark conservative dress, was everything one might expect from a senior public servant. It led those who did not know him to suppose he was an official who performed his duties with a puritanical zeal and a man who had no personal regard for anyone who did not adhere to his own exacting standards. Ezra Twigg knew differently.

Behind the prim façade there resided a man who was fully and often painfully aware of the responsibilities he carried on his slim and elegantly clad shoulders. Read was indeed dedicated to his job. He was also dedicated to the men who worked for him. The Chief Magistrate knew the dangers facing his officers. The Runners were an elite band and few in number. They were thinly stretched and, by the nature of their assignments around the country, often placed in harm's way. Read knew them to be highly competent, resourceful and sometimes ruthless. It wasn't unusual for an officer to remain out of contact for a time. But that didn't stop Read from feeling concern for their welfare or their safety.

And Read's pensive look told Ezra Twigg all he needed to know.

The Chief Magistrate was worried.

"Is there anything I can do for you, sir?"

Read looked up. His face remained serious and thoughtful.

"Yes, Mr Twigg, there is. I'd be obliged if you could deliver a message for me."

"Very good, sir." Twigg waited expectantly. After a pause, he said, "And to whom am I delivering this message, sir?"

Read told him.

Twigg's eyebrows rose. "Do you think he'll come?"

Read nodded. "He'll come."

"I'll leave right away." Twigg made for the door.

"Mr Twigg?"

The clerk turned. "Your Honour?"

"Please tread carefully," Read said.

Twigg permitted himself a small smile. "I always do, sir."

Read nodded. The clerk closed the door behind him. Read looked at the clock in the corner of the room. He took a watch from his pocket and consulted the dial. Walking to the clock he reached up and moved the minute hand to a quarter past the hour.

Perhaps it was an omen, he thought. Time *was* ticking away.

In the outer office, Ezra Twigg sent the waiting courier on his way and reached for his hat.

He wasn't sure if he should offer a prayer for his safe return before he left.

For he was, after all, about to pay a visit to the Holy Land.

The Hanged Man public house lay in a dark alleyway behind Buckbridge Street. It was not the sort of establishment frequented by gentlemen or ladies of a genteel disposition. It catered mostly for those who lived on the edges of conventional society, the borderland between the criminal and the lawful. Gamblers, tricksters, forgers and debtors; opportunists, seducers, procurers and paramours all frequented its dim-lit, beer-steeped, smoke-filled interior.

At the back of the main room on the first floor, four men wreathed in tobacco fumes were playing dominoes. The men's faces were serious as they concentrated on the game before them. Their moves were brisk and confident. There was little banter. The position of the counters in front of each player – face down, in two rows of three – and the pile of coins by each participant's elbow testified to the spirit in which the game was being played.

One man seemed to be ahead in his winnings. He was stocky, with a craggy face and short, pewter-coloured hair. His back was to the wall. When he was not concentrating on his counters, his eyes watched the room. There was no fear in his gaze but there was caution. A glass of brandy stood by his right arm. Every so often he would raise the glass to his lips and take a sip before laying his counters down. Despite his watchfulness, he gave the impression of a man at ease with himself, his insalubrious surroundings and with the company he was keeping.

Occasionally, his gaze would pass over a solitary male customer seated at a table at the top of the stairway leading down to the ground floor. The man sat with his back to the panelled wall. He was young, with a strong face and dark, intelligent eyes. Whenever he raised his drink to his lips, he performed the movement with such economy it suggested his partaking of the spirit was purely a means of keeping his hand and arm occupied rather than a desire to savour the contents of the glass. The moment a customer ascended from the pub's lower floor, he would place his drink carefully on the table before him, leaving his hands free. Sometimes, he caught the grey-haired man's glance, but mostly he kept his eye on the stairway. The young man's name was Micah.

A new round commenced. Counters were laid down in quick succession, interspersed with a rap of knuckles whenever a player was unable to follow on. Table stakes notwithstanding, the atmosphere was friendly and relaxed.

With one domino left in his hand and with a line of counters snaking unevenly across the table top, the pewter-haired man undertook his reconnaissance, scanning the departures and arrivals, faces unknown and familiar, assessing whether they were likely to be friend or foe.

His eyes moved to the table by the stairs and he stiffened imperceptibly. Micah was no longer alone. Standing next to his table was a small, bow-legged, bespectacled man dressed in a black coat and breeches and wearing a faded three-cornered hat. A powdered wig which had seen better days poked from beneath the hat's folded brim. The older man was talking. Micah was listening. Finally, Micah nodded, turned and looked towards the domino table.

The pewter-haired man laid down his final counter and collected his winnings. Pushing his chair back, he stood up and swept the pile of coins into his palm and then into his pocket.

"Thanks for the game, boys. Deal me out of the next one – business calls." Ignoring the protests of the other players, he stepped away from the table and headed for the stairs.

Ezra Twigg watched him approach.

As the pewter-haired man reached his table, Micah rose to his feet.

"Well now, Mr Twigg –" Nathaniel Jago gazed down at the clerk and sighed heavily – "your being here can only mean one thing. What's the daft beggar gone and done now?"

The four riders crested the rise and urged their mounts towards the edge of the wood. Moonlight dappled the men's features and the foliage that concealed their passing. Their attention was focused on the outline of a low-roofed cottage which lay some three hundred yards away, set back from the road. The rest of the village lay beyond it, perhaps a dozen houses in all. Another one hundred paces separated the cottage from its nearest neighbour.

"Looks quiet," McTurk murmured. The observation made, the Irishman hawked up a gobbet of phlegm and spat the result into the bushes.

Lasseur wrinkled his nose in disgust.

"See anything?" McTurk whispered to the horseman on his left.

The horseman, whose name was Croker, shook his head and growled, "Coast's clear, I reckon."

McTurk turned to Hawkwood. "You set?"

"We're wasting time," Hawkwood said. "Let's get on with it."

They coaxed their horses out of the wood and back on to the path, riding two abreast, McTurk and Croker leading the way.

A soft breeze caressed Hawkwood's cheek. It brought with it the scent of the sea, which lay less than a mile distant. He thought he could hear waves lapping against shingle, but dismissed it as his imagination, though when he looked to his right, he could see the occasional shimmer of moon on water through gaps in the trees.

McTurk and Croker did not speak and Lasseur was silent beside him. Progress was marked by the steady perambulation of the horses and the faint gleam of candlelight from the houses ahead of them.

It had been a while since Hawkwood had ridden. The last time had been in Spain, when he'd fought alongside the *guerrilleros* in hit-and-run raids against the French. He had never considered himself to be anything other than an average horseman, with an ambivalent attitude to the animal as a species. Yet when he'd lifted himself into the saddle in Morgan's stable yard and thrust his boots into the stirrups, it was as if the years had rolled away.

Lasseur looked perfectly at home, handling the reins as if he had been born to it, which he probably had, Hawkwood concluded. He recalled Lasseur telling him how his wife had died and Hawkwood suspected that the privateer, despite his chosen profession, was an accomplished rider and had probably accompanied his late wife on early morning gallops whenever he was home. He knew that Lasseur's unease was due to the morality of their task and not the fear of falling off and breaking his neck or being trampled to death by flying hooves.

A night bird called out from the darkness and the horses' ears pricked up. Hawkwood laid a calming hand on his mount's neck and felt the muscles relax beneath the smooth brown pelt. They were some two hundred yards from the house when Lasseur leaned over and whispered in French, "I have no stomach for this, my friend."

"And I told you that I'd take care of it," Hawkwood said, in the same language.

Lasseur sat back in his saddle and fell silent, his face thoughtful.

Hawkwood didn't think the men ahead spoke French, but he watched them for any sign of reaction. There weren't any, though it could have been because they were good actors.

"I'm sending two of my best scouts with you," Morgan had told Hawkwood. "You say you want Captain Lasseur at your shoulder, but Pat and Jack know the paths and they'll identify Jilks. After that, it's down to you. If you do run into trouble, which I doubt you will, they're good men to have at your side in a skirmish."

Hawkwood had been expecting one man to accompany them. Morgan's announcement that there was to be a second was unwelcome news, as was Morgan's next proviso.

"It's possible Jilks may have a woman with him. I don't wage war on women. She's not to be harmed."

"Wife?"

Morgan had shrugged. "Housekeeper. Does it matter? She's not to be touched. I have your word on that?"

"I don't wage war on women either," Hawkwood said, and thought about the murderess, Catherine de Varesne, and how he had put a bullet into her throat on a London quayside.

They halted. The cottage was less than one hundred paces away. Somewhere in the darkness a dog barked and Hawkwood soothed his mount once more. At McTurk's signal, they guided the horses off the path into the shelter of a spinney where they dismounted.

Hawkwood looked towards the cottage. There was no movement. A light was showing in one of the downstairs windows. He drew the pistol from his belt and turned to McTurk. "We go together. Croker stays here with Captain Lasseur to guard the horses and keep watch."

McTurk didn't look too happy at being on the receiving end of an order. His eyes narrowed as he considered his response. Finally, judging that Hawkwood's command made sense, he glanced towards Croker and nodded. He was an inch or two shorter than Hawkwood; sinewy but strong, with dark Celtic features. His own pistol sat in a holster secured to a bandolier across his chest. A stout wooden club was thrust in his belt. He looked, Hawkwood thought, agile and tenacious.

In contrast, Croker was stocky with large hands and a hard face that would not have looked out of place on the neck and body of a pugilist.

Hawkwood spoke to Lasseur in French. "Keep an eye out and watch your back."

"You, too," Lasseur said, his face grim.

Hawkwood jerked his head at McTurk and switched to English. "Let's go."

Hawkwood took the lead. Using the spinney as cover, they moved in a line towards the trees at the back of the cottage. There was a small outbuilding, which Hawkwood assumed was a stable. He could smell wood smoke and for a second he was reminded of his first sighting of Jess Flynn's farm. A twig cracked behind him and he stopped and stood still. When he looked around he found that McTurk had drawn his pistol.

The light was coming from a side window. It guttered as Hawkwood and McTurk moved forward and Hawkwood had a vague image of a shadow passing between the flame and the glass, and then the light dimmed further as a curtain was drawn across, obscuring the view within.

As they drew closer to the back door, McTurk reached inside his waistcoat. When his hand emerged it was holding two cloth hoods. He held one out to Hawkwood and pulled the other one over his head. Even close to, the painted skull was frightening enough to make the heart lurch. Hawkwood steeled himself and put the hood on. The sense of claustrophobia as he lowered it over his head was immediate, as was the familiar tightening of his throat muscles. Then his eyes found the holes denoting the skull's eye sockets and, as his vision was restored, the moment of discomfort passed. He adjusted the material over his face and heard the brittle ratchet sound as McTurk cocked the hammer of his pistol.

Hawkwood stood aside as McTurk placed his hand on the door latch. McTurk looked at him and Hawkwood nodded. McTurk raised his boot, lifted the latch and kicked.

The door flew back with a crash. Hawkwood and McTurk,

pistols held high, stepped through together, McTurk to Hawkwood's right.

The kitchen was not large. There was a hearth and a cooking range, with pots and pans and cooking utensils hanging from hooks. A table occupied the centre of the floor. A man was seated at the table in shirt and breeches, his waistcoat unbuttoned. A fork was poised halfway to his lips. A uniform jacket hung over the back of his chair. He stared at his hooded visitors, his jaw dropping in shock and the blood draining from his face at the sight of the guns. His eyes moved briefly to the top of a sideboard upon which lay two pistols.

"No," McTurk warned, his pistol pointing unerringly at the seated man's head. "Don't."

McTurk nodded at Hawkwood and released the hammer of his pistol. "He's all yours."

McTurk realized his mistake in the quarter second it took for Hawkwood to slam his pistol barrel against the front of McTurk's skull; by which time it was far too late. McTurk went down as if pole-axed, the unfired pistol slipping from his fingers. The seated man was out of his chair; the fork dropping with a clatter, as Hawkwood swept his pistol round, pulling back the hammer as he did so. "Sit down."

Shaking, with the muzzle of Hawkwood's pistol pointed at his forehead, the man at the table retook his seat.

"Sit on your hands," Hawkwood said. "Palms down."

The man did as he was told. His eyes remained wide open. He had a long, lined face, with close-cut fair hair and well-tended sideburns that reached almost to his jawline. Hawkwood estimated he'd probably aged ten years in the last three seconds.

Hawkwood reached up and removed his hood. He knew there wasn't much time.

The seated man's eyes widened further.

"You *are* Riding Officer Henry Jilks?" Hawkwood said.

The seated man nodded mutely. His eyes moved from Hawkwood to the body on the floor. He looked utterly bewildered. Keeping his pistol trained on Jilks's chest, Hawkwood stuffed the hood inside his jacket, then retrieved McTurk's weapon.

"Don't look at him," Hawkwood said. "Look at me. Don't speak; just listen."

Jilks's head lifted.

"I mean you no harm. My name is Matthew Hawkwood. I'm a special constable. I work for Chief Magistrate James Read of the Bow Street Public Office in London."

Hawkwood watched the astonishment blossom across Jilks's face.

"There was a plot to kill you tonight. Ezekiel Morgan is the man behind it. He doesn't like the way you've been interfering in his business. The one on the floor is Patrick McTurk. He's one of Morgan's lieutenants. There's another man close by, so we don't have much time."

At the mention of McTurk and Morgan, Jilks's face lost more colour.

"Pay attention," Hawkwood snapped. "I need you to convey a message for me."

"Message?" Jilks found his voice and frowned, and then his jaw sagged. "To London?"

"Chatham," Hawkwood said. "To the dockyard; the Transport Board office, for the attention of Captain Elias Ludd."

"Chatham? Why Chatham? I don't understand." Jilks shook his head in confusion.

"You don't need to understand," Hawkwood said curtly. "I told you; all you have to do is listen. I don't care how you do it, but you're to contact Captain Ludd. You tell him that Morgan and his men are planning to steal a consignment of bullion from the Admiral's residency in Deal in three days' time. He is to take all necessary precautions. Tell him the message came from me. He's the one who will understand."

The man at the table stared at Hawkwood aghast.

Hawkwood said to Jilks, "You've a horse in the stable outside?"

Jilks nodded.

"Warn Ludd. It's imperative. Have you got that?"

"Yes," Jilks said, though indecision still showed clearly in his face.

"What?" Hawkwood said sharply.

Jilks flushed. "Forgive me, but how do I know you are who you say you are?"

"You're still alive," Hawkwood said. "That's the only proof I can give you."

At that moment a sound came from the shadows beyond an open doorway in the corner of the room.

Hawkwood turned.

"In here, now!"

There was no response.

"I said now, damn it!"

The woman who stepped into the room was wearing work clothes and an apron. She was several years younger than Jilks. Her hair hung loose about her face. She moved to the table and stood behind the seated man's shoulder, staring at the pistols in Hawkwood's hands as if held in some kind of thrall.

"What's your name?" Hawkwood demanded.

"Esther." Her voice was a whisper as she stared at the body on the floor; hand moving to her mouth when she saw the painted skull where McTurk's face should have been.

The woman Morgan had told him about. Housekeeper? Wife? Lover? There was no time for an interrogation.

A groan sounded from the floor. The woman jerked back. McTurk was stirring.

Hawkwood addressed Jilks. "You know what you have to do?"

Jilks released his hands. His expression grew quizzical. "What about you?"

Hawkwood grimaced. The scars on his cheek burned white. "I'm making it up as I go along."

Another groan sounded from the floor.

Hawkwood turned, aimed his pistol at the body on the floor and fired. The ball tore through the soft hood, entered McTurk's right eye socket, and burst from the back of his skull with a spray of blood, bone and tatters of black cloth. McTurk's corpse jerked with the impact before settling into the floor in an ungainly heap.

Jilks jumped, releasing his hands, and the woman let out a cry. They stared down at the body, the horror on their faces as much a reaction to the speed of events as to the violence they had just witnessed.

"Why?" Jilks asked hoarsely.

"I couldn't leave him alive. I have to report back to Morgan."

"What will you tell Morgan?"

"That you fought back and got away."

The woman stared at him in disbelief.

"It's the best I can come up with," Hawkwood said. "Wait until we're gone, then you ride. Travel light; you'll make better time." He turned to the woman. "You'd best make yourself scarce, too. If you know what's good for you, you'll forget what you've seen here."

Hawkwood placed the spent pistol in McTurk's bandolier. "Quickly – give me a hand to lift him up."

Jilks hesitated and then moved to help. Hawkwood got his arm under McTurk's armpit and together they lifted the corpse up so that it appeared as if it was resting across Hawkwood for support after a heavy night out.

"Grab a pistol." Hawkwood nodded towards the sideboard. "When I say fire, you fire."

Jilks moved to obey. "What am I shooting at?"

"As long as it's not me, I don't give a damn," Hawkwood said. "Ready?"

Jilks nodded.

"Now," Hawkwood said.

Jilks aimed his pistol into the hearth and pulled the trigger. The pistol jerked in his hand.

The woman flinched.

Hawkwood aimed his remaining pistol at the window and fired. A ragged hole appeared in the glass, which did not shatter.

"Don't delay," Hawkwood said. Tucking the pistol in his belt and taking the dead weight on to his shoulder, he hefted McTurk's body towards the open door.

Back in the trees, Croker grinned at the sound of the first pistol shot. "That's the bastard done for!"

Lasseur did not respond. He felt the knot tighten in his belly.

When the second shot cracked out of the night, the horses shied and Croker turned towards the cottage. Moonlight illuminated the look of disquiet on his face. The third shot, coming in quick succession, caused him to curse violently and draw his pistol from his belt. His eyes tried to pierce the darkness. "Something's up."

The dog barked again, but it was the only sign of life beyond the cottage, implying that none of the hamlet's human inhabitants had either the desire or the nerve to venture out and investigate the disturbance.

Lasseur followed Croker's line of sight and looked towards

the house. A dim light was still visible through the curtained window but the glow from the open doorway was interrupted as two figures, bound together, stumbled into the open.

"Shite!" Croker spat fiercely. He took a hard grip on the horses' reins and pulled them round.

Fifty paces from the cover of the trees, Hawkwood adjusted his hold around McTurk's shoulders and tried quickening his pace. It was never easy, hauling dead weight. That was the trouble with corpses; they had no sense of coordination. He heard a snuffle in the darkness and saw Croker and Lasseur guiding the horses towards them.

"What the bloody hell happened?" Croker snarled. "Aw, Jesus!" he gasped.

"The bastard fought back." Hawkwood feigned shortness of breath. "I thought this was supposed to be easy? McTurk's hit. I don't know how badly." Hawkwood pretended to lose his grip and cursed as McTurk's body slid from his grasp.

Croker bent down and hurriedly drew the hood off McTurk's face. He stared at the ruin that had been the back of McTurk's skull. "Christ Almighty! He's dead!" He looked at Hawkwood, his expression hard. "Jilks did this?"

Hawkwood nodded. "He had a pistol. Took Pat by surprise. We both got a shot at him, but he made a run for it. With Pat down, I thought it best to get out before the neighbours started creating. What should we do?"

Croker stood up. "We get the hell out of here, that's what."

Lasseur stared down at the body. "What about him?"

Croker, beset by indecision, chewed his lip.

"He's your mate," Hawkwood said, turning the screw.

"Christ's sake!" Croker spat angrily. "Bloody Christ's sake!" Then he said, "All right, get him on to his horse. See if there's a tie in the saddlebag. We'll take him with us. Anyone comes after us we'll have to leave him. Make it quick!" Croker tossed the hood aside.

They lifted McTurk across his horse and secured his arms and legs together by passing a cord beneath the animal's belly. They left, leading McTurk's mount behind them. As he mounted his own horse, in the darkness over his shoulder, Hawkwood thought he heard the sound of a latch dropping into place.

It might have been the sound of a stable door closing.

Henry Jilks reloaded his discharged pistol and felt the sweat break from his armpits as he recalled the moment the two men had stepped through his door. His gaze moved to the floor and the dark stain that showed where McTurk's brains had leaked through the hood and on to the tiles. Jilks thought about the dark-haired man and the lack of emotion he'd displayed when he'd pulled the trigger, dispatching McTurk into whichever afterlife he'd been assigned. Jilks assumed it was Hell. Either way, he knew he would shed no tears, even though McTurk's death had not been a merciful one.

He thought about the man who'd sent Hawkwood and McTurk to his home and his pulse quickened. Jilks had been under no illusions about the dangers when he'd taken the post of Riding Officer. The life was hard and poorly paid. Intimidation was commonplace, as were the opportunities for despair and corruption. For every officer who had been forced to flee his post because of threats to his family, there were half a dozen who had succumbed either to drink or bribery.

Jilks's last but one predecessor had been a former cavalryman called Haggard. Haggard had left the area with his wife and daughter after they had returned to their house one day to find their daughter's pet kitten hanging from one of the rafters in the kitchen. In contrast, Haggard's successor, a sexagenarian drunkard by the name of Rigsby, had spent more time in his cups than on his horse, and had expired in a drunken haze in a local drinking den after a night carousing with a group of men known to be tub carriers and scouts for one Ezekiel Morgan.

It hadn't taken Henry Jilks long to discover the degree of influence Morgan exerted over the local Trade. Knowledge, however, was not proof. Aware that the chances of finding Morgan's hand in the jar were remote, Jilks had concentrated on keeping his head down but his eyes and ears open. His perseverance had begun to pay off. In the time he had been patrolling his district – an area extending six miles inland from and including the stretch of coast between Shellness Point and South Foreland – his successes had been few in number though incrementally significant, as had been confirmed by the amount of contraband seized and the fact that Ezekiel Morgan considered him enough of a liability to have dispatched men to kill him.

Jilks wasn't sure whether he should feel aggrieved or flattered.

He did know, however, that the wisest option was to follow Special Constable Hawkwood's directive and make himself scarce. He thought about the information that Hawkwood had asked him to deliver. It sounded too fantastical to be true, but the look in Hawkwood's blue-grey eyes had been too persuasive to ignore, as was the realization that, if it was true, then he had been granted a unique opportunity to bring Ezekiel Morgan's reign to an end once and for all.

Jilks buttoned his waistcoat, pulled on his jacket and gathered both pistols. It was time to go. Esther was in the stable, having slipped out earlier to saddle his horse. He thought about Esther, who had become more than a housekeeper.

He thought about asking her to go with him and wondered what her answer would be. He could send for her later, when he was safe.

Which brought him to the matter of which direction to take. Riding Officers were required to conduct regular patrols by day and by night, and Jilks had come to know the back roads well. The Wingham Road was the best route, he decided, and then on to Boughton. With luck he'd be at the dockyard gates by morning, if he didn't push the mare too hard.

He paused before letting himself out of the cottage. It had been a good ten minutes since Hawkwood had left with McTurk's body. He wanted to be sure the coast was clear. It sounded quiet. Jilks took a deep breath, opened the door and headed for the stable.

The mare was in her stall and fully saddled. She snorted softly when Jilks entered.

"Easy, girl," he whispered, and stroked the mare's haunch, wondering where Esther had got to. He placed the pistols in their holsters on his saddle. It was then that he noticed his sabre was missing. The scabbard was there, hanging from the saddle, but it lay empty. Curious, Jilks thought, trying to recall if he'd taken it into the cottage with him.

"Esther?" he called.

He heard a footstep behind him, and turned.

The sabre thrust took Jilks by surprise, piercing his waistcoat and entering his belly with ease. At first, he felt nothing, but as the sword-point continued on its path the pain took him, spreading through his body like liquid fire. Jilks clasped his hands to his stomach, curving them around the blade in a desperate effort to prevent the sword from penetrating further, but all he felt was numbness in his fingers as the tempered steel bit into his flesh. Jilks stared at his killer, an expression of stupefaction on his face, as the sabre blade was withdrawn. His hands felt suddenly warm. He looked down and watched, curious, as the dark stain spread across his waistcoat and the blood dripped on to his boots. With a groan, he fell forward on to the straw. It was odd, he thought, how his hands were still warm while the rest of him was so cold. He was still thinking that when his eyes closed for the last time.

The gatehouse picket stepped forward and lifted up McTurk's head. Gazing at the shattered eye socket and the matted mess at the back of the skull, his face clouded in grim recognition. Wordlessly, he let the head drop and moved aside.

Croker led the horses through the archway in silence and in single file.

The journey back to the Haunt had been accomplished without incident, save for the one occasion when they thought they had heard hoofbeats coming up behind them in the distance, not long after leaving the cottage. They had taken cover in a thicket, but after an anxious ten-minute wait, with no evidence of pursuit, they had continued on their way.

The lanterns were burning as they entered the yard. Light issued from the stable doors. Hawkwood had no timepiece, but he knew it was late. He wondered if there was a run on or perhaps there were difficulties with the new foal. There had been no ghostly friars on the road.

Morgan appeared through the stable doorway as they dismounted, wiping his hands with a cloth. His eyes moved to McTurk's horse and the body across its back. He looked to Croker.

"It all went to shit," Croker said savagely. "That bastard, Jilks – he did for Pat."

"What happened?" Morgan sounded remarkably calm, Hawkwood thought.

Croker nodded towards Hawkwood. "Ask him."

"I was about to." Morgan regarded Hawkwood. "Well?"

"Your man Jilks is what happened. He put up more of a fight than we were expecting."

"Explain."

"What's to explain? He heard us coming. He shot at us. We shot at him. McTurk's dead. Jilks lives to fight another day. My guess is he's still running."

"We thought it best to bring Pat back with us," Croker said, avoiding Hawkwood's gaze. "Didn't seem right to leave him behind."

Morgan turned abruptly. "Bring him inside."

Croker took the bridle of McTurk's horse and led it into the stable, pulling his own horse after him. Hawkwood and Lasseur followed.

The groom, Thaddeus, was in the first stall, wiping down a bay mare. He looked up as the men entered, saw McTurk's corpse and his hand stilled.

Morgan nodded towards the body. "Help Jack lift him down."

Hawkwood and Lasseur tethered their mounts as Croker and the groom undid the ties and laid the corpse on the straw. In the lantern light, the groom's lined face looked cracked and yellow.

"Looks as if you had a lucky escape," Morgan said as Hawkwood and Lasseur stored their saddles across the top rail of the stall.

"No thanks to McTurk," Hawkwood said. "He made enough noise to wake the dead."

"Really?" Morgan said, stepping away. "That's not what I heard. I heard he went quietly and the poor sod didn't even know what hit him. When you're ready, Cephus."

Pepper emerged from the shadows, a pistol in his right hand. He was not alone. A slight figure stepped out behind him and Hawkwood knew that his troubles were only just beginning.

"You've met Esther," Morgan said.

She had forsaken the dress, swapping it for a short coat and breeches. Her hair was tied in a ribbon at the back of her neck. Her eyes blazed with anger. "He's the one," she said, pointing at Hawkwood. Her voice was cold.

Hawkwood looked for an escape route. The only way out was through the main doors, and that wasn't an option because the two men who had been concealed behind the doors walked into the light. Both carried cocked pistols. Each had a cudgel in his belt. One of them was Del.

"Move and you're dead," Morgan said. "You, too, Captain Lasseur."

Hawkwood stood still. There wasn't much else he could do.

Lasseur raised his hands and looked around. "What is happening here?"

Croker rose to his feet, equally perplexed. "What the hell's going on?"

"We've been deceived, Jack," Morgan said. "We've another fox in the run." He looked at Lasseur. "Maybe two."

"What?"

"Seems our Captain Hooper's been a tad economical with the truth. Turns out he's not an escaped prisoner after all. He's probably not even a captain. He sure as hell isn't an American."

"What are you talking about?"

"He's the law, Jack; sent to spy on us. His name's not Hooper, it's Hawkwood. And according to Esther he's a special constable working out of – where was it? – Bow Street? You know what that means? I reckon we've gone and caught ourselves a bloody Runner!"

"Jesus!" Croker, teeth bared, clapped a hand to the butt of his pistol.

"No!" Morgan said sharply. "Not here. Take their weapons."

"He killed Pat," the girl said, her thin face all angles and shadows in the lantern light. "Shot him in cold blood, the murdering bastard!"

"*That's* why we're taking their weapons," Morgan said patiently. He gestured to the men by the door. To Hawkwood and Lasseur, he said, "Take out your pistols. Fingers and thumbs only. Lay them on the ground. Step away."

Hawkwood and Lasseur did as they were told. Morgan's men retrieved the guns.

Lasseur stared at the girl. "Who is this woman? What is she saying?"

Morgan feigned surprise. "Of course, I forgot. Esther, this is Captain Lasseur. Captain, allow me to present young Esther. She's family; daughter of a cousin of mine. Grand girl, smart as a whip, takes after her mother, God rest her soul. Esther's father was killed by the Revenue, five years back. Her brother, Tom, was sent down two years ago; seven years' transportation. Coincidentally, he was three months in the hulks before they shipped him off. Small world, isn't it? Means she has no love for the Revenue or the law, so it's no use trying to appeal to her better nature – she hasn't got one. That's why we placed her in Officer Jilks's employ. Got her a job as his housekeeper so she could keep an eye on him for us. What is it they say? Keep your friends close but your enemies closer? Been a mine of information, Esther has.

"Oh, and by the way, Captain – Officer – Hawkwood, whatever the hell it is you call yourself, just so you know: Jilks won't be delivering your message. He didn't make it. Esther made sure of that. Don't feel bad, though. It wasn't your visit that hastened his end. His days were already numbered."

Morgan smiled. "Remember that conversation we had when you asked me about the Warden affray and I told you we always have reinforcements standing by? Well, that's our Esther. She was all set to deal with Jilks, but it seemed a good idea to have you and Captain Lasseur save her the bother. Goes to show how hard it is to find good help these days.

"I have to say, Esther did the business. Even took his horse and rode here to warn us. She was worried she'd run into you on the road, but we were lucky, she took another track. Managed to beat you to it. That's Jilks's mare over yonder, the one Thaddeus is rubbing down."

The hoofbeats they had heard: Esther overtaking them in the darkness.

"The Frenchie's in on it?" Croker grated, turning flint eyes towards Lasseur.

Morgan gazed at Lasseur, a thin-lipped smile on his face. "Now that's a very good question."

"Captain Lasseur didn't know," Hawkwood said.

"Is that right?" Morgan turned. "You really had no idea your Captain Hooper was really a police officer?"

Lasseur stared at Hawkwood.

"Oh, I admit, he's a cut above the rest of them," Morgan said brightly. "Posing as a Yankee and speaking French the way he does, but it doesn't alter the fact he's a damned infiltrator. He'd have sold us all down the river and not thought twice about it."

Hawkwood shrugged. "Nothing personal, Captain. It was business."

Morgan looked pensive. "I've got to be honest; I can't see what your motive would be for helping him; which makes me inclined to believe Officer Hawkwood here is telling the truth when he says you were in the dark as much as we were. It's a dilemma, right enough."

"One way to find out," Pepper said. He threw Morgan a penetrating look.

"There is?" Morgan said. Then he smiled as Pepper passed him his pistol. "Now, why didn't I think of that? There you go, Captain. Be my guest." Morgan held out the gun.

"What is this?" Lasseur said.

"Your chance to make things right. If you are who you say you are, then he's played you for a fool. Are you going to let him get away with that? Go on, take it. Kill the son of a bitch."

Lasseur hesitated. Then, slowly, he took the gun. Croker looked sceptical. He took out his pistol and trained it on Lasseur.

"Kill me," Hawkwood said, "and they'll only send someone else."

Morgan laughed. "They'll be too bloody late."

"They'll hunt you down, Morgan. You'll be in a world of trouble."

"Funny, that's what that navy lieutenant said. I've forgotten his name already. Remind me, Cephus."

"Sark," Pepper said.

"No, not him. The first one."

"Masterson?"

"That's the one! Kept telling us that, if we killed him, the navy would only send someone after him."

"They did," Pepper said. "They sent Sark."

"And look what happened to him!" Morgan grinned at Hawkwood. "I'm guessing they sent you to look for the other two – am I right? Wonder why they sent a Runner? Perhaps the navy's out of lieutenants. God, you'd have thought they'd have learnt by now, wouldn't you?" He turned to Lasseur. "If you're going to do it, Captain, now's the time. Might as well put the poor bugger out of his misery."

Lasseur faced Hawkwood. His expression was as bleak as a winter sky.

He raised the pistol and fired.

18

"You're telling me he's been gone for twelve days?" Jago asked.

James Read nodded.

They were in Read's office. The Chief Magistrate was seated at his desk. Jago was standing with his back to the window. It was late in the evening. Outside, darkness had fallen, reflecting the mood in the room.

"Not exactly a lifetime. The captain's a grown man. He can look after himself. When was the last time you had word of him?"

"The last positive news was six days ago, though not from Hawkwood directly. We received a dispatch from Ludd advising us that Officer Hawkwood and the privateer, Lasseur, had escaped from the ship." Read paused and then said, "Ludd informed me that they left rather a lot of chaos in their wake."

Jago was about to retort, *No change there, then,* only to be forestalled by the look on the Chief Magistrate's face.

"What sort of chaos?" he asked guardedly.

"Five dead, including a child."

Jago stared at Read aghast. "What?"

"I'm led to understand that the child – a young boy – was in severe jeopardy. Hawkwood and Lasseur went to his aid. They were forced to defend themselves against serious assault. At least that's the explanation that was given to the ship's commander. Captain Ludd is still ascertaining the facts. It seems the commander, a Lieutenant Hellard, chose to deal with the incident in a manner that went beyond the boundaries of Royal Navy discipline, as it applies to the treatment of prisoners of war. He is to face a Board of Enquiry and is unlikely to emerge unscathed. If he thought that commanding a prison hulk was the lowest depth he could plumb, he is going to be sorely disappointed."

Jago, still shaken, looked pensive. "And that's it? That's all you know?"

"There may be more."

"Meanin' what?"

"Ludd also reported that, on the night of their escape, there was an incident on the opposite coast. A place called Warden. A force of Revenue men supported by a small company of dragoons intercepted a landing party. In the mêlée that ensued, several men were wounded. One of the Revenue men was watching through a spyglass. He couldn't be certain, but he thought there were two members of the smugglers' gang who stood aside and appeared to play no part in the landing of the contraband, and when the shooting started they did not seek to conceal themselves ashore, but instead hurried to board the smugglers' boat as it pulled away. He also said that, unlike the rest of the smuggler crew, they seemed to be unarmed. He thought that was . . . unusual."

"And you think it was the captain and the Frenchie?" Jago said, looking doubtful. "Any of the smugglers caught or questioned?"

"Unfortunately, it was the smugglers who emerged victorious. They were able to call up support; as a result it was the Revenue who were forced to retreat." Read pursed his lips. "I know it's not much to go on, Sergeant. In fact, it might be nothing at all, but it's the only lead we have."

Interesting that he still calls me sergeant, Jago thought.

He suspected it was the closest Read would come to granting him the courtesy of a title. He doubted the Chief Magistrate would ever address him as "Mister". *Mister* inferred respectability, and Jago suspected that, while James Read was willing to overlook the more nefarious aspects of his commercial activities in the interest of quid pro quo, the magistrate wasn't yet prepared to accept Nathaniel Jago as a fully paid-up member of legitimate society.

"If you ask me," Jago said grimly, "it sounds like a complete bloody mess."

Read nodded, thin lipped. "From all I've heard so far, I'm inclined to agree. It adds up to a very unpalatable brew, especially if one takes into account the fate of the two naval lieutenants I told you about: one dead and one missing."

"So, what is it you're asking me to do, exactly?" Jago asked, not a little warily.

Read steepled his slender fingers. "I know you to have knowledge of that part of the country. Certain avenues are open to you that would be inaccessible to the authorities. I'm hoping you can use your contacts to discover Officer Hawkwood's whereabouts and perhaps pick up his trail."

Jago's eyebrows rose. "You don't want much, do you? You do realize that if it *was* him getting on that boat, he's probably in France by now? I've got contacts all right, but they ain't *that* widespread."

"I take your point, but we cannot be sure that it was him. It's possible that Hawkwood, along with Lasseur, is still in the locality, in which case it's also possible that he is in difficulty and unable to send word."

Jago sighed and then nodded. "All right, suppose I do go looking and I find him. Then what?"

Read lowered his hands. "I'm prepared to leave that to your discretion."

Jago fixed the Chief Magistrate with a jaundiced eye. "That's mighty trusting of you. I take it this doesn't mean I'm on the payroll?"

Read allowed himself a wry smile. "That suggestion was put to me in the light of your assistance during the William Lee affair. I'm told you found the idea humorous, as it would represent a considerable drop in your earnings?"

"Aye, well . . ." Jago shrugged, "just thought I'd ask. You do realize, if you'd come to me in the first place, you might have been able to save yourselves a deal of bother."

"In hindsight, you may well be right," Read conceded. "At the time we considered that the fewer people who knew of Officer Hawkwood's assignment, the better. We –"

"What you're tryin' to say is that you thought there might be a conflict of interest on account of my occasional dealings with the import trade," Jago said.

"There was that possibility, yes," Read agreed solemnly.

"But now that his nibs's assignment has gone tits up, it's because of those dealings that you'd like me to help you out?"

"In as much as we have no firm evidence to suppose Officer Hawkwood *is* in extremis, that is correct."

"Well, at least you're honest," Jago said. "I'll grant you that. But you've got a bloody nerve."

There was a pause.

"So, you'll do it?" Read said.

Jago did not reply immediately. He turned and looked out of the window, gazing down on the dimly lit windows of the street below before raising his eyes to stare out over the steeply tiled, moon-flecked rooftops.

Finally, he nodded.

"Of course I'll bloody do it."

The gunshot echoed around the stable like a thunderclap, causing the horses to shy and stomp in fear. The powder smoke dissipated.

"Now, there's a pity," Morgan said. He stared at the pistol muzzle, which was aimed at a point over Hawkwood's left shoulder.

Lasseur lowered the gun. His eyes met Hawkwood's and he gave a wry smile.

Hawkwood said nothing. The distant booming sound was not an echo from the shot, he realized, but the pounding of his own heartbeat slowing to a crescendo.

Morgan held out his hand. "It wasn't loaded anyway, Captain. It was to see what you'd do with it. You didn't think we'd actually *give* you a loaded weapon, did you?"

Morgan looked almost sorrowful as Lasseur, silent and stone-faced, handed over the pistol.

"Better the devil you know, eh?" Morgan said. "Though I'd be a liar if I said I was surprised. It's a damned shame. I had high expectations for you two. Now I'm three men down." He shook his head. "It'll be interesting to hear what Captain Lasseur's compatriots say when I give them the news. Maybe I should let *them* deal with you, Captain, the same way they do on the hulks. Know how they punish traitors on the prison ships? It's not pretty. They use needles and gunpowder to tattoo the words *I betrayed my brothers* on the forehead. They tell me there's a severe amount of discomfort. Still, let's not jump the gun." Morgan smiled mirthlessly and turned to Del and his companion. "Either of them so much as farts – shoot him."

Croker didn't look happy with that proviso. "Can't we kill them, anyway?"

"Not yet. We'll find a use for them later. Maybe give the dogs a run if Captain Lasseur's friends don't care to pass sentence. That'll be after Cephus and I have a few words with Officer Hawkwood, of course."

"I'd like to be in on *that,*" Croker said.

"Don't look so disappointed, Jack, my boy. If you behave yourself, you'll get your chance. All in good time. For now, Thaddeus has just put clean straw down and it'd be a pity to mess it up. Besides, it'll disturb the horses and we've spooked them enough as it is. I don't want the mare panicking and stepping on that foal, not after the trouble I've been through."

To Hawkwood, Morgan said, "Gave you a bit of a fright, did we?"

Croker sneered. "Smells like he's soiled his breeches."

Hawkwood shook his head. "Not me. That'll be Del. I've known sweeter-perfumed middens. I thought you said he wasn't allowed inside?"

Del wrinkled his nose. "What's he on about?"

"Your boss thinks you smell," Hawkwood said. He eyed the pistol in Del's hand. Getting the weapon wouldn't be that hard, but Croker was too eager and Del's companion looked useful and Hawkwood wasn't prepared to gamble with the odds. There was Pepper, too, to contend with and Pepper was the unknown quantity. Not to mention the girl; she'd proved her worth by killing Jilks. Hawkwood wondered how she'd done it. He recalled the pistols on the sideboard.

"Ignore him, Del," Morgan said wearily. "He thinks he's being funny."

"Ain't me," Del said, looking pained. "It's the bloody paint. How many times do I have to tell you?"

"You're not wearing any paint," Hawkwood said.

"Ha, bleedin' ha," Del said, though he still looked doubtful.

He turned to Morgan for instructions. "Where d'you want them?"

"Out of my sight. Take Sol; put them in one of the cellars. Let them stew for a while. Jack, you go with them. There's safety in numbers. Don't give either of them an inch – I mean it. Soon as they're locked away, Del, I want you back watching the road. Better send word to Asa Higgs, too. Use one of the carrier birds. Tell him there's a burial that needs arranging." He looked at Hawkwood and Lasseur. "Possibly three."

Morgan tossed Pepper his spent pistol and turned to the girl. "Esther, you get Jilks's bay back in her stable before it gets light. Make sure you rub her down. We don't want her looking like she's been ridden hard. Once you've done that, give it till morning, then make out you just found him. Not too tearful; just enough to make it look good. You know the drill. If you go now, you should just make it. Thaddeus'll give you a hand to saddle up."

The girl nodded.

"Good," Morgan said. "You all know what to do."

Croker picked up a lantern. "All right; move your arses." He pointed the muzzle of his pistol at Hawkwood's cheek. "Just give me an excuse."

"Enough, Jack," Morgan said. "You'll get your chance."

Croker looked as if he couldn't wait that long.

Sol, carrying a lantern of his own, led the way out of the stables, across the yard and down a series of steps into a dank, vault-like passage beneath the foundations of yet another outbuilding from the ancient priory complex.

Croker halted them outside a closed door and withdrew the bolt. He pulled the door open and gestured Hawkwood into the room. Hawkwood was halfway through the doorway when Croker's boot slammed into the back of his calf, folding his leg and pitching him on to the hard stone floor.

"Watch the Frog," Croker snarled and launched his boot towards Hawkwood's groin. Hawkwood twisted aside, leaving his thigh to catch the brunt of the strike. It was still hard enough to make him cry out with the pain. Two more kicks in quick succession found their mark before Croker stepped away; finally heeding Sol's warning that their employer was unlikely to be happy if the bastard pegged out before he'd been questioned.

Holding up the light, he gazed down at Hawkwood, his eyes black with hate. "You're a dead man," he said.

He turned. "Get the other one in here."

Del pushed Lasseur forward and Croker exited the cellar. Lasseur had barely enough time to move to Hawkwood's side before the door was slammed shut behind him, leaving him cocooned in darkness, with only Hawkwood's ragged breathing for company.

It was several minutes before the pain subsided and Hawkwood was able to sit up. He did so gingerly, thankful that Croker had aimed for his lower torso. None of the kicks had landed on the previous wounds sustained from the duel in the hulk.

He couldn't see a thing. The interior of the cellar was as dark as a tomb.

"Matthew?" Lasseur's disembodied voice came out of the blackness.

"Still here," Hawkwood said.

He felt a hand on his arm. "Are you hurt?"

"I'll live."

"I should quote Charbonneau. What was it he used to say? 'The Lord loves an optimist'?"

Ignoring the pain in his belly and his thigh, Hawkwood got to his feet and heard Lasseur do the same. He reached out and took hold of Lasseur's sleeve. "The door's to our left, yes?"

Lasseur thought for a second. "Yes."

"Let's make sure," Hawkwood said. "Back up until we reach the wall."

It took five paces before their spines touched the cold stone.

"Now, what?" Lasseur asked, intrigued.

Leaning flat against the wall, Hawkwood took his bearings, picturing in his mind the things he'd seen in the cellar before the door closed and the light vanished. Croker's keen desire to inflict punishment had provided him with valuable seconds in which to take stock of his surroundings, the dimensions of the room and some of the objects immediately to hand.

Uppermost were the position of the door and a shelf to the left of it bearing a candle stub and what had looked like a tinder box.

"Don't move," Hawkwood said.

Holding his hands out in front of him, moving painfully, he set off towards the opposite wall. A vision struck him of soldiers blinded in action and reduced to begging on street corners, enclosed in perpetual darkness. I'd rather be dead than blind, he thought.

When his hands finally touched stone, he paused. Knowing the dark would have caused some disorientation he debated whether to move left or right. He chose left. The shelf had been set low, he recalled, and at waist height. Tentatively, he began to edge along the wall. After a few side steps his fingers encountered wood; moved on, and found metal. It was the tin. Hawkwood fumbled awkwardly with the lid, eased it open and probed the interior. Yes! He breathed a sigh of relief and ran his fingers over a flint and steel, and something with the consistency of thistledown. He heard Lasseur's exclamation at seeing the spark as he struck the flint. Looking down, he saw not only the tinder but two short lengths of taper lying on the shelf next to the candle stub.

A few seconds later, they had light.

Extinguishing the tinder, Hawkwood placed the fire-starting tools back in the tin and slipped it into his pocket. "We need a way out or something to fight with. Preferably both."

"You still have your knife?" Lasseur said, remembering.

"It won't be enough," Hawkwood said. He looked at Lasseur. "Why didn't you try and shoot me? You had the chance to save yourself."

Lasseur, trapped by the candlelight, looked surprised by the question. "You still owe me four thousand francs, remember? I was protecting my investment."

"Now, who's the optimist?" Hawkwood said, and winced.

His discomfort did not go unnoticed. Lasseur frowned. "I thought you said you weren't hurt."

"No, I said I'd live. I hurt like hell."

"You can't blame Croker. You killed his friend."

"I might just kill Croker as well," Hawkwood growled. He paused. "Why *are* you doing this, Captain? What's the real reason?"

Lasseur smiled and then his face grew serious. "I said you were an honourable man. I also said there was a darkness within you. I believe both statements to be true. You proved it by fighting by my side to protect the boy and when you saved my life on the beach. For those acts alone, I will always count you as my friend. As a general rule, I do not kill my friends. Did Morgan speak the truth? You really are a police officer?"

Hawkwood nodded.

"You had me fooled."

"But I didn't *take* you for a fool," Hawkwood said. "It's not the same thing."

"No," Lasseur said. He looked thoughtful. "I don't believe it is."

The candlelight confirmed there was only the one door and that the cellar held nothing lethal enough to use as a weapon. A dozen half-anker tubs were stacked against the far end of the room. Six bigger barrels rested on their sides next to them. Adjacent to the large barrels were several glass demijohns containing what appeared to be, in the dull candle glow, a coloured liquid. Next to the demijohns were some wooden crates containing dozens of glass bottles, all of them empty. The smell was enough to tell them what the barrels contained. Hawkwood nudged the small kegs. Their weight told him they were full. He presumed the six tubs Asa Higgs had transported from Jess Flynn's farm were among them, though there was no way to know for sure as they all looked the same. Morgan was taking a risk keeping them on his property, Hawkwood reflected, if the Haunt was ever raided by the Revenue, though that seemed an unlikely prospect given the pickets and the representatives of officialdom Morgan supposedly had on his payroll.

There was a spigot in each of the large barrels. Hawkwood held his hand under one and turned the tap. He let the clear liquid run and took a sip. He had taken it for gin, but it was water he could taste.

"At least we won't die of thirst," Lasseur said.

"Depends which barrel you sup from," Hawkwood said. "Pick the wrong one and you're more likely to die of alcohol poisoning."

"What?" Lasseur's eyebrows lifted.

"Not all the brandy that's brought in is drinkable. A lot of it's seventy per cent over proof. They have to add water. Some of it comes in clear, so they add caramel syrup to darken it. I'm guessing that's what's in those." Hawkwood indicated the demijohns and then the kegs. "You drink that stuff undiluted, it'll likely kill you."

"There might be worse ways of going," Lasseur said. He stared wistfully at the kegs. Then his eyes shifted to a large wooden tea chest. "What do you suppose is in there?"

More smuggled goods, Hawkwood guessed, though it was unlikely to hold tea, as the duty on tea had been heavily reduced decades ago. It was more likely to be lace, or gloves, or rolls of silk. There was no lock. He undid the clasps and opened the lid.

Nothing to get excited about; bundles of material, though none of them were of lace or silk. Hawkwood was reaching down to feel if there was anything concealed beneath the layers when something about the material struck him as vaguely familiar. He held the candle close then placed it to the side and lifted one of the bundles out. When he unrolled it, he was holding a jacket and a pair of breeches. The jacket was dark blue with a red collar and cuffs. The trousers were a grubby white.

He heard Lasseur give a grunt of surprise. "That's a French infantry uniform."

Hawkwood nodded. "Company of Fusiliers."

"You're familiar with French army uniforms?"

"It's a long story," Hawkwood said.

"These aren't new." Lasseur pointed to a hole in the tunic. "That was made by a musket ball."

Or maybe even a bullet from a Baker rifle, Hawkwood thought.

There were upwards of two dozen more uniforms in the chest. What was Morgan doing with them? He couldn't begin to guess, but he wasn't going to lose sleep over it. He tossed the uniform back in the chest and closed the lid.

"I think we've exhausted our possibilities," Lasseur said. "It looks as if your knife's the only weapon we've got."

Hawkwood looked around.

"Not necessarily," he said.

Lasseur frowned. "What did you have in mind?"

Hawkwood told him.

Lasseur considered Hawkwood's idea.

"The darkness returns," he said grimly.

Footsteps, followed by the rasp of metal catching on metal.

Hawkwood, senses alert, opened his eyes. It didn't make any difference. He still couldn't see a damned thing. He wondered if it was morning already. Had he slept? It didn't seem as if five minutes had passed since they had been locked in.

He heard voices behind the door but the words were indistinct. He assumed Lasseur had heard them, too. Acting quickly, using the flint and steel, he set light to the tinder and transferred the flame to the candle. Slipping the tin into his pocket, he squatted down with his back to the wall, the flickering candle on the floor by his hand. He glanced across the room to where Lasseur was crouching. The privateer nodded.

The sound came again; a door bolt being released. The door swung open. Croker stood on the threshold, a pistol in his hand. Sol, also armed, was behind him with the lantern.

Hawkwood saw it was morning. Beyond the doorway, grey light from outside was filtering along the passageway.

Croker jerked his head. "You – lawman – on your feet, now! The Frog stays put."

Hawkwood remained where he was.

Croker raised the pistol. "You bleedin' deaf? I said outside! Mr Morgan wants to see you."

"I don't think so," Hawkwood said. "I prefer it here."

Croker moved forward. For the first time, he appeared to notice the candle flame. "Would you look at that, Sol?

They found themselves a light. Afraid of the dark, were we? How sweet. Keep your eye on the Frog while I deal with his nibs."

Croker stepped further into the cellar, Sol close behind him, holding the lantern high and looking wary.

The cellar had always carried the smell from the kegs. It was nothing new, but it wasn't until Croker looked down and noticed the lantern reflecting off the wetness on the floor and the dampness on his boots that it occurred to him the smell might be stronger than usual.

Which was when Lasseur kicked over the opened brandy keg and Hawkwood touched the candle to the edge of the puddle.

Croker let out a yell as the floor and his boots and breeches erupted in blue tongues of fire.

Hawkwood knew the flames might not last long, depending on the strength of the liquor, but he was counting on Croker's initial panic to give them the edge. Pushing himself off the wall, Hawkwood slammed the knife towards Croker's throat. The blade entered Croker's neck with devastating force. Croker's eyes widened with astonishment. As he toppled backwards, the pistol still held fast in his hand, Hawkwood swept the knife sideways before tugging it free. Gravity did the rest.

Sol turned too late and screamed as Lasseur rose and smashed the empty bottle on to the bridge of his nose. The lantern fell from his hand. As Sol went down, Lasseur levered the pistol from his grip and swung his boot into Sol's crotch. Sol joined Croker on the floor. Lasseur tossed the bottle aside, ignoring the sound of breaking glass. Croker, prostrate, brandy-soaked and burning, tried to bring his pistol to bear and died, choking on his own blood.

Placing the knife inside his boot, Hawkwood prised the pistol from Croker's hand. Already, the flames were dying.

Lasseur was in the passageway. Hawkwood slammed the door shut and rammed the bolt home. He caught up with Lasseur at the bottom of the stairs.

"If we can get to the stables," Lasseur urged, "we can steal a couple of horses."

But Hawkwood shook his head. "No time. If any of Morgan's crew are in the stables we'd have to deal with them *and* saddle up. Even if we managed to get clear, we'd still have to get past the pickets at the gatehouse. We can assume Morgan's briefed his men. They'll hear us coming and seal us in. So far, no one knows we've broken out. The longer we can keep it that way, the better. We're better off going over the back wall and heading for the woods."

"Morgan has men on the perimeter."

"They'll be spread out. We can deal with them."

Hawkwood thought about the palisades. They were the only weak spots he'd seen. They would have to cross open ground but when weighed against being on horseback in full view and making noise, to Hawkwood's mind, the option still made more sense. It wasn't much of a choice, either way.

Lasseur contemplated Sol's pistol. "Then, let's hope this one's loaded."

They halted at the top of the steps. The yard was empty. The stable doors stood enticingly ajar. Hawkwood felt a twinge of doubt.

"Ready?" Lasseur murmured.

He found he was talking to himself. Hawkwood was already on the move.

"What are Croker and Sol playing at, for Christ's sake?" Morgan shook his head, half in anger, half in bafflement. "It would have been quicker sending Del."

"We should have gone ourselves," Pepper said. "At least, if there's a mess, it'll be easier to clean the cellar than the carpet."

They were in the main house. Morgan was at his desk. Pepper was leaning against the hearth.

Morgan thought about that. He stared at the carpet. What Pepper said made sense. He nodded. "You're right." He picked up the blackthorn walking stick. "Come on."

Pepper retrieved a pistol from the table and followed Morgan out of the room.

They headed for the stable yard.

There was still no sign of either Croker or Sol en route. Morgan tried to ignore the seeds of doubt germinating deep in his gut. He wondered whether Pepper was experiencing concern, too. If he was, there was no sign. But that was the thing with Pepper: he rarely showed any outward emotion. It didn't matter if the news was good or bad, Pepper's expression hardly ever seemed to change.

The two men crossed the yard and descended the cellar stairs.

It was Pepper who sensed it first.

"What?" Morgan said.

Pepper raised the pistol and approached the cellar door. Cautiously, Morgan tugged back the bolt and pulled the door open.

"God damn it to hell!" Morgan's features distorted with rage as he stared down at the carnage. His knuckles whitened around the blackthorn. "Useless bloody sods!"

Croker lay on his back. His clothes were singed; his eyes were open and sightless. There looked to be a lot of blood. Sol was on his side with his knees drawn up, clutching his balls with blistered hands and whimpering. One eye was closed. Blood and snot from his broken nose was dripping on to the floor. The cellar reeked. Pepper took in the opened brandy keg, the shards of broken bottle, the discarded lantern and the extinguished candle stub.

Clever, he thought. He glanced towards the other tubs at the back of the cellar. It was a good job Hawkwood and Lasseur had concentrated their escape strategy on this immediate area and that the flames had extinguished themselves before they'd had a chance to spread to the rest of the kegs.

"Sound the bell," Morgan said. "They can't have got far."

Pepper was already running for the stairs.

Hawkwood and Lasseur had the perimeter wall in their sights when they heard the clamour. Fortune had been on their side. Using the ruins as cover, they had made it as far as the windowless shell where Hawkwood had encountered Morgan's dogs.

Cautiously, Hawkwood raised his head and looked through one of the empty window frames towards the main house, where several men were hurrying towards the sound of the bell, which was becoming more insistent with each successive clang.

"I think we can assume they've found Croker and Sol," Lasseur said drily.

"And they'll be looking for us as soon as that bloody bell stops," Hawkwood said. He turned, eyes probing the line of the wall, trying to recall where he'd seen the nearest breach.

He saw it and pointed. "There, close to the trees. There's a break in the stonework. Morgan's plugged the gap, but we can use the tools to break through."

They ducked out from the ruin, using it as a shield, keeping low. The bell stopped ringing when they were twenty paces out from the ruin. The first pistol shot rang out ten paces further on. It did not come from behind them but from one of two men who appeared out of the trees one hundred paces to Hawkwood's right.

When he saw the men break cover and heard the cry, it dawned on Hawkwood that both he and Lasseur had underestimated the discipline of Morgan's perimeter guards. At some point, Morgan must have issued a directive telling his pickets to remain at their stations in the event of an alarm, in case it signalled a breach of the defences. While the rest of Morgan's crew had been answering the summons behind them, the pickets had been moving into position. Their readiness to engage and use weapons against them was proof that Morgan had alerted his men to Hawkwood and Lasseur's indiscretions.

Hawkwood swerved to one side, though he knew eagerness had forced the picket to fire too soon and from too great a range. There had been no risk of the ball finding its target.

He kept going.

There was another cry, this time from the direction of the main buildings. The sound of the pistol shot had travelled, alerting the rest of Morgan's crew that their quarry had been sighted. There was no need for caution now. Hawkwood risked a look over his shoulder. Beyond the ruin, he could see a dozen men were racing towards them. Some with cudgels, others armed with pistols. Two looked as if they were carrying muskets. Reassuringly, they were still some distance away.

He turned back to see Lasseur steady himself, take aim with Sol's pistol and fire. There was a sharp cry fifty paces away as the second picket staggered back clutching his shoulder. Lasseur tossed the weapon aside.

Twenty yards from the palisade, Hawkwood saw that he might have miscalculated. The wooden stopgap was more substantial than he had anticipated.

Hawkwood passed Lasseur the pistol he'd taken from Croker. "Make it count. It's all we've got to hold them off."

The advice sounded pitiful even to his own ears. But Lasseur merely nodded as he received the weapon and turned to face the oncoming threat.

Hawkwood ran to the pile of tools, looking desperately for something to prise the stakes of the palisade apart. There were some shovels, two picks, a selection of mallets and a crowbar. He reached for the crowbar, knowing in his heart that they had run themselves into a dead end.

We should have gone for the bloody horses, he thought.

And then he saw it, resting lengthways against the base of the wall, partially concealed by the lime and sand bags.

A ladder.

He ran towards it even as he heard Lasseur's urgent warning: "They're closing!"

Hawkwood jammed the ladder up against the wall. As he did so, he heard a distant report – a musket shot – and ducked instinctively, though he guessed the shooter was still too far back. It was when they got to within a hundred yards that he would start worrying, though he knew that time could only be seconds away.

Holding the ladder in place, he yelled at Lasseur. "Come on, damn it!" And saw that the first picket, who had stopped to snatch up his wounded companion's firearm, was coming in fast.

Lasseur turned and ran. The picket fired. An invisible finger plucked at the sleeve of Lasseur's jacket. Hawkwood heard the privateer grunt as he threw himself forward and began to climb. With a bellow of anger at having missed his target, the picket drew his cudgel and came on.

Lasseur turned on the ladder rung and levelled the pistol.

"Stand still!"

Lasseur's command rang out and stopped the picket in his tracks.

"I will shoot you dead if you move," Lasseur said.

The picket stared at him.

"Don't make me kill you," Lasseur said.

Hawkwood looked back to see that the rest of Morgan's crew were gaining considerable ground. They had skirted the ruin and were now a little over a hundred yards away. One of the men was kneeling. A musket cracked. The ball struck the rung by Hawkwood's right hand and he felt a splinter slice into his wrist.

Lasseur was astride the top of the wall. He was still pointing his gun at the picket, who was less than thirty yards away, holding his ground in the face of Lasseur's threat. He had seen Lasseur's first shot cut his companion down from a greater distance and had no wish to suffer the same fate.

"No!" Hawkwood yelled. "Don't wait! Go!"

But Lasseur ignored him, stuck the pistol in his belt and stretched out his arm.

Seizing his opportunity, the picket sprinted towards them. Hawkwood grabbed Lasseur's hand, hauled himself up and threw himself across the top of the stonework. Another shot sounded as Hawkwood reached down for the ladder. He hunched his shoulders and felt the wind as the ball churred past his ear and thudded into the wall.

The picket was only feet away.

"No time!" Lasseur gasped when he saw what Hawkwood was trying to do.

But when Hawkwood bent down and hooked his hand around the ladder's top rung, Lasseur did the same.

The picket leapt forward, hand outstretched.

And was left clutching air as, together, Hawkwood and Lasseur hauled the ladder up and out of his reach and pitched it over the wall.

As the ladder toppled, more shots rang out. Chips flew from the stone as Hawkwood and Lasseur let go. There was no time to consider the consequences of a nine-foot drop. Hawkwood jumped, missed the falling ladder by inches, hit the ground and rolled. Then he was up and running and Lasseur was following him into the trees.

The woods closed in around them. There was no discernible path; only sporadic gaps in the undergrowth. They ran on; tree roots snapping at their heels; brambles tugging at their clothes. A small clearing appeared. They darted across it and a pathway opened up before them; a deep-sided gulley, overhung with branches. A deer track, Hawkwood supposed, judging from the slot marks; crisscrossed by even narrower funnels that suggested regular use by fox or badger.

They plunged into the gulley, moving as swiftly as the uneven surface would allow, careful not to lose their footing, finally emerging into an even denser patch of woodland at the bottom of the slope. They paused for breath, sucking air into their tortured lungs. Hawkwood tried to look back up the hill but his view was obscured by swathes of foliage.

When they had first entered the trees, a jabber of birdsong had announced their presence to the wood's more elusive inhabitants. Now, the wildlife around them had fallen silent, evaluating this new invasion of their territory.

They moved off again, knowing their sole purpose was to put as much distance as possible between themselves and their pursuers. Secure in the knowledge that Morgan, far from giving up the chase, would be marshalling his forces, it made sense to stay on the deer trail for as long as possible. Better that than try to blunder through less accessible tracts of woodland, thus allowing the hunters to catch up. Hawkwood estimated they had probably travelled a little over a mile since scaling the wall. It wasn't far enough. But as long as they had the advantage of cover and could move at speed they had a chance.

It was warm, even under the shade of the trees. Both of them were soaked in sweat when Hawkwood called another halt. Heart thumping, he remained still, and listened. Sunlight filtered down through the overhead canopy, creating shadows among the thickets. Bird calls were the only sounds that broke the stillness.

"I think I saw Masson and Leberte," Lasseur gasped, chest heaving.

Hawkwood frowned and found his breath. "Where?"

"Back at the wall. They were among the men chasing us. Leberte was carrying a musket."

"That's probably how come I wasn't hit. I never rated French marksmanship." Hawkwood smiled.

"Perhaps he missed on purpose," Lasseur said, still panting.

Hawkwood considered the possibility and wondered if Lasseur was grasping at straws.

"And perhaps we'll never know," Hawkwood said.

It was then that he heard it. The noise came from somewhere up behind the trees, beyond the gulley, in the direction of the Haunt.

The baying of a hound.

He saw the colour leave Lasseur's face when a second dog took up the chorus.

Hawkwood had a sudden vision of Thor and Odin, fangs bared. His heart ran cold at the prospect. He looked at Lasseur. The privateer's shirt was soaked in sweat.

"We have to move," Hawkwood said.

Lasseur nodded dully. He looked up, squinting through the canopy, then stuck out an arm and pointed. "That way."

"What's in that direction?"

"The river."

"You're sure?"

"Yes."

"Then we'd better run faster," Hawkwood said.

The deer trail petered out a couple of hundred yards further on. The woodland was becoming less dense; the gaps between the trees more frequent. Through them, Hawkwood could see the beginnings of pastureland, smooth green meadows dotted with sheep. He could see hedges and a stile and a house in the distance.

And all the while he could hear the hounds. He could hear shouts, too. They sounded a lot closer than they had before. The hunters were still behind them, and they were gaining. It seemed to Hawkwood that there were more than two dogs chasing them, but he wasn't about to stop and check.

Lasseur closed his eyes, as if he was trying to block off the sound, or not think of the consequences if they allowed themselves to get caught.

They were approaching a wide clearing beyond the trees ahead. As they drew closer, Hawkwood realized the significance of the clearing's width. It wasn't a clearing. It was a lane. They stumbled to a halt, dropping to a crouch behind a small clump of alders.

Hawkwood wondered if it was the same road that had taken them to the Haunt on that first night. In the moonlight, all stretches of road had looked the same. He craned his head. The track was lined with wheel ruts, which meant it was a well-established route. He could see cattle tracks, too.

He eased forward cautiously. Fifty yards to their right, the lane bent out of sight, but showed empty in both directions. A bark sounded from behind them.

"They're catching up!" Lasseur tugged urgently at Hawkwood's sleeve. "Come on!"

He was on the point of stepping out when Hawkwood pulled him back down. Lasseur was about to protest when he felt the vibrations. He ducked. Three seconds later, two horsemen appeared around the right-hand bend, riding hard. Their heads were low over their horses' necks as they galloped past.

As the hoofbeats receded, Lasseur raised his head. "How did you know?" he whispered.

"Practice," Hawkwood said.

"Morgan's men?" Lasseur suggested.

"We'll have to assume so."

They crossed the lane and stepped quickly into the woods on the other side. Behind them, they could hear the shouts of the dog handlers. It sounded as if they were beating the underbrush for game, as if they knew they were drawing close to their quarry.

The trees began to thin out once more. Hawkwood and Lasseur moved forward as if walking on glass. At the edge of the woods, they stopped. Hawkwood could see the river. It lay beyond a strip of meadow, less than a pebble's toss from them. It was broad, at least thirty yards in width and shaded by trees on both banks. He looked to his left. Two hundred yards away there was an ancient stone bridge. He could see the parapet and beneath it a keystone and the curve of an arch. He could see the tops of reeds, too, and he could hear water rushing over a weir.

A series of howls, sounding ever closer and rising in volume, reminded them why they had sought out the water. If they could make it to the river, it would be hard – hopefully impossible – for the dogs to track them.

They stepped from the trees.

And a twig snapped at the edge of the wood behind them.

Hawkwood and Lasseur froze. Hawkwood was aware of a shadow moving to his right. His nostrils caught a familiar whiff.

"Got you now," Del said. As he moved into the open, his mouth formed a grotesque gash in his thin face. He was dressed in work clothes. There was no ghostly skull, nor a monk's robe. Just the pistol gripped in his hand.

Another chorus of baying came from the woods at their back and Hawkwood knew with sickening finality that Morgan's men had finally managed to close the gap.

Del grinned again. "Saw you coming. You were making a real racket. Now we'll have some fun," he said. His voice seemed to change, to take on a darker, crueller tone. Suddenly, Del didn't seem quite so oafish.

"No," Lasseur said. "I don't think so. Not today."

It was the timbre in Lasseur's voice that alerted Del to the imminent danger. His response was immediate, driven by panic.

Hawkwood was standing to Lasseur's right and thus partially blocking Del's view as Lasseur drew the pistol from his belt. With an alacrity that belied his doltish looks, Del raised his pistol and fired. Hawkwood felt the impact of the ball against his skull. As he went down in a vortex of pain, he heard Lasseur return fire. His last memory was of seeing a bright flower bloom in scarlet abandon across Del's chest.

Before the world ended.

19

At one point it felt as if he was falling, the next as if he was floating, drifting at the mercy of a weak tide, ebbing back and forth without purpose, never quite breaching the waves and never quite reaching the shore. One moment he was cold, the next he was bathed in perspiration. During each of these episodes there had been a strange taste – bitter, but not unpleasant – which had lingered on his tongue and at the back of his throat.

He'd also been vaguely aware of shadows and voices. But the shadows, like all shadows, had been without definition and the words he thought he'd heard had been like dry leaves rustling in the wind. Sometimes they had seemed close and almost audible, at other times they were no more than whispers, as if the speakers were far away and afraid of being overheard. He'd suspected they were talking about him and had strained his ears to hear better, but the harder he'd tried the harder it had been to mark the conversation clearly.

He also had a hazy recollection of a cup being placed against his lips and of swallowing, but with no clear memory of what he might have ingested. Once, he thought he heard a dog bark and a cry started in his throat, but then the sound faded abruptly and the tightness in his chest began to ease and the moment passed and he did not feel so afraid.

When he opened his eyes he thought for one terrible moment that he was back in the hulk's sick berth. The stinging sensation along the side of his skull, although mild, seemed horribly reminiscent, until the feel of a cool, damp cloth and gentle fingers smearing something on his scalp began to soothe the hurt away and he heard a woman's voice say softly, "He's awake."

The voice sounded vaguely familiar.

Maddie? Hawkwood thought.

He turned his head. He was lying in a narrow bed. Alongside the bed was a night stand upon which stood an unlit candle in a holder, a bowl and some small blue-glass jars. He could not tell what they contained.

A woman's face was looking down at him. It did not belong to Maddie Teague.

"Hello, Captain," Jess Flynn said.

"About time," Lasseur said, appearing from behind Jess Flynn's shoulder. "How do you feel?"

Hawkwood stared at them both and wondered if he was dreaming. He touched fingertips to his skull and winced. "Tired of getting hit on the head." He took his fingers away. They were sticky, as if they had been dipped in beeswax. He rubbed the ends of his fingers together.

"Don't worry, Captain, it's only an ointment. I make it myself from special oils and herbs," Jess Flynn said. "It reduces the pain and encourages healing. The ball grazed your skull, which was why you lost consciousness. You were very lucky; there was some bleeding and you were feverish for a while, but that's all."

"Good thing it was only your head," Lasseur said, smiling. "Anywhere else and I'd have been worried."

Hawkwood realized he had felt no residual pain when

he moved. Encouraged by the discovery, he tried to sit up. His effort was rewarded with only minor discomfort. He looked around. The room was small with a sloped ceiling. There was a half-open window, through which he could just see the underside of the eaves. There was a simple mirrored dressing table upon which sat another bowl and a pitcher. A chair stood in front of the dressing table. A narrow wardrobe rested against one wall.

He looked down. He appeared to be wearing someone's nightshirt. There was no sign of his clothes, though he could see his boots propped on the floor beside the wardrobe.

"It was my husband's," Jess Flynn said, indicating the nightshirt. She exchanged glances with Lasseur and smiled. "I'll leave you to talk." She squeezed the cloth out into the bowl and stood up. Her hand brushed Lasseur's as she walked towards the door. Lasseur watched her go before pulling the chair to the side of the bed and sitting down.

Hawkwood still couldn't quite believe what he was seeing. "How in the name of God did we get *here*?"

Lasseur grinned. "By boat."

"*What?*" Hawkwood felt another brief twinge.

Lasseur laid his hand on Hawkwood's arm. His face was full of concern. "How much do you remember?"

"I saw you shoot Del. After that . . . not a damned thing. What do you mean, 'by boat'?"

"It's a long story. Do you remember me carrying you to the river?"

"No."

Lasseur had left him on the bank while he returned for Del's body, hauling it to the edge of the water in the hope of putting the hounds off the scent. The ruse had worked, but it had been a close thing. Daubing their faces with mud, Lasseur had dragged Hawkwood into the reeds moments before the dogs burst from the trees.

Lasseur frowned at the memory. "I could hear them baying and the men searching. I didn't know if you were alive or dead beside me. I waited until the searchers moved off, then pulled you ashore; still breathing, thank God. And that's when I saw the boat. It was almost submerged. When I found the oars beneath it I thought I was seeing things, and when I examined the hull and realized it was sound, I couldn't believe it. I think the owner must have sunk it deliberately so people wouldn't think it was worth stealing. Fortunately for us, it was.

"I could still hear the dogs, but they were heading downriver. Morgan's men must have assumed we'd try to get to the coast. I knew we needed to go in the opposite direction, so I raised the boat and took us upstream. It was easier than carrying you across country. Del's body was still there when we left. I heard them say they were going to send the gravedigger to pick it up later." He looked at the expression on Hawkwood's face. "What is it?"

"I was going to ask you why we came *here*, but something tells me that would be a stupid question."

"We were close; I knew we would be safe here and the Widow Flynn might have some means of treating your wound. I was right. She's the one who's been looking after you with her medicines and broth."

Which explained the bitter taste on my tongue, Hawkwood thought. To Lasseur, he said, "Don't think I'm not grateful, but are you sure those were the *only* reasons?" Then, for the first time, he noticed the privateer's clothes. "I don't recall you wearing that shirt before."

Lasseur smiled. "I'm happy to see your head wound has not robbed you of your powers of deduction. You're right; like you, I am the happy beneficiary of the Flynn family slop chest."

"It's a good fit," Hawkwood observed laconically. "You

know, our being here places her at serious risk. If Morgan finds out she's harbouring us, it will go badly for her."

Lasseur's face grew immediately serious. "I know that, my friend. Believe me; I know that only too well."

Hawkwood watched the worry lines on Lasseur's face deepen. "And how the devil did you find your way back here? Higgs transported us at night."

Lasseur's features lightened. "I'm a sailor, Matthew. Did you think I was sleeping when the gravedigger took us to the Haunt? I was reading the stars. It was a clear night, remember? I knew the course we were taking. I knew where and when we crossed the river, and I knew the farm was upstream. In daylight, it was simple. Some day, you must let me teach you the finer points of celestial navigation!"

"And no one saw us?"

"Not to my knowledge. Though, if our pursuers hadn't had the dogs it might have been different. I might not have heard them coming. All I can say is that the gods must have been with us." Lasseur straightened. "Thomas Gadd knows Jess has taken us in, by the way. He helped me get you upstairs. He also took the boat back downstream. We've been here ever since."

The room was warm but Hawkwood suddenly felt a cold chill on his back. "What do you mean; *ever since*? How long have we been here?"

Lasseur hesitated. Something moved behind his eyes. "You've been confined to your bed for just over twenty-four hours."

It took a moment for Hawkwood to absorb the shock. "What?" Then his mind did the calculation and he started to push the sheet back. "Jesus!"

Lasseur's eyes widened in alarm. He placed a hand on Hawkwood's chest. "What are you doing?"

Hawkwood thrust Lasseur's hand aside. "I have to get a

message to the authorities! I've got to warn them about the attack on the Admiral's residency! It's tomorrow night!"

Lasseur grasped his arm. "Wait! Tom Gadd told me that Morgan's men are still searching for us. There's a price on our heads. If either of us sets foot off the farm there's a risk we'll be seen. Besides," Lasseur added urgently, "look at you! You're in no fit state to go anywhere."

"I'll take my chances." Hawkwood pushed Lasseur's hand away once more, swung his legs round and placed his feet on the floor. "Where are my bloody clothes?"

Lasseur's eyes flickered to the wardrobe.

Hawkwood stood up. The room swam before his eyes. He sat down again, quickly.

Lasseur threw up his hands in despair. "You see? You can hardly walk. You need to recover your strength."

"There's no time for that!" Hawkwood looked towards the window. It was like looking through a gauze veil. "What the hell *is* the time?"

"It's late; nearly six. Are you hungry? You've eaten nothing solid for a while."

"No, I'm not bloody hungry!" Hawkwood pushed himself off the bed again. The room tilted dramatically, but only for a moment or two before returning to its true axis. He took a deep breath, crossed unevenly to the wardrobe and discovered his jacket, shirt, breeches and underclothes suspended from hooks and hangers. He leant on the wardrobe door and studied them. They were suspiciously clean, considering they'd been immersed in a river, and certainly when compared to how he remembered them from the day before, following their breakneck run through the woods.

He pulled the clothes out, took off the nightshirt, and began to dress. He bent down and picked up his boots. Light-headed, he sat on the end of the bed and attempted to pull on his right boot. The knife, he saw, was still in place. He caught a glimpse of himself in the mirror and almost didn't recognize the unshaven individual staring back at him. He had to admit he'd looked in better health. He turned away and found that Lasseur was watching him with a look of worry on his face. When he made no offer to help, Hawkwood guessed the privateer was trying to make a point.

Lasseur tried again. "Matthew, listen to me. You're not thinking properly. Morgan won't go through with the raid on the gold anyway. Not at this late stage. He daren't. If he hasn't tracked us down, he has no way of knowing if you were able to get word to your people. For all he knows, the army's going to be there waiting for him. He'll only go ahead with the theft if he can silence us first, and then only if he has time to spare. You're more likely to prevent the attack by remaining here and keeping him guessing. That way we'll all be safe."

"We won't ever be safe! Not from Morgan. We've damaged him too deeply. He'll be angry at losing face." Hawkwood reached for his other boot. "I have to do this. The bastard's that bloody cocky, I wouldn't put it past him to still go through with it. In which case, I've no choice. It's my duty to try and stop him."

Lasseur sighed. "Then I ask you for one favour. At least wait until sunset before you leave. You'll reduce the risk of being observed while you're still close to the farm."

Hawkwood shook his head. "I can't do that. I'll be careful, but I can't wait until dark. I have to get to Barham while it's still light."

"Barham?" Lasseur frowned. "What is Barham? And why do you need to be there before dark? I don't understand."

"It's an Admiralty telegraph station."

Hawkwood had been briefed on the telegraph by Ludd, in case he needed to take advantage of it. The Admiralty had devised the system to allow it to communicate directly with its bases around the south coast. It consisted of a line of shutter stations placed on high ground across the country. Each station consisted of a large rectangular frame comprised of six shutters arranged vertically in two columns of three. The shutters could be opened and closed at will, with the positions of the shutters representing letters of the alphabet. Ludd had taken Hawkwood up to the roof of the Admiralty building to show him the signalling mechanism in action. It was an ingenious contraption. Ludd had boasted that, given good visibility, a message could be relayed from Portsmouth to Whitehall in less than ten minutes. Preparatory signals could be acknowledged in a quarter of that time, which was impressive, given that it had taken almost five minutes for Hawkwood and Ludd just to reach the roof.

There were two lines of shutter stations in Kent. One ran from Sheerness to Faversham – Hawkwood assumed notification of his and Lasseur's escape had been sent down that route. The other line ran from the roof at Whitehall via a dozen stations, including Chatham and Faversham, all the way to Deal.

Given the farm's location in relation to the coast, Hawkwood estimated the Shottenden telegraph was the nearest. It was probably no more than seven or eight miles away, but it lay across country. Barham, the next station down the line, sat on the main Canterbury to Dover Road. The distance was perhaps a mile or so longer, and it was a route Morgan was probably monitoring, but the journey would be quicker. Hawkwood knew if he could get to Barham, he could alert both the Admiralty and the Deal authorities at the same time.

"Then wait until morning," Lasseur argued. "That's still more than enough time for the signal to be seen. You need to eat and you'll be fully rested. If you leave at first light, you're less likely to find Morgan's men on the road, and you'll be in better shape should you need to take evasive action."

Hawkwood pulled on his left boot and reached for his jacket, which he had laid on the bed. It was more of a struggle than he had anticipated. He felt slightly nauseous and the bitter aftertaste of the Widow Flynn's tincture was suddenly strong at the back of his tongue. His clothes were beginning to feel tight around him, too, after the looseness of the nightshirt. He had the sudden, intense desire to rest his head on the nearest pillow.

In his heart, he knew there was sense in what Lasseur was telling him. His body was warning him that it needed rest. He hadn't eaten in a long time. He was in no condition to sit astride a horse and endure a nine-mile ride or deal with any threat that came at him.

He nodded reluctantly. "All right – you win. I'll leave at dawn."

When Pepper walked into the room, Morgan was at his desk, going through the accounts ledger. He was not having a good day. Despite the upheaval – in particular, the threat posed by the disappearance of the Runner and the Frenchman – work had to go on. There were still things that required his attention: runs and meetings to arrange, people to manage, deliveries to supervise, accounts to be maintained, both the legitimate ones and those "off the books". He looked up. There was no warmth in his gaze. "Cephus."

"Ezekiel," Pepper said, closing the door behind him.

Morgan glowered at his lieutenant. "Well?"

The severe expression on Pepper's face told him all he needed to know.

Morgan slammed his pen down on to the table. His features

darkened. "God damn it to hell! Somebody must know something!" He shook his head in anger and exasperation. "That bastard Runner can't have made it home. There's been no sign that an alarm's gone out. Deal's quiet. There's no extra troop activity. The place would be crawling if the Admiralty or the army had been alerted."

"We're still on, then?" Pepper said. He stood as if awaiting orders.

Morgan glanced towards the unlit hearth, where the two mastiffs were stretched out, hogging most of the carpet. Useless bloody animals, he thought, and felt more anger building. The dogs did not look up. It was as if they were trying to avoid eye contact, knowing they were the objects of Morgan's displeasure.

"I haven't decided." He tried to keep his voice steady.

"We're cutting it fine," Pepper said.

"I bloody know that, Cephus!" Frustrated, Morgan pushed the books to one side. So much for keeping calm. He knew he was running out of time; the decision could not be put off for much longer. As a result he could feel the tension welling up inside him like a dam threatening to burst. He chewed his lip. "What's happening with our guests?"

"Restless. They want it over and done with."

"Don't we all."

"They keep asking if we've news of Lasseur."

"They miss him?"

"No," Pepper said. "I think they want to kill him."

"Then they'll have to join the bloody queue," Morgan snarled. He sat back. "I suppose we should be thankful *their* loyalty isn't in question."

"It won't be, not as long as they think they're going to make money," Pepper said.

"Just so long as they keep thinking that," Morgan said, rising from his desk.

Walking across to the side table, Morgan reached for the bottle of brandy and poured a measure into a small, ornate glass. He downed the brandy in one swallow. He did not offer a drink to Pepper.

Pepper said nothing. He waited.

Without warning, Morgan picked up the bottle and hurled it at the wall above the fireplace. He followed it with the tumbler. As the bottle shattered and the glass and spirit rained down upon them, the dogs shot to their feet and fled towards the shelter of the desk. "God damned bastard sons of bitches!" Morgan roared. Globules of spittle flecked his beard. He picked up another bottle and threw it at the brindle mastiff, catching it across its rear end. The dog yelped and tried to hide behind one of the chairs.

"Ezekiel?" Pepper said, moving towards him, halting abruptly when he saw that Morgan had retrieved one of the loaded pistols from the table.

Morgan cocked the pistol, aimed at the fawn dog, and fired. The dog howled and fell away, paws scrabbling impotently on the carpet. Suddenly, it began to shake, its back legs kicking uselessly. The howls became whimpers. The dog's flanks stopped moving. Blood pooled on the floor beneath it.

"For the love of God, Ezekiel!" Pepper cried as the brindle mastiff padded cautiously out of hiding and started to lick the blood off its companion's hindquarters.

Morgan lowered the gun. He stared down at the dog, then walked purposefully across the room and laid the pistol on the desk.

He turned to Pepper. His face suddenly composed. "Get someone in to clear that mess up." Morgan pointed to the dead mastiff.

Pepper hesitated then nodded silently. He could hear footsteps and muted voices outside; people wondering what was happening.

Morgan stepped around the corpse. Absently he stroked the brindle mastiff's ears before sitting back down at his desk. He felt, he realized, remarkably at peace now.

"And, Cephus?"

Pepper halted by the door.

"The Runner and the Frenchman – I want them found; I want their balls served up on a plate."

"We're looking," Pepper said.

"Look harder. Lasseur will be making for the coast. He'll be trying to get home. I want every fisherman, every skipper, anyone with a bloody rowboat between Rye and Rochester to keep his eyes peeled."

"And the Runner?"

"He's the dangerous one. He'll want to tell everyone what he's heard here, whereas the Frog'll want to keep his head down." Morgan hesitated. "You can't deny they're damned effective as a pair. It could be the two of them will stick together at first, so they can watch each other's backs. Increase the reward. I want people on their toes, so start pulling in markers. Everyone who owes us – and that's *everyone* from shit shovellers to magistrates. Any bugger kicks up a fuss, do what you have to do. Billy Hollis reckons the Frenchman might have been nicked before they went over the wall, and it's possible Del did some damage before they killed him. Get Rackham to have a word with some of his cronies. They might have received a couple of visitors looking for medical assistance."

"I'll do that," Pepper said. Rackham was Morgan's pet surgeon. His surgical skills wouldn't win him any kudos at Barts or St Thomas's, but he was discreet, and that was what counted.

"All right," Morgan said.

Pepper let himself out.

Morgan returned to his books but found it impossible

to concentrate. Restless, he stood up and moved to the window.

The door opened behind him.

"Ezekiel."

It was Pepper again. There was something in his voice. Morgan turned.

Pepper wasn't alone. He stepped aside to allow the figure behind him to enter.

Morgan stared at his visitor's face.

The brindle lifted its muzzle and growled threateningly.

Pepper closed the door. "I think you should hear this."

"Hello, Mr Morgan," Seth Tyler said. His eyes widened when he saw the dead dog and the blood around the brindle's massive jaws. The scratch marks from the besom showed livid across Tyler's face. Some of them still looked raw. He swallowed nervously. "Heard you were looking for information. Reckon I've got something that might interest you . . ."

"At last you see sense," Lasseur sighed. "I was beginning to think I was talking to myself."

Hawkwood pulled on his jacket. A thought struck him. "Do Jess and Tom Gadd know I'm a police officer?"

Lasseur hesitated. "They did not hear it from me, but Thomas knew."

"Morgan put the word out."

"Undoubtedly."

"And they still took me in?"

"It seems, my friend, that they trust us more than they trust Morgan."

"God Almighty," Hawkwood said.

Lasseur smiled. "It must be my Gallic charm."

They made their way downstairs; Hawkwood less energetically than Lasseur, though it felt good to be back on his feet, no matter how precariously. Jess Flynn was at the kitchen table cutting up vegetables and placing them in a cooking pot. A familiar shape was sprawled half in and half out of the back door. The dog looked round, its eyes hidden by its fringe, and wagged its tail at the new arrivals before turning back to protect the herb garden.

Jess Flynn regarded Hawkwood with a critical eye. "You should be in bed."

"It's thanks to you I'm not," Hawkwood said.

A small smile touched her face, though it might have been a little forced. She still had problems with that errant strand of hair, Hawkwood saw. "You've nothing to fear from me," he said.

There was a pause. The tension seemed to leave her and she nodded. "I know." She glanced at Lasseur. Her face softened and then she turned back and frowned. "Should I still call you Captain? Please, sit down before you fall down. You need some food inside you. There's some broth on the hob and a fresh loaf and butter on that platter beside you. Help yourself." She gestured to a chair, brushing the hair off her face, and busied herself at the fire.

"I *was* a captain once," Hawkwood said, taking a seat. "In another life."

"You really were in the army?" Lasseur asked. He looked genuinely surprised as he sat down opposite Hawkwood.

"The Rifle Brigade. The British regiment, not the American one."

Hawkwood leant back as Jess Flynn returned to the table and placed a bowl of broth and a spoon before him.

"Eat," she ordered.

The smell rising from the bowl was wonderful. Hawkwood broke off a piece of bread.

"And you fought in Spain?" Lasseur asked.

"Yes."

"At Ciudad Rodrigo?"

Hawkwood dipped the spoon into the bowl and raised it to his lips. Chicken, potatoes, carrots and herbs; flavours exploded across his tongue.

"No, that was after my time."

He ate some bread and took another spoonful, savouring the taste. He could feel the torpor slipping away with each mouthful.

"And now you're a police officer. What was it Morgan called you? A Runner – I do not know what that means."

At the mention of the word, Jess Flynn's eyes widened. Presumably Gadd hadn't revealed that little snippet of information.

Hawkwood broke off some more bread and dipped it in the bowl. "It means I'm a special kind of police officer."

"You hunt smugglers?"

"Not just smugglers."

"Ah," Lasseur nodded. "You mean you hunt people like me: escaped prisoners. That's why you were on the ship."

"Not entirely. I was investigating the disappearance of two naval officers."

Lasseur's brow furrowed. "The men Morgan mentioned? I forget their names."

"Sark and Masterson."

"Morgan had them killed?"

"Sark's body was never found, so we didn't know for sure. But after what Morgan told us in the stables, I'm prepared to take his word for it."

"And you plan to bring him to justice."

"If it's the last thing I do," Hawkwood said. He took another piece of bread and used it to soak up the broth. It tasted as good as the first mouthful. He rested his spoon, looked down and was surprised to find he'd emptied the bowl. He felt remarkably fortified. Perhaps he could make it to the telegraph station after all.

Suddenly, the dog stood up. A low grumble began at the back of its throat.

"Into the pantry," Jess Flynn said quickly, wiping her hands on her apron. "The trap's open."

The dog's tail began to wag.

"Wait," Jess Flynn said, relief filling her voice. "It's only Tom."

A minute later, Gadd limped in through the door, followed by the dog. Its nose was twitching. When the seaman saw Hawkwood and Lasseur he paused. The scar running through his cheek and eye socket looked like a slug trail crossing a paving stone. He had a muslin sack over his shoulder and a fowling piece in his hand.

"Tom," Hawkwood said.

Gadd nodded in solemn and cautious recognition. He regarded Hawkwood's unshaven features for what seemed like an inordinately long time. There was no malice in the seaman's gaze. Nor did there appear to be disapproval. It was almost as if he couldn't make his mind up what to think. Eventually, he nodded and said neutrally, "You're on your feet, Cap'n. That's good. Not sure the beard suits you."

"Captain Lasseur tells me I've you to thank for helping me up the stairs." Self-consciously, Hawkwood drew a hand across his jaw. He thought about the razor the woman had given Lasseur. It was back in the cell at the Haunt. Lasseur's facial hair also needed a trim, but because he already had a goatee, it seemed to suit his face.

Gadd shrugged. "Aye, well, you were there to help Jessie when she was in trouble. Reckoned I owed you. Besides, digging a grave's too much like hard work. And Morgan's still after your blood, by the way."

"Tell us something we don't know," Hawkwood said.

"He's upped the bounty. That good enough for you?" Gadd reached inside the bag and brought out two rabbits.

He went to the open pantry door and suspended the game from a hook in one of the beams. He propped the gun against the wall by the door. Behind his back, the dog's nose continued to twitch.

"I'm flattered," Lasseur said.

"You should be," Gadd responded. "It's a tidy sum. McTurk and Croker were two of his best men. Plus there was young Del. Morgan don't take kindly to someone removing three of his crew. Word's spreading that he's willing to pay over the odds for information, which means people'll be on the lookout. You're safe here for a while, but there's no telling for how long." Gadd nodded towards Hawkwood. "And you, Captain, or Constable or whatever it is they call you, are a long way from home."

"Funny," Hawkwood said. "That's what people told me when they thought I was an American."

"Aye, well," Gadd said morosely. "Just so's you know."

"The captain was not solely responsible," Lasseur said.

The privateer glanced towards Jess Flynn as he spoke and Hawkwood saw a look pass between them. He wondered how much Lasseur had told her. She didn't look shocked by the admission.

"That's as maybe," Gadd said. "Not that it matters. Morgan wants the two of you found. And he wants you dead. Probably planning to do it himself. Rumour has it that he likes to keep his hand in. He thought you'd try for a boat, so he's got his people making enquiries along the coast. He's got 'em watching the roads, too. I haven't seen this much activity since the army thought Boney was going to invade back in '04. Word is, he can't believe you've lasted these past two days without being seen. You'd've thought . . ." The seaman's voice trailed off, rendered mute by the look on Hawkwood's face.

Lasseur's head lifted.

Hawkwood stared at the old seaman. "*How* long did you say?"

"How long, what?" Gadd said.

"How long did you say we've been here?" Hawkwood stood up.

Gadd looked at Jess Flynn, whose hands, dusted with flour, had stilled at the coldness in Hawkwood's tone.

"Since the day before yesterday. The captain brought you by boat. Jessie and I thought he was too late. You were in a bad way, all covered in mud. Looked like you weren't breathing. Had the devil of a job lugging you up the stairs. Captain and me had to peel your clothes off, they were that damp. You smelled something rotten, too." Gadd paused. "Why're you asking?"

Hawkwood stared down at Lasseur as the significance of Gadd's words struck home. "You told me we'd only been here a day. We've been here two days. That means the robbery's not due tomorrow; it's tonight!"

It hit him then, like a hammer blow to the ribs.

"My God, you *want* them to go ahead!" Suddenly everything had become clear. "That's it, isn't it? You actually want Morgan to go through with it!"

At first the privateer did not respond. Finally, he spread his hands in an admission of defeat. "You have me." He gave Hawkwood a look of wry contrition. "What can I say? I knew you'd discover my ruse eventually. Though I had hoped it would take you a little while longer." His eyebrows lifted as he met Hawkwood's gaze. "You look shocked, my friend. But what would you do if the situation was reversed and you had the chance to relieve your enemy of the means to feed and equip his army? Would you take it? I think we both know the answer to that. I'm a patriot, Matthew, and for that I make no apology. I told you I looked upon you as my friend, but I love France. And France *needs* that gold."

"Gold?" Gadd said. "What bloody gold?"

"You're siding with Morgan?" Hawkwood said, ignoring Gadd's look of confusion. "You'd do that, *knowing* he sent his men after us? Two of your own countrymen tried to kill you! How does that fit in with your definition of patriotism?"

"Jessie?" Gadd said. "Do you know what they're on about?"

Jess Flynn stood still, her eyes flicking between the two men. She was obviously as bewildered as Gadd by the sudden turn of events.

Lasseur shook his head. "I'm not the one who's important. It's for the greater good."

"That's why you were so concerned for my health," Hawkwood said. "And why you were persuading me to stay put. If Morgan does go ahead with the raid tonight, you knew any message sent from Barham in the morning would be too damned late."

He pushed the chair back angrily, his eyes moving to the open door. Sunset was a little over two hours away. There was still time to get to the telegraph station at Barham and use the shutters to send a warning to the authorities at Deal and the Admiralty before darkness rendered the system impotent.

But would Morgan be making his play tonight? Would he take a chance, knowing that his quarry was still free? Hawkwood knew he couldn't take the risk that Morgan wouldn't go through with his plan.

He spun towards Jess Flynn who was still staring at them both as if mesmerized. "I need a horse, Jess! Now!"

"Would somebody mind tellin' the rest of us what the bloody hell's going on?" Gadd implored. "What's all this talk about gold?"

"Morgan's planning to attack the Admiral's residency at Deal and steal the army's pay chests," Hawkwood said. "Then he's going to sell the gold to the French. It's possible he's going to do it tonight. Captain Lasseur here would like to see him get away with it. I'd like to stop him."

"Bloody hell!" Gadd took a step backwards.

Hawkwood turned to Lasseur. "What now, Captain? Is this where you try and stop *me*?"

Lasseur smiled sadly. "I did not think it would come to this, my friend."

"Me neither," Hawkwood admitted truthfully.

Lasseur started to rise from the table. "I am sorry, Matthew."

"No!" Jess Flynn cried.

Hawkwood tensed; thought about the knife in his boot and how quickly he could reach it.

"Best stay where you are, Cap'n. I'd hate to have to shoot you."

"Tom!" Jess Flynn said urgently.

Hawkwood looked around. Gadd had retrieved the fowling piece. The muzzle was pointed at Lasseur's chest. Tom Gadd's finger was curled around the trigger.

"It's loaded, Cap'n, in case you were wondering. I keep it that way on account of I always need game for the pot and you never know when something's going to come flying up out of the barley. So before you try anything stupid, you can rest assured there's no way you can move your body from behind that table faster than I can squeeze this trigger."

Lasseur showed his palms and lowered himself into his seat, the half smile still hovering on his face.

"That's the way," Gadd said. "Make yourself comfortable while the rest of us try and figure things out. Army pay chests, you say?"

"For Wellington's troops in Spain," Hawkwood said.

"And Morgan plans to give 'em to Bonaparte?"

"No, he plans to sell them to him."

Gadd sucked on a tooth. "Can't say as I like the sound of giving Old Nosey's gold to the French. I've smuggled a few guineas in my time, but we never stole 'em from our own lads. Seems to me you've got to draw the line somewhere. And if Morgan's fingers are in the pie, you'd have to be bloody stupid not to know he's featherin' his own nest at the same time. Heard you mention Barham. You talking about the telegraph?"

"That's right."

Gadd drew himself up. "Best get going then. You leave now, you'll still make it before dark. There's two horses in the barn. Take the mare. She's the quicker. The cob's more used to pulling a cart. You want the Dover Road; take the track through the bottom wood till you reach the church, then turn south. That'll take you all the way to Barham Downs. You'll see the shutter station on top of the hill. Can't bloody miss it. We'll keep the captain here while you're gone. Maybe enjoy some of Jessie's cooking and a wet at the same time. That sit all right with you, Jessie?" Before she had time to reply, Gadd turned. "You still here, *Constable*? Best get your finger out. Time's a wasting."

Hawkwood looked back at Lasseur. "Safe journey, Captain," Lasseur said, making it sound almost as though he meant it.

Hawkwood left the kitchen at a run.

And saw the flash at the top of the slope as he turned towards the barn.

Too damned late, he thought, knowing that it had to be the sun glancing off a spyglass lens. He'd experienced the phenomenon too many times for it to be anything else.

Reacting instinctively, he was already ducking back into the house as the first of the horsemen broke silently from the edge of the trees above him.

Then the dog began to bark.

20

Pepper had been watching the farmhouse for a good fifteen minutes before there was any noticeable sign of movement. Letting the reins of his horse hang loose, he raised the telescope to his right eye.

A slight figure was making its way to the back door. Pepper recognized Thomas Gadd. There was no mistaking that limping gait. He wondered what was in the sack. It was bulging, so there was something wrapped within its folds. Game of some description, most likely. Pepper could see the gun in Gadd's hand.

He saw the dog get to its feet. Its tail began to wag and he watched as Gadd ruffled the animal's fur and led it into the house. The dog had been Pepper's main concern. He'd remembered it wasn't in the first flush of youth, but that didn't mean its sense of smell wasn't acute. Pepper and his men had taken pains to conceal themselves downwind, but breezes were fickle. They could change direction at any moment.

"What are we waiting for?" Seth Tyler spat into the dirt and fingered the butt of the pistol in his belt. "Are we going down there or not?"

"We go when I say we go," Pepper said, without moving the glass from his eye.

Tyler flushed at the put-down, made more potent by Pepper not even bothering to lower the telescope, but he knew better than to answer back.

The wounds on Tyler's face still pained him. Some of the shallower cuts had turned into scabs; the deeper ones remained tender and sore to the touch. Tyler's explanation that he'd sustained the scratches after falling into a patch of briars on his way back from the Duke's Head had been generally accepted, given his reputation as a man who liked a drink. He'd used the same story with Ezekiel Morgan and Cephus Pepper when he'd gone to pass on information about the two men Morgan was looking for.

Tyler's rage had been simmering since the day he'd been run off the farm, and his bitch of a sister-in-law had threatened to take the gun to him if he set foot on her land again. Who did she think she was? Leading him on with her sly glances and then turning all coy when he made his move. She wanted him; he knew she did. And she had to be craving it; her husband in the ground these past three years. The way Tyler saw it, he was doing her a favour. She ought to be bloody grateful. Instead, she'd come on all contrary and rejected him. And it was probably her doing that Annie had started acting up every time he tried to get *her* interested. He suspected Jessie was trying to turn her sister against him, and the thought of that made Tyler angrier still. She'd pay for all the trouble she'd caused him, he'd see to that.

And then came word that Ezekiel Morgan was willing to pay good money for information leading to the apprehension of two men. It had been the men's descriptions that had caused Tyler to sit up and take notice, for they matched those of the duo who'd given him a drubbing at Jess Flynn's farm. A chance meeting with Asa Higgs over a pint at the Blind Hog had revealed to Tyler that they were indeed the same men who'd been transported from the Flynn farm to the Haunt a few days previous. At this point, Tyler's ears had perked up. With those two on the run, Jess Flynn would be on her own at the farm.

Still smarting, and fortified by several measures of grog, Tyler had decided it was time to teach the cow a lesson. This time there would be no interference. But when he got there, he'd discovered Jess Flynn wasn't alone. The men were back. Or at least one of them was; the one who'd attacked him in the kitchen; the one with the accent. His companion, the tall one who'd wielded the besom to such murderous effect, was nowhere in sight. That didn't mean he wasn't around, but he'd not shown himself once during the time Tyler had stood spying on the farm from his vantage point at the edge of the wood. And then he'd watched Jess Flynn and the other man embrace, and the plot that had been fermenting in his brain reached fruition.

All it would take was one word to Morgan or Pepper and he'd be in Morgan's good books, he'd make himself some money, he'd have his revenge on at least one of his attackers, and he'd get the Widow Flynn all to himself.

And with McTurk and Croker out of the picture, Morgan would be looking for a new lieutenant. Tyler's opportunities were expanding by the minute. He hadn't been able to get to the Haunt quickly enough.

He heard Pepper sigh beside him. Tyler looked down towards the house. A man was leaving hurriedly by the back door.

Pepper peered through the glass.

"Well?" Tyler said, unable to keep the eagerness out of his voice. "Was I right or was I right?" He knew the answer already. It was the other bastard. He'd been at the farm all along.

The jangle of harness and the sound of teeth snapping

down on bits came from the riders on either side of him. The others were growing restless; the horses as well.

A faint breeze touched the back of Pepper's neck. *Not what we need,* he thought, knowing what it meant.

Pepper watched the Runner pause and look back towards the top of the slope. He saw the dog raise its head. When he saw Hawkwood spin back towards the house, Pepper collapsed the telescope against his thigh. He consigned the spyglass to an inner pocket, took up the reins and urged his horse forward.

"Now," he said.

The dog's barking had already alerted the others, but it didn't prevent them from exhibiting varying degrees of disbelief as Hawkwood stepped quickly back into the kitchen, dragging the dog by the scruff of the neck. The muzzle of the fowling piece wavered alarmingly. "What –?" Gadd began.

Hawkwood slammed the door shut and released the dog. "It's Pepper," he said. "They've found us."

He watched the shock explode across Lasseur's face. The privateer rose swiftly to his feet, drawing Jess Flynn to his side. She did not resist and neither Hawkwood nor Gadd moved to intercede.

"How many?" Lasseur asked.

"Eight, maybe ten," Hawkwood told them.

Lasseur absorbed the news. He looked thoughtful.

"Are you with us?" Hawkwood asked.

"The enemy of my enemy is my friend, Matthew. Don't you know the saying?" There was no humour this time.

Hawkwood nodded. "So be it."

"Bloody hell!" Gadd said suddenly from the window. "It's Seth Tyler."

Jess Flynn's head came up. She gripped Lasseur's arm.

"I knew I should have killed him," Lasseur murmured. "Ten against two? Not good."

"Worse if we don't have any bloody weapons," Hawkwood said. He eyed the fowling piece. It wasn't enough.

"Ten against three," Gadd said, turning from the window and brandishing the gun. "Though I reckon having Seth Tyler on their side will be the same as them losing two good men." The seaman grinned. The scar made him look positively demonic.

"It's my fight too," Jess Flynn said.

Hawkwood shook his head. "It's not you Morgan wants."

"If Seth is out there, then it is my fight," Jess Flynn said.

"HELLO, THE HOUSE!"

The shout came from the front.

"That's Pepper," Gadd said. "Reckon he must be vexed. He doesn't usually raise his voice. Sounds like they want to parley."

Hawkwood peered through the window, careful to stand sheltered by the wall at an angle to the glass.

The riders were arranged in a semi-circle twenty paces from the door.

Hawkwood turned to Lasseur. "Do you still have Croker's pistol?"

Lasseur nodded. "It's not loaded."

"They don't know that," Hawkwood said. "Hold on to the dog."

When he opened the door he did so cautiously, the pistol cocked and extended in front of him. Several of the men sat up straight in their saddles. Tyler was at the end of the line; Pepper was in the centre. Hawkwood stayed in the doorway and aimed the pistol at Pepper's chest. Pepper looked unconcerned by the imminent threat. Unarmed, he walked his horse forward a couple of paces.

"Constable," he said evenly.

"You're all under arrest," Hawkwood said. "If you get down from your horses and surrender your weapons, we'll say no more about it."

Pepper's mouth twitched.

Hawkwood shrugged. "It was worth a try. How's Mr Morgan?"

"Not happy. You've caused him a great deal of bother," Pepper said drily, eyeing the pistol. "He's anxious to make your re-acquaintance."

"I can imagine," Hawkwood said.

Pepper did not smile. "Didn't expect you'd end up back here. We thought you'd be across the water by now."

"How'd you find us?"

Pepper jerked his head. "Seth here told us he happened to be in the neighbourhood, thought he'd pay the widow a visit on account of they're related and saw Captain Lasseur loitering with intent. We figured you'd not be too far away." Pepper put his head on one side. "You all right, Constable? You know, you don't look too well."

"It's *Officer* to you, Pepper, and no, it's nothing serious. Just something I ate." Hawkwood looked along the line of men. "You've brought a lot of help. Worried about coming on your own?"

"Best to be prepared," Pepper said.

"And I suppose you'd like me to give myself up?"

"Got it in one," Pepper said. "Captain Lasseur as well, if it's not too much trouble."

"You know, that's what I miss about you, Pepper: your sparkling wit."

"It'll go badly for you if you don't."

"I suspect it'll go badly for us if we do," Hawkwood said.

"True, but then the Widow Flynn and the old man get to walk away."

The inference was clear.

"I thought Morgan didn't make war on women," Hawkwood said.

"Sometimes he's willing to make an exception. You want time to think about it?"

"No," Jess Flynn said. "We don't."

A look of surprise began to fan across Pepper's face, then the air was ruptured by the blast of a gun behind Hawkwood's right ear. He stood transfixed as every horse started in fear and Seth Tyler, arms outflung, mouth forming a perfect oval, was catapulted backwards. As Tyler's corpse landed among the herbs, the remaining horsemen scattered, drawing weapons. Pepper, showing commendable dexterity for a one-armed man, wheeled his horse about as Hawkwood threw himself through the open door, dragging Jess Flynn and the rifle with him. He heard a chorus of sharp reports and the sound of the balls striking the wall behind him. Somewhere a window shattered, the noise sounding as if it might have come from upstairs. The dog began to bark.

Lasseur kicked the door shut.

"Looks like the parley's over," Gadd muttered sardonically.

Hawkwood handed the pistol back to Lasseur and took the rifle from Jess Flynn's shaking hands. It was a beautiful gun; a double-barrelled Manton with grooved barrels. Not a light weapon by any means, yet she had wielded it well and clearly hit what she'd aimed at. He remembered then her threat to Tyler.

"Rab, hush!" Jess Flynn called the agitated dog to her.

"Tom's right, Jess," Hawkwood said. "You killing Tyler means Pepper's through talking. He's got nowhere else to go."

"You certainly did for the bugger," Gadd said, peering out of the window. "Can't see the others, though."

"They're there," Hawkwood said. "They'll be *coming*." He

suspected Pepper and his crew had found sanctuary behind the barn.

"Let them." Jess Flynn raised her chin defiantly, though her face was pale. She stroked the dog's head. It began to quieten. The barks turned to deep growls.

"Four against nine," Lasseur said. "That evens it up." He stretched out his left arm and Jess Flynn moved into his embrace and rested her head on his shoulder. The dog, still restless, prowled the room.

"You any good with that?" Hawkwood nodded to the fowling piece.

Gadd grinned. "Got those two coneys, didn't I?"

"Rabbits don't shoot back," Hawkwood said. He held out the Manton. "Do you have any more ammunition for the rifle?"

She moved away from Lasseur's embrace. "Only what's in the second barrel."

Hawkwood felt his heart sink. "Tom, what about you? Any refills for the Mortimer? What about powder and shot?"

"I've powder. Only a few shot though. Not enough for all *them* –" Gadd nodded towards the window.

Better than nothing, Hawkwood thought. But not by much. "What's the bore?"

"She's only light. Twenty."

Be thankful for small mercies, Hawkwood murmured to himself. "Then they'll fit the pistol. We can divide the powder and shot between yourself and Captain Lasseur."

He turned to Jess Flynn. "Are there any other weapons in the house?"

"There's a pistol. It was Jack's. He brought it back from the navy." She pointed to the dresser in the corner.

Hawkwood went to investigate. The pistol was in a drawer next to a small flask of powder and some squares of cotton wadding. The gun was military issue. It was in good condition though it didn't appear to have been oiled in a while. He found tools for making ammunition but there was no lead or spare shot. Theoretically, since it was a larger bore than the Mortimer, it would take the smaller ball, provided more wadding was added. Failing that, it could always be used as a club in the last resort, Hawkwood supposed.

"No other guns?"

She shook her head. "No."

"Then we'll make do with these," Hawkwood said.

While Jess and Tom Gadd kept watch, Hawkwood and Lasseur attended to the guns at the kitchen table. The fowling piece was already loaded, and there was enough ammunition for an additional five shots between them. As Hawkwood had expected, the balls cast for the fowling piece were of a smaller bore than the service pistol. Hawkwood compensated by wrapping one of the balls in a thick wad of cotton. When he used the rod to ram the ball down the pistol's barrel it felt tight enough, but there was no way of knowing if it would be effective when the trigger was pulled. He would just have to make sure the target was close enough to be certain of his shot. They divided the remaining ammunition between them.

Hawkwood considered the layout of the house. The downstairs was effectively one large space divided in two by a central chimney breast which effectively formed the wall between kitchen and parlour. Each room had one window facing the front of the house and one facing the rear. There were two ground-floor entrances: the front door, which led into the parlour and the stairs to the upper floor, and the back door, which opened into the kitchen.

"We should barricade the front door," Hawkwood said.

"What about the windows?" Lasseur asked.

"We need to see them coming, but we don't have enough

guns to cover all points so we'll block one off. The front window in the kitchen will be the easiest." Hawkwood pointed to the nearby dresser. It was almost six feet tall. "We can use that."

"It seems to me you've done this before," Lasseur said as they manoeuvred the dresser across the floor. The room darkened immediately as the light from outside was obscured.

"Once or twice. Sometimes I've been the one trying to get in."

They moved to the parlour, upended the settee and propped it against the front door. They used the long-cased clock to obscure half of the parlour window at the front. It wasn't much, but it was better than nothing.

"We need a redoubt," Hawkwood said. "Somewhere to make a stand."

"Don't like the sound of that," Gadd said.

"There are more of them than there are of us, and I'm guessing they're a lot better armed. They're going to get in, sooner or later." Hawkwood indicated the kitchen table. "We can retreat to the pantry and block off the door with the table to restrict their access point. Maybe we can use the cellar as a last resort. Does it have another entrance?"

"No."

"Then we'll deal with that problem when we come to it."

They up-ended the table and laid it lengthways in front of the pantry door. As a place to make a last stand, it was wretched. Hawkwood knew that, if Pepper and his men got into the house, a kitchen table wasn't going to alter the outcome.

"We could always give ourselves up," Lasseur offered, reading his mind.

"No," Jess Flynn said. "It's too late for that."

Hawkwood knew she was thinking of Tyler.

"I'll take the Manton, Jess," Hawkwood said. "You take the pistol. We've still got one shot left with the rifle. I want to make it count before they get too close."

No sooner had he spoken than there was a bang from outside and the rear kitchen window shattered.

Everyone ducked. No one was hit.

"They're probably trying to draw fire," Hawkwood said. "Let *them* waste ammunition." He looked down at the dog. "Put Rab in the pantry, Jess. We don't want him to get in the way."

Hawkwood waited until the animal had been removed, then he picked up the rifle. "To your places. The second you realize you can't hold your position, fall back to the redoubt."

From the corner of his eye, Hawkwood saw movement out of the window.

"Here they come," he said.

Pepper peered round the corner of the barn. He could see Tyler's body in the dirt in front of the house. He looked for Tyler's horse, which had bolted from the scene, and spotted it in the field where it was grazing contentedly, oblivious to the carnage.

Tyler's death had come as a shock – and not just to Tyler. It was clear from his reaction that the Runner, Hawkwood, had also been taken by surprise. Pepper didn't think it was a lucky shot either. The woman had been deliberate in her aim. Her calmness and the cadence in her voice when she'd pulled the trigger had been proof of that. Pepper wondered what had led Jess Flynn to kill her own brother-in-law in cold blood.

He'd been intrigued by Tyler's request as they'd ridden from the trees: *Leave the woman to me.* It sounded as if Tyler had been harbouring some kind of vendetta against the Widow Flynn. Jess Flynn's uncompromising declaration of hostilities had confirmed that the ill feeling was mutual. Whatever her motive, by killing Tyler she had aligned herself with the two men Pepper and his crew had been sent to eradicate. Knowing Thomas Gadd's history with the late Jack Flynn, Pepper felt it was safe to assume that Gadd, too, had chosen sides. It was just as well he'd brought the number of men he had. Which brought him full circle back to Tyler. Pepper had never liked the man. He'd long considered Tyler to be a liability. So he did not feel bereaved by his death, only inconvenienced at being a man down so soon.

A shot rang out. Pepper heard a window break.

"Hold your fire!" he called. They were too far out of range for a pistol to do effective damage.

He was suddenly aware that his left arm had developed a ferocious itch. He reached to scratch it and then remembered there wasn't anything there to scratch. It had been ten years since he'd lost the limb to a cutlass slash and yet the phantom tickles persisted. Sometimes, the sensation was so real he had to take a look to convince himself his arm really was gone.

Suppressing the impulse to grind his stump into the wall of the barn, Pepper surveyed their objective. The front of the house was a killing ground, as Tyler had found out to his cost. The safest approach would be via the rear, using the outbuildings as cover. From the nearest shed it was only a scurry over the vegetable garden to the back door. The side wall was reachable through the orchard. From there the attackers could plant themselves in the lee of the building, where the angle of the wall would offer protection against shots fired from the windows.

Behind him, Pepper's crew checked their weapons. Each of them had a brace of pistols. A couple carried cudgels. Four had short cutlasses held in scabbards on their belts. Hard, seasoned men, they had all served their apprenticeship either as escorts, bat men or tub carriers. The four cutlass bearers had all served in naval press gangs before joining Morgan's organization. Good men to have at your back in a fight, which was why Pepper had chosen them. He was prepared to forgive the errant shot a few moments ago. Seeing one of your number gunned down like that would spook anyone.

Pepper wondered about the opposition. Outnumbered they may be, but Hawkwood and Lasseur had proved themselves. The woman, too, though there was no telling how she would fare in the event of an assault on the house. As for Gadd, he'd seen action before, but he was old and he was a cripple. How effective would he be? Pepper knew that they had weapons – at least two long guns and a pistol – but did they have anything in reserve? Pepper doubted it.

The safest option would have been to wait it out, but Pepper and his crew had an appointment to keep, and it wouldn't do to be late. Certainly not tonight of all nights. Best to get the matter over with as quickly as possible.

Pepper drew the pistol from the holster across his chest.

"Billy, you stay with the horses. Keep them calm. Deacon, Roach and Clay – you're with me. The rest of you, go round the front. It's the Runner and the Frog we're after. As far as they're concerned, it's no quarter given or expected. If the widow and the old man get in the way, that's their misfortune."

Pepper waited as the four men he'd dispatched to the front entrance worked their way to the other side of the barn and ran in single file towards the corner of the house, using the orchard as cover. No one shot at them.

"On me," Pepper said. Pistol half-cocked, he stepped out from the wall. With Deacon, Clay and Roach at his heels, he ran towards the nearest outbuilding. They made it without incident. Pepper took stock. He could see that the other half of the crew had reached the orchard and were making their way through the trees. Two of them had drawn their cutlasses. Pepper looked towards the back door and the broken kitchen window. He could see vague movement inside the kitchen, but the rays of the low-hanging sun were reflecting off the remaining glass and the gloom inside the house prevented him from making out details.

The second outbuilding – the one nearest to the house – was only a few paces away. An eager Deacon sidled out from the wall. Pepper, seeing a dark shape move behind the broken window, opened his mouth to hiss a warning only to be silenced by a sharp report. Deacon's body was flung back against the outhouse wall. It remained motionless for several seconds, as if suspended from a hook, before toppling to one side like a puppet with severed strings. As Deacon hit the ground, blood seeping from the wound in his chest, a volley of small-arms fire sounded from the front of the house.

Hawkwood lowered the Manton. The gun wasn't as comfortable in his hands as a Baker rifle. Thankfully, the target had been an easy one. He had been hoping to get a clear shot at Pepper, but it had been one of Pepper's crew who had showed himself first, and beggars couldn't be choosers.

That left eight.

All they had now was the fowling piece and the two pistols, and not enough shot between them to make much of a difference. As he laid the rifle down, Jess Flynn passed him the pistol. A second later he heard Gadd yell in the other room and then the seaman's cry was obliterated by an explosion of gunfire and the splintering of glass.

Hawkwood took the spare ball from his pocket and laid it next to the sink with the flask of powder and one of the squares of wadding. It looked as insignificant as a pea left at the side of a dinner plate. Knowing he probably wouldn't have time to reload anyway, Hawkwood drew back the pistol hammer and spoke over his shoulder. "If one of us goes down, you pick up the gun. Make each shot count."

Jess nodded nervously. "I understand."

Now let them come, he thought.

And they did.

At Pepper's nod, Roach broke from concealment, and Clay poked his head round the side of the outhouse and aimed a covering shot towards the kitchen window. As the pistol cracked, Roach, his cutlass drawn, veered left, heading towards the parlour end of the house.

Clay loosed off his second pistol and ducked back behind the outhouse to reload.

Pepper waited to see what would happen.

From the kitchen, Hawkwood saw Roach come into view. He heard the report and saw the puff of powder smoke by the corner of the outhouse wall, and ducked just as the ball broke the surviving window pane and thrummed past his ear. He heard a plate break into pieces on the dresser behind him.

Before the shattered china hit the floor, Hawkwood's pistol was up, tracking the running man. As the man's companion let off his second shot, Hawkwood fired. The ball struck the running man in the groin, pitching him to the ground with a ragged cry. His companion's pistol ball buried itself in the wall beneath the window frame.

Pepper emerged from cover, pistol in hand and running towards the corner of the house, as Roach went down.

Hawkwood stepped back from the window, rammed the ball down the pistol barrel, placed the powder in the pan and snapped the frizzen in place. His hands were steady as he thumbed the hammer back. By the time he was done, Pepper had disappeared from view.

Hawkwood swore.

Behind him, Jess Flynn was crouched by the fireplace. From the other side of the chimney breast came the sound of somebody trying to kick in the front door.

"Jess, find out what's happening out there!" Hawkwood whispered.

In the parlour, Tom Gadd had been busy proving he could hit more than rabbits. Another of Pepper's crew lay dead, his throat pumping blood into the dirt beneath one of the apple trees. Gadd had whooped aloud as the ball from his fowling piece struck home, only to have his exclamation of triumph cut short as the dead man's companions returned fire with venomous fervour.

The window and the clock case took the brunt of the damage, but it had been a close shave. Gadd recalled Hawkwood's remark about rabbits not shooting back. Crouching by the wall, the old man tapped powder into the muzzle of the fowling piece and reached into his pocket for his final round. He glanced across at Lasseur and grinned, only to lose the grin as the front door shook under a bombardment of boots. He looked up as Jess Flynn called his name from the kitchen.

"Stay where you are, Jessie!" Gadd called back. "We're all right."

At the sound of Jess Flynn's voice, Lasseur turned away from the rear window. As he did so, he saw Gadd's eyes widen in alarm at something behind him. Lasseur swivelled just in time to see the cutlass blade hammer the pane into a thousand shards and a pistol muzzle appear in the opening. Lasseur swung his arm up and fired in the same instant as the attacker. The room was lit by simultaneous flashes and two thunderclaps. A shriek of pain sounded outside the window and a body dropped away.

"THOMAS!"

Lasseur spun back at the sound of Jess Flynn's cry of horror.

The fowling piece had dropped from Gadd's hands. The seaman was slumped back against the wall, clutching his shoulder. The blood on his shirt looked almost black in the half-lit room. Jess Flynn was scrambling towards him on her knees.

Lasseur sprang across the room. Shouts sounded from outside. The attackers had heard Jess Flynn's cry. From the anguish in her voice they had guessed someone inside had been hurt.

"Quick!" Lasseur looped his arm under Gadd's shoulder, ignoring the wounded man's wail of agony. Between them, they half-pulled, half-carried Gadd back into the kitchen.

"Tom's hurt!" Jess Flynn cried. She opened the pantry door. The dog leapt up at her.

"Down, Rab!"

Hawkwood turned to see Jess Flynn lift the flap to the cellar and push the dog down into it. Closing the trap she reached out to support Gadd as Lasseur lifted the seaman over the table and into the pantry.

Then Lasseur yelled.

Hawkwood turned and his throat went dry at the sight of Pepper, teeth bared in anger, curving the axe blade towards the window.

Hawkwood hurled himself backwards. The heavy blade demolished what was left of the glass and a good portion of the lattice. As Hawkwood's spine hit the floor, Pepper threw the axe to one side, pulled the pistol from the holster at his chest and fired through the open window. Hawkwood rolled and felt the wind from the ball as it struck the floor by his head. Pepper let out a roar of frustration. Hawkwood brought his pistol up and fired, but he was too late, Pepper had gone.

From the parlour came the sound of a window frame being turned to matchwood and from the upper floor the breaking of glass.

And then the back door reverberated to the sound of axe blows.

Hawkwood backed away from the door and joined the others behind the table. "How bad is he hit?"

The back door was shaking under the onslaught.

"The ball went through his shoulder," Jess Flynn said.

Lasseur reversed the pistol in his hand. "I'm out of powder."

Hawkwood looked towards the powder flask he'd left by the sink. Maybe he could still retrieve it.

The wood around the door lock was splitting. Suddenly the axe head appeared in the opening, then withdrew, tearing a great chunk of wood away with it.

Maybe not.

"Me, too," Hawkwood said. "But they don't know that."

Lasseur smiled.

"Stay down, Jess," Hawkwood said.

Then, suddenly, as if time had come to a halt, it went quiet. The blows on the door ceased. There was no sound from the front of the house either, except for a faint crackling.

"I smell burning," Lasseur said.

With a crash, the back door swung inwards.

The straw bundles were well ablaze. Three came through the doorway in quick succession, landing in a fiery cascade of sparks. One broke apart, scattering tendrils of fire in all directions. The noises in the parlour intensified as more burning straw was tossed in through the broken windows. Flames reached for the curtains and the furnishings, running up towards the roof beams in ribbons of fire. Smoke began to weave across the floor.

"Out!" Hawkwood yelled. He ran to the door and felt the breeze from the pistol ball as it thudded into the wall. A second gun cracked and he knew then that Pepper did not intend to let them leave the burning building.

Another plate tipped off the dresser and smashed behind him. In the other half of the house, the parlour was well alight and flames had begun to devour the underside of the ceiling. Plaster was splitting from the wall. The smoke was getting thicker and more acrid.

"The cellar!" Hawkwood yelled.

Lasseur pushed the table out of the way. Jess Flynn flung open the trapdoor and as the dog came out like a shaggy brown missile shot from a cannon, she grabbed a handful of fur and hung on tight. The dog yelped and tried to pull free, but with grim determination she strengthened her hold and bundled the protesting animal, claws skittering, back down into the cellar with her. Lasseur bent and scooped Tom Gadd up in his arms. The wounded man groaned as Lasseur carried him down into the darkness.

Hawkwood was about to follow Lasseur down the stairs when his eyes fell on the pail beneath the sink. He guessed it was used to carry water from the stream and as a reservoir for the sink, but he couldn't recall if he'd actually seen water in it. For a split second he hesitated as he heard Lasseur call his name. Then, the decision made, he crossed to the pail. It was half full. Grabbing it, Hawkwood retreated to the pantry. He thought he heard the sound of a shot behind him. Pepper or one of his men must have seen movement within the smoke. Eyes watering, with the heat of the flames lapping at his back, he descended the cellar steps and shut the trapdoor behind him.

"We thought Pepper had got you," Lasseur said. He sounded angry. "What were you doing? What's that you've got?" His expression changed when he saw what was in the pail.

Jess Flynn had lit a candle. She handed it to Lasseur, who held it over Gadd's wound. "Keep it still," she said.

Gently, she lifted the blood-soaked shirt off the wound and examined closely the rent the pistol ball had made in the material. She pressed the torn edges of the cloth together. Hawkwood knew from experience that she was checking to see if any of the material had travelled into the wound. If it had, there was more risk of Gadd dying of infection from the dirty cloth than of expiring through trauma and blood loss. The bloody edges of the tear fitted together perfectly. She breathed a sigh of relief.

Hawkwood took out his knife and cut a flannel-sized strip of material from the hem of Gadd's shirt. Jess took it from him and dipped it in the pail then began to clean the blood from Gadd's shoulder. Gadd groaned and his eyes flickered open.

"It was Jed Cooper who shot me," he murmured. He peered at Lasseur. "Hope you got the bastard."

"Take it easy, Tom," Hawkwood said. "Don't speak."

Gadd lapsed into silence, flinching as the cloth skirted the edges of the wound.

Hawkwood looked around. The cellar wasn't large; about the size of the kitchen above it. Punnets containing fruit and vegetables rested on shelves around the walls.

"I don't know if we're that safe from the fire. This cellar's stone-built, so it won't burn; but if too much smoke gets in here, we're dead. We'll run out of air, which means we'd have been better off letting Pepper shoot us. If you've got any petticoats under there, Jess, we can cut them into scarves to soak in the water and cover our faces. I'm told it's what heroines are supposed to do."

She dabbed the last of the blood from Gadd's shoulder,

wetted the cloth again and squeezed out the moisture. Then she held out her hand. "Knife."

She cut four strips of material from her underskirt and dropped them in the pail.

Hawkwood got up and examined the underside of the trapdoor. It was heavy wood banded with iron. Though a snug fit, it would not keep out a determined fire. If the flames grew hot enough, the metal would warp and the wood would burn and smoke would infiltrate the cellar and kill them where they lay. There was no sign of the grey demon yet, but it was up there, searching, and eventually it would find them.

A crash came from above. Hawkwood wondered if part of the ceiling had come down. He returned to the others. The dog was pacing back and forth, whining and uttering plaintive yips of distress. It looked at Hawkwood and gave a tentative wag of its tail before lying down next to Jess Flynn with its head on its paws. It did not remain still, however, but kept raising its head and staring dolefully towards the cellar roof.

More noises came from within the burning house. The dog's ears twitched.

They stubbed out the candle to conserve air and their one source of light. And then, in the darkness, in silence, they waited.

Hawkwood wasn't sure whether he had been sleeping or not. He hadn't been conscious of closing his eyes, and in the absolute blackness of the cellar it wouldn't have made any difference, but it occurred to him that he felt curiously rested. He knew that in the absence of light the mind could play strange tricks. Once the candle was extinguished, his thoughts had been full of random images; all of them, without exception, violent and bloody and fearful. But then, as the time passed, the darkness had begun to have a palliative effect. His body ached, but there was no pain. He wondered if it was because his mind had accepted the inevitability of death. His fate had been ordained, so why fight it?

But so long as he was thinking, he was still the master of his own fate and nothing was inevitable.

He was conscious of movement close by and of a panting sound. It was the dog, suddenly on its feet and making faint gruffling noises at the back of its throat. Then it let out a bark. Hawkwood heard a flint strike and then there was a spark and the candle flickered into life. Jess Flynn's face materialized out of the shadows.

Lasseur said uneasily, "I smell smoke."

Hawkwood could smell it, too. He wondered why he hadn't been aware of it sooner. He looked up, but couldn't see anything untoward. The stone at his back was still cool to the touch. Retrieving one of the strips of cloth that had been soaking in the pail, he tied it around his nose and face, then he picked up the candle.

The dog broke into a fit of frantic barking. In the confines of the cellar, the cacophony was so intense that Hawkwood thought his eardrums might burst.

As he approached the trapdoor, despite Jess Flynn's soothing words, the noise behind him grew more abrasive.

The smell of smoke was stronger now. He suspected it was because it had been building up steadily over the time they'd been down there, which indicated they'd been underground for a while.

There was no sign of burning on the underside of the trapdoor, but the smell of charcoal was pervasive. As he reached out to touch the iron banding, he heard a scraping noise above him followed by a heavy thud.

Instantly, he paused.

Pepper! Returning to finish the job.

He realized he had no weapon, save for the knife and that was behind him, with the woman.

But then he thought wearily, what did it matter? They were dead anyway.

The trapdoor swung open. A large shadow filled the opening.

Hawkwood tensed.

"Well, you look like seven miles of shit," Jago said.

21

“I’d lose the beard,” Jago said. “It puts years on.”

They had emerged to find that dusk had fallen. They had been in the cellar for nearly three hours. All four of them must have fallen asleep for some of the time. The smoke had not infiltrated the space because the outer wall of the pantry had collapsed in on itself, leaving that side of the house exposed, so that the smoke was allowed to dissipate in the air.

The rest of the house was in a similar state of ruin; a shell of scorched brick and blackened timber. None of the furniture had survived. Most items had been reduced to charcoal and ash. The stench of smoke was overpowering.

Jess Flynn knelt on the ground supporting Tom Gadd as he drank from the canteen Jago had filled in the stream. The old man swallowed eagerly. His eyes were open and moving. He seemed more alert now that he was out in the open air. Lasseur sat beside her with his elbows on his knees, surveying the wreckage. The dog lay with its head on its paws next to them.

Jago turned to the two men at his back.

Hawkwood saw an individual of similar build to Jago; thick set and sturdy with a heavy face and farmer’s hands. The second man was younger. Well set, with a strong, clean-cut face and dark eyes. He regarded Hawkwood in cool appraisal.

"You remember Micah?" Jago said.

"Of course," Hawkwood said.

Micah nodded. "Captain."

"And this here is Jethro Garvey." Jago nodded towards the first man.

"Jethro," Hawkwood said.

"Take a look around," Jago instructed.

The two men turned away.

"Who's Garvey?" Hawkwood asked.

Jago thought about it. "He's what you might call my local representative."

"How the devil did you find me?" Hawkwood was having difficulty believing it really was Jago standing in front of him and not some figment of a dream or an extension of the images he'd experienced in the cellar.

"Magistrate Read was worried when he hadn't heard from you. He sent for me. Obviously thinks you can't cope on your own."

"He did what?"

"Told me about your assignment, too. Your man Ludd sent Bow Street a dispatch about a possible sighting of you and the captain boarding a boat at Warden. I figured that was as good a place to start as any. I had a quiet word with the local landlord, Abraham. Very accommodating, he was. Seems it's a well-used route for escaping prisoners – and not just foreigners, either. Anyway, he confirmed that an American and a French officer had boarded a lugger bound for Seasalter on the night in question."

Hawkwood wondered about Jago's definition of a "quiet word".

"But how did you find this place?" Hawkwood asked.

"You familiar with a culley named Higgs?"

Jess Flynn's head came up.

"The gravedigger," Hawkwood said.

Jago nodded. "That's him. Abraham told me he was the next man down the line. I tracked him to his local; place called the Blind Hog – a right bloody hovel. He was a bit reluctant to talk at first, but it's amazing how a drop of grog'll loosen a man's tongue, once he's in the right mood."

From the expression on Jago's face, Hawkwood suspected the "right mood" might have been helped along by Jago's hand clenched around Higgs's testicles or a threat to cut off his remaining fingers.

"Our Asa," Jago said, "let slip all manner of interestin' gossip 'bout how he'd delivered the Yankee and the Frenchman first to here and then to this Ezekiel Morgan's place. What was even more fascinating was that Morgan was now offerin' a reward for the Yankee and his mate. Seems he wasn't a bloody Yankee at all but a poxy Runner!

"Then he told me about a drinking session he'd had with some arse-wipe name of Tyler. Seems Tyler had been all ears when he heard that Morgan was after the blood of the Runner and Frenchie. Started saying it would serve the Frog right for sniffing around our women."

Lasseur and Jess Flynn exchanged glances.

"Higgs thought Tyler might have had a particular woman in mind, on account of it was his sister-in-law's farm the two captains had been staying at. He said he'd had a feeling, when he came to pick you up, that the widow and the captain were a bit more than landlady and lodger, if you get my drift. And that got me thinking: if I was on the run, looking for somewhere to hide out, where would I run to? Somewhere I'd find a friendly face, that's where. So I decided Mrs Flynn's farm might be worth a visit, even if it was only to see if I could dig up some more information. Turns out it was a sound stroke. Mind you, if we hadn't heard the dog barkin' we might have missed you. We were just about to head back."

So Higgs had seen Lasseur and Jess Flynn's tactile goodbye, too, Hawkwood thought. One small gesture that had led to consequences unimagined.

"Nathaniel –"

Jago turned. It was Garvey. He was on his own, his face grim. "You'd better come and take a look at this."

Jago, Hawkwood and Lasseur left Jess with Tom Gadd and accompanied Garvey towards the barn.

Micah had found a lantern. He held it high so they could see.

The bodies were covered with straw. There were six of them. Three lay face up, the others lay face down.

"That's Tyler," Hawkwood said, pointing to one of the corpses that was lying on its back.

Tyler's mouth was still wide open, as were his eyes; a man surprised, even in death. In the lantern light, his face was the colour of rancid cheese.

"You know them, Jethro?" Jago asked.

Garvey looked down at the corpses. He nodded grimly.

Hawkwood wondered what Jago had meant by local representative.

"I'm assuming this is all your doing," Jago said. "Want to tell me about it?"

"Later," Hawkwood said.

"They left the horses, too," Lasseur said. He was standing outside the barn door, looking into the paddock.

"Why would they do that?" Jago asked.

"They were in a hurry," Hawkwood said. "They were probably planning to come back for them later."

"Who's 'they'?" Jago asked.

"A man called Pepper and three surviving members of his crew."

Garvey's head came round.

An owl called from the nearby woods.

Jago said, "That wouldn't be Cephus Pepper?"

"You *know* him?"

"I know *of* him. Why would they be in a hurry?"

"They had an appointment."

"With who?"

"Morgan," Hawkwood said.

"Something else you're not telling me?" Jago asked.

"Plenty, but there's no time."

"Why's that?"

"I've got an appointment, too."

"Don't tell me," Jago said. "Same place?"

"Yes."

"And where's that?"

"Deal."

"An' I don't suppose it can wait?"

"No."

"You going to need any help?"

"Probably," Hawkwood said.

"Christ," Jago shook his head. "I should definitely be on the bloody payroll. Micah, bring the horses round."

"Someone has to get Tom Gadd to a doctor," Hawkwood said.

"That'll be Jethro. Did you hear that, Jethro? I saw a cart round the side. Take the lantern. Go hitch it up. Then collect Mrs Flynn and the old 'un and take them to wherever she tells you."

Garvey nodded. He took the light and left.

"Good man." Jago studied Hawkwood's face. "I meant it when I said you looked like shit. Are you going to be all right? It's a fair ride."

"You know the road?"

"'Course I know the bloody road!"

Jago had been raised in a small village on the Kent marshes. As a young man, he had tried his hand at a variety of jobs – some legal, some more dubious in nature – all over the county before finally accepting the two-guinea signing-on fee from a recruiting sergeant at a Maidstone fair.

"How long?"

Jago looked thoughtful. "Depends how fast you want to push the horses. Sky's clear and it's a good moon. Our best bet'll be the Dover Road down to Green Street. Then across country through Eythorne. It ain't going to be a stroll in the park. I reckon it'll take a fair while."

"The horses that Pepper's men left will be fresh."

"Good point. We'll still have to walk them some of the way."

"I'll go and pick out the best ones," Lasseur said.

Jago looked at Hawkwood and raised an eyebrow.

"Best to have him inside the tent," Hawkwood said.

"Your call," Jago said. He watched as Lasseur let himself into the paddock.

"He's a good man, too," Hawkwood said.

"For a Frog, you mean?"

For the first time in a while, Hawkwood smiled.

Micah returned with his and Jago's mounts. There was no discussion as to whether Micah would be riding with them. Hawkwood had had dealings with Jago's lieutenant before and had been impressed with the man's quiet efficiency.

Jago and Micah retained their own horses. Lasseur had picked out the best of Pepper's string: a russet mare and a blue gelding.

Garvey, meanwhile, had taken the cob from the barn and backed it on to the cart, then tied his own horse to the rear. He was now sitting ready with the reins. Gadd was lying on the flat boards, covered up to his chest with a horse blanket. The dog's head lay across his thighs.

Hawkwood went over and took Gadd's hand. "You did well, Tom. You made a difference. I won't forget."

"Won't be forgettin' you in a hurry either, Cap'n." Gadd smiled weakly, though some of the fire was back in his eyes. "You going to make them pay?"

"Count on it," Hawkwood said.

"Especially Pepper."

"Especially him." Hawkwood leant in close. "I've a question for you, Tom: Morgan mentioned a ship that would be waiting for him off Deal. Any idea what that ship might be?"

"That'll be the *Sea Witch*. He uses her for special runs. She's an ex-navy cutter, fast; schooner-rigged and black-painted. You can't miss her."

At night time, you would, Hawkwood thought. He looked up at the sky.

"Sounds as if that'll be the one. Thanks, Tom. Take care of Jess, you hear?"

"I will, Cap'n. Good luck to you."

Hawkwood climbed on to the mare. Jago and Micah were already mounted. Lasseur stood with Jess Flynn.

"By the way," Jago said. "Thought you might need this –" He reached into his saddlebag and lifted out Hawkwood's baton, the ebony tipstaff containing his Runner's warrant.

"Where the hell did you get it?"

"Don't ask," Jago said, and winked.

Hawkwood gripped the baton, enjoying the feel. It was like greeting an old friend. He looked over to Lasseur. "We have to go, Captain."

He watched as Lasseur and the woman embraced. Lasseur whispered something in her ear and waited as she climbed up beside Gadd. The cart moved off and she raised her hand in silent farewell. Lasseur stared after her for a moment, then climbed on to his horse.

As the cart started up the track, Hawkwood, Jago, Micah and Lasseur turned their horses about and rode for Deal.

It was after midnight when they finally arrived.

It had been a hard ride. They had joined the Dover Road to the south of the church at Blean and made good progress along the ten miles between there and Den Hill. The road had been firm and it had been a straight run, though they'd had to temper their speed through Canterbury, walking their horses part of the way through the town. Jago had used the opportunity to ask Hawkwood what was going on. Hawkwood had told him.

"Can't leave you alone for a bloody minute, can I?" had been Jago's response.

The route had continued south through Barham Downs. It had been too dark and too late to send a signal by shutter, but Hawkwood had seen the station outlined against the night sky at the top of the hill as they rode past.

They had been making good time until Wooten, but then the journey had taken a turn for the worse. The roads had become little more than narrow winding tracks, barely wide enough for a wagon, forcing them to ride in single file. Some stretches had taken them across moonlit fields. Hawkwood suspected it might have been quicker riding all the way to Dover and then taking the main road north, but Jago had argued that their chosen path was five miles shorter.

They entered Deal through the toll gate on the western end of the town. They could tell by the lights and the frantic activity that they were too late. In truth, Hawkwood had suspected that would be the case from the moment they had left the ashes of the farmhouse.

True to his promise, Morgan had taken his revenge. In

doing so, he had left a trail of death and destruction behind him.

The attack had not been subtle. If Morgan's only intention had been to instil fear and confusion, then he had succeeded admirably. Six wagons and more than two dozen men had taken part in the assault on the Admiral's residency. The handsome two-storeyed building with its large windows either side of a pillared and porticoed entrance didn't look like the sort of place where bullion was stored. To the right of the pillars stood a manned sentry box. A pair of heavy doors formed an effective barrier to the street. Or at least they had done. Morgan's attack had left them hanging from their hinges, blown apart by twelve-pound shot fired from a 6-cwt carronade that had been mounted on the heavy horse-drawn, flat-bedded wagon that was now parked at an oblique angle across the road.

The carronade was an effective weapon, short-barrelled, utilizing a variety of calibres – of which the twelve-pounders were the smallest – but it had its flaws. One being that it was prone to violent recoil. The stubby, nozzled tube of metal resting on its side next to the wagon told its own tale.

A four-man military guard stood watch over the gun and the two horses, now waiting placidly in their harnesses.

"Nathaniel, you and Micah have a word with the guards," Hawkwood said. "See what you can find out. Captain Lasseur and I will pay our compliments to the Admiral."

Jago looked Hawkwood and Lasseur up and down. "That's if he doesn't have you both arrested for vagrancy first."

After running a gauntlet of curious stares, Hawkwood's warrant got them through the door and into a cold marble-floored room with an impressive domed ceiling, where a harassed army lieutenant called Burden identified himself as the officer in charge of the bullion escort. He and his troops had been in their quarters in the castle when Morgan launched his assault.

Rear Admiral Foley had not been in residence at the time, Burden explained. A galloper had been sent to Dover, where he was attending a meeting with his fellow Port Admirals, to inform him of the night's events.

"Who was in the residency?" Hawkwood asked.

Hawkwood could tell that Burden was still wondering who he was, but the warrant gave him the authority to ask questions, and Burden knew it, irrespective of the fact that Hawkwood looked like the bastard son of a low-class bordello keeper and the town drunkard.

There had been six people in the house: the admiral's secretary, the cook, the housekeeper and three armed guards, who rotated shifts in the sentry box under the portico. The unfortunate sentry manning the box when the carronade round demolished the entrance doors had been Private Hobley. His body had been found, face down and badly mutilated, twenty feet from the entrance. It was still lying there now, awaiting removal to the dead room next to the castle's infirmary, where it would join the night's other casualties.

Throughout his report, Burden kept casting surreptitious looks in Lasseur's direction. The Frenchman had remained silent thus far, but Burden's interest had been piqued; no doubt because Lasseur, with his goatee beard, didn't have the look of an Englishman. And, like Hawkwood, he was bloodied and bruised and reeked of smoke.

To satisfy Burden's curiosity, Hawkwood introduced Lasseur by name but described him as a Bourbon loyalist officer on special detachment to the Home Office. He could see that Burden wasn't entirely satisfied with the explanation, but that was something the lieutenant would just have to live with.

Then Burden said to Lasseur, "You'll have to forgive me, Captain, but after what we've seen tonight, my men and I ain't feeling too well disposed to your countrymen."

"What are you talking about?" Hawkwood asked.

Burden gazed at him in puzzlement. "You mean, you don't know?"

"Know what?"

"It was a French raiding party that did this."

Hawkwood felt cold fingers caress the back of his neck.

Burden explained, with another sideways glance at Lasseur, that the men who'd invaded the residency had been wearing French infantry uniforms.

"They killed two of my men, the murdering bastards," Burden said, unable to keep the anguish from his voice.

In addition to the sentry, Corporal Jefford, one of the guards stationed in the inner lobby, had been killed. His body was lying next to Hobley's, under the same blanket.

The lieutenant in charge had spoken in English, summoning all the building's occupants to assemble before him. Then he had demanded the key to the strong room. The admiral's secretary, the individual entrusted with the safety of the key in his master's absence, had, in a laudable but ultimately futile display of defiance, refused to comply. At which point, one of the lieutenant's men, a short, broad-shouldered sergeant somewhat older than his comrades, had shot Corporal Jefford stone dead.

The key had been produced within minutes.

And then the raiding party had commenced emptying the strong room.

It had taken some time to remove the bullion boxes, but the Frenchmen had worked with quiet, speedy efficiency. According to the surviving guard, Private Butcher, it looked as if it was something they did every day.

When the last box had been taken, the lieutenant had

locked the staff in the strong room. He and his men had then departed with the bullion.

"Where was the army?" Hawkwood demanded. "What the devil were you doing while all this was going on?"

The army, Burden told him miserably, had been out-manoeuvred.

Following a tip-off that two major contraband runs involving hundreds of men and ponies were planned for that evening – one to the north at Sandwich Flats, the other to the south at Margaret's Bay – the Revenue had turned to the town's regular contingent of troops, modest at the best of times, for assistance. Only a handful of soldiers had been left in Deal.

Hawkwood realized then how well Morgan had played his cards. He had obviously started the rumours himself, instructing his agents to spread the word the runs were taking place. With the troops out of the way, his men had soon sealed off the town's three major access roads: the Dover Road to the south, Five Bell Lane in the west and the turnpike road to the north.

Burden coloured. "And we were stuck in the bloody castle. We were able to return fire, but I'm still not sure if we hit any of them."

Deal Castle lay at the southern edge of the town, close to the Dover Road toll gate. It had been besieged once before, during the Civil War. Since then it had remained inviolate, its massive circular bastions standing guard over the town and the coast, a monument to Tudor engineering.

Like the carronade, however, the fortress had its flaws. Its primary use was as a defence against attack from the water, not from the land. Its guns faced the sea. The second major flaw was that, like all castles, it had only one main entrance: the gatehouse.

Access to the gatehouse was by a narrow stone causeway.

Morgan's men had turned the causeway into a killing ground, blockading it with another of their heavy wagons and a pair of mounted swivel guns opposite the entrance.

When the carronade opened fire on the Admiral's residency, a patrol had immediately set out from the castle to investigate. The soldiers made it only as far as the causeway before Morgan's men, dressed in their French infantry uniforms, opened fire to lethal effect. Four men dead, six injured, out of a force that hadn't been large to begin with.

"We couldn't get at the bastards," Burden said. "And all they had to do was keep us confined. We couldn't get out by the moat either. They had the postern gate under their guns, too."

"What about the Naval Yard; aren't there any troops there?"

Burden shook his head. The Yard lay next to the castle. It was small by Admiralty standards and its main role was to victual ships with bread and beer and ballast from the local beach. Enclosed by high walls and with only three entrances, it had been easy to seal off. In any case there were no troops stationed there beyond a couple of sentries manning the gates.

With his wagon crews effectively in control of the town, Morgan and his raiders had driven the gold straight down to the beach where his ship had been waiting. They had used a fleet of small boats to ferry the bullion boxes from the shingle beach out to the ship.

"She was flying the ensign," Burden said heavily. "In the dark, we thought she was one of ours."

With the gold on board, the ship had weighed anchor and Morgan's wagon crews had melted away in the night, leaving the strong room bare and the town in a state of shock.

That had been nearly two hours ago, Burden told them.

Morgan had put the army to shame. And he had done it with a precision the army would have been proud of. Even down to executing the robbery at night so that the Deal telegraph station would not be able to send a shutter message alerting the next station down the line that the residency was under attack.

The time had come for Hawkwood to add to the lieutenant's suffering.

It wasn't the French, he told Burden, at which the man seemed to age a thousand years in front of their eyes.

Leaving the shattered lieutenant in the empty strong room to contemplate what remained of his career, Hawkwood and Lasseur made their way to rejoin Jago and Micah.

"Perhaps he'll shoot himself," Lasseur said. "It would be the honourable thing."

"I think someone will probably do it for him," Hawkwood said.

Outside, the bodies of the dead were being lifted on to a cart.

Jago nodded towards the soldiers guarding the overturned carronade. "There are some bodies on the beach and the corporal told us there are more up by the castle," he said, then paused and looked at Lasseur. "They're French." Jago turned back to Hawkwood: "I thought you said Morgan and his men were behind this?"

"It's only the uniforms that are French," Hawkwood said. "It was Morgan's crew."

Jago shook his head. "The ones I saw were definitely French. They had tattoos. I'd know that eagle anywhere."

"You've seen them?"

"Beach is that way –" Jago pointed. "And you won't even get your feet wet."

"Show me," Hawkwood said.

The bodies had been laid side by side, face up, on the

shingle, ready for disposal. In the moonlight, in their dark tunics, shakos and dirty breeches, and with their faces already grey and misshapen by death, they looked like bloodstained ragdolls left by the tide.

Le Jeune looked about a hundred years old. The tattoo was visible just below the crook of his arm. The tunic was too short for him and the sleeve had ridden up. Next to him, in complete contrast, Louis Beaudouin looked about twelve. Souville resembled a skeleton already; Rousseau wasn't much better.

Jago had referred to another lot of bodies found by the castle. Hawkwood was willing to wager he knew the identities.

"He killed them," Lasseur breathed. "He killed them all." The breeze ruffled his hair as he gazed down at the corpses in disbelief.

"They'd served their purpose," Hawkwood said, and then wished that he could take the words back, even though he knew it was the truth. Morgan had used Frenchmen in French uniforms; hearing them conversing and giving orders and probably exhorting their comrades to greater effort in their own language, any witnesses present would have been left in no doubt that the gold had been stolen by a French raiding party.

And dead men in French infantry uniforms gave added credence to the lie. In the confusion, it would have been assumed that some of Burden's beleaguered troops had managed to fight back.

Leaving Morgan's men to steal away scot-free.

Sooner or later the truth would have come out. Morgan kept his people on a tight leash and the hardened members of his crew knew how to keep secrets, but this was huge. Eventually, over a glass of grog or a pipe of tobacco, the story would be told. But by then it would be too late.

Wearily, Hawkwood lowered himself to the pebbles and rested his hands on his knees.

What had it all been for?

Jago sat down next to him and let out a sigh. "Don't know about you, but I'm getting too old for all this runnin' about. A man of my age, it ain't good for my health."

Hawkwood could hear cries behind him and the sound of tramping feet. Pretty soon the army, having learned that its pay chests had been stolen not by the French but by someone much closer to home, would begin hammering on doors.

To what degree, Hawkwood wondered, had the town's inhabitants been involved? Morgan could not have deployed his crew or distributed the weapons – especially the carronade – without reconnoitre or support. And there were the wagons and the horses to consider, too. Morgan had once boasted that there would never be a shortage of men willing to do his bidding. Did that mean he could recruit an entire town? Deal folk were a close-knit community, and they had seen their livelihoods overturned by the authorities on more than one occasion. They didn't like the government or the army, and a share of Morgan's profit from the gold would keep families housed and fed for a long time to come, ensuring their loyalty. He even had the bloody judges in his pocket, and half a million pounds bought a lot of protection. The authorities – and that included the army – would have their work cut out.

"Now what?" Jago asked.

Hawkwood looked back at the town. Lights were flickering on. He could hear shouts, more running feet. "See if we can find ourselves beds for what's left of the night. Leave someone else to clear up this damned mess."

"I could use a wet," Jago said, getting to his feet. "I've got a throat like a tinker's crotch. Let's go find ourselves an inn."

Lasseur, standing to one side, continued to gaze out over the water. His expression was as black as the waves.

Hawkwood stood. "Looks like you got what you wanted."

Lasseur looked at the line of bodies. "Not like this."

"But your Emperor will get his gold."

Lasseur shook his head, saying nothing. He looked deep in thought. Then he said, "They can still be caught."

"What?" Hawkwood said, not quite hearing.

"I said they can still be caught."

Hawkwood laughed. He couldn't help it. "I don't think so, Captain. It's the navy's task now, and it'll take them the rest of the night just to get their bloody breeches on. The bastards are long gone. Besides, no one knows what port they're heading to."

"I do," Lasseur said. "I know exactly where they're going. We might be able to catch them."

"It's too damned late. They'll be across the water before anyone can raise a sail."

"Not necessarily," Lasseur said. "Not if this breeze stays on the same heading."

Hawkwood fixed him with a stare. "What do you mean, 'We'?"

Lasseur turned slowly. "I mean my ship, the *Scorpion*."

"Your ship?" Hawkwood said. "What the devil's your ship got to do with it?"

And Lasseur smiled.

22

Hawkwood's warrant got them out of town, through the army-manned toll gate and south, on to the Walmer Road.

The horses were flagging, despite having been rested, and Hawkwood knew they would not be able to go much further. It came as some relief when, after only a couple of miles, Lasseur led them off the road, turning east towards the sea. A signpost, standing crooked in a hedge, read *Kingsdown.*

They walked the horses through the sleeping village and on to a shingle beach lying at the foot of a tall, grey rock face. Hawkwood could see the raked outline of an even higher slab of headland beyond it and another beyond that, and he knew this was the beginning of the long line of pale cliffs that stretched all the way along the coast to Dover.

Just discernible against the night sky, some three hundred yards from the shore, a dark-painted, three-masted schooner lay at anchor. No lights showed upon her deck or from within her hull. It was possible, Hawkwood thought, that if they had not been looking for the vessel, it would have taken them some time to realize it was there.

"I need a pistol," Lasseur said.

Jago reached into his saddlebag. "It's loaded," he warned.

Lasseur took a long breath, pointed the pistol into the air, and pulled the trigger. The powder flared and the report rebounded from the cliff above them. As Micah calmed the horses, Lasseur handed the pistol back and Jago stuck it in his belt.

The water looked dark and cold and deep. Hawkwood was reminded of the night they had sailed from Warden. He could see the lights of two vessels far out in the Channel beyond the black-hulled ship and he wondered if one of them was Morgan's *Sea Witch*.

The privateer had employed Tom Gadd as his messenger. On their first day back at the farm, while the widow attended to Hawkwood's fever, Lasseur had sent Gadd to visit his agent in Ramsgate; the same man Lasseur had been trying to reach when he'd made his dash for freedom prior to his arrival at Maidstone Gaol.

The agent had dispatched Lasseur's message to his crew in Dunkerque by carrier pigeon; informing them their captain was free and awaiting their arrival. They were to sail *Scorpion* to the Kent coast, and lie at anchor in the waters off Kingsdown for two hours either side of midnight. They would do this for five nights, from the time of the message's receipt, and look for Lasseur's signal.

"It all depends," Lasseur had said, "whether my men got the message in time."

It seemed they had.

Hawkwood looked towards the ship. A small object had detached itself from the hull and was heading towards them. Slowly, it drew closer and Hawkwood saw the hunched backs of the rowers and heard the light splash of the oars.

Lasseur came to life. He stepped towards the water.

A soft cry came out of the darkness. *"Scorpion!"*

Lasseur waded into the water. *"C'est moi!"*

"More bloody Frogs!" Hawkwood heard Jago mutter under his breath.

The rowboat continued its steady approach. Finally, it

grounded against the shingle. The dark-haired man who leapt from the boat was about Micah's age, and of similar build. He was not wearing a uniform but was dressed from head to toe in black, as was the seaman manning the oars at the stern of the boat. Eyes laughing and smiling broadly, the dark-haired man clasped Lasseur's arm in a firm grip.

Lasseur grinned. "This is my first officer, Lieutenant Marc Delon."

The young lieutenant nodded a greeting, though he couldn't disguise his curiosity at the presence of three strangers. Hawkwood wondered if Delon thought they were all fellow escapees.

Lasseur nodded towards the man seated in the stern. "Henri, *comment va cela*?"

The oarsman grunted an inaudible reply.

Lasseur clapped his lieutenant on the back. *"D'accord, allons!"*

Delon scrambled back on to the boat.

"Let's go, my friends!" Lasseur urged. "Hurry!"

"Anything left in your saddlebags?" Hawkwood asked Jago.

"Nothing that I'll miss," Jago said.

Lasseur climbed into the boat. Hawkwood and Jago followed him. Micah remained on shore. The smiling lieutenant picked up his oars and the boat pulled slowly away from the beach.

Micah remained standing motionless at the edge of the water. Jago raised his hand. Micah nodded once, then turned and walked up the shingle towards the horses. He did not look back.

Hawkwood caught Lasseur's eye. "Does Jess know?"

"No," Lasseur said. He looked over the bow towards the open sea, and lapsed into silence.

* * *

Lasseur's crew made no secret of their joy at his return, lining the rail to welcome him. Once on board *Scorpion*, however, Lasseur wasted no time in giving his lieutenant the order to depart as quickly as possible.

As the crew sprang into action, Hawkwood looked out over the rail. He could see the long line of chalk bluffs extending into the darkness behind them. They looked close enough to touch. Of Micah and the horses, there was no sign. He looked over the bow towards the line of the horizon, but there was nothing to see except the dark curtain of night. The lights of the vessels he had seen earlier had disappeared.

Her anchor stowed, the ship began to swing round. Sails were being raised as Lasseur led them below. In the chart room, a lantern swayed from a beam as Lasseur pulled a chart from a nearby locker and opened it out upon the table.

"Morgan will be heading here –" he said, pointing with a pair of compasses. "Gravelines."

Hawkwood looked over the end of the compass points at the lines and squiggles. The name sat halfway between Dunkerque and Calais on the northern coast.

"Why there?"

"They call it *la ville des Smoglers.* The port was chosen by Bonaparte to accommodate free traders and their ships. They've built a special enclosure with stores, warehouses and lodgings. The whole place is protected by gun batteries. There's even an English quarter. They say that up to three hundred English free traders use it at any one time. The Emperor has granted merchants special licences to import and export goods using the smugglers. Any contraband landed along your southern coast will have started its journey here."

Lasseur tapped the chart table with his knuckle. "This is where the guinea boats deliver their cargoes. The trade is controlled by the Rothschild family. Head of operations is Nathan Rothschild, the banker; he's based in London. His brother, James, arranges for the transfer of the gold from Gravelines to Paris, where it is changed back into English bank notes. It's then that the smugglers and their backers make their profit. Morgan's heading for Gravelines, I'll stake my life on it."

"And you still think we can catch him?" Hawkwood asked.

"If any ship can, it's this one."

"Back in Deal, you said something about the breeze. What did you mean?"

"The wind's from the east."

"I don't understand," Hawkwood said.

"One of the reasons Morgan chose to carry out the raid when he did was to take advantage of the tide. Cutters have deep draughts and are not usually good for close inshore work, so he needed a high tide to enable him to load the gold on to his ship and then make his escape.

"To get to Gravelines, however, he would first have to steer south to avoid Les Sables – what you call the Goodwin Sands." Lasseur tapped the chart. "During that part of his journey, the tide would have been against him; with the wind driving him against the shore, his progress would have been very slow. Once he cleared the Downs and reached the southern end of the Sands, the tide would have been more in his favour, but so long as this wind holds, he'll find it hard to make headway. Even if the breeze remains gentle, he will have to tack constantly. Cutters are fast; that's why the free traders use them. Ordinarily, a cutter could probably outrun a schooner, but in a headwind he will not have got very far. *Scorpion* will be faster – she can defeat the wind. I believe we can catch him."

"I thought ships couldn't sail into the wind," Hawkwood said.

"*Scorpion* can," Lasseur said confidently.

"How?"

"She has a special type of sailing rig. I designed it myself. It's based on the rigs of the xebecs, the ships used by Barbary pirates. They robbed European vessels and escaped by sailing *into* the wind, leaving escorts unable to chase them. I studied the design when I was in the Mediterranean. *Scorpion*'s rig has been adapted so that she can use the same tactic. You saw how her main mast is square rigged? Those sails provide the forward motion, thrusting her through the waves. The xebec sails were triangular and set between bowsprit and foremast. I use the same principle, but instead of one large sail I use two, between my fore and main masts. With the jibs, they create a lifting motion; soon as they're raised, you'll see that they are cut flatter than normal. That allows her to go to windward and to glide over the waves with ease."

Hawkwood tried to look as if he knew what Lasseur was talking about. He was pleased to see that Jago didn't appear any the wiser.

"What have you told your crew?"

"That we seek the enemy. It's what we do."

"Won't they wonder what Nathaniel and I are doing here?"

"We've been together a long time. They will not question my actions."

There was a discreet cough. Lasseur's lieutenant stood in the doorway.

Lasseur acknowledged his lieutenant's presence and laid the compasses on the chart. "Forgive me, gentlemen," he said crisply. "I need to be on deck. Let me show you to my quarters."

Lasseur led them through the ship towards the stern. The schooner was small, Hawkwood saw; a minnow compared to the *Rapacious*. Curiously, even though he had to duck his head beneath the beams, there seemed to be a lot more headroom; he realized it was probably due to the ship having only the one lower living deck. Several crew members, who'd already welcomed Lasseur topside, were seated at the tables in the mess area and their faces lit up as Lasseur entered. He greeted each one by name as he passed through. It was impossible not to notice the renewed spring in his step now that he was back on board his ship.

The stern cabin was tiny, with two narrow berths and a table and a seat beneath the window.

"Make yourselves comfortable," Lasseur told them. "I'll have Raoul bring you something from the galley. It will be cold on deck later, so we'll find you some extra gear."

When Lasseur had left, Jago lowered himself on to the window seat and ran a hand over his cropped hair. He looked at Hawkwood and sighed.

"Remind me again why we're here."

Hawkwood sank on to a berth.

"Because I'm damned if I'll let Morgan get away with it. This is the only chance I've got of catching him."

"Of getting killed, more like! Morgan's gone. Couldn't you just admit that you've lost him? You can't win them all."

"I haven't lost him yet," Hawkwood said.

"No, right, that's how come we're sailing to France with a Frog privateer. You couldn't just cut your losses, hand Monsewer over to the authorities and go back to London with Micah and me?"

"I can't hand him in, Nathaniel. Not when it means sending him to the hulks. I wouldn't do that to any man. You wouldn't, either, if you'd seen what those places are like. He saved my life. I owe him. I reckon he's gotten this far, he deserves a chance. In any case, I don't see as I had much choice."

"You've always had a choice!"

"It's not that easy."

"From where I'm bloody sitting, it is," Jago snapped back. "Have you asked yourself why Lasseur's doing this? Way I see it, it's in his interest to give Morgan a clear run. The Emperor will get his gold, Lasseur gets to go home. All we are is bloody ballast! You do know you ain't going to get the gold back?"

"I don't give a damn about the gold! It's Morgan I want. The bastard's responsible for the deaths of two naval officers, a Revenue man and at least two British soldiers. Not to mention the inconvenience he's caused me."

"And the Frog prisoners?"

"I'll leave them to Lasseur's conscience."

"He's got one, has he? What's to stop him delivering us up to the Frog authorities? Could be all you've done is exchange an English hulk for a French one. That's if they don't shoot us for being bloody spies."

"He won't do that."

"Who says?"

"He did. He gave me his word."

"And you believe him?"

"Yes. Besides, it's not in his interest to give me up." Hawkwood smiled. "I still owe him four thousand francs."

"Well, that's all right then. There was me thinking he was being swayed by the thought of four tons of gold bullion swelling Boney's coffers. How daft is that? I still don't see why he's so damned fired up about catching Morgan before he reaches France. Why doesn't he wait till after Morgan gets there and then denounce the bugger?"

"Because as soon as he lands, Morgan will disappear into the English enclave. They're Morgan's people. He has friends there. There's also a good chance the French will protect him. He delivers Bonaparte twelve million francs and they'll probably think he's someone worth protecting. Maybe they'll think if he can do it once, he can do it again."

"He killed eight Frenchmen. You telling me they won't hold that against him?"

"Morgan gets to Gravelines first, his story is going to be that they died in the execution of their patriotic duty – that's assuming he even bothers to mention them. By the time Lasseur gives his version, Morgan will have become the Emperor's blue-eyed boy. Twelve million francs buys a lot of favours. And there's no proof he killed them. Who's to say they weren't shot by redcoats? It'll be Lasseur's word against his and Lasseur wasn't there."

"So Lasseur's planning to catch up with Morgan on the high seas?"

"That's the way of it."

"And mete out some justice of his own?"

Hawkwood said nothing.

"And we're going to help him?" Jago pressed.

"You didn't have to come along," Hawkwood said.

"'Course I had to come along! Christ, you get these Tom-fool ideas into your head, someone has to watch your back!"

"And that's you?"

"Yes, it's me! It's always bloody me! And, might I say, you've come up with some crack-brained ideas in your time, but this one takes some beating. You're willin' to go to all this trouble just so's you can serve notice on a bloody smuggler?"

"The damned gold's lost anyway. This way at least I've a chance of making sure Morgan doesn't profit from it."

"Any likelihood we can steal it back from Lasseur's clutches?"

"Just the two of us?" Hawkwood said drily. "I doubt it."

"Worth considerin'. So Lasseur and his Emperor get twelve million francs while you get one murdering bastard free trader?"

"Some might call that a bargain."

"Only if they've lost their bloody wits. And have you given any thought to how we'll get home?"

"Lasseur will see we get back."

"You're settin' an awful lot of store in the man."

"I told you, he's worried he'll lose the money I owe him."

Jago shook his head in exasperation. "You can joke, but you realize if anything happens to Lasseur and we end up in bloody Verdun or one of those other Frog prisons, we're well and truly buggered."

"That why you sent Micah home?"

"I thought it best that someone back there knows where we are."

"You're saying he'll come looking if he doesn't hear from us?"

"If he doesn't hear from *me*, he will." Jago fell silent, then said, "Jesus, this is a rum business. You must really want the bastard."

"I do," Hawkwood said. "But it's not business. With Morgan, it's personal."

There was a rap on the door, then a seaman entered bearing a tray loaded with bread and cold beef, two mugs, a pot of coffee and a bottle of brandy.

"Avec les compliments de Capitaine Lasseur, messieurs."

Placing the tray on the table, the cook departed.

Jago poured the coffee and added a generous measure of brandy to each mug before passing one of them across the table. "Get that down you."

Hawkwood took a swallow. The liquid was scalding. He waited for his throat to cool and then said, "Tell me about Cephus Pepper."

Jago grimaced. "He's Morgan's right-hand man, though you already knew that. I heard he used to be first mate on a blackbirder, runnin' slaves to the West Indies. Ran foul of a rival ship off Havana – back in '02, I think it was. Lost his arm in a deck fight. They say he escaped by going over the side. Not a man you'd want to cross in a hurry, as you found out."

"How long's he been with Morgan?"

"Eight years, or thereabouts. You think he was there with Morgan tonight?"

"You can count on it. You know Morgan, don't you?"

"We've never met, though I reckon I know enough about him not to turn my back. He likes to tell folk he's a descendant of Henry Morgan, the buccaneer, which I bloody doubt. Far as I know, he's the son of a farmer from over Ruckinge way. Family was in the Trade for years. Morgan's father used to run with the Callis Court mob. Morgan quit the farm when he was a lad. Rumour was he ran off to sea to escape the law, but that could be a story he put around. Same way he's supposed to have been a bo's'n on the *Britannia*; though that'd explain why he's so good at runnin' things and why a lot of his crew are former navy men. It's probably why he and Pepper make a good team. He came back and took over the business when his old man died; built it up from there. Got no Welsh blood in him at all, unless his great-grandfather was caught buggering a ewe. He say anything about that to you?"

"He must have forgotten to mention it," Hawkwood said. "Ever taken advantage of his services?"

"You referring to my business interests?"

Hawkwood smiled.

Jago shrugged. "Probably have, indirectly, given the control he's got. My line of work, you don't always know the provenance of the goods. Mostly I try and deal with the Sussex branch of the Trade."

"Don't think I care to know too much," Hawkwood said.

"Just as well."

"And Garvey, does he work for Morgan?"

"No flies on you, are there?" Jago said, taking a sip from his drink and smacking his lips in appreciation.

"*Local representative?*" Hawkwood said. "Come on! He knows Pepper, he recognized the bodies in the barn, and he obviously knows his way around that neck of the woods. It doesn't take a genius."

Hawkwood leant back against the bulkhead. His limbs, for some reason, had started to feel as heavy as lead. Added to which, he had the sudden overwhelming desire to close his eyes. He knew he mustn't fall asleep, for that would be fatal. If he nodded off, there was a very good chance he'd never wake up. He tried to fight the rising tide of weariness that was creeping over him.

"Aye, well," Jago said. "Not that it matters. He's one of Morgan's errand boys; delivers messages about upcoming runs and the like. Morgan also uses him to pay people off, so he knows where some of the bones are buried. We go back a ways; if ever I've a mind to visit my old hunting grounds, I get in touch. Just as well, too." He paused and took a sip of coffee and glanced across the table in time to see Hawkwood's eyes droop and the mug begin to slip from his hand.

Jago sighed. He put down his own drink and, reaching across swiftly, rescued the falling mug. "'Bout bloody time," he murmured. He placed the mug on the table, grabbed the blanket from his bunk and draped it across Hawkwood's sleeping form. He stared down at the scarred and unshaven face, his brow creasing as his eyes took in the new wounds and the state of Hawkwood's clothes. He shook his head, returned to his seat and picked up his drink. "No bloody stamina, some people," he muttered softly.

* * *

The touch of a hand on Hawkwood's arm brought him jerking awake. For a moment he wondered where he was. Then his ears picked up the creaks and groans and the cry of a crewman from somewhere on the deck above and his brain began to function. He looked up to find Jago's craggy countenance looming over him. He sat up quickly, nearly crowning himself on the underside of a deckhead beam in the process.

"Captain wants us up on deck. There's a sail off the larboard bow, whatever the hell that is."

Hawkwood scrambled to his feet and almost lost his footing as the deck pitched unexpectedly. He cursed, grabbed the edge of the table and felt his stomach turn.

He followed Jago up the canted stairway on to the schooner's deck and immediately felt the bite of the wind and the lash of spindrift on his cheek. The hiss of the waves against the ship's hull and the crack of canvas filled his ears. It was not yet light, but beyond the bowsprit a band of sienna-coloured sky was slowly widening across the horizon. Running along the lower edge of it was a long uneven smear which Hawkwood knew was land. It was too far away to pick out details.

Lasseur was braced against the port rail, peering through a telescope, shoulders thrust forward. A cheroot was clenched between his teeth. He looked like a wolf scenting prey; a man in his element.

"Home," he said, following Hawkwood's gaze. "Mine," he added. "Not yours." He gave a lupine grin.

"How far?"

"Twenty miles, maybe a little less."

Hawkwood looked over his shoulder. Beyond the stern, the sky was much darker and it was harder to differentiate between sea and land, if there was any land out there.

"There's a sail?" Hawkwood said.

Lasseur nodded. He handed Hawkwood the spyglass and pointed ahead, towards the distant smudge of coast.

"Two miles off the bow."

Hawkwood wedged his hip against the rail, tried to ignore the water sluicing over his boots, and jabbed the glass to his eye. At first, all he could see was a dark swell of blue-black waves. He lowered the glass, took his bearings, aimed at the band of light coming up over the bow and tried again. He bit back a curse as the eyeglass slipped once more, but his perseverance was rewarded when suddenly a dark, angular silhouette slid across his line of sight. The vessel was low down, running close-hauled on a port tack, her fore- and aft-rigged canvas braced tight.

"I see it!" He felt a surge of excitement move through him. "Morgan?" He passed the telescope to Jago.

"She's a cutter," Lasseur announced confidently. "And Gravelines lies almost dead ahead of us. It will be dawn in an hour. We'll know for certain then."

"She's not showing any colours," Jago muttered, peering through the glass. The telescope looked very small in his hands.

"Neither are we," Lasseur pointed out, taking the glass back and stealing another look. "If they've seen us, which they may not have done, they'll be wondering who we are, though they might guess from our rig that we're not a British ship. The British don't have many schooners. Some of the ones they do have were captured from us, but they're nothing like *Scorpion*, so he's probably not too concerned at the moment. That gives us the edge."

Hawkwood looked up. The schooner, like the cutter, seemed to be carrying a huge amount of sail for her size; Lasseur's Barbary rig. He peered over the side at the water rushing past the hull. The ship was slicing through the swells like a knife. Spray burst over the bow. The sense of speed was exhilarating, and as the eastern sky turned from reddish-brown to golden orange, and as the coastline drew ever nearer, *Scorpion* continued to overhaul her quarry.

The three men remained at the rail. Hawkwood was impressed at the speed with which the schooner was bridging the gap. In no time at all, it seemed, the cutter was barely three cables ahead of them. The sky had grown considerably lighter and he could see figures moving about her deck.

"If she didn't know we were interested in her before, I'd say she does now," Lasseur said. He raised the telescope. *"Bâtards!"* He swore suddenly and handed Hawkwood the glass.

Hawkwood's first wild thought was that they had been following the wrong boat. Then a black-painted hull swam into the foreground; increased in size now, but still dwarfed by the spread of her canvas. Hawkwood remembered Gadd's description of the *Sea Witch*. He searched for a name on her counter, but the jolly boat suspended from the cutter's narrow stern obscured his view. Three men stood by the rail at her starboard quarter, close to the tiller man, staring back towards the *Scorpion*. Two of them were wearing blue coats and white breeches. When Hawkwood saw the third man standing between them, the boat's name became irrelevant. Tall and grey-bearded, the man was holding a telescope to his face with one hand: his right.

Pepper.

And then as Hawkwood and Lasseur watched, the three men separated. Activity on the cutter's deck suddenly took on a new urgency.

"Jesus, they're running out bloody guns," Hawkwood cursed as the cutter's crew began to remove canvas sheets from the cannons that lined the sides of the cutter's hull. Six in all, from what he could see, three to each side. He handed the telescope back to Lasseur, who took another look.

"Merde!"

"What are they?" Hawkwood asked. He wasn't well versed in the bore sizes of naval ordnance. As if it mattered. Cannon were still bloody cannon.

"What you would call six-pounders, from their look. Your Revenue uses them. They're accurate to about two hundred and fifty yards, with the right elevation. Fortunately, we have the advantage. We've got more of them."

The possibility that the *Sea Witch* would be carrying heavy armament had not occurred to Hawkwood. He'd assumed that Morgan and his men would be equipped with small arms; swivel guns at a pinch – indeed, he had seen one mounted on the cutter's bow – but not carriage guns, though the carronade used in the storming of the residency should have been warning enough. He wondered how well versed they were in combat at sea. It wasn't that much of a leap to suppose that Morgan would have some gunners among the ranks of the former seamen that he employed.

Lasseur was clearly surprised, too. He spun away. *"Tous les marins sur le pont!"*

A bell began to clang loudly. The deck echoed to the volley of pounding feet.

Scorpion rose on the swell and plunged forward.

"Préparez les canons!"

Within seconds, sand had been laid down, guns run out, personal weapons distributed, and neck cloths transferred to the men's right arms. As Lasseur explained, his crew knew each other, but everyone, especially Hawkwood and Jago, had to be able to identify friend from foe. A split second's hesitation could mean the difference between life and death.

"You definitely plannin' on boardin' her, then?" Jago

asked, running his thumb down a cutlass blade as Lasseur passed Hawkwood a pistol and tomahawk.

"I doubt Morgan will surrender to a hail," Lasseur said grimly.

Her crew primed and at their stations, *Scorpion* swept on.

The cutter, now less than a cable's length off the bow, started wearing to port. Her sails flapped as her bow turned through the wind, then the canvas filled quickly as her sheets were pulled taut. She looked, Hawkwood thought, strikingly top heavy.

Lasseur barked out orders. The nautical jargon meant nothing to Hawkwood. Lasseur might just as well have been yelling in Chinese. But as men hauled eagerly on ropes, reducing canvas, and as the helmsman swung the wheel hard over, it was clear that the privateer was attempting to match the cutter's manoeuvre. *Scorpion* began to come round.

There was a distant bang and a puff of smoke appeared on the cutter's deck, then a waterspout erupted five yards off the schooner's starboard quarter.

Someone cheered derisively.

Lasseur snorted contemptuously and yelled at his first officer to fire on the up roll.

Hawkwood remembered being told that English gunners generally fired on the down roll so that any delay would cause the ball to bounce off the water and ricochet into the enemy's hull. French gun crews usually aimed for the rigging. As a consequence, the French tended to suffer greater casualties. Hawkwood knew the last thing Lasseur wanted was to sink the cutter, especially given the cargo she was carrying, so in aiming at the cutter's rig the privateer was following tradition. Hawkwood tried not to think about the rest of it.

As *Scorpion*'s starboard rail swept past the cutter's tapered stern, Delon dropped his arm.

The gunner hauled back on the lanyard and the explosion

took Hawkwood by surprise. It was sharper and louder than he had expected, more an ear-splitting crack than a roar. The sound pierced his brain like a skewer and he saw Jago flinch beside him.

Hawkwood looked for the fall of the shot and saw nothing.

They bloody missed! he thought angrily, and then he watched as the top quarter of the cutter's mast began to topple sideways in a jumble of rigging.

A loud whoop rang out from the gun crew, who were already sponging down the barrel in preparation for the next firing. The cry was taken up by the rest of the men on deck as the mast collapsed upon itself in a tangle of ropes and spars.

Lasseur had used chain shot. He yelled again. *"Feu!"*

Another detonation. This time Hawkwood saw the shot hit, tearing away the gaff, ripping into the sail and shattering what remained of the mast. Halyards gone, main sail shredded, the cutter's rig lost all integrity. As the man in the stern wrestled with the tiller, the vessel began to wallow.

But her crew were fighting back.

A double report sounded from across the water. Hawkwood saw the twin billows of smoke dispersing along the cutter's deck – one from the swivel gun. He hunkered down instinctively as a section of the schooner's starboard rail disintegrated under the impact, heard a whimper as the ball went past his ear and ducked again as splinters pierced the air like arrows. Screams rang out. Hawkwood saw one man spin away, hand clamped around his throat, blood pumping from between his fingers.

A roar of defiance erupted from *Scorpion*'s crew.

"Au tribord!" Lasseur screamed at his helmsman.

The helmsman hauled down on the wheel and *Scorpion* obeyed the command. Her bow dipped. Water boiled along her length and foamed across her steeply sloping deck as she swung towards the cutter's hull. Her stern lifted as she slewed to starboard. There was another blast of cannon fire and Hawkwood saw one of the cutter's gun crews split asunder in a welter of blood and smoke and splinters and tumbling bodies. And *Scorpion* was beam on to the cutter's port side. Only yards separated them.

Lasseur screamed at his men to steady themselves. The hulls were less than two cannon lengths apart when the first grappling hook curved over the cutter's gunwale. A rain of metal claws followed. With their comrades providing covering fire, the men on the ropes began to haul in. Hawkwood felt Jago's strong hand on his shoulder, held on to a shroud and braced for impact. It wasn't dissimilar to an attack on a breach in a wall, he thought, as the distance between the vessels closed. The principle was the same: people were trying to kill you. So, eyes forward, keep your wits, don't bloody fall over.

"It's possible they'll match us in numbers," Lasseur had told them. "But my men have done this before. Watch your flanks."

Powder flashes lit up the faces lining the cutter's rail. A seaman to Hawkwood's left gave an explosive grunt and fell back, a red orchid blossoming across his front.

The hulls met with a shuddering crash and a groan of timber, and *Scorpion*'s crew, screaming like banshees, leapt over the schooner's side and hurled themselves towards the cutter's deck.

Where they were met head on with ball and steel.

As Hawkwood jumped, he caught a glimpse of grey-green water swirling in the gap below his feet. Then he was over and the deck was rushing up to meet him. He landed hard, slithered in a pool of dark blood, brought the pistol round and fired point-blank at a body coming in, sword held high. He saw a red mist envelop the attacker's skull and then the corpse was falling away into the mêlée. Hawkwood reversed the pistol and drew the tomahawk from his belt. The air rang with the clash of steel and the crack of small-arms fire.

He looked for Morgan but couldn't see either him or Pepper. In the uproar and the noise and with powder smoke roiling across the deck, all he could see was a confused mass of struggling bodies. Hawkwood searched for anyone not wearing a neckcloth on their bicep. He saw Lasseur, fighting with knife and sword, turn his blades towards a blue-jacketed man, his face a mask of fury. A good number of Morgan's men were still wearing their French uniforms. Lasseur had briefed his crew. They were making good use of the information. The blue tunics made easy targets.

A huge figure – one of the cutter's crew, from his lack of an arm band – appeared on Hawkwood's right, in his hands a musketoon designed for close-quarter work. The gun's maw looked about a foot wide. Hawkwood saw death staring at him and then Jago was there, cutlass hacking down through the man's wrist before he could pull the trigger. Hawkwood followed through with the tomahawk, felt the blade bite into muscle, tugged the weapon free and scrambled on.

The battle raged. It was brutal and bloody, and it was becoming increasingly perilous underfoot. Detritus from the vessel's broken rig had turned the deck into a morass of cordage, black rigging, torn sailcloth and broken spars. The bodies of the dead and wounded were adding to the debris.

Then, through a gap in the fighting, Hawkwood saw Pepper. Morgan's lieutenant was at the cutter's stern, hacking a cutlass at a knot of rope wrapped around an arm of the jolly boat hoist. The tiller man lay dead by Pepper's feet.

Bastard's trying to go over the side again, Hawkwood thought. But Pepper wasn't alone. Another man was attempting to free the ropes on the hoist's other arm. Hawkwood didn't recognize Morgan immediately. His black beard was gone, but his shape gave him away. He looked up, saw Hawkwood, swallowed his shock and redoubled his efforts. Like some of his men, he was still wearing the blue tunic and white breeches. Hawkwood saw diagonal stripes low down on the tunic sleeve as Morgan raised his arm and in a moment of clarity heard Lieutenant Burden's voice in his ear describing the broad-shouldered sergeant who had shot Corporal Jefford stone dead in the residency lobby.

His eyes swept the deck, trying to pierce the smoke. He saw Lasseur, caught the privateer's eye and pointed. Lasseur followed his gaze and his eyes took on a new intensity. Sidestepping over the mess of fallen canvas and ignoring the press about him, the privateer, teeth bared, clambered towards the jolly boat.

Hawkwood saw Pepper look up. Morgan's lieutenant had spotted Lasseur moving towards him. Beneath his beard, Pepper's cheeks hardened. He edged away from the hoist, cutlass in his hand. Behind Pepper's back, Morgan continued to attack the rope. Suddenly the strands parted and the jolly boat's bow dropped. Morgan transferred his energy to the second hoist.

Hawkwood heard Jago bellow. Another of Morgan's men chancing his arm. He turned and whipped the pistol butt into a startled face. Regaining his balance and with the fighting raging about him, he headed for the stern.

Pepper gripped the cutlass and waited for Lasseur's attack. He looked unconcerned, confident. The cutlass was his weapon.

Lasseur ran in, Pepper scythed the cutlass towards Lasseur's sword arm. Lasseur parried, driving the strike away with the side of his blade. As Pepper's weight carried him round, Lasseur went low and ripped his knife through the tendons behind Pepper's right knee. His *hamstrings* severed, Pepper collapsed on to the deck, his expression one of bewilderment, shock and pain. Head thrown back, his mouth opened, but the scream was cut short as Lasseur rammed his sword point down and through the exposed throat.

Lasseur placed his boot on Pepper's unmoving chest and tugged the blade free.

"*Crétin!*" he hissed.

Morgan was almost through the last rope when he saw Pepper fall. The sight of Lasseur and the Runner on the bow of the schooner had been shocking enough. Seeing his lieutenant killed so suddenly and with such ruthless efficiency was even worse. One second Cephus was there, guarding his back, the next he was on the deck with a gaping wound in his throat, leaking blood. It didn't seem possible things could happen that quickly.

But they had and Morgan had seen the look in Lasseur's eye and he knew what it meant. So, ignoring the dead tiller man and the pool of blood that was seeping into the deck, he continued with his frantic attempt to free the jolly boat from its cradle, knowing it was futile.

He heard a voice say, "It's over, Morgan," and turned, breathing heavily.

Lasseur and Hawkwood were standing shoulder to shoulder. Beside them stood a stocky, hard-faced man with gun-metal hair, carrying a bloodstained cutlass.

"It's over, Morgan," Hawkwood said again. "You lost. Your men are finished."

Morgan saw that Hawkwood spoke the truth. Those members of his crew that were still standing were laying down their arms in surrender and lowering themselves to the deck, hands on their heads. Lasseur's men were moving among them, collecting weapons. It was clear from the lack of cloth bands on the bodies littering the deck that the cutter's crew had been overwhelmed by sheer force of arms. The *Sea Witch*'s scuppers were slick with blood.

"Reckon this is what they mean when they talk about rats tryin' to leave a sinkin' ship," Jago said.

Morgan let the sword slip from his grasp. His chest rose and fell.

"We're still fifteen miles off the coast," Hawkwood said. "Did you really think you'd make it?"

"The Lord loves an optimist," Lasseur murmured.

"Can't blame a man for trying," Morgan said.

Hawkwood stuck the pistol in his belt, tossed the tomahawk aside and drew the knife from his boot.

A flicker of doubt crossed Morgan's face. His jaw tightened.

The man looked strange without the beard, Hawkwood had decided. His face looked rounder and at least five years younger, and not so aggressive. In fact, Hawkwood thought, there was something else about Morgan that was different. He looked more portly round the chest, which was a bit odd, and his movements looked . . . ponderous.

Before Morgan could react, Hawkwood jabbed the knife point beneath the front hem of Morgan's tunic and with effortless ease sliced the blade towards Morgan's chin like a surgeon opening up a cadaver. The tunic cloth parted like grape skin.

"Well, would you look at that!" Jago said in wonderment. "Haven't seen one of them since the old king died."

It was a waistcoat, but it wasn't like any Hawkwood had seen before. It was lined with pockets and every one of them was bulging.

Hawkwood reached out and with another flick of his wrist performed a second filleting along one of the pocket seams. The cloth split and the weight of the contents did the rest. A gold ingot clattered to the deck.

Hawkwood slid the knife back in his boot and picked the

ingot up. It wasn't very big, about half the size of a tinder box, but it was heavy nonetheless. Impressed into the dull metal were some numbers and a round stamp bearing the words Rothschild & Sons.

From the size of him, Hawkwood guessed there were pockets in the back of Morgan's waistcoat, too, and there was a suspicious bulge across his lower back. Lasseur used his sword point to lift the back of the blue tunic. A bustle-like garment was tied around Morgan's waist.

"You might want to check inside his breeches, an' all," Jago said. "They used to carry thigh pieces, back in the old days."

"We get the picture," Hawkwood said. "Check Pepper."

Lasseur did so.

"The same," he announced, realizing that the weight had contributed to Pepper's sluggishness and inability to repel his attack.

"The old tea waistcoats used to hold about thirty pounds weight," Jago said.

"Judas got silver. You got gold," Hawkwood said. "You go to all that trouble and all you end up with is a bloody waistcoat. Hardly worth the effort."

"What do you want to do with him?" Lasseur asked. "I give him to you. My gift."

"Let him have the gold," Hawkwood said.

"What?" Lasseur's jaw dropped.

Hawkwood shrugged. "Let him take his chances."

"You ain't bloody serious?" Jago said. "After all you said?"

Morgan's head came up. "You're not arresting me?"

"Arrest you?" Hawkwood laughed. "You've a bloody high opinion of yourself. No, I've a mind to let you keep your waistcoat. I don't think the army will miss thirty pounds of gold, do you? Far as I'm concerned, you make it to the coast, you damn well deserve to keep it. There's only one condition . . ."

"What's that?" A tiny light flared in the dark eyes. Hope springing eternal.

"You have to swim."

Hawkwood half turned and slammed his boot into Morgan's belly.

The kick rocked Morgan on to his heels. The edge of the bulwark caught him across the back of his legs and momentum did the rest, sending him backwards over the cutter's side. He hit the water with the look of incredulity still glued to his face. He was still trying to recover his breath as the sea closed over him, taking his encumbered body down into its cold and lasting embrace.

It was over so quickly, there was no trace of his passing. Hawkwood stepped back.

"That's taken the weight off his mind," Jago observed. "Though you had me worried for a while. Thought you'd gone soft."

There were more splashes from behind. Under the supervision of Lieutenant Delon and his men, the remnants of Morgan's crew were tipping the bodies of their dead comrades into the water.

"Time to go, I think," Lasseur said, turning on his heel and sheathing his sword. He called his lieutenant to him.

"When they've disposed of their dead, lock them below. Get our men back on *Scorpion*; including casualties. Keep a small crew behind to clear the deck, then rig a sail. We'll escort you in. She's not much of a prize by herself, but her cargo's worth more than a king's ransom." Lasseur looked at Hawkwood and grinned.

And Hawkwood said, "You'll have to be sharp about it."

He wasn't looking at Lasseur. He was looking over the bow.

At the same moment Lasseur's man yelled, "Sail to the north-east!"

"British frigate," Hawkwood said. "But that's just my guess. Probably on blockade patrol. She's damned close, too. If I were you, I'd shoot your lookout."

Lasseur sprang to the rail.

The frigate was bearing down fast. She was closer to the French coast than *Scorpion*. Yards braced, with a full spread of sail, she was running before the wind. Lasseur could even see the water creaming at her bow.

"Save yourself or the gold," Hawkwood said. "Don't think there's time for you to do both. If they catch you, it'll be the black hole for sure. They'll likely throw away the key this time, the mayhem you've caused. Interesting dilemma."

"It's a bugger, right enough," Jago said.

Lasseur stared hard at the approaching man-of-war.

He turned and looked at the wreckage that was strewn across the cutter's deck; at the bodies that were still being lowered over the side, at his own ship and at the exhaustion on the faces of his men, who would be unable to withstand another pitched skirmish.

He gnawed the inside of his cheek and came to a decision.

"Merde," he said.

EPILOGUE

"Nice night," Jago said.

Hawkwood couldn't disagree. There were no clouds. The sky was dotted with a thousand stars and moonlight speckled the blue-black water. The only sound to be heard was the soft wash of the waves along the shore and the steady creak of oars. It was a sound Hawkwood had become used to.

But he'd had his fill of midnight meetings on moonlit beaches. He'd had enough, he decided, to last him a lifetime; several lifetimes.

But maybe this one was different.

The two men walked down to the water's edge, their boots crunching into the pebbles. They waited for the black-hulled rowboat to draw closer, stepping aside at the last minute as the bow glided out of the darkness and on to the beach.

Lasseur stepped ashore.

He smiled and held out his hand. "Captain." He shook hands with Jago. "I'm happy to see that you both made a safe return. You'll have forgiven me for my hasty departure, I hope."

"Couldn't be helped," Hawkwood said. "Business called."

"Indeed. I trust the army was suitably generous in its gratitude?"

"That'll be the bloody day," Jago said.

"No reward?"

"Just the thanks of a grateful nation," Hawkwood said. "I'm inclined to think you came out of it better than we did."

Lasseur grinned.

"I hope you gave Pepper a decent burial," Hawkwood said as they left the boat and walked towards the top of the beach where a wall of grey rock rose from the shingle and a line of tall cliffs stretched away into the darkness.

Lasseur nodded. "Wrapped in sailcloth with a six-pound ball at his feet."

"More than the bastard deserved," Jago muttered. "Mind you, it'll give Morgan someone to talk to."

"I'm assuming he wasn't wearing his waistcoat," Hawkwood said.

Lasseur shook his head. "On the contrary, we let him keep it. Without the contents, naturally."

"Spend them wisely," Hawkwood said. "That might be all you'll get for a while. I hear deliveries may be curtailed."

Lasseur had left them the rest of the gold. The British warship had been too close and coming in too fast for *Scorpion*'s crew to pilot the damaged *Sea Witch* to a safe harbour or transfer the bullion before being apprehended. Even Lasseur's Barbary rig wouldn't have saved them, not given the frigate's heading and speed and the proximity of her eighteen-pounders.

Leaving the frigate to salvage the cutter and what remained of her decimated crew, along with the two individuals who'd been left on her bloodstained deck, *Scorpion* had reset her canvas and made for the nearest French port.

When the frigate's captain dispatched his second lieutenant to investigate the crippled cutter, he had little idea what his officer would discover in the vessel's hold. He had been forced to admit it had been the biggest prize he'd taken in his career. Though *prize* wasn't strictly the word for the army's own missing bullion.

They recouped all of it save for the ingots that Morgan and Pepper had attempted to carry ashore. The recovery of the bullion, Hawkwood learned, had not resurrected the career of Lieutenant Burden, for whom the stores depot at Fort Amherst beckoned unenticingly.

"Will they hang them all?" Lasseur asked, referring to the cutter's crew.

"They're up before Maidstone Assizes in two weeks' time. Morgan's not around. His lawyer won't be able to save them. It'll be a meeting with Jack Ketch or else transportation."

"So Morgan's organization is starting to unravel. Cut off the head and the beast withers?"

"I wouldn't say that. More arrests are being made, including the admiral's cook – she was the one passing Morgan information about the layout and people in the house. But the Trade's like a spider: you break its web and it spins another one just as fast. Someone will be along to take Morgan's place."

"The king is dead, long live the king?"

"Something like that," Hawkwood said.

A low whistle came from the darkness.

The three men turned towards the sound. A small horse-drawn cart appeared. The cart drew to a halt and Jethro Garvey dismounted. "Sorry we're late," he said. He walked to the back of the cart and took down a valise.

Lasseur helped Jess Flynn down from the cart. Taking her hand, and without speaking, he held it to his lips and then to his cheek.

While Garvey stayed with the cart, Hawkwood took the valise and he and Jago accompanied Lasseur and Jess Flynn down to the water.

At the edge of the beach, she looked round. "Come on, you," she called softly.

There was a scrabble of paws and the dog jumped down from the back of the cart and loped slowly down the shingle towards them, tail wagging.

"We'll have to teach him French," Lasseur said.

"Just speak loud and slow," Jago said.

Jess Flynn smiled. "He's not deaf, Nathaniel. He's getting on in years, that's all."

"Like me," Jago said.

Hawkwood placed the valise in the boat.

Jess Flynn let go of Lasseur's hand and kissed Hawkwood's cheek.

"Thank you," she said.

Lasseur helped her into the boat then lifted the dog in beside her. With Hawkwood and Jago's help, he pushed the boat off the shingle and climbed aboard. Slowly the boat pulled away. The last sight before darkness swallowed it was of Lasseur raising his hand in a silent farewell.

"What do you reckon?" Jago mused. "You think the real reason he gave up the gold was so's he could come back for her?"

"Maybe," Hawkwood said.

"Daft sod," Jago muttered.

They turned and retraced their steps.

Garvey was still waiting by the cart.

"Thanks, Jethro," Jago said. "Mind how you go."

As the cart trundled off, Hawkwood and Jago walked to where they had tethered the horses.

"You do realize the only person to get anything out of all this was a bloody Frenchman," Jago said. "Bugger sailed away with a pile of gold *and* the girl."

"Not strictly true," Hawkwood said. He paused and reached into his pocket. "Here, catch –"

The ingot he'd cut from Morgan's waistcoat landed neatly in Jago's hand.

Jago raised an eyebrow.

"Expenses," Hawkwood said.

Jago stared at the ingot in his hand. "What's it worth?"

"No idea. A lot."

Jago handed it back. "The wages they pay you, you need all the help you can get."

They mounted up and turned their horses away from the beach.

And the sound of a single bark echoed over the darkened water behind them.

HISTORICAL NOTE

Over the course of the Napoleonic Wars, Britain incarcerated thousands of prisoners of war in both mainland gaols and hulks; former men-of-war of British and foreign origin that were considered too old and too unseaworthy for active service. By 1814, the population of the prison ships had reached its peak of 72,000 souls. The majority of these vessels were moored at Portsmouth, Plymouth and the Medway towns.

Of all the prisoners that lived on the hulks, the most feared were the Romans and the most despised were the Rafalés. Duels were fought as described in the novel, and there are records confirming that bodies were indeed cut up and disposed of through the ships' heads.

The majority of the deaths on the Medway hulks were due to consumption and fever. The corpses of both civilian convicts and prisoners of war were buried along the fore-shore. When Chatham Dockyard was extended in 1855–56, the remains of over 500 prisoners were discovered on St Mary's Island. These were disinterred and re-buried under a stone memorial that may still be seen in the grounds of the old naval barracks.

Accounts vary, but in the period between 1811 and 1814, it's thought that between 300 and 450 French officers made successful escapes. Most of them would not have made it home without the aid of the British smuggling fraternity, who charged escapers up to 300 guineas for the journey.

The favour was returned in the support that English free traders received from Emperor Napoleon Bonaparte. Bonaparte is on record as declaring that "during the war, all the information I received from England came through the smugglers". He was so enamoured of the service they provided – including the delivery of newspapers which, upon arrival in France, were taken by courier to the Minister of Police in Paris – that he designated the port of Gravelines the exclusive entry point for British free traders. Thus the City of Smugglers was established.

"Free trading" has always been a very profitable enterprise. The audacity of the smugglers, particularly those who operated along the Kent and Sussex coastlines during the eighteenth and early nineteenth centuries, was nothing short of remarkable. The landing of contraband was not confined to a couple of jack-the-lads and the odd rowboat. The Trade was carefully controlled and financed, in many cases, by London merchants. Smuggling gangs operated with impunity, often in broad daylight. Hundreds of men and beasts of burden could be employed at any one time, forming caravans that delivered the goods from the coast to warehouses on the outskirts of London. Pitched battles between smugglers and Revenue men – who relied on troops for support and who were often outnumbered – were not uncommon, resulting in many casualties and deaths on both sides.

One of the most profitable aspects of the smuggling business, however, was the deployment of the guinea boats. The trade, most of it conducted under the guidance of the house of Rothschild, was carried out in the manner described. The sums involved beggared belief, with rowing galleys carrying up to 30,000 guineas at a time. In 1811, smugglers transported a total of almost 1,900,000 guineas or 49,000,000 francs. In today's money, that would equate to nearly £65,000,000.

Fanny Burney, the eighteenth-century diarist, referred to Deal as a *"sad smuggling town"*. I doubt the townsfolk saw themselves in such a melancholy light. Deal's reputation for free trading was second to none; its ties with the Trade went back to the early 1740s, and the town remained a thorn in the side of the authorities well into the next century, with Deal boatmen playing a crucial role in both general smuggling and the guinea trade. As a result, in 1784, under the direct orders of Prime Minister William Pitt, a regiment of troops torched the entire Deal fleet as it sought sanctuary from a storm on the shingle beach. The galleys used by the guinea traders were so integral to the Trade that in 1812 the British Government banned their construction.

The character of Ezekiel Morgan is based loosely on the Kent smuggler, George Ransley, leader of the Blues, one of the county's most infamous gangs. Ransley, like Morgan, employed his own surgeon and a firm of lawyers. In 1826 Ransley and his cohorts were convicted of the murder of a quartermaster of the Coast Blockade (a forerunner of the Coast Guard); Ransley was transported to Tasmania, where he ended his days as a free settler in Launceston.

Many of the locations in the novel are real and were indeed used by smugglers. The Smack Aground pub and the church at Warden Point on the Isle of Sheppey, did exist but are now long gone, demolished due to severe coastal subsidence. But Warden Manor, home of Sir John Sawbridge and his pigeon loft, is still there.

The Admiral's residency at Deal was located on Queen Street; its strong room was the repository for both navy and army pay chests, with bullion regularly being landed in the town. In 1813, for example, HMS *Bedford* deposited 25 tons of gold and silver in bars, dust and coin. The building was demolished in 1936 to make way for a cinema. A night club now occupies the site.

The oyster platforms at Seasalter and Whitstable were frequently used to offload French prisoners of war so that they could be transferred ashore. I took the inspiration for Jess Flynn's smallholding from Pye Alley Farm near Seasalter, which was one of many houses that provided escapers with food and shelter. That farm still stands.

Should anyone wish to delve more deeply into the world of the smugglers, I would recommend the splendid website run by author Richard Platt. The site's address is www.smuggling.co.uk.

Rochester Museum is an excellent source for anyone wishing to know more about prisoners of war and their life on the Medway hulks. The museum has under its roof a mock-up of a prison hulk, complete with a "black hole", and is well worth visiting. I'm indebted to the museum's curator, Steve Nye, who very generously took time off from his busy schedule to answer my questions and give me the guided tour.

I'm also grateful to Gavin Daly from the University of Tasmania, whose article "Napoleon and the City of Smugglers 1810–1814" set me on the right track.

Little has been written on the lives of prisoners in the hulks. Two books of note, however, are Louis Garneray's *The Floating Prison,* translated from the French by Richard Rose, and *The English Prison Hulks* by W. Branch Johnson.